WATER IN HER VEINS

Books by Shannon Schuren

The Virtue of Sin

Water in Her Veins

Where Echoes Lie

WATER IN HER VEINS

BY SHANNON SCHUREN

VIKING

VIKING
An imprint of Penguin Random House LLC
1745 Broadway, New York, New York 10019

First published in the United States of America by Viking,
an imprint of Penguin Random House LLC, 2025

Visit us online at PenguinRandomHouse.com.

Library of Congress Cataloging-in-Publication Data is available.

ISBN 9780593621431

1 3 5 7 9 10 8 6 4 2

Manufactured in the United States of America

BVG

Design by Anabeth Bostrup

Text set in Perpetua MT

For my dad—
There are still days when I wish I could pick up the phone
and share some amazing news with you.
This is one of those days.

"We are linked by blood, and blood is memory without language."

—Joyce Carol Oates

"Sometimes it's blood memory . . . not the blood your mother and father gave you . . . but that which stretches back two or three thousand years."

—Martha Graham

"But chains made out of blood and memory were a thousand times more difficult to sever than those made of steel, and the past could overtake a person if she wasn't careful."

—Alice Hoffman

CHAPTER 1

My first memory is of blood. I was maybe four, playing outside with my friends underneath the old elm tree on the edge of the empty lot that probably belonged to the Presbyterian church next door, but the neighborhood kids have always treated it like it was ours. Jesse lived around the corner, and with his shaggy curls and Converse sneakers, he was easily the coolest boy I knew. In my recollection, he's much older—practically a teenager—though since we eventually went to the same high school, he couldn't have been more than seven or eight.

All the same, I loved him. We all did.

While my friends and I would play with our dolls, building houses among the roots, he'd climb high onto the branches above us. Sometimes I'd catch a flash of his blue eyes between the leaves; other times he'd call down suggestions for our play. Most involved taking off the Barbies' tiny halter tops, but I ignored those. Wasn't it enough that he wanted our attention? This older, shining boy who climbed so close to the sun, who was wild and free and used the word "boobs" without so much as a giggle? He was a star above us and we were content to bask in his presence back on earth.

And yet I wasn't as shocked as he seemed to be when he plummeted from a weak branch and landed at our feet. Even as a preschooler, I understood the basic properties of gravity. What goes up comes down. You climb a tree, eventually you will fall. Even cute boy-gods. And truthfully, I was a little bit thrilled. He'd never joined our game before and now here he was, so close I could count the freckles on the bridge of his nose. It wasn't that I didn't care. But this was Jesse. He was invincible. I wasn't happy that he'd fallen, but I certainly wasn't scared.

Not until I saw the blood. Thick and rusty, soaking his jeans and pooling beneath his leg, which we later learned was broken in two places. He tried to sit up, shooting a dazed look in my direction as I rocked back on my heels, clutching my Barbie doll. He grabbed at his leg, then reached out to grab my hand, his own slick with blood. He missed, catching Barbie's golden tresses instead, streaking them crimson.

That's where the memory stops. Because that's when I fainted.

A crash jerks me from my daydreaming, and I tear my gaze from the kitchen window, where the elm tree is just visible at the corner of the lot. The movers must have dropped something. Again. Their voices echo loudly through the house as they reassure Mom that nothing's broken.

I rub the throbbing space above the bridge of my nose. I'm never at my best in the morning. Waking up is brutal, like clawing my way out of a deep, dark cave, leaving me raw and achy and emotional, even on a good day. And today is not a good day.

As the Keurig burbles to a stop, I dump sugar and nondairy creamer into my travel mug before heading to the front porch. One of the movers, a scraggly Men at Work wannabe in denim shorts and an orange running vest, nods as he holds the screen door. This small act of chivalry pisses me off and I glare at him, resisting the urge to toss my coffee cup in the bushes and chase him down before he can load the truck with all of my worldly possessions.

"Wow, it's early. Who knew there was a six o'clock in the morning?" Mom's voice is husky with fatigue as she joins me on the porch swing.

It's an old joke, but I force a smile and take a gulp of coffee. Neither of us is a morning person. Left to our own devices, we'd probably sleep till noon. But Kurt says you waste half the day that way, so he's gone ahead and booked the movers for this ungodly hour. And Mom, being her usual supportive self, has tried to rally behind him. She's already dressed and pulled her hair back into a ponytail instead of the wild tangle of curls she usually sports right out of bed.

I turn away from the door, ignoring the movers, and try to focus on the sunrise as it paints the sky in hues of softest pink. The night shadows slink back to reveal Mom's hydrangeas bent low, as if in prayer, the blooms so full they drag on the ground.

My throat aches for all this beauty. For all the time I've wasted. For all that we're leaving behind.

Behind me, I hear a scrape and a crash, followed by a muttered curse word.

I wince but refuse to look. "I dreamed about Erma's," I say instead, clearing my throat. "I wish we'd gone last night. One last time."

When Mom doesn't comment, I turn my head in time to see her dash a tear with her index finger as the movers drag her bedroom vanity down the steps.

"Never mind," I say. "No big deal. I'm sure they have ice cream in Colorado."

She reaches over and squeezes my hand. "I'm sure they do. But not like Erma's." She smiles, and for a second, things feel like they used to—me and Mom against the world. Life may knock us down, but it wasn't anything a watermelon freeze or a peanut butter sundae couldn't fix.

"I'll bet we'll find something even better than Erma's. Something dairy-free and delicious!" Kurt lets the screen door slam behind him as he comes to stand in front of us, hands on hips, a ridiculous grin plastered across his face.

Then again, some things even ice cream can't sweeten.

Mom gives my hand another squeeze before dropping it and hopping up to wrap her arms around her new *husband*. I can barely think of the word without gagging.

It's not that I didn't want her to ever get married. I just thought she'd choose someone more like her. From the tip of her wild curls and his military-precision crew cut down to her thrift-store Crocs and his Air Jordans, they're polar opposites. He's also ten years younger and almost an inch shorter. Mom says none of that matters, but I think we both know she's lying.

"Erma's is our happy place," she says, resting her head on his shoulder.

"Was," Kurt says, kissing the top of her head. "New town, new start, remember? And who knows? Maybe the mountain air will be so healing, Lola can try a regular diet again. With real ice cream!"

My face flushes. *I'm right here, you moron.* But my new step-dick's superpower is the ability to make me feel invisible—even when the conversation is about me.

"The diet helps," Mom says, smiling brightly at me. "It's just so restrictive. But maybe you're right." She pats his chest. "We can try reintroduction. Slowly. Depending on what this new doctor says."

"Or maybe it's time you took a step back. Like we talked about. See what happens when you give her some breathing room."

"I'm her mother!" And then, maybe feeling guilty for her tone, she adds, "I know you mean well. But you don't know what it's been like this past year, since she's gotten sick . . ."

She's right. He has no idea. Not only because he wasn't even in our lives a year ago, but also because he hasn't bothered to ask what it was like. I cannot listen to his bullshit one second longer. I jump up, slamming the swing against the porch rail, and push past them into the house.

"One hour!" Kurt hollers over the slap of the screen door. "As soon as the movers get the truck packed, we're heading out."

We're heading out. He says it so casually, like we're running to the store, not leaving the only home I've ever known.

I lean unsteadily against the newel post of the stairway, my skin puckering at the sight of the living room, empty save for the dusty outlines where the furniture used to be. The curtains are gone, and the bay window spills sunshine across the bare cherry floor like a stain. I need to say my goodbyes. Or try, anyway. I run my fingers over the scratch marks in the kitchen doorway where Mom had marked my height over the years. The new owners will paint over that first thing, so I snap a photo.

These guys work quick. The rooms are already so empty, my echoing footsteps all that's left of the life we lived here. Soon strangers will move in, painting and decorating and changing, putting all their things on top of our memories.

I walk slowly up the stairs and push open the door to my bedroom. Everything is gone, packed away into the van downstairs. All my books, all my clothes, my desk. My dresser. My favorite quotes, printed and framed. The only one remaining is the one Mom and I stenciled onto the sloped ceiling when I turned ten and she declared it was time to give me a more grown-up room. Ten-year-old me was hovering somewhere between childhood and now, because when it came time to choose the words for my wall, I picked Winnie the Pooh: *You're braver than you believe, and stronger than you seem, and smarter than you think.*

I still love reading these words each night, which comfort me when my courage fails. Remind me that I'm a fighter.

And now I have to leave them behind.

I reach behind the door and grab the carryall I've packed for the drive. A few days of clothes, pajamas, toothbrush, hairbrush. A few books. My laptop.

Another bump and another curse from somewhere downstairs. I stick in my AirPods and use my phone to pull up my Spotify playlist, settling on "Blues for Annie." Supposedly, my dad suggested naming me after this song. Instead, Mom named me Lola Joy after each of my grandmothers, Dolores and Joyce, two more dead relatives I've never met.

All of my grandparents died young.

I sometimes picture the moment my parents met, wandering the Michigan campus, both orphaned and alone before they found each other and became a family. Until my dad died in a car accident, leaving Mom alone, eight months pregnant. By the time I was born, he was gone. So all the memories I have of him are not my own. They belong to my mother; to the stories she's told me, over and over, until I had them memorized and could play them like a movie in my head; and to the photographs—stories themselves, of moments captured in time. I used to carry them around the house and match them up, the existence of that chair or lamp or bookshelf evidence that these moments happened. He sat on our oversized chair with my mother on his lap, his hand wrapped protectively around her pregnant belly. He lit a fire in our fireplace, on some long-ago night so cold the window in the corner had frosted over. He drank coffee leaning against our kitchen sink, out of a mug that read WORLD'S GREATEST HUSBAND.

The mug is long gone, and just as well; Kurt would have chucked it in the move.

Sometimes I imagine I can feel my dad's presence—looking over my shoulder as I walk down the hallway, or a whiff of cologne in the bathroom. But those phantom memories are all tied to this house. And this house is no longer ours.

The song ends, and muffled reality trickles back in. Kurt is still harping on my medical problems, loud enough that I can hear him from the stairs. I pull out an earbud in time to hear, "All I'm saying is, she's nearly an adult. What if you stopped fighting all her battles for her? Maybe that should be your new goal. For our new start."

I shove the earbud back in, readjust my backpack, and gulp my lukewarm coffee, trying to push back the bile in my throat. Kurt is *very* invested in our "new start."

He works from home, some kind of internet broker thing that I never bother to try to understand whenever he explains it. Basically, it means he could uproot himself from Ann Arbor when he and Mom hit it off as easily as he can pack up and move to Colorado. Especially now that he has a stepdaughter with her own house there.

I step onto the porch and they break apart, faces red. "Ready? Finally?" Kurt asks.

It's that last word that does it. I don't answer; I just take off.

My hometown is small. Just a lot of foursquare houses and two-lane roads. We didn't even have a traffic light until a few years ago. Probably because Foxfield,

Michigan, isn't on the way to or from anywhere. Smack dab inside a triangle formed by three highways, but no direct exit from any of them. We're like the Bermuda Triangle, minus the boats.

I don't have a conscious destination in mind, but I'm not surprised when I end up at the tree. I lean up against the rough bark, panting and trying to catch my breath. I haven't moved that fast in ages, and even though I was barely jogging, my body is not going to thank me for it. Already, my joints are screaming in protest, but I ignore them as I trace the crude heart carved into the trunk. *LB + JP*. Lola Boyd and Jesse Parker. Not to be confused with the half dozen other hearts. *MA + JP. TC + JP. CD + JP*. The poor tree didn't deserve our abuse any more than Jesse probably deserved our adoration.

But don't most things live on bright and shiny in our memories, long after life has tarnished them? Happy or not, after today these memories are all I'll have.

When I've caught my breath, I cross the street and walk on past the high school, then cut through the empty parking lot. Not only is it early in the morning, it's August. School doesn't start until next week, and for now, the grass is still untrampled, the sidewalks free from litter, the building dark and shuttered. Not that I care—I said those goodbyes a long time ago.

It's the track I need to visit one last time.

I'm sure the cross-country team has already started their practice season, but thankfully, they aren't meeting this morning. I slip through the gates and across the grass, and once my feet hit the rubberized surface, my calves contract as if by reflex. My body aches to sprint down that long stretch, proving my muscle memory is just as out of touch with reality as that little girl who defaced the tree.

I dig in my heels and clench my fists, taking in as much of the mix of hot pavement and fresh-cut grass as my lungs will hold. The morning is silent, so sweltering and muggy not even the birds have the energy to chirp. But when I close my eyes, I can still hear the excitement of competition days. The laughter of my teammates, the calls of the crowd. It used to annoy me, how hard I had to fight to drown it all out. Once I did, though, once I found my rhythm? Pure bliss. The sound of my own breath, the rhythm of my heart pumping in my ears, the thump of my feet against the track as I hit my stride. It's that feeling that I'll miss—that I already miss—more than anything.

I've always been a runner. I took it for granted, the ability to make my body do whatever I wanted. Back then, I could push myself to extremes with only minor muscle aches as punishment.

It was a no-brainer for me to join cross-country and track my freshman year.

The first time I remember feeling not quite right was during a 400-meter dash, when I got hot and woozy and then went down hard.

Coach and I chalked it up to dehydration.

I was out for over a week with that first bout of whatever, dizziness and body aches ravaging my body and leaving me so spent I could barely lift a spoon to my mouth. When I returned to practice, I was weak and shaky but determined to push myself back to where I'd been. Better, even.

But that didn't happen. What did was a season of confusing lapses, of itchy pain in odd places and fatigue I couldn't shake. I stopped pushing myself in practice in hopes of being able to push myself in my events, even when it meant I wouldn't be able to function for the next week. I started skipping classes the days of our meets, hoping that sleeping fifteen hours before I ran would be enough rest to get me through.

It wasn't.

It was Coach who pointed out that I was in violation of the code of conduct. That my class attendance had dipped too low to allow me to compete. It wasn't fair to the others, she said, if I was allowed to be "lazy." What about the rest of them, who were giving it their all? Who had to show up to school *and* run? Why did I think I was so special?

That was the part that stung the most. I was barely holding my head up by then, between the fatigue and the brain fog that never quite lifted. I felt worthless and awful and terrified. I definitely didn't think I was special.

Even so, track was the thing I clung to longest, my last pillar of normalcy. I could still participate, Coach finally decided. But I couldn't compete, not when I'd be taking a spot from someone who deserved it more. Who'd worked harder.

If only she knew the effort it took to get out of bed most days. I worked as hard as all of them, if not harder. But I didn't fight it. How could I? I knew how it looked. At that point, my own doctor barely believed me. Why should she?

I quit the team, and without that last bit of hope keeping me anchored, nothing else mattered.

I open my eyes and blink against the glare of the sun, the track wavering in front of me like a mirage. I long to run, one last time, but I'm not that girl anymore. Instead, I huff out a choking breath, bending to wipe my sweaty palms on my knees. *Everything has an ending.* This is the mantra I'm supposed to repeat when I'm dealing with a wave of pain that feels like it won't ever stop. But it applies to good things, too.

Nothing lasts forever.

A brown rust-bucket Mazda wheezes to a stop beside the fence and my best friend climbs out, the slam of a car door shattering the quiet. Bryn's blood-red hair is spiky, more likely from bed than styling, and they're wearing a flannel coat and rhinestone-studded sunglasses despite the fact that it's already eighty degrees out and barely daylight.

Bryn and I met in middle school, when they were the only person to attend the family history club I tried to start. Eventually, we stopped holding meetings and just started hanging out at our houses. We've been best friends ever since. They're the only one who stuck by me after I quit track at the end of freshman year and then switched to virtual school last year, with the rest of my so-called friends promising to keep in touch even as they were deleting me from our friend group chats.

"What are you doing up this early?"

"An early-morning walk is a blessing for the whole day!" they cry with a sweeping gesture.

"Thoreau," I call. "And you drove."

"Shut up," Bryn says, closing the remaining distance between us and throwing their arms around me. "Like I wouldn't come to say g—" They catch a look on my face. "Au revoir?"

I hug them back. And find it hard to let go.

"Damn it," I say, pulling away. "This is why I told you not to come. I didn't want to do this."

Bryn pulls their sunglasses down. "I swung by the house. Inert Kurt's worked himself into a bit of a snit."

I roll my eyes. "Pissed I took off?"

"Nah. He was more worried about showing the movers how to properly do their jobs."

"Of course he was. Probably hasn't even noticed I'm gone yet." I brighten. "Maybe if I stay away long enough, they'll just leave without me."

"Aren't you the dreamer?"

"The future belongs to those who believe in the beauty of their dreams," I reply.

"Eleanor Roosevelt!" Bryn crows.

"Damn it. You set me up for that one."

"I did. And you fell for it. We make a perfect team. Which reminds me." Bryn pulls out a slim, square box. "I brought you something."

I tear off the bow and open it. A copper bangle bracelet is nestled on a cotton pad, a single filigree leaf gleaming in the sunlight.

"Wow," I say around the lump in my throat. "Thank you. It's gorgeous."

"Easy to put on," they say, showing me how the two ends of the bangle wrap around. "Just slides over your wrist. So you don't have to bother with the clasp. I know you have trouble with those lately."

Trouble. Meaning sometimes my fingers are so swollen, I can't bend them.

"It's a leaf from my family tree," Bryn continues. "So when you wear it, you can remember that no matter where you go, you'll always have family back here."

I slide it on and touch the leaf.

A hot, dry wind rushes over me, searing my face and pushing out the mugginess of the day. At the same time, pain pierces my lungs. I stumble and claw at my chest, struggling to take a breath. Roaring fills my head and I have to push to get the words out: *Help me! I can't breathe.*

Instead, I say, "As sure as this tree will shade you, so too will these waters heal you."

My vision goes red and I begin to shake, not with fear but with rage. "You bastard," I hear myself hiss.

Bryn grabs my wrist and my body jolts, as if jerked back into place. I blink in the sudden brightness of the day and take a deep, gulping breath before I go down on one knee.

"Shit. Do you not like it? Or is it the pain? Has it come back? Shit. I've got a water bottle here. Somewhere." They yank open the passenger door and lean in.

I clutch the cotton of my tank top. My breath comes easy again, but my heart is racing. "I'm . . . fine. Just . . . give me a minute."

Bryn shoves a lukewarm Fiji water at me and watches closely as I gulp from the bottle. "Are you all right? That was . . . weird. Bastard?" They wrinkle their nose. "That's so patriarchal."

I choke on a mouthful of water. "Sorry. I don't know why I said that. I was . . . thinking about something else."

"Right. As sure as this tree . . ." Bryn rolls their hand. "I give up. Where's the quote from?"

I swallow hard as I stand up. I remember saying the words, but they're already fading, like a memory too old and tenuous to grab on to. "I don't remember. It just popped into my head. Because I'm thirsty, I guess." I can also feel a killer headache coming on.

"Come on," Bryn says. "I'll drive you home."

Home. But it's not anymore.

"Don't," Bryn warns, snapping their fingers in my face. "If you lose it, I'm going to lose it, and what fucking good will that do us? Trust me, if there was a way we could live in this moment forever, I'd make it happen. But I've got no working knowledge of space-time physics or temporal realities, and besides, you need to get to Colorado and find your dad's people. So let's just get in the goddamn car."

I'm hovering on the lip of a deep well of grief, on the brink of falling apart, but I trust Bryn to pull me back. And they're right. As usual. I can keep wallowing, or I can pull myself together and say a proper goodbye to my best friend in the whole world.

So I lean my head on Bryn's shoulder and close my eyes, willing this memory to stay. I have a feeling I'm going to need to hold on to it in the days ahead.

CHAPTER 2

Bryn is possibly even more obsessed with genealogy than I am, originally trying to chart their ancestors so they could "prove I'm descended from royalty to get my mother off my ass." Since we started high school, their agenda has evolved into a determination to get heritage sites to change their hetero-gender-normative default settings. They're also the only person who fully understands my desire to learn more about my dad.

A month ago, I had no idea that my father owned an ancestral home in rural Colorado. Much less that he'd left it to me. Once I turn twenty-five, it's mine. Until then, it's held in trust and has been since before I was even born, according to the stipulations in my dad's will.

Mom never told me. She had her excuses: "I was waiting until you were older, and then you got sick" and "It wasn't like we needed another house."

Until we were dead broke.

By then, Kurt was in the picture. He was the one who found the property tax bill among the growing pile of medical bills. After grilling Mom on why she owed thousands of dollars for the upkeep of a house in another state, he quickly pivoted to trying to sell it so Mom could use the profit to pay down her debt.

Fortunately—or unfortunately, depending on how you look at it—Dad's trust prevented that. When the dust settled on the bankruptcy, our next best option became our only one—Kurt would sell his house and we would sell ours, and we'd use that money to pay off our creditors before moving across the country to my dad's family home.

A house so big it even has a name. My name. Boyd Manor.

Since her marriage to Kurt last week, Mom isn't a Boyd anymore, which means I'm the only one left.

Unless I can find some relatives in Colorado.

Kurt is bugging the movers with corny dad jokes when we pull up, and to their credit, they're smiling politely instead of punching him. Probably still holding out hope for some kind of a tip. If I know Kurt, unwanted daytime talk show mantras are all they're going to get.

"Hey, Mrs. G!" Bryn calls to my mom, who is wrestling a box off the porch and into the car.

I try not to wince at the new initial.

"Bryn!" She slams the trunk and throws up her hands. "You came to see us off! How lovely!"

"Lovely," Kurt echoes. "Last night would have been even lovelier."

Bryn says something under their breath that sounds like "asswipe," then quickly covers it with a cough.

Both moving guys grin and use the interruption to break free from Kurt's rambling about proper packing being a metaphor for life, loping back into the house for another load.

Mom takes my hand, twisting the bracelet toward the light. "Is this from Bryn?" When I nod, she adds, "It looks like an aspen leaf. Native to Colorado. You've done your homework." She taps the leaf once more and murmurs, "Beautiful," as a wave of dizziness washes over me and my words from earlier echo in my head. *As sure as this tree will shade you, so too will these waters heal you.*

Where the hell have I heard that quote before?

"Thanks, Mrs. G. Respect."

Bryn pulls me and Mom close, and I wrap my arms around both of them and squeeze my eyes shut.

Kurt clears his throat.

Bryn takes the cue. "I should go. Let you guys get on the road." They hug Mom once more, then look at me.

"I can't do this," I say. I'm in severe danger of becoming a blubbering mess, or worse, throwing myself on the hood of Bryn's car and begging them not to go.

"Of course you can. You're braver than you believe—"

"Are you fucking quoting Winnie the Pooh to me right now?"

Bryn laughs. "Just trying to lighten the mood. Listen, I'm gonna scoot. Call me when you get there and we'll start planning my first visit."

"I'll probably call you before."

Bryn nods, their eyes hidden behind the dark glasses. "Peace, Boyd family. Er, Gundersons."

I watch their car rattle down the road and out of sight, until Kurt says, "You should go pee."

I turn. The movers are standing on the sidewalk, shuffling their feet and trying not to smile, while Mom is staring at him with an expression I can't read. Maybe she's marveling at the fact that just when we think he can't get any worse, he finds a way to surprise us all. But I'm projecting.

"I don't have to go, actually," I say, my cheeks reddening as one on the movers barks a laugh.

"We're not stopping before Battle Creek, so you better empty everything now."

"I'm not sure that's the way it works," Mom says.

"Your only other option is going to be peeing in a cup!" Kurt sounds far too cheerful. But before I can protest, or ask what his plan is if I need to do more than pee, he's paying the movers and Mom has gone inside.

I hurry in after her to grab the last of my things, and then the house is empty and we're leaving. Mom pulls the door shut behind us, pausing and laying a hand on the frame before knocking softly, once. Then she straightens her shoulders. "All set."

But set for what? My entire life lies behind that door. I swallow hard and try to speak around the giant rock in my throat.

Kurt, already behind the wheel of the U-Haul, honks the horn as if sensing things are about to get emotional. Mom looks over, away from me, and the moment passes.

So that's it. Pretty sucky, as far as goodbyes go. We get into the car, and I look back one last time as Mom pulls the Nissan out of the driveway.

"And we're off," Mom says. "God, I'm tired."

I groan. "It's so early."

"Butt early!" She grins at me. "Get it? Like b-u-t-t, butt? Your dad used to call it 'the butt crack of dawn.' And then he shortened it. Butt early."

I love it when she shares these details, so tiny and so intimate. Things only they knew. Like a secret language. I also know there won't be many more. They slide away as time passes, and now with Kurt in the picture, our time together is passing, too. Once it was the two of us against the world, now we're three. Or they're two and I'm the third wheel.

"Fresh start," she says, as if reading my mind. "I know we keep saying it, but it's true. This is going to be good for us."

Every time she says this, it sounds less like she's trying to convince me and more like she's trying to convince herself.

"New town, new home. New family." She doesn't look at me as she says this, but I know she's gauging my reaction.

I wish I could be as happy as she needs me to be. She deserves every good thing. I've never been in love, but I understand how it works. And I know how much she loves Kurt. Despite his many flaws, I see how he takes care of things, taking the burden off her shoulders. How he treats her like she's the most beautiful woman in the world.

But knowing all this doesn't quite stop me from hating him.

It's not like he's an incontrovertible asshole. Mom would never have fallen in love with a guy like that. Uptight, yes. Control freak, big yes. A bit too enamored of the white-horse fantasy he's cast himself and my mother in? Absolutely. Clueless about raising a daughter? *Ding, ding, ding!*

It's the last one I'm struggling with. I don't need a father. I made it this far without one, and Mom and I have always been fine on our own. Still, it would be nice for him to acknowledge that we're a package deal, instead of treating me like a tacky accessory Mom had picked up before they met. Like a gaudy purse.

Mom reaches over to grab my hand. "Please give him a chance, Lo. For me." She squeezes. "He's not as bad as you want him to be. And I love him."

I swallow hard and squeeze back. I'm not a monster.

Mom has always told me I was enough of a family for her, but I know a part of her still missed my dad. I'm sure she's looked ahead to the future and thought about being alone in an empty house when I head off to college. Now she doesn't need to worry about any of that. Even our financial problems have been solved, with the help of this short little man who stole her heart.

I pull out my phone and plug it in, then thumb open Google Maps, clicking until I'm zoomed in on an aerial view of our new house, perched on a rocky hill outside of Claret Creek, Colorado. There's no street view, but luckily, the caretaker sent us pictures.

I open those next, staring at the gigantic house where my dad grew up. I've looked at this so many times in the past few weeks, I've memorized every stone. It's huge, probably four times the size of what I'm used to. Dad's house has a wide front porch, which is tucked under the first story, with four towers on each corner supporting the second and third floors. Additional twin columns hold up the front edifice, a single massive piece of stone carved with the face of a lion.

"Have you ever seen it?" I ask when I catch Mom sneaking a glance at my screen.

She hesitates. "In pictures," she finally says. "It was already sitting empty by the time we started dating. His dad—your grandpa, John Henry—he died while

Daddy was still in college. And Teddy wanted to finish his degree before he moved back home to sort everything out."

"But then he met you," I prompt.

"Then he met me," she echoes softly. "He used to go out west to check on it every so often. We sometimes talked about me going with him but . . ." She swallows hard. "It always feels like you have more time, you know?" She blinks as she stares at the road ahead, but I know she's really lost in a past I can't see.

"His mother had always insisted it had to stay in the family," she finally says, lifting a shoulder. "And our lives were in Michigan. So Daddy rented it out for a while. And when that family moved out, he hired a caretaker." Her face clouds over. "That's what he was doing out there, that last time." She tightens her grip on the wheel. "When he had the accident."

An electric shock runs up my back, nearly pushing me out of my seat. "What do you mean? He'd been away on business, you said."

She nods once, stiffly. "Business with the house."

I'm speechless. I mimic her posture, straightening in my seat and staring out the windshield. My dad died driving somewhere along this same route. Out of town, I'd always heard. When I'd gotten older, I'd tried to look up details of his accident, but the closest I got was some county in the middle of Nowhere, Colorado.

"Do you know where?" I ask. "Exactly?"

She puffs out her cheeks, then lets the air out slowly as she shakes her head. "I have a rough idea, but that's it." She reaches out to squeeze my hand. "It was a long time ago. I don't like thinking about it."

The first day of our trip is boring and uneventful. We stop to refuel and pee at regular intervals, my bladder quickly becoming attuned to Kurt's schedule—yet another way my body has chosen to betray me. I try to sleep as best as I can, though my muscles scream at being crammed into the same position for hours at a time. I get up to stretch whenever we stop, scouring the shelves at every convenience store for something that at least partially adheres to my limited diet. I settle for a granola bar and a hard-boiled egg in Battle Creek, a day-old hot dog minus the bun in Illinois, and a packet of peanuts and an iced coffee that I nurse through Iowa before we finally call it quits in Omaha. By then, it's late, inky dark, and Mom is pissed, though she's trying to hide it.

"Almost halfway, babe!" Kurt declares, throwing open the door to our room at Super 8. He throws his arm around Mom's shoulders and lands a big kiss on her cheek. "You're a trooper. Best to push on while we're still fresh, right?"

"Speaking of fresh, I need a shower," she says, gently disentangling from his embrace. Kurt watches as she drops her purse on the puke-colored bedspread, then turns to me. "Hey, Lola, why don't you go check out the pool? Take your time."

Ugh. Gross. I know money is tight, but they couldn't have sprung for a second room? I'm dead on my feet, but I will definitely go to the pool. I may sleep there. Or in our car. Anything to get me away from the two of them *together*.

The outdoor pool is empty, the surface scattered with dead bugs. I watch the cars pass by on the interstate as I wait for Bryn to pick up my FaceTime call, the line of tiny lights stretching back into the distance. Back toward home. Winston Churchill once said, "The longer you can look back, the farther you can look forward."

I used to love that quote. Now it just feels like meaningless tripe. I can't see anything except for what I'm losing.

"They just got married. This is technically their honeymoon," Bryn reminds me after I bring them up to speed. "And they're spending it at some cheap-ass motel. Your mom is probably just as unhappy about it as you are."

"You're wrong. My mom is happy. Deliriously so. Which is the only way to explain why she married him in the first place. Is this my life now? Getting booted so they can have sex while they pretend I don't know what they're doing?"

Bryn tilts their head. "No. This is temporary. Soon, your life is going to be sneaking around and having sex behind their backs while *you* pretend *they* don't know what you're doing."

I bark a laugh. "Your ability to make lemonade out of shit is truly inspiring."

"If at first you don't succeed, suck lemons. You'll suck seeds."

I pause, but I don't recognize the quote. "Nope. I'm stumped."

"It was a cheat," Bryn confesses. "Something my dad loves to say. But mark my words—you're going to meet a gorgeous cowboy out there. Unless pop culture has betrayed me, Colorado is absolutely brimming with eligible men in boots and flannel and leather chaps."

"Right. Because it's all exactly like on TV." I heave a sigh. "There aren't going to be any cute cowboys. It'll just be me and Kurt, alone in that big house while Mom goes off to work."

"Look on the bright side," Bryn says.

I raise an eyebrow.

"The leather chaps! I swear, it's like you're not even listening. But seriously, this is a good thing. You're getting what you've always wanted."

"I'm waiting for the punch line."

"You're moving to your dad's hometown. Into his fucking childhood home. You've wanted to learn more about him and his family as long as I've known you, and you're about to hit the mother lode."

I feel myself relax a tiny bit. "Is that a mining joke?"

"Damn right!"

"It was better than the leather chaps."

Mom and I both sleep through Kurt's alarm, which does not please him, and he makes us pay for our fatigue by stretching the time between our bathroom breaks to three hours. Mom gets her wish from the day before—lunch in the car—and

I nearly have to resort to peeing in my Big Gulp. Tempers are running high by the time we stop in Denver for dinner.

The diner is right off the interstate, one of those '50s throwbacks that looks like it was built out of an old Airstream trailer. Or a tin can. Kurt makes a show of stretching his arms out across the back of the red leather booth with a loud groan. Even the waitress looks annoyed as she comes over with a coffee pot, which somehow cheers me. I love it when even strangers find him ridiculous.

Mom waves her off. "No, thank you. I need to get some sleep tonight."

"Drink up, love. We've still got another four hours or so to go."

The waitress fills my cup instead, jumping back when Mom slaps her plastic menu on the table. "Four hours? I thought once we hit Denver, we were 'practically home.'" She makes air quotes around the phrase Kurt has been repeating for the past half hour over Mom's Bluetooth.

"It's four hours. Three and a half if we push it. We're in the home stretch," Kurt insists.

But Mom is already shaking her head. "I'm not driving that tonight. In the dark? Absolutely not. I'm exhausted."

Kurt opens his mouth to argue, and I hold my breath. Maybe this is it. The Big One. The fight that will let her know, once and for all, what kind of egomaniac she married.

Before he can drop whatever asinine wisdom he's intending, Mom turns to me. "Lola, honey. Can you wait outside while we sort this out?"

I take a gulp, the coffee scalding my throat. I'm starving. And I'm exhausted. But sure, I'll leave.

I shove my own menu aside and crawl out of the booth, snagging the chipped diner coffee mug as I go. The waitress eyes me sympathetically as I shove through the door, sloshing hot coffee on my hand.

Bryn doesn't answer my call, so I perch on a picnic table in a dirty strip of grass beside the parking lot and stare at the mountains rising up in the distance. I've only seen them in pictures before, and nothing has prepared me for the overpowering feeling of sitting in their shadow. I feel very small and very alone. Like God herself is throwing up a warning. *None shall pass.*

Maybe we should heed it.

Mom comes out just as I drain the last dregs of my coffee. I stand and dust off my shorts. Kurt trails behind her, then veers off suddenly to jump into the U-Haul.

"What the f—" I swallow the curse. "I don't even get to eat now?" The jolt of caffeine on an empty stomach has me shaky and lightheaded, but that could also be the anger.

The squeal of Kurt's tires drowns out Mom's reply.

I turn to watch him peel out of the parking lot, and when I look back, Mom waves toward the motel at the other end of the parking lot.

"I got us a room. And I left the tab open, so you can get some food." Her mouth is set in a grim line; her face is pale and drawn. "I've got a headache. I'm going to the room to lie down."

I blink at her, trying to process what's just happened. We've got a hotel room. And clearly, Kurt is going on without us. I've got a million questions, but Mom looks too tired to answer any of them. This is what I wanted, after all. Just her and me, no Kurt breathing down my neck. I just wish she didn't look so devastated.

I wake to find Mom sitting at the table in our hotel room, hands wrapped tightly around a coffee mug and papers spread out in front of her.

"Morning," I say, blinking blearily at the weak sunlight streaming through the window. I stretch gently, trying to work out the kinks from the long car ride and the unfamiliar mattress. "Did Kurt make it to the house?"

She nods, her face turned toward the window so I can't read her expression.

It irks me that he's gotten to see it before me, but there's nothing I can do about it. "So, what's the plan?" I grab my phone from the end table, swiping up to see the time—7:12. "We're only a couple hours away, right?" I calculate quickly in my head. Shower, breakfast, on the road by 8:00?

"Get there by noon, maybe?" My stomach turns over—upset or excitement, I'm not sure. In just a few short hours, I'm going to see my dad's house. *My* house.

Mom clears her throat. "Yes. We're close." Her hands seem to tremble as she lifts her mug, and I rub my eyes, trying to focus. Is she still upset about her fight with Kurt?

"I've been planning our route," she says, gesturing at the map spread in front of her. "I think I've found a better way. It will add a bit of time, but I think it will be nicer."

"How much time?" I ask, sounding like Kurt and hating it.

She bites her lower lip. "Maybe an hour or so."

My morning-fogged brain struggles to make sense of this. "You want to go an hour out of our way?"

"You've never driven on mountain roads, Lola. They're dangerous. I'd rather be safe than fast." She stands abruptly and crosses to the bathroom, ending the discussion with a decisive click of the lock.

I shower and dress as fast as I can, mentally trying to make up the additional time. Now that we're so close, Kurt's insistence from the night before doesn't seem that unreasonable. Though I would never admit to agreeing with him, we really are in the home stretch.

I toss my bag into the trunk and find Mom standing in front of the passenger door.

"Would you mind—I've still got such a headache. Could you drive? I'm sure it will be fine. I've programmed the new route. You'll be fine." She holds out the car keys, trying to reassure herself as much as me.

I take them as she stares at me intently with a look I know well. As if she's trying to peel back the layers around my brain and peer inside. I've seen this expression before. If she could just get a good look under the hood, she'd be able to figure out what pains me.

If only it were that easy.

"You don't have to, you know. If you aren't feeling up to it. We could get another coffee—"

"I'm fine, Mom. Happy to drive."

It's true. I love driving. There's a power in being able to get in and go, wheels and fuel taking me farther and faster than I could ever run. In Michigan, it was windows down, music up—the fresh air its own kind of freedom. But I've never driven for longer than an hour or farther than Ann Arbor.

And very shortly, I discover that Mom is right. The mountain roads are different. And sometimes terrifying.

Especially when I hit the stretches where the cliff seems to drop away beyond the guardrail. Looking down into all that space makes me dizzy, and though I have an unsettling urge to nudge the car closer to the edge so I can see how deep the drop is, I resist the impulse. Instead, I move to the far lane, which has no shoulder, just a thin strip of aluminum separating the road from the sheer rock wall of the mountain rising up beside me.

My hands sweat on the steering wheel as I aim the car down this road that feels more like a tightrope suspended between two equally fatal possibilities. Meanwhile, Mom sits ramrod straight in her seat, one hand clutching the door handle and the other braced on the dashboard. She's not the best passenger under normal circumstances, but today her anxious silence is especially annoying.

"Maybe you can find something on the radio," I tell her.

As she presses the button with shaky fingers, her phone buzzes. She stares at the screen and takes a deep breath before answering, which is how I know it's Kurt.

I don't want to listen in on her conversation, but we're sitting right next to each other. Kurt sounds enthusiastic and overly friendly, while Mom gives him clipped, one-word responses.

"Yes. No. Lola. By two."

If Kurt's surprised it's taking us so long, to his credit he doesn't say so. The navigation app mounted on the dash flashes, and I squint at it: *Alternate route. Will save you 46 minutes. Would you like to apply?* I glance over at Mom, who's hunched in her seat whispering into the phone. What the hell. Forty-six fewer minutes of this white-knuckle, anxiety-riddled ride? Yes, please.

I punch the button and the map reroutes, taking us around a sharp bend that hugs the mountain. The sheer rock wall to my right is impossibly tall, the canyon on my left endless and deep, and I suddenly remember that somewhere near here is where my dad lost control of his car.

My head goes woozy and I blink, my vision going out of focus for a second or two before clearing. I reach for my travel mug, but it's empty. Maybe I should pull over. Only there's nowhere *to* pull over.

I take a breath, slow and even, and ease off the gas pedal. I'm being ridiculous. So the road is a little twisty. And maybe I'm not as rested as I thought I was. I've driven tired before. I've never had blackouts. I don't faint.

Except that one time, with Jesse.

Don't think about that.

Don't think about blacking out, about the car veering into the other lane and over the side of the cliff, or smashing through the guardrail and straight into the side of the mountain.

Is that what happened to Dad?

Do not think about Dad! Don't think about him behind the wheel, or his last thoughts, knowing he was about to die.

I fumble with Mom's water bottle in the other cup holder, not wanting to take my eyes off the road. When I finally free it, I take a long drink and it slips from my sweaty hand, dumping cold water into my lap.

"Shit!" The car sways into the other lane as I shove the bottle into the cup holder.

"Lola!" Mom drops her phone and clutches the dash.

"It's fine. I dropped my water." I glance down at the water soaking my jean shorts.

"Eyes on the road," Mom barks.

A green sign rises up, towering above me, its white stickers gleaming in the sun: CLARET CREEK, 150 MILES.

"Wait. Where are we?" Mom asks, her voice hoarse. "Did you change the route?"

I don't answer her. We're nearly in Claret Creek. My dad's hometown.

"Lola, answer me!"

I don't want to die here.

The words float into my mind, unbidden. I'm driving, but the hands on the wheel are someone else's. Older hands, bigger knuckles. A wedding ring. Instead of sunshine through the windshield, there's only rain. Ceaseless, pouring rain.

Jesus, Teddy. We need to get off the road. It's not safe here.

I jerk back against the seat, blinking in the sudden brightness as the vision recedes. My hands shake. The view through the windshield is blurred, and I can't catch my breath.

I catch sight of the turnoff from the corner of my eye and yank the wheel at the last second—onto the ramp that tilts steeply up the mountain, intended for runaway trucks.

I slam my foot on the brake. The tires lock as the car skids across the gravel and rock for another second before shuddering to a stop.

CHAPTER 3

Blood doesn't scare me anymore. I don't know why it did when I was younger. With the tree incident, it had felt like the fear was coming from somewhere outside of me; that panic was so deep it engulfed me, swallowing me whole. It wasn't that I thought Jesse was dead, or even that he was in pain. It was something else, some primitive response from the lizard part of my brain telling me blood equals bad.

Mom is having the same response. "Lola! You're bleeding! Oh my god! What happened?" She reaches for me, but her seat belt has her trapped. She fumbles with it, her hands shaking. "Shit. Are you all right? Answer me, baby!"

"I'm fine," I say, hands still gripping the steering wheel. "I got . . . dizzy. So I pulled off." Her expression is one of such pure panic, my stomach lurches. *Am* I okay? What the hell *was* that? Another new symptom? It felt like a memory, but from someone else—Teddy, my dad—and from some other time and place. A memory that doesn't belong to me.

Or maybe it's a warning.

It's not safe here.

We're not very far up the ramp, which pitches steeply in front of me. I turn around in the seat and get caught by the seat belt, so I jab my thumb to release it. I have to pee. Or did I already? My shorts are wet. I'm weak and shaky and my head feels fuzzy, stuffed, like there are too many thoughts crowding it and they aren't all mine.

I dumped my water bottle. Right. I remember now.

"You're bleeding," Mom says again.

She's succeeded in unbuckling herself, and she leans over to press a hand to my face. I swat it away automatically, then pull down the visor to look at myself. My nose is bleeding. "Did I hit my head?"

"Did you?" Her voice is shaky. "Do we need to go to the hospital?"

I shake my head, tentatively at first, then more vehemently when it doesn't throb. "No. I'm fine." Stronger this time. I might be convincing myself at least, if not her.

I grab a wad of napkins from the console, then turn around again, trying to gauge how we're going to get out of here. Getting back on the road should be simple, only a slight backing up before the ramp widens, and then I can make a reverse Y-turn and pull back onto the highway.

"What are you doing?" Mom asks sharply as I put my hand on the gearshift. "You're not driving."

She has a point. What if it happens again? Whatever it was. The . . . hallucination. It felt like I was . . . channeling my dad. Feeling his feelings. Thinking his thoughts. Maybe his final thoughts.

My stomach lurches. No. That's not possible.

I shove the car door open, nearly falling into the dirt in my haste to get out of the car. I brace myself against the door as another wave of dizziness hits me, the bright sun flashing over and over, blinding me.

Not the sun. Lights.

A police car pulls up behind us.

The officer takes his time climbing out of his vehicle, sunlight glinting off his mirrored sunglasses. He's tall and lean, with dark hair shorn so close I can see the bumps of his skull and skin weathered like a piece of beef jerky.

"Everything okay?"

"Y-yeah. I just got . . . um, dizzy," I stutter. Have I done something illegal? Maybe these pull-offs are only for trucks.

Mom slams her door and hurries around the car. "Officer. Thank you for stopping."

He gives her a curt nod and gestures at the license plate. "Out of state?"

I put up a hand to block the relentless glare of the sun. "Yeah. We're moving."

"Where to?" He directs this at Mom, but she's staring down the highway and doesn't seem to hear him, so I answer.

"Claret Creek?" I've no idea why it comes out like a question.

"Ah. The waters." Is it just me, or does his mouth twist distastefully as he says it?

Is that a reference to my wet shorts? "W-what water?" I stutter, tugging at the bottom of my T-shirt.

"The creek." He pronounces it like "crick." "I thought that had all died out."

Does he mean the town? Or the creek? I try to catch Mom's eye again, but she's staring at the road with such intensity that it looks like she's trying to stall traffic with her mind.

"Is one of you sick?" he asks. I can't tell if he's concerned about our well-being or convinced I might not be competent to operate a vehicle. Then again, why would he assume we've driven a thousand miles for creek water? Has he never heard of the Great Lakes? And how could he possibly know about my illness?

I gape at him for a beat, then realize he's asking which of us was driving. "It was me," I say. "I got . . . disoriented." It's better than hallucinate-y. "What did you mean by died out?"

"Altitude," he says, nodding firmly, as if the word sums up everything. "Light-headed? Disoriented?" He points at the license plate. "Highways can be treacherous if you aren't used to driving in the mountains."

"Are there a lot of . . . accidents," I force out, "on this stretch?"

He shrugs. "All roads can be dangerous if you aren't paying attention." He mutters something under his breath, then raps on the trunk with his knuckles, jerking Mom's attention back to us. "You let me know when you're ready, and I'll help guide you out."

"Thank you, officer. I'll . . . I'll drive. I think it will be better if I drive." Mom doesn't sound like she believes that, but I'm not going to argue with her.

I climb into the passenger side and wait for her to get in. "Sorry about the wet—" I begin, fumbling with some napkins, but she sits down without looking. "I'm sorry I scared you," I say, fiddling with the leaf on my bracelet.

"I don't want to talk," she snaps, then softens her voice to add, "I need to concentrate."

She flexes her hands on the wheel, then adjusts the seat and the mirrors before turning the key. The radio comes to life, softly, but she jumps and stabs a finger at it as if she's been shocked. Her face is as pale as her gray hair and her knuckles tense on the wheel as she watches the cop car behind us. He reverses first, then angles his car into the first lane with his lights going, leaving a break for us to pull out.

He never answered my question. *I thought that had all died out*, he'd said. All this time, I've been focused on the house and my dad. I hadn't given much thought to the town. Or if there is one.

But of course there is. Claret Creek exists. There are road signs. Mom has a job lined up there. I turn, watching the cop watch us. He was just weird. Off, somehow. The way he'd asked "Is one of you sick?" instead of "Who was driving?" or "Did you feel sick?" like a normal person would.

We cruise slowly down the highway in silence, and it's probably just as well. I'm not sure I want to talk to Mom, either. What would I say to her? I was tired? That part was true. But "I hallucinated my father's accident" is harder to say and even harder to believe. That can't be what happened.

I'm tired. And stressed. And thinking about my dad. Hell, I've had his music on repeat this whole trip. Maybe that's what it was—a stress reaction. Triggered by a song he loved. When I put it like this, it doesn't seem so implausible.

I lay my head against the glass and give in to the relentless tug of fatigue.

Mom shakes my shoulder. "Lo, wake up. We're here. Well, almost."

I sit up, yawning so big my jaw cracks as I rub the grit from my eyes and try to focus. The scenery has changed from twisty road to flat, and from rocky alcoves to evidence of suburbia—scrubby lawns, a few trees, fences lined with bikes and big wheels. A sign proclaims WELCOME TO CLARET CREEK—HOME OF HEALING WATERS.

What is that? A waterpark?

The town has an old-timey, antique feeling. Like we've been plopped down at some unspecified time in the past. The diner has a tin sign hanging in the window advertising Coke for a nickel, but the fact that it's tucked in between a vape shop and a tattoo parlor only accentuates how hard they're trying—and failing—to hang on to the past. It's like a poorly designed movie set.

"Welcome to Claret Creek," Mom says, and I can't tell if she's being serious or reading it off the sign. "The house is on the outskirts of town, so we won't get to see downtown proper. We'll have to take a tour later. But there's the library." She idles at a stop sign and leans over me to point down the road to a tall brick building with white paned windows and a dome on top. I'd say it feels out of place, but I'm the one who's out of place here.

"When do you start work?"

"Tomorrow."

"Did you want to stop now? Peek inside?"

"No," she says, then more confidently, "No. Not today. I'm a mess. Better I meet everyone when I'm cleaned up and put together."

She straightens and keeps driving, crossing a bridge over what I can only assume is the eponymous Claret Creek before turning off on a long, winding, shoulderless road that cuts through a grove of aspen trees planted so close together it seems their branches have started to intertwine. They stand like sentinels, silent and blocking my view.

"Aspen. Quaking aspen, actually," Mom says.

"What are they afraid of?" I shoot back, but maybe it's better I don't know.

"Do you see the turn?" she asks when the GPS instructs us to turn right.

I can't see anything through this damn cluster, but I strain forward. "Maybe up ahead? Around the curve?"

As we round the curve, a stone pillar appears on the right and Mom jerks the wheel. The driveway is easy to miss, tucked between the trees, but once we're clear of the foliage, the house comes into view.

It's so much bigger than in the pictures. And so much more forlorn. It's evident to me that the photos I have of it had been taken much earlier, maybe even when my dad was still alive. Mom's been paying a caretaker to rent it out when he can, as well as do minor repairs and keep an eye on things, so nothing is collapsing. The stone pillars supporting the deep front porch are darkened with age but look solid, and the tangled bushes around the house have been trimmed recently, as evidenced by their uniform flat tops. The wide, smudged windows lining the second and third stories are all intact.

Still, there's an air of abandonment about it. The stone lion above the porch is green with age, his eye sockets leaking moss from the corners as if he's weeping. Like he's sad. Like the house itself is sad. Like it's stood empty for so long, loneliness is seeping out of it.

I'm out of the car before Mom, intent on getting inside as fast as possible. Instead, I freeze at the bottom of the steps.

I am standing where my dad once stood. This is where he grew up. That was his porch. He walked those stairs countless times. Peered through these windows. Slammed that big front door. The feeling of connection clutches at me, squeezing so tight that for a moment I can't catch my breath.

I blink back dark spots, and Kurt is in front of me.

"It's going to be a bitch to heat, I can tell you that," he says, hands on hips as he blocks my entry.

I want to slap him so badly my hand tingles. *That's* the first thing he says to me? No hello? No "How was the drive?" *We almost died, thank you very much.* But I don't say it. It's over-the-top bitchy, and I promised Mom I'd try to get along.

It's just that I'm so tired. And I cannot stand the fact that this . . . man, this relative *stranger*—who never met my dad, who wasn't even in our lives up until a few months ago—he got to spend the entire first night in my dad's childhood home. Without us. I know I'm being ridiculous, but I wanted to be the first one to walk on my dad's floors. To touch his things. To breathe his air.

I can't help but feel like it's all been tainted by Kurt now.

Like everything else.

"I've seen photos," I tell him, clenching my fists at my side. "There are fireplaces. You don't have to pay for heat."

"Where do you think the wood comes from?" he asks, grinning and shaking his head.

"It grows on trees?" But my sarcastic comment is lost to the desert wind as he catches sight of Mom and sprints down the stairs to greet her.

I close my eyes, not wanting their reunion to intrude on this, my first introduction to Boyd Manor. My dad's home. And now mine.

When I open them, there's a wild animal running straight toward me.

CHAPTER 4

It's a bear.

I've been here in Claret Creek all of thirty seconds, and I'm about to be mauled by a bear.

My heart thuds dully in my throat as my life flashes in a technicolor blur before my eyes.

"Orson!"

A strange voice halts the bear and he skids to a stop in front of me, tongue lolling out. On second glance, I realize he's too small to be a bear. But the fluffy cinnamon fur, tiny round ears, and dark snout are definitely bear-like.

"Orson's completely harmless." The boy comes up behind me, grabbing for the bear-dog's collar.

Having to hold your dog back does not inspire confidence in the phrase "completely harmless," but I don't say it. I can only manage a nod, because up close it seems ridiculous that I mistook him for a bear. He's just a big, adorable dog.

And his owner is even cuter, which maybe explains my sudden lack of vocal cords. He has a mop of curls and an easy grin that widens into a dimple. The first thing that pops out of my mouth is "Labradoodle."

The boy laughs. "Actually, he's a Chow Chow. I'm Fletcher. Fletcher Hart." He leans over to pick up a tennis ball, which he lobs into the distance; Orson chases after it. "And you're Lola, right? I'm so stoked you're finally here."

He beams at me with such joy that I smile stupidly back, though I'm not sure why. Why would he be this excited to see me? He's acting like we know each other, like this meeting was arranged and I'm late. It's like some kind of reverse déjà vu;

instead of feeling familiar, it's like I've been dropped into the middle of a play and I'm the only one who doesn't know my part.

"He scared me," I blurt, then wince. *Really, Lola?* I follow up with "What are you doing here?"

Smooth. Now he thinks I'm a coward *and* abrasive.

But his relentless cheerfulness is not easily dampened. He waves a hand toward the house. "We wanted to make sure you had a warm welcome." He adds, "My dad and I," as my mouth forms the word "we."

That doesn't clear anything up.

"I see you've met the welcoming committee," Kurt says, his voice booming with fake heartiness as he and Mom head up the driveway toward us. Looking tired and wan, she doesn't speak but ducks Kurt's arm as he tries to put it around her.

While I love watching her give Kurt the literal cold shoulder, this time I feel bad for him. I know she's mad because Kurt left us behind, and she's blaming him for my incident on the drive. But there was no way he could've known something like that would happen. Whatever *that* was.

It's not safe here.

I shake my head like I'm brushing off a bug and cross my arms to hide the goose bumps.

Fletcher looks equally thrilled to see Mom, which seems even weirder than his excitement at my arrival. "Welcome, Mrs. Boy—I mean . . ." Fletcher falters on the greeting but extends a hand, his eyes darting between Kurt and Mom.

"Please, call me Tress."

"We're so glad you're here!" he repeats.

There's that "we" again.

"Lola and I are both juniors," Fletcher continues. "We'll probably have at least a couple classes together."

Uh-oh. I stare at Mom, willing her not to say anything about my health or my school situation. I hate explaining it under the best of circumstances, and this—the first time meeting this cute, eager boy right after that hellish car ride—is hardly the best-case scenario.

Mom gives me a half shrug, but we're both saved from whatever she might have said as another man comes around the side of the house. He's at least six inches taller than Kurt, with dark hair and an easy smile—basically an older version of Fletcher with a beard. When he sees us, his blue eyes brighten and he dumps the load of sticks he's carrying, dusting off his hands on his jeans. "Tress! You made it! Good to see you a—"

"Thanks so much for meeting us!" she says, too bright and too loud. "This is my daughter, Lola. Lola, this is Dominic Hart. He's the caretaker. And a good friend of your father's."

"Great to meet you, Lola," he says, holding out a hand. "I've heard so much about you. You look like Teddy. Around the eyes." He circles his own with a finger. "I see you've already met Fletcher."

He turns to Mom. "And you. You look great." It's clearly a lie, but he manages to make it sound sincere.

Mom twists the end of her ponytail between her fingers. "Thanks. You look great, too. It's good to meet in person, isn't it? Finally. After all those Zoom calls."

Dominic frowns, two lines like quotes furrowing the space above his nose.

There's something oddly intimate in the look that flashes between them, but my curiosity is overridden by more pertinent information. Dominic was a good friend of my father's. Besides Mom, I've never even met anyone who even knew my father, much less one of his good friends.

Kurt takes the awkward lull as an opportunity to steer the conversation. "Dominic and I met earlier," he says. "He's given me the whole rundown. So I think we're set." He pastes on a fake smile.

"How is it?" Mom asks, staring up at the house.

"Well, it's going to need a ton—" Kurt begins.

"You said 'habitable.'" Mom speaks over him, turning to Dominic and pulling a face. "That's a pretty broad interpretation."

Fletcher's dad rocks back on his heels as he laughs. "So serious, Tress. I should have been more specific. I'd say she's in better shape than you might be expecting. Teddy did a lot of upgrading, before . . ." He clears his throat. "The electrical and the slate roof are in good condition. I also went ahead and had the gas switched on for you. The tenants were here through the winter, but it's been off for the summer. I took a walk-through earlier and everything looked to be up and running, but definitely let me know if you have any problems."

"Thank you." Mom doesn't move, and I wonder if she's afraid to go inside, if she thinks there will be too many reminders of my father the minute she walks through those doors.

It's the same reason I'm itching to do exactly that. I'm about to ask if we can see it when Mom says, "Can you walk us around the grounds?"

Dominic checks his phone. "Sure. If you're not pressed for time. I know you've had a long drive. There's also that tax issue we have to discuss, sooner rather than later."

"I think later is best. Tress and I need to get settled," Kurt says, stepping toward the porch.

I notice he hasn't included me in this scenario, and maybe Fletcher notices, too, because when I sneak a glance at him, he's watching me with a puzzled smile.

"Let's walk," Mom says, winding her arm through Dominic's. "I need to stretch my legs. Lola, come with us? You're going to love the creek."

I'm torn. I'm dying to see the house. On the other hand, Dominic was a friend of my father's. What kind of stories does he have to tell?

It's an easy choice. "Sure," I say, following them around the side of the house. Fletcher matches his steps to mine and Orson brings up the rear. Kurt, who has not been included in this invitation, sets his shoulders and hurries past us, trying to catch up to Mom and Dominic.

The house is perched on a sloping hill overlooking a sandy yard dotted with patches of scrub brush. The mountain looms over us, casting a long shadow, and I'm relieved when we manage to leave it behind and emerge into bright sunlight. I feel like I should make conversation with Fletcher, but my mind is blank. "So," I begin, and he turns that bright smile up another watt. "Your dad and my dad were friends."

"Best friends," Fletcher says promptly. "Teddy and Dom. Dom and Teddy. They were like Dave Grohl and Taylor Hawkins. Mick Jagger and Keith Richards. Daryl Hall and John Oates?" He adds the last as a question.

"You're into music," I say, gesturing to his Pink Floyd T-shirt and wishing everything that came out of my mouth didn't sound completely asinine. Of course I know who Mick Jagger is. I'm still stuck on his first words. *Best friends*. Which means Dom is Dad's Bryn; he knows everything. He's—what had Bryn called it?—the mother lode.

Fletcher offers his hand and I hesitate a second before taking it, but the land pitches steeply, giving way to red rocky soil that shifts beneath my ill-chosen flip-flops. We half walk and half slide to a stop beside the bank of the creek, Fletcher catching me before I stumble into the water. I hurry to disentangle myself, conscious of our parents standing only a few feet away, but they aren't looking at us.

Since I'd heard the name of the town, I've been half picturing a red river. But Claret Creek is crystal clear. Sunlight pools on the water like liquid gold, while river rocks gleam like jewels beneath the surface.

It's breathtaking.

"This is ours?" I ask, then flush. I sound impossibly greedy. "I don't mean all of it, obviously. But this spot, it's on our land?"

"Your land, your water," Dominic says.

The day is hot, but tall trees shade the rocky bank on both sides and the slight breeze makes me shiver as I think of the cop earlier, so sure we were coming for "the waters."

How did he know?

"Are you okay?" Fletcher asks as I rub my arms, trying to dispel the goose bumps.

"Fine. Just a little . . . overwhelmed, I guess. It's not anything like I imagined."

It's so much more.

It's *real*.

"Be careful of this," Dominic says, looking back at us as he points to a crumbling rock structure set a few feet back from the creek. "It's dangerous. Fletcher knows already. Not a spot for you guys to explore. It's all rot."

"What is it?" I ask.

"It's the foundation of the old building," Dominic says. "It burned down a long time ago."

I squint. Now that he's said "building," I can trace the crumbling stone into the outline of a square, roughly the size and shape of our house back in Michigan. Only one wall is still recognizable as such, and even that only stands waist high. In the center, in what would have been the interior, thorny weeds choke the ground.

"What was it?" I ask.

"The doctor's office," Fletcher says. "He lived in the big house and saw his patients down here."

The doctor. Something niggles at the back of my brain, like a tiny mental itch I can't scratch. Who is the doctor?

"We should have it bulldozed," Kurt says. "For safety."

Dominic winces. "I'm afraid you're going to run into some interference if that's your plan. This place is part of Claret Creek history. You don't want to mess with the creek, or do anything that might contaminate the water. People won't like it."

"I'm not sure that *people* should get to decide what I do with my"—Kurt cuts a look at me and softens his tone—"our house."

Dominic stares at Kurt for a beat and I wait for Mom to intervene, to say something to break the tension, but she's somewhere else, staring at the creek with a sorrowful expression that makes *me* want to cry.

"Did you guys hang out here? You and my dad?" I ask, because I want to know, of course, but also to break this weird spell that suddenly hangs over us, over this place, almost like a fog.

"We sure did," Dominic says. "Played at treasure hunting in the ruins, even though we weren't supposed to."

Fletcher rolls his eyes. "Way to set an example, Dad."

"I can think of no better example than our stupidity," Dominic says softly, and Fletcher flinches.

What's that all about?

Dominic continues, "Mostly, we played in the creek. Catching crayfish. When we were kids, Teddy was convinced we'd net a talking one. Grant us wishes, maybe." He shakes his head and laughs. "I guess his thinking was, magic water, magic fish."

"Magic?" The word comes out muddled as my head goes fuzzy and my vision blurs. It's like this sometimes—fatigue comes on so abruptly. I have a finite amount of energy, like a battery, and when it's gone, it's gone. And I hate that I can't control it.

I sag against the closest tree.

"Lola?" Fletcher leans in, concerned, but I wave him off.

"I'm just . . . it's been a long day. And it's so . . . warm." I pluck at my top, sticky with sweat. My skin feels like it's on fire.

"Let me find you some wa . . ." Fletcher's words fade as another, stronger voice takes over, drowning him out.

"As sure as this tree will shade you . . ."

Son of a bitch. Not this again.

My fingers scrabble for purchase against the rough bark. I fight to turn my head, but I can't. The cluster of people on the bank are blurry, unfocused. A man leans over me, so close I can smell his rank sweat. He raises a bottle.

". . . so too will these waters heal you."

"You bastard." I hiss the words through my clamped teeth.

He glares at me as he takes my chin in his rough hands, tilting my head back, shoving the bottle to my parched lips.

I slap it from his hands.

CHAPTER 5

Fletcher scrambles to retrieve the water bottle from the ground as Mom kneels beside me. Her hands are everywhere, fluttering like a moth as she pushes the hair off my face and pats my cheek and massages my wrists.

She's become adept at ministering to me in the past year, since the mysterious aches and pains began.

But whatever's happening here is something different.

"Lola, honey, answer me. What's wrong? What do you need?"

Fletcher manages to right the bottle while there is still liquid inside, but this time instead of offering it to me, he hands it to Mom.

"Here. Sit up. Can you drink something?" She peers intently, her eyes probing mine as if trying to read my thoughts.

Good luck. I don't know where these thoughts are coming from, but they aren't mine.

"We should get her inside," she says, craning her neck to look up at Dominic. "Somewhere cooler."

I lean against the trunk, legs splayed awkwardly as they all hover over me like some kind of human umbrella. Squinting up at their faces makes me dizzy, so I stare at the water bottle instead. "Mom, stop," I say quietly as I try to push myself to my feet.

Orson whines and rubs his head against my butt as if to give me a boost.

I dust off my legs and fan my face. "I'm fine. Honest. But I do want to go back to the house." She takes a step toward me and I hold up a hand. "I don't need help." I shoot her a pleading look, but it's Fletcher who comes to my rescue.

"Why don't I take Lola up to the house? I can give her the tour, and you can all discuss your boring adult stuff. Like drainage pipes and taxes and whatever."

Mom looks like she wants to argue, but Dominic touches her arm lightly and says, "There are a few other things we need to talk about. And Fletcher knows the place well. She'll be in good hands. Won't she?" Dominic narrows his eyes at us.

"Yes, sir."

I just want to be away from this place. Preferably alone, at least until I can pull myself together. But Fletcher is offering my only out, so I take the arm he offers.

We make our way back up to the house mostly in silence, for which I'm grateful. I know what Fletcher must think of me—some weird girl who's too weak to even walk up and down a hill by herself—but I'm helpless to change his opinion. I'm just glad he hasn't asked what's wrong with me. Because I don't even know myself. These . . . episodes, or dizzy spells, or whatever they are, they're not like anything I've dealt with before. One more symptom to add to a growing list for my new doctor. Will it help with a diagnosis? Or just muddy the waters?

So too will these waters heal you.

"Why did you say that?" I ask Fletcher, pulling him to a stop beside me. "About the water?"

"You said you were warm. I thought you might be thirsty." He looks flustered. "I didn't mean—"

"So too will these waters heal you," I repeat, the words foreign on my tongue, though I've heard myself say them twice now.

Fletcher's jaw goes slack. "I didn't . . . That's not what I said. Where did you hear that?"

Okay. So it was a hallucination. *Another* hallucination.

I hallucinate now. Great.

Fletcher is still staring at me. "Are you sure you're all right?" he asks.

In the early days of my illness, Mom and my doctor thought it was all in my head. They ordered a mental health screening to make sure I wasn't depressed, which wasn't a terrible idea. I *was* depressed, because I felt like shit and no one believed me. Worse, a lot of my classmates thought I was just some attention-seeking brat. Which is exactly why I don't want Fletcher to know about any of it. No need to scare off the cute boy with my weird medical drama.

I take a breath and paste on a smile. "I'm fine," I repeat, pulling my hand away. "It won't happen again. You can relax. You look like you're afraid to blink."

His cheeks go pink. "I'm sorry. It's just . . ." He rubs his finger against his nose. "You're bleeding. Right here." He reaches toward my face, but then pulls his hand away.

I touch my nose. Blood. "Damn it."

He pats his pockets and scans the ground, as if a tissue might appear before us. Then he pulls his T-shirt over his head. "Here."

Now *my* cheeks are pink. I know because my face is burning as I try not to look at his naked chest. "I'm not going to bleed all over your shirt," I say, pulling up the neck of my own shirt and pinching it over my nose. "Please get dressed before you burn. I doubt your pasty-ass can handle these atomic levels of sunshine. And I already drank all your water."

The minute the words are out of my mouth, I regret them. "Oh my god, I'm sorry. I don't know why I said that." It's something I might have said to Bryn, but not this boy I've just met. It's not even true—his skin is more like golden honey.

Fletcher bursts out laughing and pulls his shirt back over his head. "That's fair," he says. "I do burn easily. And it's hot today. Maybe not atomic level—that was last week." He busts out his dimple again and runs his hands through his unruly curls.

My stomach flip-flops, and this time it isn't the heat.

"Do you know which window was my dad's?" I ask, turning away from his perfect smile and changing the subject.

"I do, actually." Fletcher points to the big windows over the porch. "That front room was your grandparents'. Teddy's room was in the back," he continues, tracking his finger toward one of the corner towers before continuing higher. "But according to Dad, their hangout spot was in the attic. Like Eric Foreman's basement, only nineties style. Less weed, more Nintendo. Or so he says."

"Their hangout." The words catch in my throat like a prayer as I tilt my head upward. This is what I've wanted, for so long. Real stories about my dad.

"Come on," Fletcher says, tugging gently on my hand and breaking the spell. "I'll help you carry in your stuff."

I get my carryall from the car, which Fletcher takes from me. Does he think we're in a Hallmark movie? But before I can protest, he's leading me up the wide stone steps and pushing open the double doors that Kurt has left ajar. I guess he's not worried about the cost of running the A/C.

"Welcome home!" Fletcher cries.

We step into a small entryway, the floor decorated with tiny black and white tiles. A large staircase rises in front of us, winding to the second-floor balcony. Beyond it, big bow windows topped with stained-glass panels look out over the mountain in the distance. On my right, a gigantic limestone fireplace rests between two doors, decorated with a set of wrought-iron fireplace tools all adorned with elaborate, loopy handles.

"This is the great room," Fletcher says, walking backward so he can face me. "It's pretty great, right?" He takes a few steps to my right. "And look, you're going to love this. Ta-da! The library!"

"Library. Right." I step past him through the doorway, expecting a bookshelf or two. Instead, I find myself in a room lined with bookshelves. A cozy window seat is tucked into a rounded niche in the corner, and French doors beside another fireplace lead to the front porch.

This house! It's unbelievable. I nearly laugh out loud. All those nights I found Mom slumped over a pile of bills, worry lining her face as she tried to figure out which she could afford to pay. And now we live in a fucking mansion. With a library.

"We have our own library." I whisper it, because if I say it any louder, this all might disappear. I blink back tears as I look at Fletcher, who grins even wider at the expression on my face. "I knew you were gonna love it." He looks as proud as if he built the place himself.

He's right. I do love it. But how could he know that? How could he know anything about me? Yet he does. Because he grew up here, with people who knew my dad and my family. And somehow, with access to all the memories I've been missing.

I should be angry. And in that moment, I do feel a flutter of something toward him. This earnest boy who is so eager and happy to show me my birthright. But it isn't anger.

"So, what else can I tell you?" He holds his arms wide and walks backward, like a tour guide. "The house is built in the same High Victorian Gothic style as the library downtown."

"High Victorian Gothic?" I ask, eyeing him suspiciously. "How do you know all this?"

He shrugs. "My mom's in estate law. I guess I just picked up some things from her."

"That's cool. My mom's a librarian."

"I know!" Fletcher says. "The library's going to feel familiar to her, for sure. Because it was built by the same architect who designed this place. And actually, the library was once owned by your great-great-great-grandfather Joseph Payne. Three greats, right?"

"I—I don't know," I say, feeling off-kilter. Usually, I'm the one geeking out over genealogy. But I don't have my whole family tree memorized. So why does he? "I'm sorry, how do you know this?"

Fletcher backs up toward the fireplace in the library before turning to gesture at a frame on the wall. I step closer to study the photo so that we're standing shoulder to shoulder.

God, I hope I don't smell as ripe as I feel.

"That's Joseph Payne," he says, his cheek brushing mine as he leans in to point to the only man in the sepia-toned photo. "He and his brother started mining limestone here in Claret Creek, just down the road. Your family is famous around here, you know. They practically built the town."

My skin tingles. *Your family.* He can't possibly know what those words mean to me.

In the photo, Joseph is standing in front of another enormous house with a woman and three young girls—presumably his wife and daughters. "Where was this taken?"

"That's the library. Back when it was Payne Manor, before they donated it to the town."

Another shiver passes over me and I rub my hands quickly over my arms.

"Are you cold?" Fletcher asks, his forehead wrinkled in concern. "Do you need to sit for a minute?"

I shake my head. I squint as I try to line up the three girls with what I know of my family tree. One of these girls must be my great-something-grandmother, but the names are swimming just out of reach. I study them carefully, looking for a family resemblance, or a feeling. Something.

But the women in these photos are as unfamiliar to me as my own father.

It shouldn't surprise me. Female ancestors are notoriously hard to track, given their name changes and the stupid laws of coverture. I can practically hear Bryn's voice in my head, railing about the misogyny and heteronormative ideals present in marriage laws.

"If the library—Payne Manor—was their family home, when did they move in here?" I ask.

"Actually, they didn't all live here." Fletcher taps the tallest daughter in the photo. "Only Rebecca. She inherited this house. From the doctor."

The doctor. "The one with the office down by the creek?"

He nods. "Dr. Frederick Clarett."

"Claret? Like Claret Creek?"

"Close. Clarett with two *t*'s. The creek and the town are both named after him. I'm not sure why we dropped the second *t*. But you might know. You're related to him, right?"

There isn't a Clarett on the family tree, at least not that I remember. "I don't think so. But Rebecca." I draw the name out, running it through my head, and surprisingly, something shakes loose. "Rebecca married a Harrison. James Harrison."

I'm shocked that I've actually remembered this, and Fletcher looks both thrilled at the new information and impressed with my knowledge.

"I only know because I went down a rabbit hole one night on Myroots. Someone researched the Harrison tree and I was able to see their work. It makes sense. The Harrisons are tied to two US presidents and Zebulon Pike."

It sounds like I'm bragging now, so I stop. It really doesn't mean anything, but I was excited as Fletcher looks when I discovered the link. He's the only famous relative I've ever stumbled upon, and though the connections are tenuous, they're there.

"I knew you'd fit right in here," Fletcher says.

A dead relative? Is that all it takes?

I'm not so sure.

I turn away from his eager acceptance to run my fingers along the cloth-bound spines tucked into the towering bookshelves. There's a set of books simply titled *Recipes*, their spines cracked and pages bulging. One of my great-grandmothers probably cooked meals with one of these very books open on the counter in front of her. Probably in this house. There's so much history—my history—packed into this place. I can't quite wrap my head around it.

The next shelf over contains the classics, with fading gold-embossed titles like *The Castle of Otranto*, *The Turn of the Screw*, *Northanger Abbey*. On the other side of the room, the shelf beside the window is entirely full of old paperbacks. I slip one from the shelf and flip through the pages.

"I wonder if this was what my dad liked to read." I tip the book toward Fletcher, who peers at the title.

"Stephen King?" He lifts his shoulders. "Looks like someone was a horror fan. Dean Koontz. Anne Rice. I'm betting the Victoria Holt was not his."

But if he was the last reader, he left no clue behind—no nameplate in the front or pencil marks in the margins. I drop it with a sharp pang of disappointment.

"What do you like to read?" Fletcher asks.

"Anything," I say. "I'm not picky. Words kinda stick in my head like music lyrics. My best friend and I, we play this game where we try to stump each other with famous quotes or passages from books we've both read." I'm not sure why I'm telling him any of this. I'm clearly overtired and off-balance and missing Bryn.

As sure as this tree will shade you, so too will these waters heal you.

I shake my head. Where the hell is that from?

"Bears are made of the same dust as we," says Fletcher.

I have no idea what he's talking about. Have I had another episode and blacked out? "Bears are . . . I'm sorry, what?"

His cheeks go pink. "Sorry. That's really the only quote I know off the top of my head. I have it on a T-shirt. It's from—"

"John Muir," I blurt suddenly.

Fletcher gapes at me. "How did you know that?"

"It was a guess," I admit. "He was the only nature writer I could think of in the moment." My face gets hotter the longer Fletcher stares at me. "Are you a Muir fan?" I ask, hoping to break the awkwardness.

"Nope. But I'm a bear fan. The animal. Not the sports team. Although you probably guessed that, right?" He rolls his hand, and for the first time since we've met, he looks unsure of himself. "Sorry. My mom says I talk about them too much. *No one's that interested in bears.*" He says the last part mimicking what I assume is his mom's voice, then grimaces.

"That's cool," I say. Not because I'm particularly interested in bears, but because I know what it's like to be obsessed with an interest that almost no one else shares. I'm definitely warming to Fletcher, which seems ridiculous. We just met.

"Want to see something else that's cool?" he asks, and without waiting for my reply, he steps around me to the window seat and pulls up the cushion, revealing a recessed cupboard underneath, piled full of old albums.

"Are those . . . photo albums?" My heart pumps with a furious excitement as he nods.

We squeeze together onto the window seat, the books balanced on Fletcher's lap. The first few are coated with dust, and my eyes water as I slowly turn the thick paper pages. Black-and-white photos stare back at us, stuck with darkening glue and with names written below in spidery script.

This book definitely warrants a closer examination. But first, I want to find my dad.

I reach for another book, a square album with a blue gingham cover. I page through slowly, hungrily devouring the images—baby Teddy in a baptismal gown; Teddy's first birthday. Teddy, age three. His first lost tooth. Teddy, age ten, in his bedroom.

My eyes burn—with tears, maybe, or because I've forgotten to blink.

"He was *here*," I say softly, pressing my hand to the photo. "God, I'm being so silly," I add, rubbing my eyes. "Hearing the stories is one thing; seeing him for myself makes it so . . . real."

"I totally get that," Fletcher says. "I grew up hearing the stories. I can't imagine what it would be like to not know." He hands me another album. "Here. This one's got both our dads."

How does he know that? Before I can ponder further, he plops it on my lap and flips it open. This one is not nearly as organized as the others; it looks like my dad might have done it himself, the pages only half-filled, with stacks of loose photos tucked in between the pages. I hold one up, where he sits on a wall with a bunch of other kids. One of them must be Dominic. And on either side of the boys, two teenage girls with poofy hair and braces.

"That's your dad? And who are they?" I ask, pointing at the girls.

"That's my mom," Fletcher says, tapping the girl next to Dominic. "And the other girl is Amber. She's a friend of the family. She and Teddy used to go out."

I wish so much I could communicate with him somehow. I stare at teenage Teddy until my vision blurs, searching for some kind of resemblance. *Around the eyes*, Dominic had said. And it's there. I can see it, the narrow droop near his nose and the thickness of his eyebrows.

"You do look like him," Fletcher says, as if reading my mind.

I slam the book shut.

I want to look at him forever, but by myself. Not with Fletcher watching me.

His face falls when I stand to put the albums away, but he rallies quickly. "Want me to show you his room?"

I grip the railing as we climb the spindly staircase. The upstairs rooms are all situated around the outside of the house and open to the balcony corridor, which overlooks the great room below. Fletcher leads me to the end of the hallway and pushes open a door. The walls are painted a faded blue gray and peppered with phantom rectangles, outlines of old posters maybe. The floors are hardwood, dusty and scuffed, but those are *his* floors. His scuff marks.

I make my way slowly around the room, running my hand across the wall as I go, catching at the edge of an old piece of tape.

I press my forehead to the window overlooking the west side of the property, which is lined with more of the overgrown trees we passed on the way in; beyond them, green foliage gives way to the browns and purples of the mountainside. From here, I can just make out the creek as it snakes around the base of the mountain, but my view of the old foundation is blocked by the trees. Strangely, I'd missed it on my Google Maps search as well.

The door slams shut and I let out a small scream, turning around in time to watch it creak back open. Fletcher stands in the middle of the room, fists clenched.

"Sorry." Kurt sticks out a foot to stop the door from shutting. "I see you found my office."

I shake my head, finally finding my voice again. "Your office? No. This is my room."

Kurt points his chin toward the ceiling. "I put you in the attic. Whole place to yourself. It'll be like having your own apartment."

He *put* me? *Stay calm. Don't let him bully you; don't let him push your buttons.* It's a sure way to lose this argument, and judging by the look on his face, he knows it.

I shake my head, unable to find the right words through the anger bubbling inside me. Fletcher looks back and forth between us, silently trying to gauge the dynamic before jumping to my defense. "I'm not sure if you've been in the attic yet, Mr. Kurt, but it's really more of a loft space. It doesn't even have a bathroom."

"We can put one in," Kurt says, clearly annoyed with the interference.

"With what money?" I shoot back. "I want to stay here. This was my dad's room," I say, slow and steady, unclenching my fist. "Fletcher and I are just going to get my stuff from the U-Haul. While you look for another office." I simply cannot stomach the idea of having Kurt's things—having Kurt—in my father's room.

"I know you're used to getting what you want—" Kurt begins.

"This isn't some bid for attention," I interrupt. "This is about my dad. His house. My house."

"And will *you* be paying the bills—"

I push past him into the hallway, barreling straight into Dominic and Mom, who must have been listening outside the door.

She takes one look at me and says, "Let's talk about this later. When we don't have company."

Dominic takes his cue. "We should go, son. Let them settle in."

"I can't thank you enough for all you've done, Dominic. I'm sure I'm going to have a ton of questions," Mom says.

"You know where to reach me," he says, touching her arm. "We're really glad you decided to come back."

Mom's eyelid twitches. "Fletcher, thank you so much for showing Lola around."

"You bet," he says. "It was fun." He sounds completely sincere, but for a moment my heart flutters in disappointment. Fun? I don't know what I wanted him to say—maybe ask for my number? But then he adds, "I guess I'll see you at school on Tuesday?"

My whole body goes hot, then cold. "I'm not—" I begin, but Kurt interrupts.

"That's right! School starts next week, doesn't it?" And maybe I only imagine that his smile widens as he adds, "Don't worry. You're already registered."

CHAPTER 6

I haven't been to school in almost a year. It's not like I haven't thought about it; I do, every day. And it's not that I don't want to go.

It's that I can't.

After I quit track, I drifted further away from everything, missing more and more classes until eventually I stopped going to school altogether. By then, I was sleeping pretty much all the time—nineteen, twenty hours a day. Bryn brought me my school assignments, along with stories about what I was missing. Which felt less important the further I withdrew. I could barely handle the physical toll this mystery illness took on my body; I was in no way up to handling the emotional turmoil of high school. Finally, Mom found a tutor to help me finish out the semester and battled the truant threats with doctor's notes. And when the summer was over, she enrolled me in self-paced online classes.

Once I was able to eliminate the physical aspects, my grades improved. Last semester, I even made the honor roll. My brain isn't the problem. It's my body that's betraying me.

I thought Mom and I were both comfortable with the arrangement. It's one of the reasons I hadn't been overly panicked at the thought of the move. Yes, it was traumatic to leave the only home I'd ever known and the best friend I'd ever had. But that had all been tempered by the fact that my daily life would remain largely the same. Online school, resting and studying on my own, occasional doctor's visits.

I hadn't factored Kurt and his motives into the equation.

I don't know if I have it in me to go back to school. Hell, it isn't even back—it's starting over. A new school, with new people who don't know me and won't give a shit about me. I can hear the whispers already. *She looks fine. What does she think is wrong with her? Did you hear that excuse she gave the teacher? Faker. Drama queen. Entitled bitch.*

I've heard them all. The insults aren't going to sound any better with a Colorado accent.

I wake with the sun in my face and my neck screaming from the unnatural angle. The movers hadn't arrived by the time I'd been ready to collapse last night, so I'd slept on the couch in the den. It didn't help my campaign to claim Dad's bedroom, but I'd been too achy and exhausted to chance the night on a cold wood floor.

I blink at the sunlight streaming through the stained glass as I gingerly test my limbs. Surprisingly, I'm in better shape than I expected, though the crick in my neck is going to need ice. And I need something to eat.

"Mom?" I call, stepping into the hallway at the back of the house, my voice echoing in a way so unfamiliar it makes me shiver. "Mom, are you here?"

In the kitchen, I find evidence that she's been up already—a plate with crumbs in the sink, half a pot of coffee cooling on the counter. I vaguely remember hearing voices earlier, but I'd stuck in my AirPods and pulled the blanket over my head.

I snag a pink Post-it off the fridge. *Lola, I'm off to work. There's bread and peanut butter and I even managed to unpack the toaster.* ☺ *I'll stop to pick up groceries on my way home. Wish me luck! Love, Mom*

"Luck," I say out loud, happy for her, for how excited she is for this new job. This new life.

I wish I could summon some of that this morning. Instead, there's a cold knot in my stomach that has more to do with dread than hunger. I pull out my phone to text her good morning, but the *searching for service* message pops up along the top. Super.

I slide it back in my pocket and pop a slice of bread in the toaster. I should make two. I know my body needs the fuel. But my appetite has gone the way of my enthusiasm. Instead, I pour myself some coffee, slosh in a generous shot of creamer from the bottle in the fridge, and go to look out the row of windows over the long countertop that lines the back wall. It's the same view as from my dad's bedroom in the back corner, but from this angle I can only see trees and the ever-present mountains beyond.

The landscape here unnerves me. I keep expecting the green fields and leafy foliage of home, but instead my gaze gets caught on spiky evergreens dried brown from the heat before hitting a wall of rock. The mountain looms over everything, all hard edges and dark shadows no matter which direction I face. I squint into the sky, impossibly blue and impossibly close as it presses down on me like a lid.

For a moment, I lose myself. I press my hands to the counter, swaying slightly. Until I hear the creak of footsteps above me. I lift my head to the ceiling, mentally tracing the crack that snakes across it.

Kurt must be upstairs. He'd better not be setting up his office in my bedroom.

The thought of having to make conversation without Mom to buffer us turns my stomach, but at least I can breathe again. I snatch my toast impatiently, smear some peanut butter across the top, and carry the plate to the stairs, pausing at the bottom. Is Kurt coming down? Am I about to substitute an awkward kitchen encounter with an even more awkward stair stare?

I hurry up as quickly as I can, ducking my head in case he's in the hallway, and pause at the top of the stairs—winded, dizzy, and unaccosted. Not that Kurt would actually do any accosting. He's not creepy or weird and he's never done anything to make me feel uncomfortable. It's more of an existential discomfort. Because I know, deep down, he'd rather I wasn't in the picture. He's crazy about my mom, that much is obvious, and has been since their very first date. He fell head over heels for her, sending huge bouquets of spiky flowers, showing up early on the weekends to do our yard work, and even hiring an Elvis impersonator to serenade her on her birthday. Flirty Kurty, Bryn had called him. Before we knew he was going to stick.

He's also never been married before and doesn't have any kids of his own, and it shows. He is not used to compromise and has definitely never had to put someone else's needs before his own. Mom has a variety of excuses and they all boil down to the same thing—Kurt's a self-centered douche who doesn't play well with others. And no amount of fake dad jokes or "tough love" posturing is going to change that.

Directly across the hall from my bedroom is another door, partially open, revealing a smaller staircase. The attic. Their hangout, Fletcher had called it. Suddenly, I need to see that. More than anything. I head up, physically pulling my body up the last few stairs with the railing.

It isn't really an attic. It isn't really a loft, either, despite Fletcher's description. It's a wide-open space, with a dust-covered floor and exposed beams overhead. An enormous skylight spills sunshine across the yellowed sheets covering the furniture. I pull one off, sending a cloud of dust motes into the air and revealing the longest, reddest couch I've ever seen. I run a hand across the nubby fabric of the arm. My dad's couch. I drop onto it and let my head fall back to look at the sky, such a bright shade of cornflower blue it makes my eyes ache.

I blink away dark spots as I finish my toast and coffee. It's peaceful up here, light and airy. I can see why my dad and his friends claimed it as theirs. Maybe I should have taken Kurt up on the offer of my own apartment. I certainly don't want him to take it over, any more than I want him in Dad's bedroom. If I'm honest, I don't want him anywhere.

On my way downstairs, I pause outside the back bedroom, taking a deep breath to brace myself for a fight before opening the door.

But Kurt isn't here. My shoulders relax. I briefly wonder where he did end up putting his office, but I don't care enough to search further. Instead, I grab my bag from the corner where I dropped it last night and pull out my laptop, scooching so my back is against the wall.

But the chat window won't open. *Unable to connect to internet* pops up on the screen.

WTF. I tap the space bar a few times. Nothing. I click on available internet connections. None appear. I slam the lid and grab my phone again. No signal.

"You've got to be kidding," I mutter. Kurt was supposed to have handled all of this. So it's his fault I can't talk to Bryn?

I head down the hall to the master suite and pound on the door. "Hey. Kurt? I can't get onto the internet." Still nothing. I crack open the door. "Kurt?"

But the room is empty.

Unease prickles the back of my neck. He was up here when I was making breakfast. I back out of the room, pulling the door closed behind me.

"Kurt?" I call, cringing at the loud echo.

My vision goes a little blurry. Suddenly the house feels impossibly big, and the long shadows stretching across the hall impossibly deep, and I need to be anywhere but here. I beeline for the stairs, gripping the handle as I rush down.

Kurt probably went downstairs while I was in the attic, to get coffee or start unpacking.

But he's not in the kitchen, or any of the other rooms I stick my head into.

The house expands around me, or I'm shrinking. I can feel it swelling, stretching, the wood and joists creaking as they breathe. Which is more than I can do.

My chest is tight and my heart is pounding way too fast.

I yank open the front door and stumble onto the porch, pressing my cheek against the cool stone parapet as I gulp in fresh air.

As my heartbeat slows and the buzzing in my head recedes, I realize the vehicles are gone. Both of them. Mom would have taken the car to work, but where's the U-Haul?

And if Kurt took the U-Haul, who did I hear walking around upstairs?

I turn slowly back to the door. It's ajar, like I left it, but a lot less inviting than it was yesterday.

Gravel crunches behind me, and I jerk around to see Mom's car pull in, Kurt behind the wheel.

"Where were you?" I ask as he climbs the steps, my voice cracking.

He makes a face, irritated that I have the nerve to question him. "I returned the U-Haul when your mom went to work." He then adds, "You're a big girl. I didn't think I needed to hire a sitter."

"You left me alone with no cell service and no internet," I say, waving my phone in his face. "What if something happened?"

Kurt peers past me into the house. "Did something happen?"

I press my lips tight. Should I say something? He isn't going to believe me.

He shoulders past before I can make up my mind, and I follow him into the great room, where he holds up a telephone. "Cell service is spotty out here, what with the mountains, so we've got an old-fashioned landline." He presses the receiver to his ear. "Working perfectly."

I'm steaming at his tone, but relieved to learn we won't be completely cut off from civilization. "What about the internet?"

Kurt frowns. "It's a problem, but I'm working on it. No one wants to come out here Labor Day weekend. It'll be up and running by next week," he says unconvincingly. "At least it better be. I've got work to do."

"I heard something," I say, the words rushing out before I can pull them back. "Earlier, I mean. Upstairs. While I was making breakfast." He watches me as I continue to ramble. "Footsteps. Like someone was walking around. I assumed it was you. But you weren't here."

He looks up at the ceiling for a moment, then heads back toward the porch. "Old houses make noise," he says over his shoulder. "I'm sure that's all it was. You'll get used to it."

You'll get used to it.

Will I? Suddenly I'm not so sure. This move, this house. School. Kurt. So many changes, and they all feel overwhelming. Insurmountable. Like I'm drowning and won't ever find a way to keep my head above water. And always the same advice. *It's a new start. You'll get used to it.*

I draw a shaky breath, trying to recall more useful advice to hang my heart on. *The secret of change is to focus all of your energy not on fighting the old but on building the new,* pops into my head. A lot of people think this came from Socrates, but they're wrong. It sounds like him; he was known for his radical rationality. But he was also executed for it.

I'll bet at the very end he was wishing he'd fought.

Mom and Kurt must've had a discussion, because Kurt doesn't argue when the movers arrive and I ask them to take my furniture to the back bedroom. And by midafternoon, I've got it mostly arranged the way I want it. I still need to decorate, but I've got sheets on my bed and books on my shelves and a couple of quotes taped to the walls, including one I took from an old *Lord of the Rings* calendar: "It is not the strength of the body that counts, but the strength of the spirit." And NCAA basketball coach John Wooden: "Success comes from knowing that you did your best to become the best that you are capable of becoming." I have a feeling I'm going to be needing a reminder of that one in the coming days.

I'm exhausted, so I lie down for a nap and when I wake, it's nearly dark out. Mom is unloading groceries in the kitchen when I go downstairs.

"Marshmallows and graham crackers?" I say, pulling the items from the bag.

"There's a fire pit at the bottom of the hill," she says, poking her head into the refrigerator. "Near the old foundation. I thought it might be fun."

"A fire? Is that legal?" Kurt asks.

His kiss lands on her jaw as she swings around and leans back against the counter, clutching a jar of spaghetti sauce to her chest. "It is. I spoke with Dominic about it."

Kurt winces at the mention of dad's friend. Interesting.

I assume they've made up since she's no longer actively spurning him, but there's a vibe between them that I can't put my finger on. Then again, what do I know about marriage?

Mom surrenders the jar of sauce to Kurt and pours a glass of wine to take to the table.

"How did everything go today?" she asks.

Kurt shoots me a look I interpret as "don't make your mom feel bad." Which is totally unnecessary. I'm not actively trying to ruin their lives, despite what he believes.

"Fine. Great," I say, not mentioning the noise upstairs. "I got my bedroom all set up."

"That's great!" She leans over to cover my hand with hers, nearly overturning her wineglass. "It's already beginning to feel like home, isn't it?"

I look around, taking in the moving boxes shoved into the corners of the room and Kurt, who is muttering to himself as he moves pots and pans from one cupboard to another. It doesn't feel like home, no matter how badly I wish it did. But I don't press the point.

"How's the new job?" I ask instead.

Kurt pauses in his banging of pots to listen as Mom presses the wineglass into the tablecloth. "It was nice. Overwhelming. There's so much to take in." She traces the circle indentation with her finger. "But the people are nice."

Nice? It's such a generic, non-Mom thing to say, and I'm about to point it out when I catch sight of Kurt's frown over her shoulder.

"New start," I mumble instead as her eyes dart away and she takes another slug of wine.

The dining room is cavernous, the table designed for four times as many people, and the walls are papered in a swirling crimson pattern that could be blood spatter and only reveals itself as some kind of floral print when I look away. Kurt brings a vat of spaghetti to the table, as if he were feeding guests at all the empty chairs. The whiff of garlic makes my stomach turn over, but I force myself to take a scoop. The last few days have caught up with me, and I'm having trouble keeping my eyes open.

We eat in silence for a while, until Mom wipes her mouth with a napkin and clears her throat. "Lo," she begins, pausing to take another drink of wine, and I know this is not going to be good.

It's about the bedroom, or school, or both maybe. How can things possibly get worse? But I don't let myself imagine. Instead, I wait, refusing to look at Kurt, afraid of what I might read on his smug face.

"I invited some people over," she finally says.

"What? Who?" I ask, dropping my fork with a clatter. "The . . . nice people?"

She tilts her head slightly and gives me a puzzled frown. "Some classmates of yours."

"I don't have any classmates," I say, but the protest is automatic and futile. I'm getting a terrified inkling of what she means, and my stomach sinks to somewhere near my toes.

Kurt is staring at my mother, open-mouthed, with a look that might just as easily be fear as admiration.

"Not yet. But you will. And I thought your transition back to school would be easier if you knew some people. Some . . . friends." Her eyes plead with mine over the rim of her glass.

"You invited people I don't know to hang out?" I can't quite wrap my head around this awkward, cringey, terrible idea of hers.

"Well, no. Not quite. You know Fletcher. And Dominic tells me his friends are all nice kids."

Kurt's hand tightens around his fork. "I didn't realize you'd spent so much time with Dominic," he says.

"He's our caretaker," she says. "I need him"—Kurt makes a choking sound deep in his throat—"to get me caught up on what all is involved with the house and the upkeep."

"I see. And I thought once we were here, we'd no longer need his services."

Mom finally clues in on Kurt's tone. "Do you not like Dominic?"

"What's not to like?" His voice has that fake heartiness he gets when he's lying. "You do realize there's no 'benevolent donor,' right? He paid off your back taxes. Which undermines our claim. I'd like to know what his angle is."

"Undermines our claim? What's he talking about?"

"Nothing," she says firmly, angling her back to Kurt and leaning in toward me. "I met a lovely girl today, Clare. She works with me at the library, as a page. And it turns out she's friends with Fletcher. She overheard me and Dominic talking and she offered to come over, too."

"Dominic came to see you at work?" Kurt's voice rises.

"Come over when?" I ask at the same time.

But before she can answer either of us, a loud bonging interrupts her.

CHAPTER 7

"That's the doorbell!" Mom hurries to the door as the long, sonorous tones continue to echo throughout the house.

"That's the loudest doorbell I've ever heard," I mutter as I trail slowly behind.

Even Kurt appears interested in this turn of events, leaving the table to watch as Mom throws open the big front door.

"Clare! I'm so glad you could make it."

Clare is beautiful, with light brown skin and glossy dark hair streaked with chunks of bright magenta. I raise a hand self-consciously, tucking the ends of my lank bob behind my ears. Why hadn't Mom given me more notice? So maybe I could have showered and combed my hair?

Clare nods at my mom and then me, her smile dimming as another girl elbows her side.

"Have you met Emory?" Clare asks, wrinkling her forehead the tiniest bit. "Emory, this is Tress. She's the new librarian. And she owns this place," she adds, her voice going hard as she gives Emory a glare I can't interpret. And anyway, she's wrong. I own this place. Technically speaking.

Emory, blond and blue-eyed, is the living embodiment of a Barbie doll, if Barbie had normal body proportions and was capable of wearing flip-flops.

"Hello, Mrs. Boyd," Emory says as she turns her attention from our foyer to my mother, flashing a smile that bares perfect teeth.

Mom falters. "Actually, it's Gunderson now," she says, half turning toward us. "This is my husband . . . Where did he go?" She looks at me and I shrug. "And my daughter, Lola. Boyd," she finishes awkwardly.

The girls both eye me with frank interest, although I'm not sure if it's due to my name—does Boyd mean something to them?—or just plain curiosity about the freak of a girl who would let her mother set up a playdate. Although to be fair, they're the ones who showed up.

Behind them, Fletcher and another boy crowd into the room.

"Hi, Tress," says Fletcher. "Hey, Lola."

"Hi, Fletcher. Thanks so much for coming," Mom says.

I'm sure his dad forced him, but Fletcher looks totally at ease when he says, "Wouldn't miss it!" He stops to wipe his palms on his jeans before leaning past my mom to give me a little wave. "Greetings and salutations!"

"Is that . . . from *Heathers*?" I ask, taken aback.

"Dude! She's right. You sound just like the psychopath in that movie!" The other boy claps him on the shoulder.

"What psychopath? No, it's *Charlotte's Web*," Fletcher says.

He's trying to play the quote game. But that isn't actually the quote.

"I love that book," Clare says, "but Charlotte never says that."

"I love it, too," I say, while Fletcher looks on with what could best be described as mortification. Until the other boy nudges him in the back.

"Uh, this is Sage," Fletcher says, introducing the muscular Latino guy dressed in athletic shorts and a Coors shirt with the sleeves cut off, exposing his tanned biceps.

Mom steps aside and motions them in. "Welcome, everyone! Make yourselves at home. I'll let Lola give you the tour while I go put together some snacks."

Tour? Snacks? Who is she, Regina George's "cool" mom? It's my turn to be mortified. This can't actually be happening. It must be one of those stress nightmares, like where I show up unprepared for a test or I'm standing in front of the class without any clothes on.

Emory wanders away from us into the library, pulling out her phone as she goes. Clare rolls her eyes at her friend's back. "Ignore her," she says. "She doesn't understand the difference between curious and rude."

"Um, did you want to see the house?" I ask, feeling panicky.

"There's a firepit. Out back," Fletcher offers. "Should we . . . I mean, do you want to start a fire?"

It sounds vaguely like an innuendo, and out of nowhere I remember Bryn's mention of chaps.

"Um, sure. That sounds good." Anything to get my mind off his adorable smile. And this awkward gathering out of my living room.

"Hold up," Sage says. "Not a good idea, bro. I think I saw a bear. On the way in."

"A bear?" I ask. "Are you guys messing with me?"

"Absolutely not," Fletcher says. "You're in bear country out here."

Sage groans theatrically. "I'm sorry I brought it up. You do not want to get Fletcher started on bears. Trust me." He pushes in between us and spins around so that he's facing us as he backs toward the stairs. "How about we hang in the attic instead?" He grabs one of my hands and tugs me forward.

Behind me, I hear Clare whisper, "I wouldn't have brought you if I'd known you were going to—"

I twist around. Emory has returned, and Claire is laying into her. But whatever she thought Emory was going to do is lost beneath my mom's voice.

"I've put some snacks together." She stands at the bottom of the stairs, holding a giant picnic basket normally only seen in cartoons with bears wearing neckties.

I start to shake my head, but Fletcher grabs the basket. "Thanks." He flips up the lid. "Looks great!"

Mom smiles and I try to return it as I let myself be shuffled toward the attic, listening in vain for any more whispers from Clare and Emory.

As we step into the attic, Sage lets go of my hand to vault over the back of the giant red couch. "I can't believe you're living here."

Clare scowls a warning at him.

"What? I didn't say anything."

I swallow. "Is there something to say? About the house, I mean."

Fletcher pulls the sheets off two of the other chairs and shakes the dust into a corner. Emory quickly claims one, throwing her legs over the arm.

"You mean, do the locals all think it's haunted? Nah. No more than any other abandoned mansion on the edge of town," he says, his grin softening his words. "I've been coming here since I was little. With my dad. Helping him with yard work and stuff. Nothing scary," he continues, "and I've never seen a single ghost."

"But there are stories?" I ask.

Clare purses her lips and tucks a lock of hair behind her ear. "I usually just hear vague sorts of warnings—don't go over there, it's dangerous. You know, the usual crap."

"Oh, it's definitely haunted," Emory says. Her sandals slap the floor with so much emphasis as she walks toward the windows, I half expect the others to agree with her. But they seem unimpressed.

Clare gives another eye roll, while Fletcher says, "Knock it off, Em. No need to freak her out."

I notice the nickname—Em. Are they a couple?

"I'm just being honest," she says. "Someone needs to be."

Implying the rest of them aren't? It's been a long time since I've spent any time with this many people—this many strangers—and I'd forgotten how mentally exhausting it can be.

"If you're scared, I'll keep you safe." Sage leers at Emory and she shakes her head, her blond mane settling back into place.

"Say that in front of my dad. I dare you."

Maybe these two are together? I study them all like they're a puzzle, trying to figure out who goes with who, until I realize it doesn't matter. They all belong together—are all friends, at the very least. I'm the piece that doesn't fit.

Fletcher sets the basket on the coffee table in the center of the room and Clare kneels down to unpack it, pulling out some bags of chips and cans of soda, along with all the fixings for s'mores.

Fletcher touches my elbow and beckons me back a few steps from the group. "Don't take Emory too seriously," he says softly.

"Okay," I say, but I don't know what he means.

"She's intense, but she's all right."

I lift a shoulder in a half shrug. "Okay," I say again, and then to prove I know more words, I add, "Are you guys together?"

He grins then, like I've said something completely hilarious. "God, no." He's still holding my arm, and when he drops it, I miss the warmth of his skin on mine.

God, no. Good. For him, I mean. Since he's so clear on the subject.

"Are you two going to keep whispering in the corner, or are you going to let us in on the conversation?" Emory demands.

I guess intense is one way to describe her.

But her bluntness shakes me out of my nervousness. She reminds me a bit of Bryn, at least in her take-no-crap attitude, and I almost smile. No one else will get the joke, because they don't know Bryn. But they don't know me, either.

For the first time in I don't know how long, I'm with a group of people who don't know about my past. Since they don't know I'm sick, they can't define me by my illness. This is my chance to be someone else, someone other than "sick Lola." The new start Mom and Kurt have been raving about.

I perch on the edge of the other chair and clear my throat before asking, "Are there really bears out there?" Sage warned me not to bring it up, but Fletcher's enthusiasm seems an easy choice compared to the awkward silences that follow anything Emory says.

"As a matter of fact, yes," Fletcher says, clasping his hands together, eliciting another groan from Sage. "This time of year, they're hungry and looking for food. The cubs are weaned and the mamas are teaching them to hunt. To fatten themselves up before winter. Bears have a keener sense of smell than dogs do, if you can believe it."

"I can't," Sage says flatly, staring up at the ceiling. "Please. Do go on."

Fletcher ignores him. "So Sage was right. If there was one nearby and we were outside, they'd smell our fire. And our marshmallows. But honestly, we'd probably be fine. They don't like humans. You just need to make noise if you're outside. And clean up after yourself. That's rule number one."

"And carry your bear spray," Sage adds.

"Bear spray? That's a thing?"

"Yeah," Fletcher says. "But it's really only for extreme cases."

"I never go anywhere without it," Sage says.

"Despite his buff appearance"—Sage flexes as Clare continues—"my brother is a bit of a wuss when it comes to wildlife."

Sage rolls over to punch her in the arm.

They're siblings.

"Oh!" I don't mean to say it out loud, but it's such a revelation, figuring out this small piece of information. Sage is here because he's Clare's brother. And Fletcher is here because of Dominic. So that leaves Emory. *I wouldn't have brought you if I'd known you were going to . . .*

Going to what?

"You haven't changed much," Emory says, but when my head snaps toward her, she's looking at the room, not at me. She doesn't even know me. How would she know how much I've changed?

Before I can ask what she's talking about, she adds, "Is your furniture still on the way?"

"This *is* my furniture," I say, a hard edge to my voice. "Or my dad's, I guess."

I can't read her expression. "And you're just going to keep it like this?"

I squirm uncomfortably, resisting the urge to snap, *So what?* Why does she care?

Clare offers Emory a soda, but she shakes her head and gets up to wander around the room, trailing her fingers across the back of the couch and peering into the dark corners.

Is she looking for something?

But she doesn't comment, and no one else so much as blinks, which endears them to me a little bit. If they're going to be my friends, or at least my classmates, it's good to know they have a high threshold for antisocial behavior.

Emory reminds me a bit of one of the girls on my track team, actually. But where Madison was always trying to find her angle and manipulating to get her way, Emory seems less calculating and more confident. As if her success is a given, so why would she waste any effort worrying about it? She looks up, as if she can sense me watching her from across the room, holding my stare with her own like some kind of challenge before turning her back to look out the window. I get the sense that Emory doesn't bother with manipulative games. If she doesn't like me, she'll probably sooner spit in my face than stab me in the back.

Weirdly, I find this comforting.

Fletcher has unearthed a pile of old CDs, and after gushing about my dad's collection—"Pearl Jam! Radiohead!"—he slips one into the old boom box, and soon we're all sitting around, listening to Guns N' Roses like . . . well, not exactly friends. But it's less awkward than I thought it would be.

"Are you all from here?" I ask, which sounds dumb, and I immediately wish I could take it back.

"Fletcher and Sage and me," Clare says, leaning back against the couch and stretching her legs out in front of her. She's got surprisingly muscular calves. "But Emory's new. Relatively speaking."

Emory plops back into her chair and scrunches up her nose. "I moved here in fourth grade," she says, snagging a marshmallow from the table. "But I guess eight years still make me the new girl."

"Not anymore," I mutter.

Her glossy hair shines as she tosses it over her shoulder. "You're right. Thanks for that."

I honestly don't know how to respond to anything she says. "Where'd you live before?"

She shoots a glance toward the door, as if maybe someone's listening. "Iowa," she finally says.

"So a Midwesterner. Like me."

"Middle of fucking nowhere. At least you had Detroit."

I shrug. "Detroit is fun, but we hardly ever visited."

Clare says, "Your mom said you're nervous about starting school." *Again* hangs in the air, unsaid, and I wonder what exactly Mom told her.

My cheeks are hot. "Yeah. It's a lot of change," I say, struggling to find words that won't make it sound like I'm insulting her and her hometown. "I'm sure it'll be fine." I bite my lip.

"It won't be so bad," she agrees, taking a sip of Diet Coke. "Claret Creek's not as cliquey as some schools. Before you know it, you'll be as bored as the rest of us. Everything new gets old eventually. Usually much faster than we'd like."

I look over, surprised by the wisdom in her statement. "Is that a quote?"

She waves a hand. "I'm sure someone said it, at some point."

"No way. That's a Clare Morales original," Sage says, pulling out his phone.

"What are you doing?" she says irritably, holding up a hand to block her face. But he isn't taking a photo—he's typing.

"I'm recording it. For posterity. Someday, when you're writing your memoir, you're going to want it and who will have had the foresight to write it down?" He thumps his chest.

"No one is going to pay any money to read our story," she says, shoving his phone away.

"Are you kidding? We're Claret Creek royalty! Descendants of the OG Creek-sters." Sage bats his thick eyelashes—which match Clare's, I realize—and looks smug as he snaps a selfie. Everyone else looks bored.

"Are you a writer?" I ask Clare.

She lifts one shoulder.

"Clare is going to be a journalist," says Fletcher, and there's a note of pride in his voice that makes me reshuffle the relationship deck one more time.

"Journalism is a dying field," Clare says as she chucks a marshmallow into her mouth. "Money's too tight to waste on a degree I'll never use."

"Come on." Sage bumps her shoulder softly. "If you aren't out there working to save us all from corruption, who else is going to do it?"

"Perhaps you can take some time off from your wrestling career and help those less fortunate."

Sage jumps to his feet. "That's it! My WWE persona! Clare-Bear, you're a genius. I will be . . ." He pauses dramatically before punching his fist into the air. "The Press!"

Clare groans, but this piques Emory's interest. "That's not bad. You can wear a fedora, with a little press badge. And your signature move can be called something like the Printing Press. Or the Typewriter!" She mimes tapping her fingers before slapping the air in a return motion. "Ding!"

"What is happening right now?" Clare asks.

"You've created a monster," Fletcher says, swapping out Guns N' Roses for AC/DC. "Highway to Hell" blares out, and he adjusts the volume.

"Better work on my catchphrase," Sage says, then grabs a marshmallow from Clare's hand as he walks past and settles on the chair beside Emory.

I stifle a yawn. I'm exhausted, but I don't want to ruin this. Chase them all away, just when I'm starting to believe this might work, that they might actually like me. I can't bring myself to break whatever magic is happening here tonight.

Fletcher leaves his post by the boom box and comes to sit on the end of the couch nearest my chair. "Should we play a game? Lola, how about that one you taught me?"

Emory does that eyebrow thing again. "When were you two playing games?"

His face goes red. "I . . . we . . . yesterday. Lola taught me. It's a quote game. Right?"

I rub the back of my neck. "It's not really a party game. It's more like a . . . thing that my friend and I did back home. Memorize quotes. And try to trip each other up."

"Ah," Emory says. "*Charlotte's Web*. Now I get it."

Fletcher crams a marshmallow into his mouth and chews furiously.

"I'll go first," Clare offers. She sits up and rests her chin in her hand for a moment, quiet and focused. "All books are either dreams or swords," she finally says. "You can cut, or you can drug, with words."

No one speaks. A lengthy guitar riff squeals to an end, and Clare speaks in the silence between tracks. "No one? Did I do it wrong?" She looks at me.

"No, you did it right. I think you win," I say. "Nicely done."

Clare shrugs. "It's Amy Lowell." She looks around the room. "The poet?"

"Jesus, Clare. Give us something to work with. At least Fletcher did that psychopath," Sage says.

"It was *Charlotte's Web*," Fletcher mutters, shifting his feet. "I've got a better one. As sure as this tree will shade you, so too will these waters heal you."

The wind goes out of me, like he's punched me in the solar plexus.

Clare tilts her head. "Why does that sound so familiar?"

Sage snaps his fingers. "It's from the plaque. Down at the park. The statue."

Fletcher points at Sage. "Got it!"

"You stumped me with that the other day," Fletcher continues, turning to me, "so I looked it up."

He looked it up. So it's definitely a quote. But where would I have seen it? I've never been to their park.

My heart pounds wildly and I walk to the window, trying not to show how rattled I am. I must have read it online somewhere. Right? I've been researching Claret Creek. That must be it.

I wipe my sweaty palms on my joggers and press my fingers to the glass. Dusk is falling quickly. I can't see where the sky ends and the mountain begins, but I can feel it looming over us. Watching. Along with whatever else is out there in the darkness.

"Creepy, right?" I jump at the unexpected closeness of Sage's voice. He rests his chin on my shoulder as he points down at the old foundation, illuminated by the bright moon.

"I kind of find it interesting," I say, taking half a step sideways.

"Interesting? I guess, if you find arson—"

"Knock it off, Sage." Fletcher's voice is mild but firm.

"Arson?" I turn from the window, bumping into Sage. Why is he standing so close? "Are you joking?"

"There was a rumor," Clare says. I can't see her face behind Sage's wide shoulders.

"It's more than a rumor, Clare-Bear!" Sage sings out. He finally steps back, releasing me, and ambles toward the couch, shoving Clare sideways as he slides down behind her. "It's a true story," he continues. "The Witch of Claret Creek."

"If you're going to lead with 'this is a true story,' you cannot have the word 'witch' in the title. It destroys your credibility," Clare says, punching him in the knee.

"But she *was* a witch! How else do you explain it?"

"Explain what?" I ask, crossing my arms against a sudden chill. I'm bothered by this more than I want them to know.

"There is a story about your house," Clare admits.

"Right. A story. As in, complete fiction," Emory says.

Clare throws up her hands.

"Just tell me," I say sharply.

"Her name was Rebecca Payne," Clare begins as a haunting melody starts to play.

My skin prickles as Fletcher adjusts the volume of the music. Rebecca Payne is one of my relatives. So whatever story Clare is about to spin, she's at least got that part right.

"She had a baby out of wedlock," Clare continues. "God forbid. So the town shunned her and called her a witch."

"That's not the story!" Sage protests. "She didn't *just* have a baby. She birthed the spawn of Satan! Right there in the creek! They say she wasn't even pregnant when she went into the water."

"They?" Emory scoffs quietly.

Sage ignores her. "She had to call on the doctor to help her—I mean, it can't be easy to give birth to the devil, right? After that she bewitched him into giving her this house. And when her sister found out, Rebecca murdered her and burned down the office, destroying the evidence!"

My heart is thudding dully in my chest, black spots swimming in front of my eyes. I've waited so long to hear stories about my father's family, and this is what they all believe? My ancestor was a witch and a murderer who gave birth to Satan's child?

"Destroyed evidence of what?" Emory asks, crossing her arms over her chest.

"Evidence of the murder." But Sage sounds less certain now.

Emory scoffs. "You're saying she lured her sister here, murdered her, *moved the body*, and then set fire to what was by then her own property. That doesn't make any sense, and you know it."

Emory paints a vivid picture. I can almost see it in my mind's eye—the old building engulfed in flames, a dark shadow tugging something heavy toward the creek. "Wait." I shake my head, trying to dislodge the images. "How do you know she moved the body?" I ask.

"Because they found it in the creek," Clare says.

"Of course she put it in the creek." Sage says. "Probably trying to bring her back to life."

Emory leans forward, her eyes flashing. "If she murdered her sister, why would she want to bring her back to life? So she could tell everyone Rebecca tried to kill her?" She throws up her hands.

"She panicked, I guess."

"What do you mean, 'trying to bring her back to life'?" I ask.

They exchange a knowing look that sets my teeth on edge. "The creek water is—" Fletcher begins, at the same time Clare says, "They say—"

But Sage interrupts them both. "It's magic!"

"Healing," Clare corrects. "At least, that's the claim. The doctor used it to cure a bunch of people about a hundred years ago."

"Cure them of what?" It comes out less a question and more a statement of disbelief.

Sage shrugs. "Of everything. It's miracle water."

Emory heaves a sigh. "How is it you know so little about actual history?" She turns away from Sage, then looks at me. "In the early 1900s, a bunch of members of the town came down with a mysterious illness."

"Are you talking about the influenza pandemic?" I ask.

She lifts a delicate shoulder. "Maybe. Whatever it was, some people died. But many of them were cured. Right here, on your property, or so they say. And what did the good doctor use to save them, this miracle cure?"

My throat is dry. "Creek water?" I manage to croak.

Emory widens her arms and tilts her head.

"And it worked? But what about Rebecca's sister?"

Emory chokes back a laugh.

"Weeeelll . . ." Sage draws out the word. "I mean, it heals illness. But it can't undo murder. It isn't . . ."

"You did say magic," Emory reminds him, and his eyes narrow.

"And what about the baby? Was there something wrong with it? Is that how the rumor started?"

"No one actually thinks it was a devil baby," Clare says.

"Speak for yourself," says Sage.

My skin is on fire. My throat is dry, parched, and the air is thick. I press a hand to my chest and clear my throat, trying to catch my breath. The words lodge in and I have to force them through.

"It wasn't the water. It was our blood."

It isn't what I meant to say, but the music is so loud, confusing me, the lyrics to "If You Want Blood" blaring in my ears. I'm dizzy and tired, so, so tired. I press my hands between my knees to anchor me as a familiar feeling of dread washes over me.

A flash of a dark room—this room—flickering with candlelight. Shadows twisting in the smoky air, coupling and uncoupling near the ceiling. Something weighs heavy on my chest and I claw at it as I labor to breathe, but there's nothing there. My friends lean toward me, their bodies wavering in the dim light as the smell of blood fills my nostrils.

"Holy shit! You're bleeding!" Dom yells, knocking a candle to the floor as Nat scrambles to extinguish the flame before it catches.

"She needs help. Get your mom," she says.

But these aren't my friends, and this isn't my voice, though it comes from my throat. "The answer is in my blood."

CHAPTER 8

"What are you talking about?" Dom's voice is sharp, though his outline is not, wavering like a mirage.

Not Dom. Fletcher.

I try to blink the blurriness away, but it doesn't help. My chest is still tight and my heart is racing and my whole body is sore, as if I've slammed into something.

Or back into myself.

So where was I before?

The others come into focus, their heads bent over me, staring, waiting for my answer. But I don't have one.

"Holy shit. Are you bleeding?" Sage leans forward.

I look down at my hands. "No. I—" My voice breaks as blood splashes onto my pants, thick and red, soaking the fabric. I press a shaky hand to my face and my fingers come away streaked crimson.

"It's all right. Just a nosebleed." Clare settles beside me and presses a napkin to my face.

"Tip her head back," Emory suggests, but Clare's hair brushes my shoulder as she shakes her head.

"You're not supposed to do that. She could choke if the blood runs down her throat."

It's already running down my throat, but I don't say this. I can't. Instead, I swallow the slick of copper, trying not to gag.

"It's all right," Clare says again, rubbing my shoulder. "Does this happen a lot?"

I shake my head, catching sight of Emory and Fletcher over her shoulder. Both their faces look distorted, their concern too big and exaggerated for what Clare called "just a nosebleed." And hovering over all of this, the memory of those words. Those people.

But I can't think about them now.

Fletcher shoves his hands into his pockets. "Maybe we should call a doctor."

"For a nosebleed?" Sage snorts.

My head is pounding, and I'm so tired I'm having a hard time holding myself upright. "No. Don't call . . . I mean, I'm okay. I just want to go home. To my room, I mean. Downstairs."

I worry I sound delusional, but they seem to understand. Clare swaps out the bloodied napkin for a clean one, tossing the other into the picnic basket. And Fletcher hurries over to help me to my feet. Only Emory is frozen in place, her stare so intense it's become unnerving.

"Em, can you clean up the food?" Fletcher asks. "Em?" He reaches a hand toward her when she doesn't respond, and she recoils.

"The food. Right. We'll clean up and meet you downstairs." She includes Sage in her directive, and he looks happy to stay with her.

Fletcher leads and Clare brings up the rear as we walk downstairs. Most of my concentration is spent on the steps in front of me, trying not to trip. I have no energy left to worry about whatever—or whoever—that vision was all about.

The answer is in my blood.

I give my head a quick shake.

"Has this ever happened to you before?" Clare asks.

Does she mean, have I ever hallucinated before? The car. The creek. *Just a few other times.*

But I don't tell her that. I don't even think that's what she's talking about. I feel odd, out of body, disoriented, and confused. But to the others, whatever I said clearly didn't sound so strange. None of them are put off, either by my words or the blood spewing from my face.

"The bleeding," she clarifies. "Has it happened before?"

I shake my head and Fletcher's eyebrows go up.

"Maybe once." I correct myself, hoping he won't say more.

Headaches, nausea, fatigue, body aches. Those are my new normal. But spontaneous bleeding? That's a new symptom, a brand-new way my body has found to betray me. Super. Nosebleeds and hallucinations. I can't help but wonder if this means it's getting worse. Whatever the fuck "it" is, this fundamental thing that's wrong with me.

How much had they heard, exactly? *What are you talking about?* Fletcher had asked, but I'm not sure if it was in reference to my first comment, or the second. Not that it matters. I don't know what any of it means. *Not water, blood. The answer is in my blood.*

As we reach the ground floor, he whips around with a concerned expression. "Where's your mom?"

She and Kurt are in the back of the house, in the room we've been calling the den. Or at least I've been calling it that. Mom has been pushing for family room, but that feels like way too much of a commitment—we aren't a family yet, despite her insistence. They're both on the loveseat, Mom pretending to thumb through a magazine but not fooling anyone, while Kurt is fixated on one of his martial art films, presumably on DVD since our internet problem still hasn't been fixed.

"Did you all have—" Mom jumps up with a pasted-on smile. Then she catches sight of my face. "Oh my god! What happened?" She cradles my chin and pushes the bloody napkins away.

"It's just a bloody nose, Mom," I say, willing her to hear me. "No big deal." I hold her eyes with mine, pleading with her not to say anymore, not to bring up my medical history now, here, in front of these possibly new friends.

Her lower lip trembles and she bites it, nodding. "Sure. I see." She presses the napkin back into place. "No big deal." Hopefully only I can hear the tremor in her voice.

"They happen a lot out here," Clare offers.

"It has something to do with the dryness," Fletcher adds.

Inert Kurt, late to the party as always, finally realizes something's going on and pauses his movie. He squints at us over the back of the couch, his face partially hidden by his popcorn bucket. "Jesus. What happened up there?" he asks. "Some bad drugs?"

It takes everything I have not to punch him.

"It's just a bloody nose," Mom says, not all that convincingly.

He shoots a glance between the two of us, perhaps trying to calculate if I'm lying. To be fair, it might be the first time I've ever heard Mom use the words "no big deal" in reference to anything medical, even if she was just parroting me. So his confusion isn't totally unwarranted.

"I'm going to go ice this," I say, pointing to my nose. I am suddenly, desperately tired, so beat I'm not sure how long I can stay on my feet. As glad as I am that they came, now I just want them to go.

Clare understands this, somehow, and turns to Fletcher. "We should head out."

Fletcher calls up the stairs for Emory and Sage, while we make our way toward the front door, Mom yammering on to Clare about gratitude and how she's always welcome to come back.

"Is she still bleeding?" Emory demands as she and Sage and Fletcher join us in the foyer.

"It's slowing," I say, afraid to pull the napkin away and find out I'm lying.

She stares at me with an unreadable expression on her face.

I try not to blink first. I don't know why, other than some inane idea that I can't show weakness, especially not in front of this peculiar girl, the only one who seems to sense that something . . . *unnatural* happened up there.

"Do you remember what you said?" she whispers, so quietly I almost miss it.

I swallow, the blood oily and bitter, and move my head back and forth, almost imperceptibly.

Her eyes narrow. She doesn't believe me. And she shouldn't.

The answer is in my blood.

The problem is, I don't know what the question is.

"Come on, Emory. We should go. Let Lola rest." Clare tugs at her elbow, lightly at first, then more forcefully, steering her out the door.

"Take care of yourself," Fletcher says, turning back to wave from the doorway.

"Thanks," I say. "And thanks for coming over and . . . everything," I say, waving my hand. "I guess I'll see you at school?"

Sage groans. "Do not mention the S-word in my presence."

They tromp down the porch, their voices fading as car doors slam and headlights briefly illuminate the front door, throwing the hallway into sharp relief.

Mom closes the door and latches it before turning to me. "Do you want to tell me what happened?"

"With my nose?" I ask, stalling for time. I don't know if I can tell her the rest. I've never kept anything big from her, especially nothing related to my health. But hallucinating is new. And scary. And maybe a bridge too far, even for her.

Still, maybe she knows something I don't.

"I had a . . . vision?" I say, stumbling over the last word. It doesn't feel quite right. Was it a vision? It felt more like a memory. Except it hadn't actually happened to me.

What it felt like most was the incident in the car. The one I hadn't told her about.

"A vision?" Mom frowns and presses the back of her hand to my forehead. "What does that mean? A vision of what?"

I fight to keep my voice steady, already regretting my words. "Or maybe it was more like déjà vu? Only it was happening to someone else. Someone in . . . the past."

"So a ghost." It's hard to miss the derision in Kurt's voice.

I hadn't heard him coming. If I had, I would have kept my mouth shut, but it's too late now. I don't expect him to understand, and I don't feel like trying to explain myself.

"No. I don't know." I pull the napkin away from my nose and look at it. The bleeding has stopped. "I'm probably overthinking it. I guess I'm just weirded out because it felt similar to what happened in the car, on the way here. When I got dizzy."

Mom's face goes completely white.

"That's enough," Kurt barks, coming up beside her and wrapping an arm around her shoulders. "I know you think you're being funny or cute, but that's enough of this shit."

I step back, my face stinging as if he's slapped me. "You think I'm trying to be cute?" The tears are always quicker when I'm tired and my defenses are down. "I'm trying to tell you—" My throat is tight and I can't get the words out before he cuts me off.

"I'm not kidding around, Lola. Knock it off. I get that you're upset. The nosebleed thing is . . . embarrassing. You were in a new place, with new people."

"That's not what happened."

"You upset your mom enough with that stupid stunt the other day. None of us want to rehash it. And as for what happened tonight, it sounds like you were fooling around, telling stories, and you got carried away."

I look from him to Mom and back. "So that's it? You can't be bothered to hear what actually happened?"

A shadow crosses over her face. "I didn't say that. But Kurt's probably right. It's been a long couple of days, and everything is new and confusing."

"And what about the other day?"

She presses her lips tightly together.

"Is this some kind of attention-seeking behavior?" Kurt asks. "Because I have been trying to figure it out, and I cannot fathom—"

"Kurt."

"No, Tress, let me finish. We're a family now, right? That's what you keep saying. And I've held my peace for about as long as I can. This needs to stop. This . . . coddling. And, and . . . crying wolf."

"Crying *wolf*? You think I'm making this up? What could I possibly gain from all this? Or do you think I'm that stupid? That even though being sick has lost me *every single thing* I love, I keep doing it because I'm too dumb to figure out it isn't working?"

"Calm down, honey."

Kurt waves his hand as Mom reaches for me. "Look, I know you're sick. I get that. But it's all a matter of perspective, isn't it? Mind over matter. It's one thing to not tire yourself out, or to try some new diet. But if you're asking us to indulge these fantasies about ghosts and woo-woo shit, I have to put my foot down. It ends now. Do you understand?"

I understand that you're an asshole. But I don't say it out loud. Less because I don't want to insult him and more because I can barely catch hold of the words in my head, much less make my lips form them. I don't have the energy to fight. So instead, I walk away.

"Lola," Mom calls softly, more like a plea.

I hesitate, but before I can answer, Kurt calls to her. "Come on, Tress. We haven't finished the movie."

She hesitates, wavering, but I turn away before she does. I should've just kept my mouth shut. Telling her was a mistake. She doesn't believe me, and worse, Kurt has drawn a line. And it's painfully obvious which side she's standing on.

CHAPTER 9

I know more about blood than any seventeen-year-old should. For instance, I know that the first transfusions were done using sheep's blood. Surprisingly, the first guy they transfused survived, which made the doctors cocky.

Many more victims did not.

Finally, someone stumbled across the idea of transfusing blood from actual humans. This isn't as surprising, though it probably shouldn't have taken them so long. But these were also the same doctors who felt that most problems resulted from too much blood. Have a fever? Let's drain your blood. Feeling blue? Too much blood! It stands to reason, with all this excess blood lying around, eventually someone would have the bright idea to put it into another person. Overall, this was more successful than the sheep transfusions, but confusingly, not all the time. They hadn't yet figured out blood types.

Another blood fact? Our bodies contain five liters. We should be sloshing when we walk. So much blood, so much information. And still, no answers. If my doctor donated my blood to someone else, my DNA would still be detectable in their bloodstream for up to two days. Blood itself is universal, but our blood cells are all different. And yet, someone else's blood cells could potentially cure me.

If anyone knew what was wrong with me.

Amazingly, I wake to discover yet another miracle of blood: dried, it apparently forms a bond to rival any adhesive. I peel the crusty pillowcase from my cheek, wincing at the rusty flakes that dot my sheets. My phone says it's 1:14—afternoon, judging by the sun streaming through the windows—but that can't be right. That would mean I've been out for fourteen hours. It feels more like four.

My whole body trembles, the way it only does when I've pushed myself far past the point of exhaustion. But even as fatigue threatens to drag me under for another round of unrestful sleep, I fight it. I need to eat something. Besides, I fear that if I sleep again, this time whatever happened in the attic will come back to me in my dreams.

The answer is in my blood.

I kick off my sheet and sit up so fast I have to hold on to the nightstand. My chest is heavy; as I pull in a breath, it catches with a sharp pain behind my breastbone. I grab for my phone to text my mom, but it slips from my sweaty grasp, and as it does, the memory of Kurt's words comes back to me.

This needs to stop.

He's right, in his own dickish way. If only I knew how to do that. What I can do is try and calm myself. That's something I've practiced, extensively. Steady breaths, in and out, until the tension in my chest eases and the panic recedes. Mind over matter. The chest pain is new, but the dull throbbing in the back of my head is all too familiar. My body needs fuel. And my heart needs Bryn, who may not know what to do but will at least know what to say.

But first, a shower. I stand under the hot water with my face uplifted, willing it to wash away not only the dried blood, but the fatigue and the fear of the night before. Let me forget how I humiliated myself in front of people I may have been able to call friends. Obliterate the vision of Kurt, face red and contorted, Mom standing silent in the background. I especially want to wipe the memories that don't belong to me, the alien thoughts that wormed their way inside my head somehow—slithering, burrowing, settling in, and forcing me to give them voice.

But no matter how hot I crank the water, I can still feel the coldness of that other room, smell the hot wax of the candles. And the blood. My eyes sting, and I'm not sure if it's the soap or tears.

Back in my bedroom, the landline trills, and a minute later, Mom calls, "Lola! It's for you."

I clutch my towel and meet her halfway down the stairs.

"When you said you were moving out west, I didn't expect you to actually fall off the side of the earth," Bryn says. "WTF. I can't believe you have a landline! Like, is there an actual cord?"

"It's cordless." I cover the mouthpiece. "I'm going to take it to my room," I tell Mom, heading back upstairs.

"Still," Bryn says, "this is some weird jujumagumbo."

"You have no idea," I say. "I've completely lost it."

"Are we sure you ever had it?"

I flop onto the bed, careful to avoid the blood-crusted pillowcase, and tell my best friend everything that happened the night before, beginning with Mom's surprise "party" arrangement and ending with the fight with Kurt.

"Leave it to Inert Kurt," Bryn says. "He's all bluster, no bite. But we already knew that. I want to hear more about Fletcher!"

"Fletcher's not . . . I mean, he is. Or he might be . . . gah! I don't want to talk about Fletcher right now. Did you even hear what I said? I had a *hallucination*. Or, I don't know, an out-of-body experience." I pause. "Kurt thinks it might be a ghost. Woo-woo shit, he called it."

Bryn snorts. "Kurt's a woo-woo shit."

"Yeah. He really lost it when I told him about the car the other day."

"Which other day?"

I'd forgotten I hadn't shared this with Bryn yet. I'd wanted to call and tell them, but I didn't have service, and it seemed too big and scary to type out over text.

"I had this . . . episode," I begin. "I was driving. I mean, I was actually driving. And then I had this hallucination that I was driving but it was night and raining and it wasn't actually *me* driving." I swallow, delaying as I try to muster up the courage to say it out loud. "Someone said, 'It's not safe, Teddy.' "

"Teddy?" Bryn shrieks. "What the actual fudgesicle are you saying? That you hallucinated your dad's accident?"

Actually, I was trying hard not to say that. "No." I bite my lip hard. "I couldn't have. Right? Because that would be—"

"Amazing?"

"I was going to say ridiculous."

"Ridiculous? That your dad is reaching out to you? From beyond—"

Every hair stands up on my body, bringing me bolt upright. "Don't say that."

"Why not? It makes sense, doesn't it? This all started right before you left for Colorado. You're the closest to him, at least in physical proximity, that you've ever been. What else could it be?"

I'm sweating, even though I'm chilled from standing too long in only my towel. I grab my robe from the back of my door and struggle into it one-handed. "Um, I don't know, a psychotic break? Hallucination due to blood loss? Or—what's that theory about the witch trials?—ergot poisoning?" I switch to speaker and drop the phone on the mattress.

"And those things sound more plausible to you?" I can feel my best friend's glare through the phone as I pull the belt on my robe too tight.

Maybe not plausible. But somehow more appealing. Instead, I say, "None of this is plausible." I sink onto the bed. "There's something else. Before the . . . hallucination last night, Fletcher and those guys were all telling me this bonkers story. About my house. Apparently, it's common knowledge around town that one of my ancestors was a witch."

"Are we talking pagan goddess, worship-the-moon type, or a black cauldron, curse-uttering variety?"

"I didn't ask. Clare seemed to think at least some of the shade was because she had a baby out of wedlock." I take a deep breath. "They say her baby was the spawn of Satan."

Bryn barks a laugh. "Figures. It always comes back to gender bias, doesn't it?"

"How can you be so casual about this? Did you hear what I said? The famous story about my family is that my ancestor had a child with the devil! Are you telling me that wouldn't weird you out? I mean, why would they make something like that up?"

"Sure I'd be weirded out. For a minute. As for why? The most likely answer is that some coward-ass Victorian schmuck didn't want to take responsibility for knocking up his girlfriend, so he blamed the devil. God forbid they ask *her* who the father was."

Right. That makes sense. A lot more sense than considering I might be descended from Satan.

The answer is in my blood.

"And get this," I say loudly, trying to drown out my own thoughts as I pace the floor, stopping to look out the window toward the creek. "The creek? It's magic. At least, that's what they told me."

"Hold up. I think you skipped a step. Did the witch, like, cast a spell on it?"

"Maybe? Sage said she wasn't pregnant when she went into the creek, and she came out with a baby."

"Let me guess—people are hooking up in the water because they think it makes them fertile."

I hadn't thought of that. "I don't think so. For whatever reason, they all seem to think the water has healing powers. It cured a bunch of people of the flu back in the early 1900s, or so the story goes. And it runs right behind my house. I mean, that's absurd, right?" As I say it, I realize there's a part of me that wants them to disagree. To tell me that there might be such a thing as magic creek water.

"Magic water." Bryn sucks in a breath. "An ancestor who's a witch, a message from your dad. A promising romance with a cute boy in leather chaps. Colorado is even more exciting than I imagined!"

"Hate to break it to you, but nobody wears chaps here," I say. "Though Fletcher did take his shirt off," I add, suddenly remembering the sight of Fletcher's bare chest.

Bryn makes a choking sound. "I know you've been through a lot, but the fact that you didn't lead with that is unforgivable."

"The only unforgivable sin is deliberate cruelty," I shoot back.

"You're mangling Tennessee Williams," Bryn counters. "And withholding of pertinent information *is* deliberate cruelty."

"It wasn't pertinent."

"Ahem—removal of clothing? Absolutely pertinent."

"It wasn't a big deal," I say, flushing as I remember the shock of the moment, surprise—and something else—flooding my body. "My nose was bleeding."

"And he literally handed you the shirt off his back to stop it? That is so—"

"Clichéd?"

"I was going to say chivalrous." A pause. "What does Fletcher think about these . . . episodes?"

Hopefully nothing. Though that's probably way too much to hope for. "Well, I didn't exactly ask him."

"Why not?" The phone practically vibrates with the force of Bryn's yell.

"I barely know him. How do I even bring it up? Hello, my ancestor might be Satan and now I think I'm possessed. Help me."

"I mean, he does seem like the helpful type."

"Actually, he did know where the quote was from. So too will these waters heal you—it turns out that's on a plaque somewhere in town."

"Aha! That weird-ass thing you said by the track. Now we're getting somewhere."

"I gotta say, feels less like an 'aha' and more like a WTF. How could I possibly have known that?"

"This is what I've been saying! It has to be connected to your dad. So too will these waters heal you? The answer is in your blood? He's from Claret Creek. He must know about the water. Maybe he's trying to send you a message."

"Even if that were true, what am I supposed to do about it?"

"I think you need to find out more about this magic fucking water."

Bryn's right. As usual.

We say our goodbyes and I end the call and flop back onto my bed. My gaze follows a crack in the plaster, from the bulb hanging above me and over to the wall behind my bed. It needs to be patched, along with half a dozen others. Painted, too, although part of me doesn't want to do it because it will cover up the evidence that my dad existed. The darker squares where his posters must have protected the paint from fading, the remnants of old scotch tape stuck to the corners. This house, this room, is the closest thing I have to a memory of him.

Unless he's somehow found a way to communicate with me.

Mom is in the kitchen when I finally make my way downstairs, leaning a hip against the counter and giving the mountains a worried frown over the top of her coffee mug. I guess I'm not the only one who can feel their malice.

"Hey," I say, forcing a lightness I'm not feeling.

"Lola!" She jerks around, sloshing coffee onto the counter. The worry lines between her eyes deepen as she opens her mouth, but before she can say anything, I interrupt.

"I'm starving. What have we got to eat?" I stick my head in the fridge before she can answer.

It's pointless to rehash last night. Either she's going to continue to back her new husband, or she's going to back down and apologize, and either way, I've decided I don't want to hear it. Her support—or lack of—has no bearing on me right now. I've got bigger things to worry about, questions that need answers, and I can't get them if we're arguing. I also can't get them if she's hovering over me, coddling and worrying and sending me back to bed.

No, I need her to believe that right now I am fine. That whatever happened last night was an anomaly, corrected by a good night's rest. From this point on, I'm wearing my game face. Perfect, normal, healthy Lola.

Kurt, with his brainless ranting, may have actually done me a favor. Without him, I'm not sure she would have bought this act. As it is, she's so grateful to put the awkwardness behind us, she doesn't look too closely for the cracks.

"Kurt made you an omelet," she says, springing forward. "It's in there, behind the butter. Let me heat it up for you."

I leave her to scrounge through the fridge and head for the Keurig, popping in a coffee pod. As the machine hums, she asks how I slept.

"Great," I lie, looking over my shoulder. "I must've needed it."

She nods emphatically. "Good. That's good. I'm glad to hear it." She frowns and reaches a hand toward me, which I duck. "How's your nose?"

I touch it lightly. "Fine. No more bleeding. Must've been some fluke thing." I stick my mug underneath the spout of the machine.

"The kids all seemed nice," she says tentatively. "Did you have a good time?"

I nod and lift the mug to my lips. "Speaking of them," I say, oh so casually, like it's just occurred to me and not like I've been waiting for this opening, "They mentioned something interesting about the history of this place."

Mom starts the microwave and leans back against the counter. "Like what?"

I force a laugh and blow on the coffee. "It sounds so silly. But apparently, one of my ancestors was a witch? Who gave birth to the devil? And maybe murdered her sister? Did Dad ever talk about that story?"

She widens her eyes and shakes her head. "What? No. That's so dark. I think I would have remembered a devil baby. But then, he never talked much about Claret Creek."

"So he never mentioned that the creek water is magic?"

"That I did hear about." The microwave dings and she pulls out the plate, dropping it to the counter. "It's the town's claim to fame." She shoves her burnt finger into her mouth and frowns. "Their only one." She catches me staring and shakes her head. "Come on, Lo. It's an urban legend, that's all."

"Emory said there was some mystery illness. A bunch of people got sick. And the water saved them."

"You know how ridiculous this sounds, right? It was influenza. A lot of people got sick. Some got better, some died. Just like everywhere else." She sighs. "But if you're that curious about the town history, why don't you stop by the library tomorrow? After school."

And just like that, the bottom drops out of my carefully constructed facade.

I'd forgotten about school.

CHAPTER 10

It's not that I hate school. I feel like any normal teenager does—given the option, I'd prefer not to spend the majority of my waking hours learning about concepts I'll probably never use again from adults who don't always see me as a person and who get to control when I can go to the bathroom. But there are layers beyond all that. There's the fact that I've gotten used to listening to my body—eating when I feel depleted, resting when I need to, not on someone else's schedule.

I'm definitely not used to being up to watch the sunrise. But my alarm went off at 6:30 this morning, and I opened my eyes to darkness. What had Mom said my dad called it? Butt early? I see his point. Technically morning, *but* . . . still dark as fucking midnight. Technically daytime, *but* . . . you'd never know because of the stupid mountains blocking the sun. Technically I've slept, *but* my body needs more rest to accomplish even basic tasks. And I'm expected to do much more today, perhaps the most dreaded task of any teen anywhere: I have to be the new kid.

Normally, I would have talked to Mom about all of this—not only the weird episodes, but my worries and doubts about going back to school. This feels like a decision she should have at least *asked* me about. But she didn't, and that more than anything tells me that alliances have shifted, and I'm not sure of the rules anymore. Our bond is loose, like an old rubber band that's lost elasticity.

Or maybe it's broken altogether.

That scares me and I can't think about it right now because if I do, I won't be able to get out of this car. She and Bryn were everything to me; yes, my world was small, but it was whole. Now it's only me, and I feel empty and alone, like that stupid plastic bag in that Katy Perry song.

It's so cliché, being nervous about being the new kid, but recognizing that doesn't make it any easier. It's been so long that I've forgotten some of the language. The rituals. The mating habits. It feels like another world, foreign and yet somehow familiar at the same time. I remember being a part of this, the groups gathered in the quad, sitting on the wall, leaning against the trees. It's the first day, and they all look excited to be back. One girl squeals as she recognizes someone across the parking lot, then runs over and throws her arms around her friend.

I was a part of all this, once. Now I'm an outsider. A scared-shitless observer.

I pluck at the skirt of my black midi dress—I finally put it on after deciding nearly everything in my closet was unacceptable for a good first-day impression—as Mom pulls the car to the curb in front of the school, behind one of the yellow buses belching diesel exhaust.

"Here we are!" Her voice is loud, the overt cheeriness adding a jarring note, like a record scratch.

Neither of us moves for a moment. I'm debating whether to ask her to come inside with me, which would be ridiculous. I don't need my mother to hold my hand. But I've also never done this, gone to a new school where everyone's a stranger, and I'm trying hard not to panic.

I can't tell what Mom's thinking, staring straight out the windshield as she grips the steering wheel like it's a life preserver.

Just go. Get out of the fucking car.

The first step is always the hardest. That's been misattributed to Confucius, and it's not even true, but it's what I need right now.

"Lola," Mom begins, her voice hoarse.

And I know that I cannot listen to whatever it is she wants to say. It's going to be too much, or too little, and either way, it's much too late.

"The first step is always the hardest," I say loudly, throwing open the car door. As I swing it shut, I look back at Mom. She's fighting back tears. I quickly turn away before I start crying, too.

"Meet me at the library after school. It's just a few blocks over," Mom calls, her voice uneven.

I wave her off without turning around and touch my hair self-consciously, which I've pulled back with a thick headband, but no one's looking at me. The first-day chaos has muffled the embarrassment of my drop-off, but it won't be long before people notice me. I duck my head and make my way to the front door.

A cute Black guy in a Nike shirt swings the door open, motioning me through with a sweeping gesture. I give him a smile, my cheeks already burning.

"Van," he calls after me, and I nod, immediately regretting it.

Was he telling me what he drives? Or his name? Should I have introduced myself? But I'm still walking and it's too late now and of all the things that my mystery illness has robbed me of, it's maybe this that stings the most—I can't quite remember how to be a normal person. How to exist in a world that requires interaction with other people. I feel like I've been away for too long, like Rip Van Winkle or maybe an astronaut who's returned from a long journey to find the landscape just slightly changed, the slang and the clothing and the interactions a tiny bit different from what I remember. Every move, every word, requires an extra second of thought, and by the time I form the correct response, everyone else has moved on.

I'm rusty and anxious and awkward, and all of those things are not good for my health. Just agonizing over whether or not I should have spoken to Van—was it Van?—is stressing me out. How in the hell am I going to do this with every single person I come in contact with today? And while I know this town is only slightly larger than Foxfield, the school seems to hold twice as many people. Or maybe more. They're everywhere, yelling and jostling, and I wish I could crawl into a hole. A nice, dark hole where no one would touch me or breathe on me or ask me questions, like—

". . . new?"

"What?" I blink at the girl who shoves her face into mine. "I mean, yes. It's my first day." I cringe. Of course it's my first day. Technically, it's everyone's first day.

"What year?"

"Junior?" Why did I make it a question?

She gives me a long once-over, taking in the dress and my short denim jacket, perhaps assessing if I am some kind of weirdo.

"Can you tell me where the office is?" I ask, hoping to cut off any more questions.

She points to the room behind us, a glass cube filled with wall-to-wall bodies. Super.

I take a deep breath, then another when the first doesn't help, and pull open the door. I can't tell if there's any organization in here. There's no line, just a crush of bodies pressed up against the counter. A few kids are scrolling on their phones. One girl is completely oblivious as someone else elbows her aside. A tall guy waves a piece of paper above his head. He's cute in a meathead kind of way, and male, so of course the secretary turns to him first. "I can't do schedule changes in the middle of this," she says, holding out her hands to encompass the utter chaos. "You want it faster, go to guidance."

"Can I get a pass?"

She shakes her head. "Just go. I'll make a note."

He turns, nearly knocking me flat in his haste to leave. I stagger backward and catch myself on the arm of a chair and the glass wall. The secretary notices, frowns, then smooths her face.

"Are you Lola?" At my nod, she waves me forward. A few of the people at the counter turn to either gape or scowl as she slides my schedule across the desk. "Here you go. You need help with anything, just ask." She turns to the person beside me before I can form my first question.

I was worried Mom might have said something about my condition, something that would involve exaggerated accommodations or long explanations. Clearly not. This woman is not the slightest bit concerned about my well-being. She assumes

I'm as capable as the next idiot at figuring things out for myself.

It's freeing, actually. This is my chance to redefine myself.

I try to read the paper, but the tiny type swims in front of me as more people elbow their way through. The secretary calls, "Wait!" and it might have been for me, but I see the door swing open and I dive for it, stepping into the relative calm of the hallway like a swimmer coming up for air.

I turn a corner and find an alcove that dead-ends at a glass wall with a view of the mountains behind the school. I know at some point I'll get used to seeing them every time I look out a window, but it hasn't happened yet. I also don't know the terrain, so it all looks the same, and though I know it's a crazy thought, it's like this slab of rock is following me. Everywhere I go, there it is.

I turn my back and look at the schedule. I register first period—History—as an electronic tone dings three times. Shit. Did the secretary not even give me a map? How in the hell am I supposed to find my classrooms?

"Lola! There you are. I've been looking all over." Fletcher grins at me, a lock of hair falling across his face. He pushes it back. He's dressed in tight jeans and a concert tee—Led Zeppelin, 1977. "Are you okay?" he asks.

"Am I . . . Oh, you mean the nosebleed?" I wave a hand. "Yeah, fine."

"Good." His grin widens. "I was going to text to see how you were doing and ask if you needed a ride to school, but I didn't have your number."

"I'm managing," I say, and his smile falters. I realize maybe that was an invitation to give him my phone number. I'm terrible at this.

"Okay, then." He points at my schedule. "Need help finding anything?"

"Yes. Everything. A map would have been helpful."

"May I?" He reaches for the schedule. "Let's see. AP History. And Bio. Impressive." He whistles. "Ooh, with Mr. Z. He's the best." He skims the rest of the paper. "And looks like we've got Spanish 3 together. Okay, here's what you need to know." He flips over the paper and sketches a quick map.

"It's basically one big square. Math and science to the northwest, language arts and the library to the northeast. Once you find your quadrant, the rooms are all in order."

"Thank you." I take the drawing from him. "This is really helpful." I squint at the couple of words he's jotted in each quad.

Another chime, this time only twice. Fletcher looks up. "We should go. Three's a reminder, two's a warning. When it's one buzz, you'd better be in class. Come on, I'll walk you."

"Are you sure? I don't want you to get in trouble."

He waves me off. "First day doesn't count, you know? It's just a trial run."

I feel myself relaxing. Fletcher seems to take our friendship as a given, which on one hand makes no sense, but on the other hand makes him surprisingly easy to be around.

"I mean, it's basically in and out, meet the teachers, find your passing route. Except for freshmen." He nods his head at a short boy in a purple shirt who scurries past. "Poor sucker. He's stuck here all day."

"What do you mean?" I ask, tracking the kid down the hall.

"They've got to stay. For 'bonding exercises.'" Fletcher notices my confusion. "That's why the first day is shorter . . . Nobody told you, did they? We've only got a half day. So you follow your schedule on the bells. First period, second, et cetera. But each class is only twenty minutes. Enough time to take attendance, find your seat, get your syllabus. Then we move on. Short and sweet. And we're out by eleven thirty."

I'm sure Mom didn't mention this. Is it possible she doesn't know? "But maybe I'm supposed to stay. Since I'm new?" Even as I say the words, I'm trying not to vomit. Spending a whole afternoon bonding with underclassmen? I cannot.

Fletcher frowns and tilts his head, considering. "If they didn't say anything when you picked up your schedule . . ."

I remember the "Wait!" the secretary hurled at my back. But maybe it wasn't my back. "Nope," I say. "No one said anything."

"Then you're free!" Fletcher says, his face lighting up. "And since you don't have any plans, how'd you like to see my bears?"

"I . . . what?"

His cheeks turn pink. "At the sanctuary, I mean. But it's fine if you don't want to. No pressure. I just thought"—he nudges the paper—"AP Bio and all, maybe you were into that kind of thing. The class always goes on a field trip. But I could show you behind-the-scenes stuff."

"You work at a bear sanctuary." Suddenly the bear banter from the other night makes so much more sense.

"Well, volunteer technically, yeah. But like I said, it's cool if you don't want to go."

"No, it's not that." I shove my hands into my pockets, reaching for my phone. Mom is expecting me at the library this afternoon. At the very least, I should text her that I'm not coming. I'm pretty sure she doesn't know about this half day.

Then again, how many things has she kept from me lately?

"My afternoon is completely free," I tell Fletcher. "I'd love to meet your bears."

CHAPTER 11

On the plus side, a shortened day means I have a better chance of getting through it. The downside is a lot—the flurry of new faces and syllabi and scrambling through the hallways, all set to the near-constant cacophony of bells.

I find the door to my fourth period class as the final bell sounds, a prolonged buzz that seems to grow louder each period. I'm the last one in and as I stand at the front of the classroom, scanning for an empty desk, a wave of exhaustion washes over me.

"Lola! Over here."

I blink and focus on Clare in the far corner, waving me over.

I make my way to her, smiling gratefully as I dump my backpack and slide into the seat beside her.

"Fletcher told me we had bio together," she says, "so I saved you a spot."

"Wow. Thanks. That's really nice of you," I say, touched that she thought of me.

She turns sideways in her seat to face me, giving me a careful once-over. "How's the first day going?"

For a second, I think she knows. Like she can see inside me, and knows how much effort it's taking to sit here, looking normal. How badly I want to lay down and take a nap. How mentally unprepared I am for all of this.

I paste on a smile, wondering how easy she is to fool. "Super."

She tilts her head, considering, her dark hair brushing the top of her chair. "You look better, but a little tired. Make sure you're giving your body enough time to recover. If you're not careful, this mountain air can fuck you up." She reaches for the papers from the person seated in front of her without breaking eye contact.

Her assessment is eerily accurate and her attention is unnerving, so I busy myself with digging a notebook out of my backpack. "It was just a nosebleed. I feel bad that I ruined the night for everyone."

"I had fun," she says with a shrug, then winces. "Not because you were bleeding, of course. But that whole 'it's not the water that's magic, it's my blood' thing. Love me some dark humor." She nods approvingly. "After Sage said all that shit about the devil baby, you gave it right back. Emory's usually the macabre one. But that was badass."

I gape at her, not sure if I should laugh or scream. She thought I was *joking*?

"Ladies!" The teacher frowns in our direction.

"Sorry, Ms. Perez." Clare turns to face the front of the room, where Ms. Perez is waiting for us to settle down.

Clare thought I was kidding. I stare down at the syllabus without seeing it. Did they all think that?

No. Not Emory.

She knew something was off. That unnerving stare. The way she'd whispered, "Do you remember what you said?" to me afterward, as if she thought there was a chance I wouldn't. Because she knew the words weren't mine.

"This is AP Biology, so we're going to be doing a pretty deep dive into some of these topics." The teacher's voice snaps me back. "That may scare some of you." A few chuckles, more groans. "Are there any questions about the syllabus?"

Clare raises her hand. "This section on genetics and environment." She waves the paper in the air. "Are we going to be covering nature versus nurture?" She sounds skeptical.

"Are you asking a biologist if she's going to entertain discussion as to whether experience outweighs genes?" she asks, eyebrow raised, and the class titters. Clare sits up straight, her face tight, and Ms. Perez relents.

"I'm kidding, Clare. You actually bring up an excellent point. The truth is, it's not either/or. That would be like asking which is more important for your car, the engine or the transmission." Her eyes flick to the back. "That was a rhetorical question, Van."

I twist around to see the guy who held the door for me earlier lower his hand sheepishly.

"You need both to operate the car. It's the same with genes. They don't operate independently, separate from their environment. They function the way they do *because* of the environment they're in. So we're going to talk about that."

"Evolution, baby!" someone shouts, and Clare rolls her eyes before turning to address the guy.

"Darwin was a white supremacist."

Ms. Perez blinks and clasps her hands together. "Some of his writings were admittedly . . . problematic," she says.

Clare snorts. "Some? Why are diseases hereditary? If Darwin's right, natural selection should eliminate them." She tosses the words at Ms. Perez like she's throwing down, her voice tight and her eyes shiny with anger.

The bell rings, saving her from answering. The rest of the class scrambles, shoving papers into folders and folders into backpacks.

Ms. Perez walks closer to us, and I get a whiff of her lemony perfume as she raps a perfectly manicured hand softly against Clare's desk. "I'm sorry I don't have a better answer for you. You're not wrong," she says. "And we'll address it. I promise."

Clare looks away and gives one stiff nod. "Thanks."

The teacher's gaze flicks to me. "Lola, right? Welcome to town." She turns away before I can respond.

"You have lunch fifth period or sixth?" Clare asks, shouldering her backpack.

"Um, next?" I say, struggling to read my schedule as she steers me toward the door.

"Me too."

We fall into step together. "It seems early for lunch," I say, although my body could use some fuel. The short day has been a blessing, but the mental activity is almost as hard. I need a snack, or at least some caffeine.

"They're just going to tell us about how it works. A la carte, blah blah blah. All you need to remember is avoid the meatloaf and the meatballs—really, anything that claims meat in the title. Salad bar is usually a safe bet, although delivery is Tuesday, so Mondays can be iffy. Mondays I usually take the pizza." She glances over. "Since you're gluten-free—"

"How'd you know I was gluten-free?"

"The graham crackers. In your mom's basket."

I mentally cringe, waiting for her follow-up questions, but she doesn't have any. "You might want to bring something from home," she says instead.

"What about coffee?" I ask.

"God, yes." She points to a window outside the cafeteria. "We've got the Red Eye Café. It's not Starbucks, but it's here and it's cheaper."

The café is located across the hall from the trophy case, and after we fill out our order slips, I wander over to look at the team photos set in between the awards and ribbons. In the chaos of the morning, I've almost forgotten the most important thing about my new school—it was my dad's school first. I scan the photos, looking for a familiar sweep of red hair, or his freckles. But I don't find either.

"Was your dad an athlete?" Clare asks.

"I don't know." I resist the urge to ask her if she does. She is eerily observant, and I'm equal parts impressed and scared.

The student barista hands over our drinks—an iced Americano for me and a chai latte for Clare. She waves at the counter, which is topped with a variety of sauces and creamers, but I shake my head and we move toward a table in the cafeteria, where the staff are just starting to wheel out tables for a buffet line.

"So, your brother," I say. "The wrestler? Is he younger? Or are you guys twins?"

Clare hoots. "He will love that that's how you remember him." She opens her cup and blows on the foam. "He's just a year younger. Irish twins, my gram used to call us."

"Are you Irish?"

Clare shakes her head. "Latina. The Irish thing has something to do with how close in age we are."

"But he does wrestle?" I ask, wondering if I got that wrong.

"He does. He's hoping to make varsity this year, but I don't know what his chances are like. He needs to either go down a weight class or up a couple. Neither is very healthy."

"Are you both athletes?"

She snorts. "Hardly." She slides into one of the bench chairs and I follow. "I'm in cross-country, but not because I'm a jock. I just . . ." She looks away and blows a chunk of magenta hair off her face. "Sometimes life is just too much, you know? And so I run to beat it back." She grimaces. "It's like, the worst metaphor. But it works. And who knows? If I work at it, I might be able to nab a scholarship."

"I totally get it." I hesitate, unsure how much I should share. "I used to run track," I finally offer. "And that's one of the things I miss most about it." That and the ability to just . . . go. Freedom. Nothing holding me back.

She studies me. "Why'd you stop?"

"It just got to be . . . too much," I say, shrugging and trying to sound casual while, inside, my stomach is churning. Part of me wants to say more, while another is screaming at me to shut my damn mouth. I've said way too much already.

But Clare doesn't press. "Were you any good?"

"I guess." Fuck it. "Actually, I was pretty good."

She nods, accepting my words, and I realize I like her. She's observant, but she isn't pushy. And she hasn't asked me to volunteer any information I haven't offered. It's a different kind of friendship from what I've had, but one I could easily get used to. Not that we're friends yet. Unlike Fletcher, who's all in, Clare seems more cautious. Like she's feeling me out, reserving judgment—and her loyalty—until she gets to know me better. If Fletcher is a puppy dog, Clare is more like a . . . well, more like me.

"Hey, about the other night. The nosebleed. I mean, before that happened. Did you notice anything . . . odd?" I ask impulsively. I'm taking a chance, putting the question out there. But Clare seems smart and not prone to bullshit. If she noticed any woo-woo crap, she'll tell me.

"Odd?" She considers for a second, her face going blank as she fidgets with her cup's cardboard sleeve. "You mean Emory? She can be a little intense, but she's all right."

"No, I—" I stop. I hadn't meant Emory, but now I'm curious about what she'll say.

"I didn't know her, before she lost her mom. But I imagine she was . . ." She pauses, searching for the words.

"She lost her mom? Oh my god, I'm so sorry. I had no idea."

Clare lifts a shoulder, acknowledging my apology. "Happier," she finally says. "I imagine she was happier."

I nod and squint toward the trophy case in the hallway. "I bet she was. I often think that about my mom. Because of my dad, I mean. He died while she was pregnant."

Clare's eyebrows go up as she sips her coffee. "Wow. That sucks. Your poor mom."

"I know, right? And now here we are, back in his hometown." I take in the cafeteria, which looks too new and modern to have been here twenty years ago. "I had this crazy idea, when I heard we were moving, that maybe when I got here I'd be able to find him." I sneak a glance at Clare. "Not literally, of course. But some memory of him." Because this is where he grew up. The place that made him. Who knows, maybe if he'd lived, we'd have ended up here before now. Would I have been a different Lola, growing up here?

"That's not so crazy," Clare says. "And Claret Creek is small. Like minuscule. You're bound to run into people who knew him."

Suddenly, I feel like an idiot. She's right. And I already knew it. But with everything that's happened, I'd forgotten all about Dominic. "Actually, I already have. Fletcher's dad."

"Well, there you go."

"Yeah, he seems cool."

"Dom? Or Fletcher?"

My cheeks get hot. Am I blushing? "Both, I guess. Fletcher invited me to the bear sanctuary. That'll be fun, right? He seems to know a lot about them."

She peels the rest of the cardboard sleeve away, then takes her time shoving the pieces into the empty cup, finishing with the lid. "Yes. Fletcher certainly knows what he likes." Am I imagining it, or is her voice cooler? "You should go. It's an experience not to be missed."

But as she pulls on her backpack and goes to throw our cups away, I can't help feeling like I'm already missing something.

CHAPTER 12

Fatigued is not the same thing as tired. Until I started experiencing real fatigue—bone-deep, brain-dead, soul-crushing exhaustion—I had no idea. Why would I? I'd get tired the way everyone gets tired. And I'd say to myself, "I'm exhausted. I've never been this tired before," without ever knowing there was another level to which I could sink, a place so dark and so deep that the very *thought* of trying to claw myself out is, in itself, exhausting.

I miss my ignorance.

The final bell sends everyone spilling into the hallway amid laughter and high-pitched chatter. It's like a holiday, or better: a get-out-of-jail-free card, on a day when excitement is already at a fever pitch. A girl at the locker next to me shrieks as she greets another classmate. Their high energy is so enticing I want to inject it directly into my veins. Mine is flagging, and I've only been here a few hours. How am I going to do a full day?

But I need to remember that this isn't a normal day. I've had a lot thrown at me. A whole new building to navigate, nearly every face a stranger. It was a full day, crammed into a few hours. Psychologically, it was far more draining than a regular day.

I hope.

I'll settle into a routine. I will. I have to believe this.

I slam my locker and follow my locker neighbor as she and her friends hurry out into the warmth of the day, a whole afternoon of freedom ahead of us.

"Lola! There you are!" Fletcher hops off the low wall that surrounds the school as I blink into the bright sunshine. "Are you ready?" His easy smile melts away most of my reservations.

"I'm ready," I say, and I almost mean it.

"Dude, wait up!"

Fletcher turns as Sage breaks away from a group of girls and lopes over to where we're standing.

Sage fakes a punch at Fletcher's arm and then slides his gaze to me. "Hey, Lola. Where're you two off to?" He turns away momentarily, clutching his heart as a tiny girl in jean shorts and big earrings walks past and flutters her fingers at him. "A bunch of us are heading over to the reservoir to partake at the waters. You guys wanna come?"

Fletcher shakes his head. "Not today, sorry. I'm taking Lola to meet the bears."

Sage tilts his head back and raises his bronze arms to the sky. "Only you would want to waste this glorious afternoon on a field trip. Besides, aren't the bears all hibernating and shit?"

"They're getting ready. That's why we're going now."

But Sage has already turned his attention elsewhere. "Your loss," he calls, backing away a few steps before turning toward the group congregating in the parking lot.

"What's the reservoir?" I ask, watching as they greet Sage with whoops of joy. The girl with the earrings dangles her keys, and Sage grabs them as someone else throws backpacks and coolers into an SUV. The flurry of organized chaos reminds me of bus trips to track meets, and I feel a pang of longing for a time that no longer exists.

"It's just outside of town," Fletcher says. "There's a beach, but we mostly hang out at the campground off-season."

"And it's near the water? Like, Claret Creek water?"

"Well, yeah. The creek flows into the reservoir." He watches me watch them. "I'm sorry. Did you want to . . . I mean, would you rather go with them?" he asks, eyes wide with concern. "I should've asked."

We're heading to the reservoir to partake at the waters.

Miracle water.

Healing.

I know it's ridiculous. This water is not going to heal me.

But ridiculous or not, what could it hurt to try it? It's just water. Besides, I did promise Bryn I'd find out what I could about this story.

"Would you mind? It sounds . . . intriguing. And as much as I want to meet your bears, I really think I should get to know some humans here. I've never been the new kid before."

"Of course! I wasn't thinking. I mean, personally I'd take a bear over most humans every day. But I'm weird." He softens his words with another of those warm-butter smiles.

"I don't think you're weird. I think you're nice. And I bet your friends are, too."

"They aren't exactly my crowd," he warns as he leads me to a beat-up Jeep at the back of the lot. "It's going to be Sage's friends, so mostly athletes."

"Are you not an athlete?"

Fletcher grins. "Do I look athletic to you?"

I give him an obvious once-over, mentally picturing him as I'd seen him that first day, toned and shirtless. "I bet you could outrun a bear."

His eyes widen. "You should never try to outrun a bear."

I hold back a grin at his sudden seriousness. "Right. I don't know why I said that. Clearly I have a lot to learn about bears. So, rain check on the trip to the sanctuary?"

"Rain check," he says, ducking his head so his curls flop into his eyes. If he's disappointed, he's putting on a brave front for me.

He holds my door, then gets in and starts the car. Mick Jagger's voice blares from the speakers.

"Sorry." Fletcher grabs for the volume knob. "Hazards of driving alone."

"You've got eclectic taste in music," I say, pointing at his shirt.

"The Stones are not eclectic," he says. "They're iconic."

He has a point. Even I recognize the song, and I'm hardly what you'd call a fan.

"And what about you?" he asks, glancing over as he takes a right out of the parking lot, heading out of town.

"What about me?"

"You don't strike me as a rock chick. Mozart, maybe."

I choke out a laugh. "What about me screams classical music?"

"I'm not sure." He shifts another glance, quickly, and I like that he doesn't take his eyes off the road for long. He's an attentive driver, calm and careful. Hopefully we aren't heading up the mountain, but I feel like even if we did, I'd be in good hands. "You just seem kind of . . . low-key," he says, then adds hastily, "In a good way. Like nothing fazes you."

I resist the urge to stare at him, focusing instead on my hands clenched in my lap. "I'm pretty sure no one has ever called me low-key," I finally say. The first time we met, I had a full-on freak-out by the creek. Not to mention my numerous nosebleeds. He's either got a terrible memory, or he's confused me with someone else.

"Really? You just did your first day at a new school and you look"—he waves a hand at me—"totally cool. Even when I was drawing you that map, you were sort of"—he shrugs—"no big deal. And the other night?"

The other night.

I can't look at him, can't even breathe. I don't want to talk about that night. I want to forget it ever happened; I want *him* to forget it ever happened.

"I mean, that was a lot of blood. And you were totally calm. No drama." He whistles as he sweeps his hand across the space between us. "Low-key."

No drama? Is he talking about the same night? The night I freaked out and told them all that the answer was in my blood? And then gushed so much blood that I shut down the party?

I force a laugh and unclench my fingers, watching as they turn pink with the blood flow restored. "Wow, I guess I've got you fooled," I say, keeping my voice light as I try to steer him toward safer ground. "Today was definitely a big deal, trust me. I've been stressed out all day."

"You did fool me," he says. "You look good." Then he blushes. "I mean, you can't tell. And also, you do look good. You smell good, too. I'm rambling. I'll shut up now." He flexes his hands on the steering wheel.

A smile creeps across my face until my cheeks hurt. "Thanks."

I'm not sure if I should be flattered or concerned that Fletcher is maybe not that bright. Either way, I'm going to try and enjoy this. I can't remember the last time I spent any time with anyone besides my mom or Bryn, let alone a cute boy who blushes—blushes!—when he says nice things to me. Even better, a cute boy who sees me as calm and in control and not as an invalid.

"Do you want to grab some food before we head to the reservoir? I didn't pack anything, and I bet you're hungry."

I want to lean over and hug him, but I restrain myself. "I'm starving, actually." I need food. I also need rest, but I'm ignoring the fatigue. This is turning into the best day I've had in a long time, and I don't want to miss any of it.

Fletcher pulls up beside a building, and I catch sight of the sign above us.

"Snarf's?"

"It's a sandwich place. The best sandwich place, in fact."

"I'll take your word for it. It sounds like something a cat threw up."

"Everything is good here, but the best stuff isn't on the menu," Fletcher tells me as he holds the door, then follows me to the counter.

Great. A place only insiders know. Can't get enough of that.

"My favorite is the Big Fat Snarf. Lotta meat."

"Sounds good. I'll take a Big Fat . . . Snarf. On gluten-free bread?" I ask, and the guy at the counter nods and I relax a little. Not even cheating on Mom's diet.

I think maybe we'll take the food with us, but Fletcher carries our tray to the dining area and gestures for me to pick, so I choose a table by the window where the sun is streaming in.

He waits for me to take a bite and shoot him a thumbs-up.

"So what did you have in Michigan?"

No one knows, I almost say. But this isn't what he's asking. I wipe my mouth on my napkin and take a sip of soda to buy myself some time. "What do you mean?"

"No Snarf's, obviously."

"We had Erma's. It was this little coffee and ice cream place. But, like, the best ice cream you can imagine. My friends and I would make these outrageous concoctions—pineapple peanut butter pumpkin with mint fudge on top."

"That sounds awesomely bad."

"That one was actually pretty bad," I admit. "But most of the time they were delicious. I mean, it's hard to go wrong with ice cream." I take another huge bite of sandwich. "Although Snarf's is winning me over."

Fletcher beams as if he made it himself. "Tell me more."

"About ice cream?"

"About Michigan. And you."

I'm flustered, and I take a moment to tear open my bag of chips. "There's not much to tell."

I'm dying to ask him about his dad—really, about my dad—but I don't want him to think that's why I came. "It's crazy that our dads used to be best friends, isn't it?" I finally say. I gesture to the brightly painted walls. "I mean, they could've even hung out here. Or someplace like it."

That's been maybe the hardest thing to get used to, the fact that everywhere I go, my dad was here first. My house, my school. Maybe even this restaurant.

Fletcher pops the rest of his sandwich in his mouth and wipes his hands on a napkin. "Yeah, they did, for sure. Only this was some kind of diner back then. Dad talks about those days all the time. Teddy this, Teddy that. Usually about some kind of trouble they got into." His smile fades when he sees my expression. "I guess your mom probably doesn't know all the stories."

My appetite is suddenly gone and I push the basket away. "She didn't tell me any stories about Claret Creek. I didn't even know this place existed."

Fletcher tilts his head. "Snarf's? Or . . . ?"

"I knew my dad came from somewhere in Colorado," I say. "But it was just a place on a map. It never occurred to me that his house was still here. Or that I owned it." The air-conditioning is blowing directly on me, and I press my hands between my knees to keep them from shaking.

"You're kidding." He drains his soda. "Your mom never told you?"

I shake my head.

"Wow. No wonder she didn't want to come back."

Something about his bewilderment doesn't sit right, but my discomfort vanishes when I feel the warmth of his skin as he taps my knee with his own. "I'm glad you're here now," he says.

I can feel his smile all the way down to my toes. "Me too."

The reservoir is on a one-lane dirt road at the outskirts of town, and far enough up the mountain that I start to wonder if I should have told my mom where I was going so she knows where to look if we drive off the edge.

"It's not much farther," Fletcher says when I clutch the door handle as the Jeep bucks over the rocky soil. Finally, we crest the hill and I catch a glimpse of the water below, the sun glinting off the surface like a postcard.

"Wow," I say. "Just . . . wow."

"The view is pretty spectacular," he agrees, parking between a rusty red SUV and a sign that reads WALK-IN CAMPING.

He comes around to hold my door, and I step cautiously toward the edge of the cliff to get a better look. The lake is at least thirty feet below and so still on this cloudless day it's like a mirror, the reflection so clear I can't tell where the mountain ends and the water begins.

I swallow back the sudden roll of vertigo and grab Fletcher's arm to steady myself.

He lays a hand over mine, his smile sliding into a frown as someone shrieks. The sound echoes off the rocks, and I follow his line of sight away from the water toward a sandy path that slopes downward between a couple of pine trees.

"How many people are here?" I should have asked this earlier, my stomach fluttering at the thought of more strangers.

"I'm not sure. But we don't have to stay," Fletcher says, watching me.

I force a smile. "No. I'm good. This will be fun."

I'm such a liar.

Their voices grow louder as we approach on the path, then quiet as they hear us coming. We break through the tree line and I see Sage standing next to Van, who held the door for me, and the tiny girl with the big earrings from in the parking lot.

"Fletcher!" Sage calls out, holding up a beer. "I didn't think you'd actually come. Hey, Lola."

"Hi. You're Van, right?" I say to the other boy. "I think we have Bio together."

Van's ditched his shirt, and I try not to stare at his abs. "With Perez," he says, pointing at me. "She's, like, way too into her job."

"I thought she was all right," I say. "I mean, it's an AP class."

Van snorts and runs a hand through his close-cropped curls as the petite girl says, "Ask Emory what she thinks of Perez." She pivots so we can see Emory lying on her back on a flat rock behind them, her tank rolled up to expose her stomach and her platinum hair spread out around her like a halo. Emory lifts her middle finger and I'm not sure if it's in greeting or in reference to the teacher.

"I'm Isa, by the way." Isa's long dark hair is pulled into two braids, and she's wearing a Claret Creek cross-country T-shirt tied into a knot so that the belly button ring nestled against her brown skin shows above her short shorts.

I feel awkward and overdressed in my dress and boots, which felt safe enough for school but are all wrong for hanging out on top of a mountain in the hot Colorado sun.

"So, what do you think of the Creek so far?" Van asks, offering me a can from the cooler, some kind of vodka seltzer. Having spent the past year as a social outcast, I haven't had many opportunities to drink. I'm not so sure it's a great idea now, given my recent episodes, but I take it. Who knows, maybe alcohol will calm my crazy visions.

I'm assuming Van is asking about the town and not the creek itself, but after the discussion the other night, I'm not positive. I settle on something neutral, just in case. "Uh, it's nice. Really great, I mean." Honestly, I've managed more enthusiasm for a blood draw.

At least Emory finds it funny. When her laughter quiets, she says, "That's how we all feel."

"Speak for yourself," Sage says. "I love it here. My great-great-granddad helped build this place."

Van rolls his eyes. "What didn't your family do?" He finishes his can in a final gulp, then crushes it in his fist and looks around for somewhere to throw it.

"Dude." Sage grabs it and chucks it back into the cooler. "Littering is not cool. Some of us still care about this place."

I press the cold can against my cheek. "I didn't mean to insult anyone. It's only been a few days. And the first day of school was—"

"The *worst*," Isa finishes. "Right? Ugh." She shakes her head and her earrings bounce against her shoulders. "I can't believe summer is over."

I point at Isa's shirt. "How's the team? I used to run. Back in Michigan."

Her face lights up and she grabs my arm. "You should totally try out. Were you any good? We've got four good scorers, but our fifth is so-so. Clare's our star."

"You know it! Morales for the win!" Sage cups his hand around his mouth.

The star. Interesting. I wonder why Clare downplayed her accomplishments when we were talking earlier.

Van bumps Isa's hip with his own. "Don't sell yourself short, Navarro. You're no slouch."

Isa cocks her head and smiles at the praise, and I use the distraction to change the subject. "Where is Clare, anyway?"

Van looks at the ground while Isa glances at Sage, who stares out over the water. "She's busy."

Weird. And vague. But I don't press it. Instead, I take a seat next to Fletcher closer to the cliff edge, where he's chucking stones toward the lake. The hot rock burns the skin on the back of my knees, so I take off my jacket and spread it before sitting down again. "I know you said we weren't going to the beach, but honestly, I thought we'd be closer to the water," I say.

"The beach is really more for kids. Families. We don't really come out here to swim. More to have a place where no one will hassle us," Isa calls, and I'm mortified once again. Sage had said "partake *at* the waters." Not *of*. This was never about the water at all. And now I've dragged Fletcher out here to hang out with a bunch of strangers, and they probably think I'm some entitled bitch.

"I didn't bring a suit. But if anyone's up for skinny-dipping, I'm in," Van adds.

Fletcher's face darkens and he mouths "sorry" at me as he chucks another stone.

"I'll pass, thanks," I say. "I didn't actually mean . . . The water just looks so inviting."

Sage cracks open another beer. "Speaking of water, Lola's living in Dr. C's old house."

"Why?" There's an edge in Van's voice that wasn't there before, a distinct "you're not welcome" tone that scorches me like a sunburn.

"Ooh," Isa says. "That place is cursed."

"It was my dad's home," I say to Van. And then to Isa, "What makes you say that?"

"Your dad?" Van squints, like he's trying to decide if I'm lying. "I just assumed you were renting. Like—"

"Like everyone else who's been in and out of there over the years," Sage adds.

"I . . . What does that mean? How many people have been in and out?" I knew that Mom had rented the place, but I was under the impression it had only been once or twice, on Dominic's recommendation. The image of a string of strangers touching my dad's stuff unnerves me.

"Who's your dad?" Van asks, ignoring my question.

"Teddy Boyd." I chug some of my vodka drink, which has already gone warm. "Why did you say cursed?"

"Because of the witch, of course," Isa says, "You must be related to her. Did you inherit her powers?" She tilts her head as she waits for my answer, her brown eyes wide with curiosity.

Is she asking me if I'm devil spawn?

"Shut up, Isa," Emory says, earning my gratitude. I've almost forgotten she's here. And why is she here? Fletcher said Sage's friends were athletes. Isa's clearly a runner, and I have no trouble picturing Van on the football field or basketball court. But Emory is a mystery. Sure, she's tall and graceful, but she lacks a certain team-player vibe.

I chug the last of my drink and force a laugh. *I'm powerless*, I want to say to Isa's question. Instead, I settle on "If I'm related to a witch, it's news to me."

Sage burps loudly and pounds his chest. "You must be. Otherwise, how'd you end up with her house?"

"It was my dad's," I repeat. What is with these people? I'm from a small town myself, but I don't remember it feeling this claustrophobic, or people being this intrusive and pushy. Or maybe it's just that I've never been on the outside.

"You all seem to know more about my family than I do." It comes out harsher than I intend, so I try for less anxious and more nonchalant as I add, "I guess I'm going to have to do some research."

"There's probably something about her in those old scrapbooks in the library," Fletcher says eagerly. Too eagerly?

"Maybe." I don't want to talk about my family anymore, at least not with these people and not the way they want to talk about it. "Tell me about this magic water," I say, gesturing toward the reservoir with my empty can.

Isa pounces like we're in the middle of an argument. And maybe we are. I can't shake the feeling that there's something I'm missing, something big and important that they all know and aren't sharing. "But it is magic," she insists. "Ask anyone. We all know someone who's been healed. My best friend's cousin's aunt had this chronic skin disease, and after she used the water, it went away. It was, like, a total miracle. Everyone said so."

"Wouldn't her cousin's aunt be her aunt, too?" asks Emory.

Isa wrinkles her nose. "What? No. I don't think so." She worries at her lip as she contemplates the question.

But I've got more important questions. "Healed how? Did she bathe in it? Or drink it?"

Isa shrugs. "You know, I never asked."

I clamp my mouth shut in order to keep from screaming at her. *Never asked?* They've got a freaking miracle in their backyard and they don't think to ask any questions?

Emory finally moves, leaning up on one elbow as she pulls off her sunglasses. Her stare bores into me, like she can read what's going on inside my head.

I unclench my fists and run a hand through my hair, trying to act like I don't believe in any of this "magic water" nonsense.

But Emory isn't fooled. "The water isn't magic," she says, each word dropping like a stone. "The town's so-called hero was just a piece of shit liar. Hung up on his own vanity. He didn't drink the water, he drank his own Kool-Aid."

Sage says, "Yes, but what you're forgetting is the Kool-Aid was *made* with the water."

He ducks as Emory chucks her flip-flop at his head. His phone chirps and, still crouching, he pulls it out of his pocket. The grin slides off his face as he reads the screen. "Shit. It's Clare. We've gotta go." He starts chucking cans back into the cooler. "Help me clean up."

"Is Amber having another bad day?" Isa asks, her voice sympathetic.

The name freezes me in place. "Amber?" My dad's friend. The girl Fletcher showed me a picture of. I turn to Sage. "Amber is your mom?"

He glares at me over the top of the cooler. "Yeah. So what of it?"

"Nothing. I just . . . heard she used to go out with my dad."

"Ages ago."

I'm taken aback by the anger in his voice. "Sure. Right. I just don't know many people who knew him."

He slams the cooler and slings it onto his shoulder. "Don't look at me. I never met him."

"Obviously." I can't keep the sarcasm from my voice, but if it bothers him, I can't tell. I want to ask if his mom would talk to me, but he's already halfway to the car and clearly this isn't a topic he wants to discuss. Or maybe he's just worried about her.

Emory hops off the rock to retrieve her sandal, then grabs on to Fletcher as she slides it onto her foot. "Are you guys heading home from here? Can I catch a ride?"

Fletcher shoves his hands in his pockets. "Uh, I'm not really sure. Lola and I were going to hang out. Maybe." He scuffs his foot against the ground.

Emory glances back and forth between us, a slight frown wrinkling her forehead. "Right. Got it. Well, you two have fun." She backs down the trail toward the parking area, only turning when Sage calls at her to hurry up.

CHAPTER 13

The quiet hits me as soon as they leave. Fletcher and I are on top of the world, alone, looking down over all this beauty and all I can think about is how removed I am from everything. Not just the water, which is thirty feet below us, but also my old life, a thousand miles away. And also this new life, which feels like a room I can't enter, like there's a velvet rope and it's VIP only.

But that's not totally fair. It's my fault, too, and the fact that I've forgotten how to do any of this, and I'm awkward and tired and a little tipsy and way outside my comfort zone. Some of them have been welcoming. Like Fletcher.

But he's been quiet from the moment we arrived, and I thought it was due to the others—I get a sense that maybe he doesn't like Van all that much—but he doesn't look any more comfortable now that they're gone.

Maybe it's me. Maybe he regrets asking me out.

If that's even what this is.

"Can we go down to the water?" I ask, just as he starts to talk. I laugh awkwardly. "Sorry. What did you say?"

He shakes his head. "Nothing. You want to go to the beach? I didn't bring a suit." He presses his lips together and blushes, and I guess he's remembering Van's comment about skinny-dipping.

"I don't want to swim," I say. "But maybe we could wade in? Unless it's too deep."

"Not too deep." He stares at the water for a moment, lost in thought. "Let's do it."

I stumble on the way to the car and hope he doesn't notice, but he shoots me a worried glance. Between all the classes and new people and sunshine and liquor, my energy is draining faster than my phone when I'm roaming. But I'm not ready for this day to be over. "Sheesh. How much vodka is in those things?" I ask lightly.

In the car, Fletcher turns the music up for the short drive down to the water, which makes conversation impossible. Whatever ease we had with each other is gone. Was it something I did or said?

I take a deep breath when he finally reaches over to turn down the volume.

"I'm sorry about those guys," he says before I can think of something to fill the silence. "And what they said. About your family. Van is . . . kind of a dick sometimes."

"You don't have to apologize for them. I mean, you did warn me." I look out the window. "Maybe we should have stuck with the bears."

He laughs. "It's not too late."

"But we're already here," I say. "And they're gone. Just us and the water." I turn in my seat to face him. "You've lived here all your life, right?" When he nods, I ask, "Is it really magic?"

"That's what they say. But it's not like anyone's drinking it to cure cancer or anything. It's hard to explain. I think for most of us, we just like to believe it could have happened, right here in our little town. The power comes from the story, not the water. If that makes sense."

I find myself nodding. "That does make sense. And I'm a little relieved, honestly." And disappointed, though I don't say that. "I mean, it sounds like Sage and Clare's mom is sick. And nobody is talking about healing her with water."

"I wish," he says softly.

"What's wrong with her, anyway?"

He lifts a shoulder. "I'm not sure. There have been a lot of tests, but I don't really . . . I'm sorry. You'd have to ask Clare. She and Sage both. They take on a lot of the care of Hunter and Rosie, their brother and sister."

"Is their dad—?"

"He died. About ten years ago."

Maybe that was why I'd felt a bond with Clare right away. Why she'd asked about my dad, and seemed to understand my need to find him.

"And Amber dated my dad, right? She was the girl in those pictures you showed me."

"Yeah, they were high school sweethearts. Just like my mom and dad."

"Really? That's cute."

He rolls his eyes, but I can tell by his smile that he thinks so, too. "Yeah, they grew up together. Best friends forever, each of them crushing on the other one but too afraid to say. I've heard the story dozens of times."

"And how about my dad and Amber? Same thing?"

He hesitates. "I mean, it's a small town. My mom did tell me once she thought they'd have a double wedding."

"Wow. That's . . . I mean . . . they were that serious?"

"Don't get me wrong," he says quickly. "My parents love your mom. And they were totally happy for her and Teddy when they got married. They just wished he had come back here. Settled here. You know." He grimaces. "I'm sorry. I talk too much."

"No! No," I repeat. "This is great. I want to learn about my dad. It's just that everything is news. Because I know so little. I think I just have to take it in small bites."

"I get it. Digestion." Fletcher pats his stomach.

"Exactly. But I appreciate you telling me this stuff. You're the only one who has." I touch his arm and he looks down at my hand and then back at my face, and for one glorious moment I think he's going to lean in and kiss me and I want that more than anything, but then he clears his throat and looks away and the magic is broken.

"Should we walk on the beach?" he asks.

He holds the door for me and then takes my hand as we walk toward the water, lacing his fingers lightly through mine.

Maybe he does like me?

He stoops to grab a stone from the sand, and our hands are tugged apart. "For you," he says, handing it to me. It's dark, with a light gray swirl through the middle that looks a little like a wave. "Whatever is not stone is light."

The rock is smooth and cool as I rub it between my thumb and index finger.

I can't place the quote, but I'm charmed by the fact that he memorized a quote for me. For a moment just like this. Giddiness pushes back at my fatigue, like my veins are filled with bubbly water.

I study his sweet face, the lock of hair falling into his eye, his dimples. His lips.

I'm aware of everything, suddenly. The kiss of air across my cheek, the heat of the sun on my neck. My blood, coursing through my body, warming my skin. The earthy smell of the water as it laps hungrily at the shore, cold and dark and endless. The sound is louder now, roaring, pushed into frothy anger as the sun leaches from the sky and the sand turns to black beneath our feet. The beach spins away from me and I tilt my head, trying to right it. The world tips, or I do, and then I'm struggling to breathe as I stumble against the trees.

Trees?

Strong hands grab me and pull me forward as my bare feet slip against the muddy grass. He's going to drown me, I'm certain of it. But I'm powerless to stop him.

"Don't!" I cry. I feel the word on my lips, as well as the effort it takes to push it out. But the voice is not my own.

And whoever he is, he doesn't stop. He yanks my arm, hard, and I lose my balance, my lace-sleeved arm reaching out to cushion my fall. On my knees now, in the water, cold, so cold against my burning skin. He dunks my head and I surface, gasping and coughing. Blood pools on my tongue.

"The water heals," he says, raising his voice for the benefit of the crowd.

I swipe a wet hand across my face, smearing blood and water together. My wet, heavy hair hangs in my face and twists around my neck like a coiled snake.

"It didn't help her, did it?" I choke out the words, taking grim satisfaction in the way he flinches.

"Lola. Lola!"

I blink, nauseated and dizzy, as Fletcher's face swims in and out of view. "Are you okay?"

"I need to sit down," I say, aware that this doesn't quite make sense.

He crouches beside me in the sand. "You are sitting."

I gape at my shaky fingers pressed against the warm sand, and the blood spattering my bare arms. Dry arms. I run my hands over my shirt and shorts, across my hair. All dry.

"I'm going to get help," he says, scanning the beach.

"Wait. Don't . . . leave."

He rests one hand on my back while fumbling in his pocket with the other. "Is your mom at home?"

I shake my head, the slight movement making me so dizzy I nearly vomit. "Library," I whisper.

He searches for the number while I focus on the water and struggle to remain conscious. Try to remember how to breathe. In. Out. Easy. Painless.

I thought it would hurt, somehow, because of the blood when I was . . . But that didn't actually happen. And it's my nose that's bleeding. Now.

Fletcher's voice fades in and out. ". . . Dominic's son." He crouches down beside me. "Fine, thanks. Listen, I'm with Lola and she's"—his eyes lock with mine and I look away—"unwell."

Unwell. So much loaded into that one word. I *am* unwell.

I'd hoped it would take him longer to find out.

CHAPTER 14

The electronic beep of an incoming call jerks me from a state somewhere between sleep and humiliation. I grab the phone from the table beside the giant red couch and stare at it in confusion. My phone hasn't worked in the house since we moved in.

I sit up quickly, head swimming, and answer it before this digital miracle is rescinded.

"Hey," says Fletcher. "How are you? I've been worried."

The aftermath is sort of a blur to me—Fletcher's phone conversation with my mom, then him driving me home, Kurt meeting us at the door with some crap comment about me being a drama queen, followed by Fletcher's awkward goodbye as Kurt ushered me inside. He'd promised to call and check on me, but I'd been convinced I'd never hear from him again.

My face goes hot, making my head pound harder. "You don't need to worry about me. Just a little too much vodka seltzer, I guess." I cringe as I wait for Fletcher's reply.

I have no idea how much my mom told him on the phone, but I'm suddenly tired of trying to hide my illness. It's not my fault my body is screwed up. Who cares what he thinks, anyway? He's just some dumb boy I didn't even know existed a week ago. Just because he's sweet and kind and gave me a stone and drove me home when I was sick and now is calling to check up on me because he's worried, that doesn't mean this is some great love story.

"It didn't seem like an alcohol thing to me," Fletcher says. "You were perfectly fine one minute and then it was like you went somewhere else. And you were bleeding. Something was definitely wrong."

I take a deep breath and it just comes out. "Look, I don't know what my mom told you, but I'm sick, okay?" It's a relief to actually say the words out loud.

"Sick how?"

"I wish I knew." I sink back against the couch cushions and it all pours out. "It started about a year ago. I got dizzy and fell during a track meet. And never really recovered, I guess. They ran a bunch of tests, but no one could figure out what's wrong. I get these dizzy spells. Headaches. Body aches. Shortness of breath. And fatigue. A lot of fatigue. Back in Michigan, it got too hard to even go to school, so I switched to virtual schooling."

The anonymity and intimacy of his voice in my ear gives me the courage to tell him everything. "My mom burned through all her savings, trying to find a diagnosis. Or a specialist who could help me. That's why we ended up out here. And Kurt—" I break off, a catch in my voice. "He doesn't believe it's real, I guess. He thinks I'm faking. And I mean, I can hardly blame him. He's not the first one to say that."

I hold my breath, waiting for his response, which is going to be something awkward, I'm sure. *You seem fine to me.* Or *But you're better now, right?*

"That must be so hard."

Do not cry. Act normal. Don't be *that* person, the one who turns into a sobbing wreck at the first sign of sympathy. Hold it together, Lola.

He continues, "So that's what happened on the beach? You got dizzy?"

I hesitate. Am I really going to share this with him? He's the first person I've talked to about my illness since Bryn. But these other episodes are on a whole different level. I don't know him well enough to trust him with my darkest secrets.

On the other hand, he knows a lot about my dad and his family. Certainly more than I do. If anyone can help figure out what's happening to me, maybe it's him. "I started having these . . . visions," I say slowly. "Like that first day, by the creek. I thought they were hallucinations at first. Some new symptom related to whatever is wrong with me. But now I don't know. They seem real. Like something that actually happened."

"When you mentioned the water," Fletcher says. "When you got the nosebleed."

"Right!" I've come this far and he hasn't hung up on me yet. Because he's being polite? Or maybe this is a by-product of the Claret Creek phenomenon. He's grown up in a town whose claim to fame is magic water. Maybe this doesn't even faze him. "This is going to sound weird—even weirder than everything else," I continue, "but these episodes, they don't feel like they're about me. It's like someone else is trying to reach me. To tell me something. Like my dad, maybe."

I hold my breath as I wait for him to reply. I have absolutely no evidence to support this theory, but I desperately want it to be true.

"What do you think he's trying to tell you?" His voice is soft and free from judgment, which isn't wholehearted support, but it's better than nothing.

"What if he thinks the water will heal me?"

"Oh boy. That's why you were asking about the water. I'm sorry, but I don't think . . . It's like I said earlier. It's not . . . We don't . . ."

"I get it," I say, not wanting to make him fumble through any more excuses or apologies.

Fletcher says hastily, "Maybe it's like a subconscious thing. You've been sick and you hear about this healing water, and of course you want it to be true."

"I'm not *imagining* all of this," I snap, though even as I say it, I realize that's exactly what I've been doing. The problem is, it feels like someone else's imaginings and not my own. "Look, remember that first day? Down by the creek? How did I know that quote? From the doctor. I'd never heard about him, or the water, before I got here."

When he doesn't answer, I know I've blown it. "Never mind. You don't believe me. Forget I said anything." *And please, for the love of God, don't tell your friends.*

"I'm not saying it's impossible. Just, if your dad wants you to try and heal yourself in the water, why'd he stop you? We were headed to the lake, right? So why send you a vision just before you got there?"

He's right. It doesn't make any sense. And though I hadn't wanted to admit it, in this last episode, it didn't even feel like my dad. It felt like I was having some other girl's memory. I can't pinpoint why exactly, or even explain it in any rational way, but she didn't seem healed by the water. She seemed frightened. And that sensation of being weak, of feeling powerless against someone older, stronger, in a position of power? It's a feeling I recognized.

"So what do I do now?" I ask.

"Look, I've always thought of the water story as more of a metaphor than anything else, but what do I know? What we need is an expert."

We?

He continues, "Someone who knows what actually happened, not just the legend we all repeat. Who was healed, and from what. And I know who we can ask: Mr. Zeller. The history teacher."

He sounds thrilled at the prospect of helping me research.

Bryn is going to love him. And they might not be the only one.

We make plans to meet before class by the big aspen in front of the school. After he says goodbye, I toss the phone onto the couch and gaze out the attic window, toward the ever-present line of rock in the distance. It isn't like me to share so much personal information, and so quickly, but I feel like I've known Fletcher my whole life. And the fact that he hasn't run screaming makes me feel like I've found my first friend here.

And maybe something more?

I just wish he hadn't dismissed the idea of my dad so quickly. Until he did, I hadn't realized how badly I want these episodes to be linked to him somehow, how desperately I want to believe he's found some way to communicate with me. I want to grab on to that moment in the car. To live there, no matter how terrifying it was. Because, what if that was him? His hands on the wheel? His voice?

But it's so slippery to grab on to a memory, even more so one that isn't rightfully mine.

My throat burns with the ache of a loss that's so far removed it's like a shadow. His absence has always brought more pain than I feel I have a right to claim. How can I mourn someone I never knew?

Then again, how can I feel whole when I was born with him missing? He's like a phantom limb, a whisper I can never quite make out, an anecdote in someone else's story. The only thing he's never really felt like is my father.

I huff out a gasp and as I do, my breath fogs the window, revealing the faint outline of a heart, traced on the glass by some long-ago finger. I press my hand to the glass beside it, careful not to smudge it, and then watch until both prints fade and the sun dips behind the mountain.

"Lola? Wake up, honey." Mom leans over me, smelling of lemons and soap. Her curly hair, still wet from her shower, drips onto my bare shoulder, and sunlight streams through my bedroom windows.

"What time is it?" I struggle to sit up.

"It's morning. I tried to wake you last night, but you were so deeply asleep, I decided to let you be." She rubs my shoulder. "Can I get you some breakfast?"

I nod slowly and touch a tentative finger to my nose, then check my pillow. No blood. "Yeah. Breakfast sounds good."

"Excellent. And after that, a shower? And maybe binge some *Grey's Anatomy*?"

I sneak a peek at my phone. It's after seven. I throw off the blankets. "I can't. I've got school."

She purses her lips. "Is that really such a good idea? After yesterday . . ."

What happened between her and Kurt while I was dead to the world, to make her drop their agreed upon "school is important" stance? The rah-rah, "push through the pain" bullshit or whatever Kurt had been peddling and she was backing?

She picks at an invisible thread on my quilt and says, "Maybe we were too hasty in sending you back. Too much change all at once."

You think? I long to fling the words in her face. Instead, I get out of bed and grab my towel from the back of my door. As tempting as it is to stay home and avoid the difficulty of another day being the new girl, it feels too easy, like a trap. Something Michigan Lola would do.

Here, I'm different. Colorado Lola goes to school. She makes friends. She shares things.

She has visions that belong to someone else.

And she needs to research those visions, which I can't do in my house with Kurt looking over my shoulder. Plus—and this is probably my real motivation—there is no way in hell I'm staying home with Kurt all day, not when I keep fainting and bleeding. School might be exhausting, but right now it's less hazardous. Less haunted.

"I can't stay home," I say. "No internet, remember?"

"But Kurt got that fix—"

"Besides, I feel fine," I say, knotting my fingers beneath the towel so she can't see them tremble. "I just overdid it a bit yesterday, what with the first day of school, and all the fresh air and sunshine. And the lake."

"Fresh air? The lake—"

"But I'm fine now. I'm rested. And I want to go to school."

"What lake?" she calls after me, but I close the bathroom door without answering.

After a quick shower, I towel dry my hair, throw on my favorite pair of jeans and my lucky pineapple T-shirt, and head downstairs. I pause in the doorway to the kitchen, trying to read the room, but either this dynamic between the three of us is too new or I'm too tired. The most I can gauge is that they aren't feeling chatty. Kurt is at the table drinking coffee and studying his phone, while Mom stares out the window over the sink.

I slide into the chair across from Kurt, where Mom has laid out a place setting for me with a big bowl of oatmeal and a cup of coffee. After a few spoonfuls of the warm, sugary cereal, my shoulders relax.

Mom turns. "You're done at three today, right? Or is it another half day?" The look she gives me is hard to read, something between frustration and concern.

"Yesterday was a fluke," I say. "I didn't know we were done early, and then Fletcher invited me to lunch."

"Lunch where, exactly?" Before I can answer, she hits me with the Mom guilt. "I'm glad you're making friends. I just wish—" She grips her mug. "Are you sure you're okay?"

I sneak a look at Kurt, but he's watching her, not me. What do they want from me, anyway? They're the ones who told me to go to school, to stop acting like I was sick all the time. To be fair, most of the "crying wolf" arguments had been Kurt. But she hadn't defended me.

"I'm fine," I say, not mentioning the storm of a headache I can feel building near my temples.

"Fletcher's phone call really scared me." Her cup trembles in her hands as evidence.

"He overreacted." I have no idea what he told her, but I decide to wing it. "I tripped, is all."

"And hit your head?"

Kurt clears his throat. "She was fine by the time she got home. Just a little shook up."

I have no idea why he's backing me up, and I don't know if I'm grateful or ashamed. Is this how it will be now? Always two against one? They form a united front against me, and Kurt and I retaliate by lying to Mom?

"What about the nosebleed? Kurt said you were bleeding when you got home."

Kurt frowns down at the floral pattern of the tablecloth but doesn't speak.

Coward. If this *is* his attempt to support me, it's failing.

"I'm not sure why it happened again. Altitude, maybe?" I rub the bridge of my nose.

"Or maybe you need more rest. Or a different diet. Should I message the new doctor? Although you do have an appointment next week. I guess we could ask her then . . ."

I've never heard her so indecisive, especially about my medical care. Even when we weren't getting answers, she was always convinced one was coming. And when it didn't, she just kept pushing forward. Tress Boyd didn't take no for an answer.

But she's Tress Gunderson now.

I go to the Keurig to refill my cup, stalling as I think of how best to appease her. "Look, Mom—"

But she's back to staring out the window.

"Come on, Lola." Kurt's chair squeaks against the laminate as he pushes back from the table. "I'll drive you to school. Give your mom some time to relax on her morning off."

I don't want to ride with Kurt. But what are my choices? Fletcher probably would've picked me up if I'd asked, but I'm running late as it is.

"Thanks," I say grudgingly. I grab my backpack and travel mug and lean in to kiss Mom goodbye.

"I didn't realize how hard this was going to be," she whispers into my hair.

My heart twists as I pull back to look at her. "How hard what would be?"

She shakes her head and turns away, but not before I see the tears in her eyes.

Kurt jangles his keys. "Let's get a move on."

I wait another second for Mom to answer me, but she doesn't, so I have no choice but to follow Kurt out the back door.

She didn't know what would be so hard? Moving? Having a daughter? Getting married?

I climb into the passenger seat and turn toward the window, praying we can do this in silence.

"So." Kurt clears his throat.

So much for the praying.

"I notice you didn't go into details with your mom. About yesterday. And I want you to know, I support that decision. One hundred percent. In fact, it shows real growth. You're thinking about her feelings for a change."

The longer he talks, the lower I sink in my seat. Does he really think this pseudo-ass-kissing is going to win me over? What does my mother see in him? Is this what she wants in a mate? A pompous jerk in love with the sound of his own voice?

I'm being unfair. I know it. And I promised Mom I would make more of an effort.

"I'm always thinking about her," I say. "Yesterday was no big deal." It's a lie, but he doesn't want to hear the truth. He heard it all yesterday. Despite my best efforts to stay cool, it had all spilled out of me like water, along with a rant about his dismissal of my earlier episode as "woo-woo shit."

I regretted the words as soon as they were out.

"It's no secret that your mom and I disagree on the topic of your . . . illness." He shifts his gaze to me and back to the road. "But now that the two of us are alone, I wanted to ask for your help. This whole thing has been difficult for her."

"This whole thing" being taking care of me?

"But I want you to know that I get it now."

What exactly does he "get"?

"And I'd like to ask if you could maybe tone it down a bit. For her sake."

My head is pounding so hard I can barely hear him, and I don't know if my anger is making the headache worse, or vice versa.

"I can't just *stop* having nosebleeds. It's not like a faucet." I can feel the anger boiling inside me, heating my blood like lava as it flows through my veins and scorches my face.

"I'm just saying, I love your mom. So do you. And I think with a little work, we can make her life easier. Working together. As a team."

Great. The first time I get to be on a team again and it's with Kurt.

But the acidic reply dies in my throat. Because however badly he is handling this, he's right about Mom. I know how hard it is for her, to watch me suffer and not be able to help. Missing work to run me to appointments, paying the endless stacks of bills every month, watching the money flow from her bank account like a drain in the bottom of a swimming pool, and still no answers. I don't want to be a burden on her, emotionally or financially. The thing is, I never felt like one until Kurt entered the picture. But maybe it isn't fair to be angry at him for making me see the truth.

"I do love her," I say. "And I don't want to hurt her. But I don't know how to get better. Believe me, I've tried."

"I'm not saying that. I know you're sick," he says, "but let's see what we can do to manage it ourselves, okay? Like we did this morning. Before we worry your mom."

When he says it like that, it sounds so simple. So I tell him that, yes, I will do my best to make Mom's life easier, whatever it takes.

He beams at me, not bothering to ask what "whatever it takes" might mean. Which is just as well. Telling him, or Mom, that I might be looking for a cure in a magic river on the advice of my dead father is probably not something either of them would understand.

CHAPTER 15

AP History is going to be too much for my first hour of my first full day of school in over a year; I can tell even before the second bell chimes. I'm tired—bone deep, as if the ten hours I'd slept were merely a product of my imagination. My headache has taken up a steady drumbeat of pain behind my right eyeball, and I want to lay my head down on my desk so badly I can taste the longing in the back of my throat. The only thing that keeps me upright is the fear of drooling.

The jangle of the tardy bell shakes me, and I press cold fingers to my brow. Among Mom's advice, gleaned from books or websites—putting pressure on certain points of the body can relieve pain and stress. Unfortunately, I can never remember which points, but since it's an action I have control over, I still do it.

"Rough night?" Emory slides into the seat beside me.

The teacher shoots us a raised-brow look but doesn't comment, turning away to write something on the board.

Emory unpacks her bag calmly, as if she's minutes early instead of late, stacking her notebooks neatly in the corner before straightening her perfectly ironed dress and running a hand over her impeccably smooth hair.

"I didn't know you were in this class." I wince at a jab of pain and move my hands to my lap. "I didn't see you yesterday."

"I work in the office," she says. "First day, I get a pass from all my classes because it's such a free-for-all in there. Everyone wanting to drop or add or bitch about their classes or whatever." She flicks her wrist. "But I'm here now. What did I miss?"

"To be honest, it's kind of a blur," I say. "Just the syllabus and—" I break off as the guy in front of me passes back a stack of papers. I take one and hand the rest over my shoulder.

"History is written by the victors." My attention snaps back to our teacher as he leans against his desk at the front of the room. "How many of you have heard that phrase or something similar?"

Mr. Zeller crosses his arms and waits, but when no one takes the initiative, he zeroes in on Emory. "Emory, can you enlighten the rest of your colleagues as to the meaning of that statement?"

Emory mutters something under her breath as she sits up in her chair. "It means the old white men get to write the books."

A flash of a smile crosses Mr. Zeller's face. "Not exactly. But close enough." He pushes himself forward and begins to pace. "This semester, we're going to dig into some real history. Learn new things about topics we thought we understood—the uncomfortable truths, the voices that those in power tried to silence. Who can give me an example of an event in history that may have played out differently than we were initially led to believe?"

"The spiritualist movement?" Emory calls, raising her hand but not waiting for him to acknowledge her.

He presses his lips together. "That wasn't exactly what I was—"

"Did you know that Thomas Edison was working on a phone to contact the dead?" She twists in her seat to face the rest of the class. "I mean, Edison was a genius. What if he'd succeeded? It would have totally changed our views of the afterlife."

"Except he didn't," Mr. Zeller says, his voice mild. Even so, Emory visibly bristles.

He tries one more time. "What I'm trying to get at here is more like . . ."

"Christopher Columbus discovering America," someone else calls, and Mr. Zeller points his finger toward the student. "Exactly!"

He strides toward the back of the room, and when he's out of earshot, Emory leans over to me. "I heard you blacked out yesterday. After we left."

I drop my pencil as my hands go numb. "Where'd you hear that?"

She stares, her expression unchanged, as if my question is too dumb to answer. Which it is. Fletcher was the only one who could have told her.

"I didn't black out," I say, the words coming automatically, which I'm grateful for, since my brain seems to have shut down from the shock of Fletcher's betrayal. "I don't know what Fletcher said to you, but it was no big deal. It was hot out and I think I just had too much"—I glance toward the teacher— "sun," I finish, swallowing hard.

What did he tell her? Did he tell her about my sickness? Or worse, my episodes? Please, God, don't let him have mentioned what I said about my dead father.

She lifts one shoulder. "He said you blacked out. And that you were bleeding. Honestly, he sounded pretty freaked out." She shrugs again. "I just figured you can't hold your liquor. Except we weren't drinking the other night at your house." She tilts her head as she stares at me. "Weird, right? That it would happen again?"

My heart pounds so hard I'm afraid it might happen another time, right here in front of her. "Bloody noses are pretty common, actually. I don't think it's weird at all."

Emory arches one eyebrow, which could mean anything—Fletcher's a jerk, I'm a liar, my constant bleeding is getting old. To be fair, all of those things are accurate.

She leans in and I take a breath, ready to dispute whatever she says. It's Fletcher's word against mine at this point, and since he clearly doesn't understand the meaning of the word "privacy," who cares about his version of events?

Instead she says, "Fletcher and Clare." She waves a manicured hand. "They're a thing. On-again, off-again. Currently off, but no one expects that to last."

My head pounds and my tongue feels too big for my mouth as I manage to parrot, "A thing?"

"We call them Flare." She does jazz hands and stage whispers the name.

Of course, they're a couple. Hadn't I picked up on some kind of chemistry between them that first night at my house? But when I told Clare about Fletcher inviting me to the bear rescue, she didn't say anything. My cheeks get hot as I remember her exact words: *You should go. It's an experience not to be missed.*

"I didn't know," I mumble.

Emory stretches out her long legs and crosses one gleaming white sandal over the other. "That's why I'm telling you."

Emory waits for me to gather my books after class, and as we exit the classroom together, I see Fletcher and Sage farther down the hall. "I need to talk . . . to Mr. Zeller," I stammer to Emory. "About . . . something . . . personal."

I can feel her stare boring into me as I duck back into the classroom.

"It's Lola, right?" Mr. Zeller says, then smiles. "Emory told me you've been spending time together. Welcome to town."

Why would Emory be telling him anything about me? I stare at his clear blue eyes, the recognition taking much longer than it should.

"Emory's my daughter," he clarifies.

"Right. Of course." Then I shake my head. "Sorry. I didn't realize . . . I just have a few questions . . ." But my mind is blank, save for thoughts of Fletcher. We'd planned on talking to Mr. Zeller together, but I was running late this morning and missed meeting him by the tree out front. I'd actually been looking forward to seeing him. Now that I know he can't keep his mouth shut, I'm not sure I can ever face him.

"I'm— My dad is from here." Does he already know this? Clare had said the town was minuscule.

But the tilt of his head indicates only minor interest.

"I actually wanted to ask you about the doctor who healed everyone. Dr. Clarett. And the creek water."

"That's an interesting local legend for sure," Mr. Zeller says. "One this town relishes. Brave hero fights off plague single-handedly, armed with only a vial of water." He spreads his hands out in front of him like he's reading the words off a marquee.

"I've heard all that," I say. "Or most of it, I guess. But is it true?"

He ducks his head. "Truth. That's exactly what I was trying to get at in class today. What is truth?"

Great. The one guy Fletcher thinks can help us—help *me*—and he wants a philosophical debate. "That's what I'm asking you," I say. "I mean, what about the so-called healing? Did that really happen? How many were cured? Surely someone knows."

"I appreciate your enthusiasm." He leans forward. "Between you and me, I'm not as convinced as everyone else about the miraculous properties of the creek. Don't get me wrong, water's great. I just think if it really cured influenza, we'd be a bigger dot on the map by now. My guess? By getting all those people to camp out by the water, Dr. Clarett inadvertently got them out of their cramped houses and away from their infected family members. Fresh air. That might've been the real hero."

"So that's it? You think people got better from the fresh air? And they were all too dumb to realize it?" I shift my books to my other arm.

"'Dumb' is a strong word. This actually gets back to what we were talking about in class. The illusory truth effect. If people hear something repeated enough times, they start to believe it. The truth becomes irrelevant."

"Not to me."

"I'm just not sure there's anything to find, beyond the story." He taps a finger to his lips and stares at the floor. "But if you're serious about getting to the heart of it, my advice would be to find a loose strand and start pulling. Any web of untruths will eventually unravel if you keep working at it. But probably not before something nasty falls out."

He meets my shudder with a small smile. "Check the local archives. There would've been newspaper articles. And burial records. I'd start there." His eyes alight with a sudden spark of interest. "You're living in the old house, I hear. Clarett's. Maybe he kept records. Those would be interesting."

The bell dings twice and Mr. Zeller points up to warn me. "Do you need a pass?"

"I can make it," I say.

"Let me know if you find anything. This could turn out to be a really interesting topic for us to cover in class."

I thank him and make a beeline for the hall with my head tucked down, hoping to avoid any contact with Fletcher. Which is silly, because I'm only buying myself time. He's in my seventh-period Spanish class. Unless something dreadful happens in the next five hours, I'll have to face him eventually.

I thought we hit it off yesterday, which is why I confided in him last night. The fact that he turned around and talked to Emory is humiliating.

I can't believe I trusted him.

And I can't believe I thought he liked me. What does that mean for my friendship with Clare? I don't want to be her rival. I'm done with petty fights, about boys or anything else. I just want to make some friends and do regular things. Why is this so hard?

The unwritten rule "Thy seat chosen on the first day must remain thy seat for all eternity" is firmly in place at Claret Creek High, because when I get to Spanish 3, the only seat left is next to Fletcher. I do a cursory scan of the room, but finding a new seat looks to be even more awkward than sitting next to him. Which I do while trying not to meet his gaze.

"I'm glad to see you," he says, turning sideways in his desk and leaning his elbows on his knees. He's forgone a band tee today in favor of one with Fozzie Bear. "I was worried when you didn't show up at the tree this morning. How are you?"

His obvious concern is both touching and annoying. I focus on the second emotion, hoping to push aside any warmth I have for him. "What did you say to Emory?" I ask, head bent as I dig through my backpack.

He leans in—to hear me or help me—and our foreheads knock as I jerk away.

"Cripes! Sorry!"

I rub my forehead and shoot him what I hope is a withering glance, not entirely sure what he's apologizing for.

"I don't like everyone knowing my business," I say, realizing I sound like a crime boss from *The Sopranos*. I lower my voice. "I told you all that in confidence yesterday. I thought I could trust you. But now everyone's talking about it."

"Everyone? I only told Emory, and only because I was worried when you weren't here this morning. I asked her to text me whether you were in class."

"None of that requires mentioning my . . . dizzy spell yesterday."

He presses his lips together, brow furrowed, maybe trying to figure out some excuse. Or struggling to figure out why I've decided to rewrite history. "But it wasn't—"The bell cuts him off and I face the front of the classroom.

Damn it. I like him—no, I *liked* him. He knows too much—and now I do, too—for us to ever be a thing.

When Profesora's back is turned, he slides a piece of folded paper onto my desk, pretending to stretch and then dropping his arms back onto his own desk.

I'm tempted to brush it into my bag without looking at it, but my curiosity gets the better of me. His handwriting is small and neat.

I'm sorry. I shouldn't have said anything to Emory.
Orson would like it if you'd give me another chance.

Below the apology, he's sketched a not-terrible drawing of his dog. I feel my face muscles working against me as I fight the urge to smile.

I write back.

What about Clare?

As he opens the paper, beads of sweat break out on my forehead. What am I, a middle schooler? Still, he should have told me they were a couple. I'm walking into this new life totally clueless, and it isn't fair.

He scrunches up his face, then scribbles something back.

Clare stayed home—her mom is having a bad day.

Did he deliberately misunderstand the question? Or am I making too much out of their relationship? I only have Emory's word on how close they were, on the on-again, off-again saga of Flare. Did I read too much into those few words? It felt like a friendly piece of advice, a window into some of the dynamics here.

But I keep forgetting that I'm the outsider. I don't have any real insight into any of their relationships. Or their motivations. I only know what they choose to tell me; that's it.

He tosses me another note before I have time to formulate a reply.

Friends?

I almost laugh. Is that what he's worried about? I'd nearly convinced myself that yesterday was some kind of date, that we were on our way to some epic romance. Hell, he gives me one rock—a *rock*—and I bare my soul. But for all I know, he is being friendly only because his dad asked him to.

Friends? I force a smile and nod.

It's not the first time I've made a stupid mistake about who I can trust, but it will be the last. I'm going to be much more careful about what I share, and with whom.

When the final bell rings, Fletcher lingers as I slowly gather my stuff. "Need a ride home?"

I shake my head. "No thanks. I've got to go to the library. To . . . meet my mom." I almost tell him that I'm going to do research on the creek, but catch myself in time. I don't need his help.

"Oh, okay. Cool." But he's still waiting. For what, I don't know. I know my social skills are rusty. But what's his excuse?

"I could drop you off. If you want?"

What I want is for him to leave me alone so as to avoid any more self-delusion about what this relationship is. My face is hot, burning, and itchy, from this awkwardness and possibly my headache, which has morphed into something stronger. I touch my nose—surreptitiously, I hope. No blood.

"It's right down the block. I can walk." He still hasn't moved, so I go around him. My chest is getting tight.

One foot in front of the other. Just get out of the building. The fresh air will help.

Behind me, his phone chirps. "Lola, wait."

I nearly scream in frustration as he catches up with me. "It's Clare. She wants to know what she missed today. You guys have bio together, right?"

I grit my teeth. "We started on the Zimmer book," I finally say, squeezing my eyes shut. "Evolution. And she handed out the supplemental reading materials."

Am I even going to make it down the block? But there is no way I'm getting into his Jeep again. Let him tease me about my taste in music. Hold my hand. Pick me up after I have another episode, just like he did yesterday. And in the attic. And down by the creek.

My eyes snap open in time to watch him walk away.

Is it just a coincidence that nearly every time I've had one of these episodes, Fletcher has been there? I've been looking for common denominators, and certainly the water is one.

But so is he.

CHAPTER 16

The Claret Creek library is built from the same kind of stone as Dad's—my—house. Which makes sense. Fletcher said this used to belong to my family.

Your family practically built this town.

My heart flutters at the memory of the first day we met and his enthusiasm for my family history, but my anger slaps it steady. He has no right to barge into my thoughts. He lost that privilege when he blabbed to Emory. And what is this obsession with my family, anyway? I found it flattering at first.

But maybe it's just creepy.

I'm expecting something more modern inside the library, but the carved desk that greets me as I enter the double front doors is from another era. The main reading room is a clear reflection of the house it used to be, with leaded glass windows and chandeliers dangling from the tall ceiling. At one end, an ornate arch opens onto a cozy grouping of chairs around a stone fireplace. A curved staircase leads to a balcony above, and through the mahogany railing I get a glimpse of crowded shelves.

To the right of the desk, opposite the fireplace, a row of public computers lines the wall. I sign the visitor's log and grab an empty seat to log in to my genealogy account. It's been almost a week and my notifications have piled up, but I ignore the itch of discovery and pull up the Boyd family tree instead.

This is familiar territory, or at least the names are. I've cultivated every one of these links, checking and double-checking newspaper articles and certificates pulled from the ether. While the papers themselves have no correlation to the blood in my veins, they make their own kind of links—a chain of my lineage that

I've managed to trace backward in time nearly two centuries.

Dad was an only child, and his parents were both dead before he ever met my mother, so she never had any information to share. All I have now is this tree.

And the photo albums in my own library back home.

I sit back in my chair. I flipped through those books so briefly that first day, enough to know they're filled with faded snapshots of my dad's childhood, along with a bunch of people I don't know. They deserve a closer look. Maybe I'll find some clues that will have some connection to these visions I'm having.

Clues. I sound like goddamn Nancy Drew.

What do I actually hope to learn? Whether or not my dead father is trying to communicate with me? In terms of research, that's a bad question. Too many assumptions.

Back it up.

Who is trying to communicate with me? But even that implies intent of some sort.

What do these episodes mean?

That's better.

For starters, all of them reference the water. Even in the incident in the attic, far from the creek, my dad still mentioned the water.

It wasn't the water. It was our blood.

They have to be tied to the story about Rebecca and the magic creek water somehow. I pull a notebook from my backpack and flip to a blank page. Mr. Zeller had suggested pulling on one thread until it all starts to unravel. So what threads do I have?

1. Rebecca
2. Had an illegitimate baby—via Satan??
3. Might have been a witch
4. Killed her own sister

5. Dunked her in the magic water
6. Bewitched the doctor to get his house
7. Burned his office

I tap my pen softly against the page as I ponder the list.

Rebecca *is* my ancestor. That's proven fact. She's right there on the screen, her name on a branch of my family tree.

Rebecca Ruth Payne, born 1897. Married James Harrison, April 25, 1917. Gave birth to one daughter, Daisy Rose Payne Harrison. Birth date, October 2, 1917. Five and a half months after her wedding.

So she got pregnant before she got married. Hardly enough to warrant being labeled a witch. Still, I find this faint whiff of historical scandal reassuring. It's not that I believed the story about Rebecca being impregnated by Satan. But with everything else going on, this evidence of a real-life, human father puts my mind at ease. I make a checkmark next to number one and draw a line through number two.

The next item is Rebecca being a witch. I don't know how to prove or disprove that, so I move on to number four—killed her own sister. This should be easy to verify. Rebecca had two sisters, Karoline and Marguerite. Karoline was older, and by 1912, she was married to a gentleman from Tucson, Arizona, where she died in 1990, presumably not at the hand of her younger sister. So it's Marguerite's entry that interests me. Born 1899, died 1916. Cause of death is listed as *unknown*.

If Rebecca had killed Marguerite, wouldn't it say something like "gunshot" or "poison"? Or at least "suspicious" or "misadventure." Something to indicate an investigation. Then again, it's impossible to read anything personal into these sparse entries. What if the coroner was just lazy? If Rebecca was an actual witch, where did I expect to read that? If someone had received creek water as a miracle cure, it certainly wasn't going to appear on a death certificate.

Damn it. I'm not getting anywhere. My head aches. I press my palm against my forehead, rubbing in a tight circle. The questions I have can't be answered by dry documents.

But.

I raise my head, blinking away spots as I stare at the screen.

Died in 1916.

That was too early for influenza pandemic. I pull out my phone and do a quick Google search. Spring of 1918 is when the first cases were announced, in an army camp in Kansas. A second, wider outbreak started in September of the same year.

I jot the dates in my notebook, underlining 1918 twice.

The timelines don't match up. According to the story, Rebecca murdered Marguerite and then put her in the water. But that would've been two full years before the doctor was curing people with his miracle water.

So how had Rebecca known about the so-called healing properties?

Someone at one of the other computers coughs loudly, and I jerk the pen across the page, leaving a long black streak of ink.

I send Marguerite's death certificate to the printer and click out of the family database.

None of it makes any sense. Maybe I have to come at it from another angle. Dig into the doctor and his mystery healings. Zeller had suggested medical records. A list of his patients would be fantastic. Who was healed? And when.

I head to the circulation desk, which is manned by a smiling librarian wearing a Colorado Rockies scarf and a name tag that reads BETTY. She holds up my document with a questioning glance, and I nod as she hands it over.

"I'm looking for some information," I say, tucking the certificate into my notebook. "I'm trying to research the story about the creek water." Do I sound like an idiot? "I've heard the gist, but I was wondering if you would have anything specific. Like Dr. Clarett's research papers? Or local newspaper stories? Obituaries?" I tick the list off on my fingers.

Betty doesn't seem to find my request unusual, which is a relief but shouldn't be a surprise. Mom has told me some of the random things people ask librarians.

"We have an archival room. Of sorts." She makes a face. "I'll be honest—it's a bit of a mess." She lifts the desk flap and ducks under. "But let's see what we can find."

The room she leads me to is not so much a mess as it is a disaster. Shelves line the cramped space, with books stacked haphazardly, sideways, and backward and minus any sort of system that I can make out. Four tables are squeezed into the middle, though the chairs are missing, possibly to make room for the folders that are stacked on and around them.

My heart sinks. I'm never going to find anything in here.

But Betty surprises me, moving straight to one of the shelves and pulling down a stack of boxes.

"I think some of these came from Clarett's estate. They say it's haunted, you know." She holds up an old photo of my house. "Don't tell your mom I said that."

Is there anyone in this town who doesn't know who I am and where I live?

But Betty's a librarian. Maybe she has actual documentation she can show me. "Haunted how?"

She pulls out a binder full of photos and flips open to one of a bearded man with a group of people, mostly women, standing beneath a tree. They look wet and disheveled, but they're all wearing huge smiles.

Except for the doctor.

"That was such a sad time for the town," she says. "So much illness. So much death. All of them looking to him for answers."

"And the ones who died?" I ask. "Do you think they're the ones haunting me—y house?"

She flips a page in the binder. "I think they haunt the whole town, to be honest. It was a horrible time in our history, one we'd all be better off forgetting. But the story is too tightly linked with the town to ever completely fade away. Like Salem and the witch trials."

My eye twitches. That word again.

She starts to flip another page, but I stop her when I read the headline.

MISS PAYNE DIES UNEXPECTEDLY

Betty tilts her head toward the hallway, where a patron is waving to get her attention. "I need to get back out front. But take as long as you need with this." She hands me the binder.

As she moves away, I read the article.

Miss Marguerite Payne, daughter of Howard Payne of 214 Main Avenue, died suddenly at 10:25 Friday evening. Miss Payne had lately been residing at the home of esteemed physician Dr. Frederick Clarett while undergoing treatment. Present at her passing was the good doctor as well as her sister, Miss Rebecca Payne. Clarett described her prognosis as good prior to an unexpected turn for the worse and could find no cause for her sudden death. A small funeral will be held on Saturday next, with only family attending.

The words swim in and out of focus. *Undergoing treatment. Unexpected turn for the worse. Sudden death.* The phrases are vague, bordering on cliché, and I can't tell if it's design or the passage of time that has rendered them virtually meaningless. The only thing the article does is confirm that Rebecca was present when her sister died.

But so was Dr. Clarett.

CHAPTER 17

As sure as this tree will shade you, so too will these waters heal you.

I uttered those very words back in Michigan, the day we left, when Bryn found me at the track and gave me the bracelet. And again, beneath the aspen tree on the bank of the creek next to the charred remnants of the doctor's office.

Sage recognized the quote from a statue in the park, which is only a five-minute walk from the library. On the way, I mentally catalog what I have and haven't learned: Rebecca didn't actually have an illegitimate child; she just got pregnant before her wedding. And while she was present at Marguerite's death, there was nothing in that article to suggest foul play.

So why label her a witch? The story had to have come from somewhere.

I'm still pondering this question when I round a corner and the statue comes into view. The bronze, life-size doctor stands atop a hill overlooking the creek, towering over all he surveys. He carries a medical bag in one hand and raises his stethoscope with the other, as if poised to listen to someone's heart.

I'd expected a jolly, smiling figure, but Dr. Clarett's thin lips are pressed tightly together in a grim line of determination. Or disgust.

My vision goes blurry.

He's definitely the man from my episodes.

Yesterday, at the beach, I felt the desperation of this doctor. And of the young woman. He was determined to drag her into the water. And she was terrified.

Because she thought he was going to drown her?

They found her in the water.

I steady myself with a hand on the base of the statue. Whatever has been happening to me—be it hallucinations, visions, memories—they're real. And from what I've seen, Dr. Clarett wasn't as benevolent as everyone has been led to believe. The man in my episodes is angry and powerful, with a sharp tongue and viselike grip.

Did that man cure people?

Or did he kill them?

I press a hand to my chest, trying to calm the erratic thump of fear and adrenaline as I lean in to read the plaque attached to the stone base:

IN MEMORY OF DR. FREDERICK JEFFERSON CLARETT, AND THE HEROIC DEEDS HE PERFORMED FOR HIS COMMUNITY DURING THE CONTAGION OF 1918. CLARETT WILL LONG BE REMEMBERED FOR HIS BRAVERY, AS WELL AS HIS SCIENTIFIC ACHIEVEMENTS.

HIS ONE REGRET WAS FOR THOSE HE WAS UNABLE TO SAVE. MAY HIS SOUL BE UNBURDENED AS HE JOINS HIS BROTHERS AND SISTERS IN THEIR HEAVENLY REPOSE. "AS SURE AS THIS TREE WILL SHADE YOU, SO TOO WILL THESE WATERS HEAL YOU."

There's no way I could have known those words before I got here. But somehow, I did.

I take a quick step back, bumping into someone behind me.

The shriek dies in my throat as I whirl around. Emory's smile manages to be somehow both bright and sarcastic at the same time.

"Calm down," she says. "This is Claret Creek. Not Crystal Lake."

She has a point, but that doesn't mean she can be trusted. I glance around.

Other than a couple of kids on the play equipment and a young mom watching them from a nearby bench, the park is deserted.

"What are you doing here?"

She crosses her arms. "I saw you walking. I had a hunch you might come here."

I don't get this girl. She's hardly given the impression that she wants to be friends. In fact, she seemed genuinely irritated at my presence the couple of times we hung out. And now?

"So you followed me?"

She shades her eyes with her hand. "He used to submerge people here, you know. Right down there," she says, ignoring my question.

I follow her line of sight to the creek bed. "Didn't that all happen at his office?"

"At first. The 'miracle cures,' at least. Once word got out, everyone wanted in. Get dunked by the doctor. It became an event. Gross, right? This dude using all that death to make himself famous." She smacks her hand against his bronze leg and I wince at the hollow sound.

"You seem to know a lot about this."

"You mean for someone who wasn't born here?" She raises her eyebrow.

"That's not what I said." But it is what I was thinking. How does she do that?

"My dad is really into history. But what's your excuse? Why are you digging around?"

"Why do you care?" I shoot back, and immediately regret it as a cocky grin spreads across her face.

What is up with this girl? She's enigmatic but cool, in a way that makes me feel muddled and disorganized—even more so than I already do. I can't say that I like her. But for some reason I want her to like me. Maybe because she's one of the only people who doesn't seem to take the magic water story as gospel.

"I'm researching the story," I say. "I think one of my family members was one of his . . ." I almost say *victims*. "Patients. And I'm not so sure the doctor helped her. What if this whole story about the water is just . . . a story? A hoax?" I float the word casually.

"Oh, it definitely is. But trying to prove it is really going to piss people off."

"Why? What is this weird obsession this town has with their water? I just want to learn more about my dad. My family."

Some emotion flits across her face at that, but I can't read it. Pity? Compassion? Understanding? "I get that. Blood is thicker than water. Unless"—she waves a hand toward the creek—"you're talking about Creek water. That's thicker than anything. The people who grew up here, they're connected in a way you and I will never be. You won't get any answers from them—they're way too attached to the town mythology."

"So what am I supposed to do?" I surprise myself with the anger in my voice, which isn't entirely for her.

"Why not ask the people who were there?"

Again, I'm at a loss for words. "It was more than a hundred years ago. Anyone who was there would be de—"

"Exactly. A séance," she says, nodding like we're on the same page. "Tomorrow night. Out at your place." The wind kicks up, blowing a lock of hair into her face, and she pushes it aside. "You want answers about this town's past, right? People died on your property. Those restless spirits are still there."

Emory's words are so close to what I've been thinking, the hair on my arms goes up.

Restless spirits.

Is she right? Whatever Rebecca or the doctor did, they did it on my property. Marguerite's tears and blood and sweat all soaked into that soil.

Is *that* what's been happening to me? Is Marguerite trying to share the truth about her death?

Or maybe my dad is trying to warn me about all of it.

Emory is staring at me in that way she has, like my thoughts are hovering in a bubble above my head and she can pluck them—and mold them—at will.

As if to prove it, she continues, "I understand why you want to keep it quiet.

You're new in town, you don't want to be labeled a freak. I get it." She leans forward suddenly, her long hair sweeping against my shoulder. "But I know you saw something last weekend, in the attic. Or felt something."

I open my mouth to deny it, but my throat is dry and the words catch. I swallow and try again. "That's not what happened. I'm . . ." I'm about to say "I'm sick" but stop myself at the last second. What is it about this girl that puts me so off-kilter that I nearly spill my biggest secret?

Then again, maybe she already knows. Not because of some magic mind-reading power. But because Fletcher told her. About my illness, and maybe even about my theory that my dad might be trying to communicate with me.

Does that explain why she's here?

I recall her questions in class earlier, about the spiritualist movement. The tightening in Mr. Zeller's—her dad's—jaw when she asked. This is important to her, though I'm not sure why.

Then again, does it matter? She's asking to do the very thing I want most in the world.

"You're what?" she asks, tilting her head to one side.

What the hell. I'm starting to think that there's not much Emory can't do when she puts her mind to it. Maybe she *can* deliver the spirits on cue.

Maybe she can help me communicate with my dad.

"I'm in."

CHAPTER 18

Emory drives me home in a tiny powder-blue Chevy. As she pulls into the driveway, I turn to thank her, but she cuts me off. "I'll be over after school. To help set everything up." She practically pushes me out of the car and slams the door in my face. "See you tomorrow!" she yells, her voice muffled by the sound of the engine as she reverses down the drive.

Mom is in the living room when I walk in, moving boxes and trying not to look like she was watching me through the window.

"How was school?" she asks, pushing at her hair with the back of her wrist. She's going for cool and breezy, but there's an undercurrent I recognize, a rigidness that almost tumbles into vibration. She's stressed, and she's fighting to hold it in check.

"Okay. I stopped at the library after school. And then Emory gave me a ride home." I drop my backpack and flop onto the couch. "How was your day?"

She waves a hand vaguely around the room, where she's unpacked a few items—my baby picture on a side table, and her wedding photo on the mantel, alongside Kurt's most prized possession, a baseball signed by the Detroit Tigers. "Oh, you know . . . You look tired. Do you want a snack?"

"Sure."

As she goes to the kitchen, I drop my head against the back of the couch. It's heavy, weighed down by a low-level buzzing, which is never a good sign. There's a certain level of fatigue that brings on a hum in my brain that nothing is able to quiet. I feel fried, like I've touched a live wire by accident, and all of the electricity has gathered in my skull, buzzing and humming and searching for some kind of release. Sleep is the only thing that really helps, but the irony is that the buzzing makes it so much harder to relax. I have to lean into it, embrace it, like falling down an endless, noisy, droning well.

"Quiet, Bea," I say. It's another one of Mom's holistic suggestions. Name the pain and take away its power. I'm not sure I believe it, but it does refocus my frustration away from my own body and onto the fatigue itself. It's not my fault I'm so tired, it's fucking Bea's fault.

I close my eyes against the throbbing in my skull. I have a thought, fleeting and ephemeral, and I try to grab on to it. Maybe I need to name these memories. They aren't mine, after all.

Are they Marguerite's?

Mom's only gone a few minutes, but it's long enough for me to fall into some state of semi-consciousness, lurching awake as she sets a plate with some apple slices and a scoop of peanut butter on the table in front of me.

"Thanks." I shift over to grab the plate and she gasps.

"You got your period," she says, gesturing at the couch.

I twist around to look at the rusty mark on the cushion. "Crap," I say, getting to my feet.

"Maybe it's a good thing. A sign your body systems are returning to normal." Her voice is hopeful. "Did it just happen?"

I shrug and shake my head. "I don't know. I've been feeling off all day. I thought it was, you know, the usual."

Since my illness started, my periods have been irregular, sometimes stopping for months at a time. It's one symptom the doctors all agree on as concerning, yet like everything else, no one has any answers. It bothers Mom more than it does me; I'm glad to not have the hassle every month. I once joked with Dr. K's nurse that they've drawn so much blood there isn't any left.

She didn't see the humor.

"This is good. This makes sense." Mom nods, her face awash with color. "No wonder you fell yesterday. You were probably lightheaded. We should start you back up on those iron supplements."

"Gah." The thought of those giant pills makes me gag, but knowing these cramps are menstrual gives me an ironic sort of relief. As painful as they are, they feel like something that's supposed to happen. Rather than one more symptom of some mysterious ailment, it's a sign my body can still perform regular functions. Though I'm not as convinced as Mom that it explains what happened yesterday.

Then again, I'd lied to her about it, so what did I expect?

"I'll get some stain remover." She hurries back toward the kitchen, returning with a washcloth for me and a can of cleaner she squirts on the cushion as I stand and watch.

"What were you doing at the library?" she asks.

I crunch an apple slice. "Research. I'm curious about Dad's family. And their connection to Dr. Clarett."

She keeps her head down, scrubbing vigorously at the stain. "I don't know how much you're going to learn," she finally says.

I frown and scuff my toe against the carpet. "They named the town after the doctor. And this was his house. I'm guessing there's got to be something of interest. Do you know if Dad had any of his old stuff? Like, medical records?" I ask, remembering Zeller's question.

"It's not going to do you any good to dig up old history."

I feel like one of those cartoon characters, the ones whose mouths fall open so far they hit the ground.

"Digging up old history is literally my favorite thing to do."

"I'm aware. It's just, what good can come of it?"

Is there something about my family she doesn't want me to find out? Or maybe she just doesn't want to dredge up the past. She's married to Kurt now, so Teddy and the Boyds aren't her concern anymore. Even if I'm a Boyd.

I struggle to find the right words. "But what if I find something that will shed some light on my condition? A . . . a cure. Or at least some kind of family history of whatever this is."

She sighs and leans back on her heels. "Poking into the town's history is not going to help, and you know it."

"How do you know?" I shoot back. "There's the water—"

"It's fake, Lo. It's all lies. Do *not* pin your hopes on impossible miracles." Her voice breaks.

"Why didn't you tell me anything about this place?"

A shadow crosses her face, and she turns back to the couch. "I don't know what you mean."

I study her body language. She's tense, on edge. Angry.

"Claret Creek," I say. "And Dad. He knew the story." I backtrack, afraid I'm giving too much away. "He had to have known it. Everyone does. Why didn't you tell me?"

She freezes in place for such a long moment that I hold my breath. "That urban legend has nothing to do with your father, or us," she finally says, her voice so low I have to take a step closer to hear her.

I feel scattered, Bea's loud and consistent drone drowning out my ability to think rationally. Mom is acting weird—twitchy and evasive. Like she's afraid of whatever I might say next.

"You hardly ever talk about him anymore," I say, rubbing my temples as I try to figure out exactly what I want to ask her.

"You know it's hard for me." She's whispering now.

"I know. But—" I struggle to find the words. "I need to know. Emory said something today. About the people who live here. How connected they are. And I can't help thinking, that could have been me. If things were different, I mean."

She presses a fist to her eye. "That's a dangerous game. Lots of things could have been different. But we'll never know. Why dwell on it?"

She sounds broken. I'm hurting her, I know. After I promised Kurt I wouldn't. It's just that the answers feel so close. If only she would open up. If only *someone* would open up. Why does the past have to be a mystery only to me? It's my family we're talking about, not hers. Why does she get to guard it so carefully?

"I'm not dwelling," I say softly, a tear slipping down my face. "I just don't understand how a person can leave so little behind. The house has been in the family for forever, right? There must be, like, a hundred years of junk. All I've found so far are the photo albums." I think about how long our clean out took, the things Mom and I had accumulated in a fraction of that time. "What happened to the rest of it?"

"What photo albums?" she asks.

"Dad's baby books. In the library."

"I'd forgotten about those," she says, pushing herself to her feet. "Your grandma Dolores was really into scrapbooking."

"Have you seen them?"

She bites her lower lip and shakes her head. "No. He told me about them, though." She twists the rag in her hand. "I'm glad you have those."

"Do you want to see them?" I take a step toward the library, but she stops me.

"Maybe some other time. I've got to get dinner going, and you should wash up." She gestures at my pants.

"You didn't answer my question," I remind her as she turns away. "Where is all their stuff?"

"I don't know! The attic? I never asked him for an itemized list." She sounds defensive. "I know there was an estate sale at one point. After your father . . ." Her voice trails off. "Dominic handled it."

I'd been picturing Dominic as a sort of weekend handyman, the guy who came over and checked to make sure the pipes hadn't frozen and the lawn was mowed. But he'd done so much more than that. I need to talk to him. I also need to do a systematic search of the house. Maybe there are documents right under my nose.

But before any of that, Mom's right. I need a shower. And sleep.

I wake to a one-two punch of blinding sunlight and stifling heat. My sheets are sweat-soaked, and my mouth tastes like I've been sucking on pennies. I must have dreamt, but I don't remember anything clearly, only fragments of slamming doors and looming shadows.

It's sunny as hell now. I raise an arm to shield the glare as I read my clock, then do a double take: 11:08.

That can't be right. Why didn't my alarm go off?

I throw off my sheet, sticky and warm. Am I feverish? No. My tampon has leaked.

Shit. I pull off the sheet and wrap it around my waist as I stumble to the bathroom to clean up. After I shower and throw on some clothes, I strip the bed and drag everything down to the washing machine in an alcove off the kitchen. I dump in some detergent, crank the dial, and let the lid fall with a soft thud.

Besides the running water, the house is completely silent. The kitchen is empty, though the door to the basement is ajar.

"Mom?" I call, flipping the switch beside the stairs to illuminate the shadows. No answer from below, which is no surprise. She'd hardly be hanging out down there in the dark. Maybe Kurt's been moving boxes around. I turn off the light and close the door.

Two coffee cups and two spoons rest on the drying rack in the sink, and there's a note in front of the coffee machine.

I hope you got some rest. Breakfast in fridge. Love,
Mom

No mention of school, or the fact that I'm already missing classes and it's only my first week.

It is only Thursday, right?

I wander slowly through the dining room and living room. No Kurt—he must be in his office upstairs. I step onto the front porch, the cement cool against my bare feet.

The car is gone.

Mom went to work and left me here without any way of getting to school. I stare down the long drive, toward the road that follows Claret Creek as it snakes into town. I know we have neighbors along that stretch, but their houses aren't visible from ours. Standing here, staring at the scrub brush and cratered rock of the mountainside, it feels like I'm the only person left on earth. The thought makes me shiver, my breath quickening as a breeze kicks up. It's hot and dry, yet I still feel clammy and lightheaded, as though I've had a beer or two.

I need to eat something. I turn back inside, slamming the door. It rattles in the frame and I look toward the stairs, half expecting Kurt to yell at me. But either he can't hear me or he's ignoring me.

Mom's work number has been programmed into the handset of the living room phone, and I push number one.

"I need to be at school. It's the first week. Do you have any idea how this looks?" I say when she answers, my words coming so fast they leave me breathless.

"It looks like you're not feeling well," Mom says, "which is what I told them when I called you out. The move has been stressful on all of us, and what with getting your period and hitting your head—"

"Oh my god, Mom. Did you say that?"

"I told them you had bad cramps and were lightheaded."

Both of those things are true, and I hate that she knew it before I did. Plus, I've got another killer headache brewing. Honestly, I'm not sure how much more I can push myself. But I don't want to give her or Kurt any more ammunition against me.

"I left a sandwich in the fridge," she continues. "Kurt has the car—he dropped me off before running some errands, but he'll be back this afternoon. In the meantime, get some rest."

"Fine. Thanks," I add, a fraction of a second too late to sound sincere.

"I love you."

"Love you, too."

I replace the handset and sink onto the couch. That explains why Kurt hasn't been on my case this morning, about the slamming doors or the sleeping in. I suppose I should be grateful. Instead, I feel unsettled.

Back in Michigan, I loved having the house to myself. On good days, I could blast music while I studied and bake cupcakes for lunch. On bad ones, I could take four showers, or sleep for ten hours straight if I needed.

Here, the stillness is different. Thicker, somehow, even though the house is so much bigger. There's more room for my thoughts to echo. The air feels stuffed full of everything I don't know, of things no one will tell me. Secrets kept, promises broken. I can hear my own heart beating hard and fast above the silence that stretches around me, wide and tall, out and up, until I'm at the bottom of a deep, dark well, with no way out and no one to hear me.

A door closes somewhere in the back of the house, the noise distinctive and loud.

Kurt must be back early. Great.

A second ago I was completely creeped out by the thought of being alone in the house, but Kurt is a poor substitute for comfort. I turn expectantly, waiting for him to come through the kitchen doorway, but he doesn't. In fact, there are no other sounds from the kitchen. No keys jangling, no cupboards opening and closing. No footsteps.

I move to the window and pull aside the curtain.

No car.

Adrenaline sluices through me like a hot blade.

There's someone else in the house with me.

I snatch up the phone, but hesitate. Who do I call? Mom? The police? And say what? I heard a door?

I did. I'm sure of it.

Almost.

I try to remember the sound, but I can't quite call it to mind. My heart in my throat, I make my way slowly down the hallway toward the kitchen, pressing my back against the wall. I go still outside the doorway, trembling so violently the phone nearly slips from my sweat-slick hand as another noise comes from the room beyond.

Bang. Bang. Bang. Bang.

I stumble backward, lightheaded with fear. It's someone pounding. Relentlessly.

Trying to get in? Or out?

The pounding continues, loud and steady. *Bang. Bang. Bang. Bang.*

Who knocks like that?

I force myself to take a breath. The back door is straight across the kitchen, which means if I can summon the courage to look, the curtainless window will give me a clear view of whoever is knocking. It will also give them a clear view of *me*.

I'm terrified of coming face-to-face with whoever this is, but I force myself to peek around the doorway.

The window is empty.

Confused, I take a step into the kitchen. The sound isn't coming from the door. It's the washing machine. The light blinks: *unbalanced*.

"Shit." I sag against the counter in relief, my legs suddenly weak. I never used to be this anxious, this scared of what amounts to my own shadow. Then again, I used to be healthy. And happy.

It's amazing the things we take for granted until we lose them.

I untangle the sheets and restart the washing machine. Then I step hesitantly to the back door, which is bolted. I twist the lock and swing the door open, then quickly shut. It closes quietly, much too softly to be the noise I heard earlier. I turn the deadbolt, grateful no one is here to witness my paranoia.

It must've been the washer I heard, switching between cycles.

What else could it have been?

I grab my sandwich and brew a cup of coffee, resting my head against the fridge while I wait. I'm still exhausted, and part of me knows I should listen to Mom and go back to bed, but I need to use this time alone wisely, without her or Kurt around to ask what I'm up to.

So instead of heading to my bedroom, I take my breakfast into the library. I'll start my search with Dad's old albums.

I love that I have my own private library. How many people can say that? It's like a dream.

Only today, it's more like a nightmare.

Because someone else has been here. And they've torn the room apart.

CHAPTER 19

Not messy like someone left some books on the table. Literally trashed. Like someone was angry and wanted us to know it.

The shelves are half-empty, the books scattered in piles on the floor, bindings cracked and pages crumpled. My gaze skitters across the destruction, first to the French doors, which are clearly locked, then to the window seat, which gapes open.

I drop my plate onto a side table and pick my way across the floor carefully, heart hammering, hoping against hope—

But it's no use. My grandmother's photo albums are gone.

I flip open the next bench, but that's empty, too.

All of my family's history. Gone.

I close the lid and brace myself against the wall. Someone was in here. Someone got into my house and ransacked this room.

I rub my arms, feeling cold and exposed. What if they're still here?

I hurry outside. On the porch, I dial 911 and tell them there was an intruder in my home, then slouch in a corner, tucking myself into the shadows while I wait for help. The stone is cold against my skin, but I don't care. I'm alone and terrified and I can't make my brain form a rational thought.

All the weird things that have been happening since I've gotten here have felt personal. Private. No one else can see them; they could all be hallucinations, produced by a brain fever or lesions or fatigue.

But this isn't a product of my imagination; this is real.

Someone did this.

But who?

And why?

They were looking for something. Did they find it?

The albums are missing. But who would want those?

Fletcher seemed overly interested in them the first day we met, but I can't picture him ransacking my home to get them. And Mom was evasive last night when I asked to show them to her. But she wouldn't have torn the room apart to get them; she could've just taken them and hidden them.

The sirens pull me from the fruitless thought circle. I stand and watch the two cars race up the drive, lights flashing.

The first officer is a woman, and she calls to me over the top of her door when she's halfway out of the car. "Are you all right?"

"I'm fine," I call back, holding my hands wide as I approach the stairs. "I don't know if anyone's inside anymore."

She nods at the three guys with her, and they all file inside while she stays on the porch with me.

"They trashed our library," I say, and she raises an eyebrow. "You'll see when you get inside." Does she not believe me? "They took my family photo albums. I can't tell if anything else is missing."

Mom's car pulls into the drive, and we both turn to watch, my heart sinking as Kurt gets out.

"What's going on? Lola, are you okay? Did something happen?"

"I'm okay," I say. "But there was someone in the house."

Disbelief clouds his features. "This again? I'm sorry, officer. This is all a misunderstanding. She's been a little jumpy since the move. Big house, strange noises. You understand."

She stares at him, her face unreadable, as I struggle to get a hold of my emotions. "Someone broke in," I finally manage to say without crying or screaming. "Go look at the library."

He moves to take a step, but she stops him. "I'd prefer you wait out here until my men are sure the house is clear."

He makes a huffing sound and pushes past her, muttering something about "his house." She rolls her eyes as she follows him inside and I trail behind, embarrassment overriding my fear.

What if Kurt is right? What if I did imagine the noises? And maybe the library isn't as bad as I thought. Maybe there was an earthquake overnight that I didn't notice.

The four cops and Kurt are all hovering in the doorway of the library. "House is clear," one of them says. "Back door and side doors are locked. Windows secured."

The female cop turns to me. "Was the front door locked before you called us?"

"I think so," I say, trying to remember. "I was outside earlier. Before I knew Kurt was gone. I went out on the porch to look for his car." Was the door locked then? I can't remember.

Kurt's been silent up until now, his jaw working. He picks up the plate and looks at me, and I can read his thoughts as if they're being telegraphed.

"I brought my breakfast in here. That's when I saw it—"

"Breakfast? It's nearly noon."

I choke back a furious laugh. Really? He wants to argue about my sleeping habits *now*?

The cop rips off a piece of paper and hands it to Kurt. "We'll need you to put together an itemized list of everything missing. You can drop that off at the station any time. In the meantime, I suggest you get some cameras installed. It'll help give everyone a feeling of security."

A *feeling* of security. As if even she knows it's an illusion.

One of the officers points at Kurt's signed baseball on the mantel as he walks through. "Mustard Maguire? That legit?"

"My pride and joy. Hometown boy makes good."

"You're from Lansing, then?"

The chief crosses her arms and raises an eyebrow as she watches this display of male bonding buffoonery, while I simply stare in disgust. Are they really discussing baseball right now?

"Nah, just a fa—" Kurt glances over and swallows the rest of his sentence, clapping his hands together. "Anyway, thank you, officers. I appreciate you coming out. Sorry for wasting your time."

He walks them all to the door, closing and locking it before he turns on me.

"I thought we were in agreement," he says, teeth gritted, and I'm taken aback by his anger.

"Agreement about what?" I ask. "The noises in the house?"

"We agreed we weren't going to upset your mother."

I gape at him. "I . . . I did. I don't—" I sputter. "What was I supposed to do? Someone *broke into our house*."

The skeptical look on his face says it all.

"I didn't do this," I say, my voice rising. "Is that what you think?"

"Well, I didn't do it. And your mother certainly didn't."

"Exactly! Someone else was here."

"The only other people who have been here are your friends," he says. "And Dominic." His voice is bitter.

"Why would Dominic . . . ? Never mind. What about the internet guy? Someone came over, right? To fix the internet?"

He shakes his head impatiently. "It doesn't matter who did it. We need to get it cleaned up. Before Tress sees it."

"So we're not going to tell her—"

"Of course we'll have to tell her. I just think seeing the library like this is going to upset her, don't you? It feels so . . . dramatic," he finally says, looking around.

I bristle but hold my tongue. "Dramatic" is usually his code word for me. He's not convinced I didn't do this. Me or my friends. But maybe I can work that to my advantage.

I ball my hands into fists and take a breath. "You're right," I say. "I'll get it cleaned up. I can invite Emory over to help me. If you take Mom out to dinner, we'll get it done while you're gone." I need them out of the house anyway, and this is as good an excuse as any.

He hesitates for so long I think he's going to argue. But finally he says, "Emory? Fine. Good." He nods and leaves the room, stomping up the stairs to his office, leaving me alone in the destruction.

He called it dramatic. To me, it feels deliberate. Like someone is trying to communicate something. But unlike the fear and desperation that underlies my visions, this message is angry. And what had Betty said earlier? *I think they haunt the whole town.*

Maybe there wasn't an intruder after all.

Maybe they've been here all along.

CHAPTER 20

In the short time between Kurt's departure to pick up Mom for dinner and Emory's arrival, I do my best to straighten the library. I told Kurt that Emory would help, but that was a lie. I can't help remembering the way she prowled around the house that first night, peering into all the nooks and crannies.

Like she was looking for something.

Until I know who I can trust, I'm not saying anything to anyone.

Besides, we have other plans for tonight.

Emory sweeps in promptly at six, dressed in a gauzy black sundress and a scarf swirled with reds and purples tossed over her shoulder. A flutter of uneasiness tickles my belly. This all felt like a game when she first asked me, like the times Bryn and I hovered over a Ouija board in the dark, pushing and pulling at the planchette. Or the slumber parties in middle school where we'd dare each other to whisper "Bloody Mary" into the mirror.

But after everything that's happened, I'm second-guessing tonight. If we're actually dealing with a vengeful spirit, is it a good idea to provoke them?

"Have you— I mean, how do you know how . . . ?" I stutter and trail off, not sure of how to ask. What I really want to know is, does she know what she's doing? But it feels rude, bordering on ludicrous, to question whether or not she believes she has the ability to conjure the souls of the dead.

She bestows upon me the cold, confident look I've come to know as "the Emory." "I've done this before, yes."

"Successfully?" But the doorbell sounds, long and resounding, and she waves me off, so I guess I have to accept her nonanswer for what it is.

Sage bounds into the room before I even have the door open all the way, followed closely by Clare and Fletcher. Together.

Flare. In the flesh.

Emory warned me, but I didn't want to see it. I still don't, so while I return Clare's smile, I avoid Fletcher's gaze altogether, waving them toward the kitchen, and Emory.

"I didn't think you were coming," Emory says in greeting.

Clare's cheeks go pink. "Why wouldn't I come?" Her eyes dart to mine.

"You weren't at school and you didn't answer my texts."

Why would she think she's not welcome? Because of her and Fletcher? Or does she have another reason to think I wouldn't want her here? Something she's feeling guilty about?

Did I imagine it, or did she just glance toward the library?

"I brought you a present," Clare says when she catches me staring. She pulls a photo from her bag. "It's your dad and my mom at their junior prom. They were king and queen, you know."

Dad and Amber are both resplendent in poofy hair and pink sequins—her in a ball gown and him in a tuxedo. Their awkward pose under the balloon arch seems to have done nothing to diminish their joy, judging by the grins on both faces. It's a fleeting moment of my dad's life, frozen in time forever.

"Wow," I say to Clare. "This is . . ." I choke up before I can finish. I want to tell her how much it means to me that she would think to share this, that she understands how much I've missed. But I can't get it out.

"The matching outfits are really something, aren't they?" Clare glances at me, her grin softening into understanding as she squeezes my hand. "Keep it. Mom has a bunch of copies."

I study this young version of my father, who at this point in his life had no idea of my mother's existence, let alone mine. Still, blood connects us. That must mean something.

Clare twines her arm through mine and rests her cheek on my shoulder. "Who would've guessed we're both related to royalty?"

"More like royal nerds." Sage pushes between us. "What's up with that hair?"

I tuck the photo behind the wedding picture on the mantel and follow Clare and Sage into the dining room, where he grabs the matches from Emory. And so our séance begins as I imagine most do, with the lighting of candles and the burning of sage. In our case, these things happen simultaneously and by accident, as Sage almost immediately singes his thumb and forefinger.

"Shit!" He drops the match, still flaming, and shoves his fingers in his mouth.

"Watch it!" Emory cries, pushing him aside to stomp out the spark before it ignites the rug.

Anxiety spikes in my chest, sharp and cold. Not only do I need to worry about angry spirits, now I'm scared we might burn the house down. "This is starting to feel like a bad idea."

"Starting to?" Clare mutters, and I blink at her. I hadn't meant to say it, and definitely not loud enough for anyone to hear me.

She gives my arm a reassuring squeeze.

"Are you sure your mom is okay with this?" Fletcher asks, his voice low as he leans toward me.

I feel my cheeks redden as I take a jerky step back. "She and Kurt are having a date night," I say, avoiding the question. It feels wrong, all the things I'm keeping from her lately, but I didn't dig this chasm between us. That rift began with Kurt.

Clare examines Sage's fingers as he continues to whimper. "Put some ice on it."

They follow me to the kitchen, where I fill a baggie from the freezer door, and Sage grimaces as Clare shoves it onto his hand.

When I agreed to let Emory do this, in the bright light of day, it seemed like a good idea. Logical, even. Find out if my dad is trying to communicate with me, and what he's trying to say.

Now that it's about to happen, I'm having second thoughts.

Especially when Emory announces, "I messaged the group."

My heart plummets so fast I feel dizzy. I'm losing control of whatever this is, and much too quickly. I hold up a hand. "Hold on. How many people are in this group?"

Emory waves me off like she's swatting a gnat. "Just us. And Isa and Van. They're on their way. And bringing supplies."

"What do you mean by supplies? Are you talking about alcohol? Or weed?" I break into a sweat as I look nervously around the room. "Because I'm not up for that kind of party. My mom is only going to be gone a couple of hours."

"Séance supplies," Emory says, disdain dripping from her voice.

"Van wrestles heavyweight," Sage says, as if this should be the deciding factor. "You unleash any evil spirits tonight, Van and I got your back." He slaps his chest and winks at Emory.

To her credit, Emory appears unmoved by this display of raging hormones.

"Nobody's planning on partying," Clare promises. "Look, I'll add you to the group chat." She pulls out her phone and opens Instagram.

"I'm sure they're cool or whatever," I say. "I'm just not sure what my mom is going to say about this many people in the house."

Clare pockets her phone and says, "So why don't we use the firepit? It's warm out, there's no breeze. Plus, we won't have to worry about anyone messing up Tress's house. Or burning it down."

Sage flips his sister off while I fight down a surge of panic. The firepit is so close to the creek, maybe too close. And with Fletcher here, the chances of this spinning out of control feel inevitable. I press a hand to my chest, which is suddenly heavy and tight. This is what I wanted—the chance to communicate with my dad. So why do I have this feeling it's all about to go horribly wrong?

When I look up, Fletcher is staring at me from across the room, his face a dark mask.

I open my mouth to protest, but Emory beats me. "Fire. Earth. Water. Darkness. Everything we need. Let's do it."

I force my mouth into a tight smile as Sage grabs a bag of chips in one hand and Emory's hand in the other.

Fletcher is at my side, his hand on my elbow. "You don't have to do this, you know. There are better ways to research Clarett and the water."

I pull away from him. How does he know what I've been researching?

"If you're uncomfortable . . ." he trails off.

What's uncomfortable is Clare's gaze on us while he touches me. But I'd let Emory open up our very own gateway to hell before I'd tell him that.

The night is clear and moonless; the stars above us hard, winking jewels in a dark velvet sky.

I haven't been back down by the creek since that first day—the first time I met Fletcher, my first nosebleed, my first episode.

Unless I'm counting the incident with Bryn. And the one in the car. Which, am I? I don't even know anymore. I don't know what I'm doing here. In Colorado. At this séance. With these people.

I'm not a member of this little group; I'm an outsider.

The air is cool and still, no hint of a breeze, but I can't stop sweating. I wipe my clammy hands on my jean shorts as the others move about apart from me. I feel detached, like none of this is real and I'm watching a play, or a movie filmed slightly out of focus. Fletcher and Emory are in charge of set design; he's building the fire, while Emory is using a stick to draw circles in the dirt. A glow of headlights and the crunch of tires on gravel send Sage sprinting to the front of the house.

I sink onto one of the logs and smooth my hair, wiping my hands on my shorts a second time.

Sage leads the newcomers down the hill, Isa first and then Van. She's wearing a UC Boulder sweatshirt and shorts, and has her hair pulled into two braids that flop over her shoulders. She greets me with a hug. "Thanks so much for inviting us," she says, plopping down on the log beside me. "I've always wanted to see this place. It's like something out of a fairy tale."

"Or a horror movie," Fletcher mutters.

"Fellow enthusiasts!" Emory calls, clapping her hands, her bracelets jangling. "Let's get started."

It's safe to say that no one here is as enthusiastic as she is. Of the seven of us, only Isa looks even mildly interested.

"First, we form a circle. Join hands," she commands, and I stand up between Van and Sage, determined not to have to hold Fletcher's hand. Van has a grip like a steel clamp, and I wince as I imagine my bones being crushed in his meaty fist.

"Lighten up," Sage whispers. "You look like you're going to a funeral. There's probably only, like, a forty percent chance someone will die here tonight."

"Thanks. That's very comforting."

"Much better odds we piss off the witch and she curses us," he continues.

"Silence!" Emory shouts, and we both jump.

Clare takes Sage's other hand, then joins up with Fletcher—of course—who reaches for Isa. But Emory places herself between them, guiding us as one entity toward the fire. Isa joins hands with Van, and our circle is complete. Without breaking it, Emory stretches her arms wide, motioning for us to follow suit. The fire dances between us like an eighth body, warm and alive, close enough that I'm uncomfortable.

I drop my hands and take a step back, but Emory's voice is crisp and cutting as she says, "No breaking the circle."

Admonished, I let Sage pull me back into place, though a second later it's

Fletcher who breaks free to tend to the fire with a long stick.

"Come on," Emory says, this time with more whine than authority.

"Sorry." He leans his stick against a log and takes her hand.

"Now. Let's get started. We are gathered here tonight, to—"

"Do you have the supplies?" Emory asks.

"Oh!" Isa bends down to rifle through her bag, pulling out a loaf of bread and a bottle with a handwritten label. "Plum wine. My abuela makes it."

"Place it near the fire. This will be our offering." Emory points to the fire ring before raising a hand in the air, dragging Isa's hand with her. "We begin now. Our hands are joined. As life, death, and the afterlife also form a circle, so too do we."

I fight back a wild urge to giggle. Emory sounds like she's conducting a marriage ceremony. The tight grip of panic around my chest loosens. That's all this is—playacting. Nothing bad is going to happen. Emory doesn't know how to summon a spirit any more than I know how to cure myself.

I don't think that's true, but I don't dare interrupt any more.

"The circle protects us," she continues. "Do not break it. In place of candles, we burn this fire. Spirits are attracted to flame, which represents the warmth and the light of the living world, things they can no longer enjoy but must constantly seek."

I have no idea where she is getting this information from, but it's mildly entertaining in a hypnotic, B-movie kind of way.

"Spirits, we offer you this bread and wine, gifts from life unto death. Please step forward, into our light, and make your presence known."

These intonations sound vaguely familiar, as though she's lifted them from a church service or an old movie. We all stand in silence, hands clasped, the light dancing, as we wait for a sign.

And wait.

And wait and wait and wait.

My legs tremble, and a low buzzing begins in my head. *Not now, Bea.*

Fletcher clears his throat, and Emory jerks on his arm.

Finally, when I've nearly gone numb from lack of motion, Sage pulls his hand free from mine.

The circle protects us. Do not break it.

But of course I don't believe that any more than he does.

The fire comes alive, hissing and spitting, as a tall flame whooshes toward the sky. Bright and brilliant, bleeding from yellow to orange to a thick, liquid red. The flames dance and reach for me, licking my face. I stumble backward and swipe at my cheeks, my hands coming away wet.

Faces shimmer in the high flame, crimson and shiny. With sweat? Or blood?

Dark smoke billows outward and up, climbing higher and higher.

I'm choking, coughing, eyes burning as the flames dance and undulate, liquid in the heat. Melting.

Bleeding.

The walls close in and I'm on the floor, the grain of the wood biting into my knees. Blood runs from my arm. A band, wrapped tight around my elbow. I try to pull it free, but my hands are weak, scraped raw and slick with blood.

"It's too much," I whisper. "You've taken too much. Stop. Please, stop."

The band pops free and I sway at the sudden release, falling against a bed. My hands stain the sheets rust red, and I grasp for Marguerite's hand, pale and lifeless.

"Restrain her, James." It's a man's voice, low and terrible, chilling for its lack of emotion.

James crouches beside me, but I push him away. "You'll . . . kill . . . her. You'll kill us both!" I force the words out, my voice gaining strength until I'm screaming, on my knees beside the fire, blood spattering the ground beside me. "You're killing us!"

". . . her space! Get back!" Fletcher is on his knees beside me, his face contorted.

I look up at the others, at their shocked, appalled expressions. Emory's hair is wild and glowing, lit by the fire behind her, while Clare's face is a pallid shade of gray, both hands clutched over her mouth. Isa is crying into Van's shoulder.

I gag, choking on my own blood. My chest burns. There's no air, only smoke, and my lungs don't work. I scrape a hand through the dirt, toward Fletcher, toward someone, anyone.

Help me.

But before they can, the world goes dark.

CHAPTER 21

"The screaming was what tipped me off. That and the blood. No offense." Emory doesn't sound particularly sorry as she says this, slouching against the window beside my hospital bed, her hands jammed into the pockets of an oversized wool cardigan. She doesn't sound particularly *anything*, really. Her account of the previous evening is dry and matter-of-fact, devoid of the sick terror that gripped me.

"Screaming?" I echo. I close my eyes as she talks, trying to match up my own tattered flashes of memory with her words. I do remember screams, and shouting. And the fire, burning much too hot. Then sirens, maybe, and Fletcher pacing, his long shadow looming above me. Clare's cold hands on my face.

Or maybe Emory is just a good storyteller.

After all, what is a memory but a story we tell ourselves.

"I thought it was you at first," she continues, "but turns out it was Isa. She wouldn't stop ranting about curses and spirits and demons from hell. I had to slap her."

"Had to?" Clare asks from her chair beside the door.

"She was hysterical," Emory says.

"She was pissed," Clare corrects, and even in my shattered state I have to give her props for calling out Emory's casual dismissal of Isa's anger. "Sage and Van had to get between them and physically hold them apart," Clare continues. Her face is pale aside from the dark smudges beneath her eyes. She flinches as our eyes meet. "Sorry. You don't want to hear all this."

"She asked," Emory says, as if I'm no longer in the room. "Anyway, after that,

Fletcher ran up to the road to find a signal to call an ambulance, and Clare . . ." She waves a hand at Clare, wrinkling her nose. "Clare got right in there."

Clare stares down at her hands. "You were bleeding. I was trying to figure out where it was coming from. I wanted to make sure you didn't have a head wound or something."

"We saw her fall," Emory says. "She didn't hit her head. Anyway, your mom showed up right after the ambulance. She went with you to the hospital and left us behind with Kurt. We offered to help clean up, but he wasn't having it. Told us to GTFO and left. He's kind of an asshole."

"God, Emory, shut up!" Clare says through clenched teeth.

"Well, he is. While you and Fletcher were off talking to Tress, he was stomping around ranting about drugs and who knows what else. He wouldn't even let me back in the house to grab the rest of my stuff."

My eyes drift shut as they bicker.

"Lola? Can you hear me?" I blink. Emory hovers above me, snapping her fingers in front of my face. "Do you need a nurse or something?"

Why is she here? Out of everyone I know in Claret Creek, she's about the last person I expected to see this morning. Clare, sure. She seems more like the concerned type. But Emory?

As for Fletcher, who knows where the two of us stand, especially now? If there was any chance he was still interested in me, last night surely put that to rest.

"I'm feeling a little out of it," I say, rubbing my forehead with the hand that isn't attached to an IV. Surprisingly, my ever-present headache has vanished. They must have some good drugs here. But it's been replaced by a ravenous thirst. "Can you get me some water?"

Clare stands and moves a wheeled tray toward me, with a pitcher and cup.

I struggle to sit upright, the IV stinging in my hand, and Emory twitches with impatience as I slop water onto the tray before Clare takes pity and pours me a cup.

"Well?" Emory finally asks.

"I don't know?" I say, which is true. I have no idea what she's talking about.

Her face turns pink as I take a big gulp of the cold water, and she shoves aside the tray to sit on the edge of the bed. "I know what's happening to you," she says, her voice low. "I know how to help."

I shudder as a wave of icy recognition washes over me.

You're killing us.

"No." I grip the cup and shake my head, hard. "I don't know what you're talking about."

"Listen to me, Lola. I know, okay?" She pauses. "You're possessed."

"Oh my god." Clare covers her face with her hands. "Are you fucking kidding right now?"

I gape at Emory, but her gaze is so intense I have to turn my head.

"I'm not possessed." I press clammy fingers against my lips, fighting the urge to say anything else. Whatever is happening to me, it isn't that. There's no spirit inside me. If anything, it's the other way around. I'm the intruder, the one who's inhabiting another girl. Or at least her memories.

"There's no possession," I say again, hoping she'll get it this time. "There's no spirit at all. That whole séance was a joke. I never would have agreed to let you do it if I'd known you were going to go full Houdini."

She rears back in disbelief. "You think that was *fake*? FYI, Houdini worked to *expose* the fakers. And besides, I'm not the one who was writhing on the ground, screaming about people trying to kill me."

Clare paces near the foot of the bed. "Come on, Em. We're here to visit, not harass her."

Emory ignores her, gripping my arm so tightly her fingers go white. "I need to know who you were afraid of. Who did you see?"

"I didn't see anyone," I whisper, shoving aside the memory of blood, all that blood. My blood. That awful voice. The lifeless girl—Marguerite—in the dirty bed.

But if that was Marguerite, who was I?

I pull my arm free, spilling the rest of the water. As it soaks the sheets, I yank at the wet bedding, stopping short of shoving Emory to the floor. These visions belong to me, to my family. They have nothing to do with her. And I refuse to give her the satisfaction of thinking for one minute that we're in this together.

"I'm done talking about this. I'm tired," I say, leaning away from her and fumbling for the call button. "I have no idea what your obsession with my house is about, but I know someone was in there yesterday. You know who it was. And whatever they took, I want it back." I'm bluffing, and she probably knows it. But she can't be sure. Just like I don't know for sure who broke in and stole my albums.

I only know that she looks guilty as hell right now.

"What do you mean, someone broke into your house?" Clare asks, but she's not looking at me; she's staring at Emory.

Some of the fire returns to Emory's eyes. "I'm not obsessed. I happen to know things about you and your house. Whether or not you choose to accept them is totally on you." She stares at me hard. "And I didn't steal anything. I'm not a thief."

"So you deny the stealing, but not the breaking and entering?"

"You're awake!" My mom stands in the doorway. Her hair is pulled back in a ponytail and her makeup has been washed off, revealing dark circles under her eyes.

She hurries to the other side of the bed, setting down her paper coffee cup to take my hand. Mr. Zeller follows her into the room, then stands awkwardly with his hands folded in front of him as Mom pushes my hair off my forehead and studies my face.

Mr. Zeller raises a hand. "Hi, Lola. You're looking much better this morning." He tilts his head toward Emory. "The girls have been up all night, worrying themselves sick. That's why I finally gave in and brought them down here. I thought it might put Em's mind at ease to see you up and about."

I'm hardly up and about, and the distraught daughter he's describing isn't the Emory I've met, but he seems sincere, if clueless, so I nod and say, "Thanks."

"Altitude sickness can be pretty serious," Mr. Zeller continues, "but at least it's easily treatable. It looks like you're on the mend already."

It takes a moment for his words to sink in, and when they do, I sit up and squeeze Mom's hand tight. "Altitude sickness?"

"I'm guessing you've been having a lot of fatigue? Dizziness, maybe? Nausea, headaches, nosebleeds?" he continues, counting off on his fingers as he lists pretty much every symptom I've had since we arrived in Colorado.

"Yes. Yes! Why didn't anyone . . . ?" My throat tightens as I remember Kurt basically telling me to suck it up. *Dial back the drama.*

Mom is openly crying now. "I'm so sorry, Lo. I really just thought it was more of—"

I interrupt her before she can say more. "It's fine, Mom. Don't cry." I press her hand to my cheek. "You didn't know. Neither did I."

Clare shifts awkwardly from one foot to the other. "We should go. Leave Lola to rest. I'm glad you're feeling better," she adds, squeezing my hand. "Text me when you get home."

"Take care, Tress," Mr. Zeller says. "Let us know if there's anything you need. We're here to help." He puts an arm around Emory's shoulder. "Right?"

"Right, Daddy. We're here to help," she echoes. "See you at school, Lola. We'll talk more then."

Emory's parting words sound more like a threat than an offer to help, but if anyone else notices her ominous tone, they don't show it.

CHAPTER 22

"Altitude sickness?" Mom clutches her neck tightly with a pale hand, as if she's trying to wring this truth from her own throat. "This place . . ."

She lurches into action, throwing open the cupboard beside the door and pulling out the clothes I was wearing last night. They stink of wood smoke, and even from here I can see the bloodstains.

"Get dressed. We're leaving."

She thrusts them toward me and I recoil. "Don't we have to wait for the doctor?"

But she isn't listening. "This was all a terrible mistake," she says, pacing near the door. She's talking to me, I think, but her words are muttered and directed at the floor. "We need to go."

I've never seen her like this, and it scares me. Beyond Mr. Zeller's explanation, she hasn't asked me what happened last night. I know I should be grateful—I certainly haven't had time to form any kind of believable lie. But her freak-out is freaking *me* out. If anyone should be upset, it should be me. What does she have to be so scared of? "I don't want to go back to the house—"

"Not to the house. Back home. To Michigan."

"But that's not our home anymore." My blurted response stuns us both into temporary silence, and we stare at each other as the heart monitor beats out the seconds it takes to register that somehow, we've switched sides.

"Knock, knock." A tall woman in a white coat wraps lightly on the doorframe. "Good morning, ladies. I'm Dr. Archuleta."

Her white coat helps tone down a riotous paisley tunic in teals and pinks, but only slightly, offering a bright contrast to her worn leather cowboy boots.

She pulls off her glasses before shaking Mom's hand, jamming them into her loose topknot. When Mom doesn't move aside to let her near the bed, she settles for a wave in my direction.

"It's so nice to finally meet you. Thank you for coming down," Mom says.

"Of course. I wish it were under more pleasant circumstances." She tries once again to step around Mom, then crosses her arms until Mom takes the hint. Point, Archuleta.

"Lola, how are you feeling this morning?" she asks, giving me a once-over before glancing down at the chart.

I shrug. "Better, I guess. Emory's—Mr. Zeller—he thought I had altitude sickness?" I don't know why I make it a question.

"Have," she corrects, then nods. "Mm-hmm. It's not uncommon. We see a lot of tourists in the ER. Most of them don't make it this long."

Mom inhales sharply.

Dr. Archuleta grimaces. "Sorry. Not because they die—that's only in rare cases. I meant, most of them seek medical treatment earlier. You really toughed it out."

I lift a shoulder, my cheeks burning. I'm too embarrassed to tell her I didn't even know I was sick. Or sicker.

"That wasn't a compliment," she says. "But I understand. For most people, it's such a shock to their systems, all the warning signals kick in. For you, a lot of this must have been old hat." She studies the chart once more. "Headaches, fatigue, muscle weakness. Just another Thursday, right?" She grins, showing off straight white teeth, and I find myself smiling back.

"Dr. Archuleta, what do we need to do? To get her on the mend, I mean. And after that, of course, I—we—have a lot of questions. You've received her medical charts, I assume? Dr. Klingbeil said—"

The doctor holds up a hand. "Please, Mrs. Boyd—"

"Gunderson."

"My apologies. Mrs. Gunderson."

"Tress."

Dr. Archuleta's smile tightens. "Tress, then. Let's all take a breath, shall we? I do have Lola's charts. I've been over them, and I definitely have some things I want to discuss with you. Both." Her eyes shift to mine. "But first things first. We need to treat this, get you back on your feet and feeling good again—whatever that word means for you, Lola. Back to baseline." She looks back at Mom. "It's no different than if she'd come in with a broken arm. I'd set it and cast it before we talked about her diet."

Mom is speechless, and for this reason alone, my impression of Dr. Archuleta ratchets up another notch.

"Now, if you don't mind, I'd like a few minutes alone with Lola. Just to chat and get to know her a bit. Would you mind? They've got some excellent coffee in the cafeteria." She takes Mom's elbow and steers her gently toward the door.

Mom glances down at the cup in her hand and then back at me. "Will you be all right, Lo?"

"I'll be fine."

Dr. Archuleta waits for the door to swing shut before turning her attention on me.

"Your vitals are all looking good," she says. "I'm very pleased."

"Uh, thank you?"

"I'm not sure how much you were aware of last night."

"Not much."

"They gave you a steroid treatment, in case there was any swelling in your lungs or in your brain. And they ran some blood tests." She's watching me, waiting for some reaction.

"I've had a lot of blood tests," I say, fiddling with the IV. "Unless someone stumbled across some radical cure while I was unconscious, I'm guessing you didn't learn anything new from that."

She tips her head back. "No, that's true. I did want to ask though, without your mom in the room, if there is anything we need to be worried about. Anything you may have ingested last night? Drugs? Alcohol?"

So that's what she's getting at. "No," I say, shaking my head. Then I pause, my recollection still fuzzy. "There was— Someone had a bottle of wine, I think. But we didn't drink it." I give her a sheepish smile. "We gave it to the spirits. It was a séance."

She nods and makes a dismissive wave of her hand. "I wanted to double-check there wasn't anything in your system we needed to be concerned about."

She pulls out a pen light and shines it in my eyes, right and then left. "How's the headache this morning?"

"Gone," I say, afraid to utter the word lest I summon it back. "For the first time in what feels like forever."

"Good. Your oxygen levels are back where we like to see them, so that should make a huge difference."

A huge difference. I do feel better. Not great, but better. The headaches, the shortness of breath, the dizziness. The memories?

She stands up straight. "You look like you want to ask me something."

I pluck at the blanket, unsure how to ask. "What about . . ." I swallow. "Hallucinations? Or, like, déjà vu? Is that a symptom of altitude sickness?"

She tilts her head, considering. "Confusion and decreased cognitive functioning, definitely. But hallucinations aren't common. Now, can I rule it out completely? No. What kind of hallucinations are we talking about?"

I haven't told anyone except for Bryn and Fletcher. And I know that saying it out loud is going to make me sound insane. But she's a doctor. If anyone is going to relieve me of that fear, it will be her. And if not, at least I'll be in good hands when she breaks the news to my mother. So I tell her everything, all the episodes, one at a time, as clearly and concisely as possible. But I've been holding so much in, for so long, this is like a dam being opened. The old cliché about a weight off your shoulder is overused for a reason. This is more like vomiting, or giving birth, all of my thoughts and feelings—bilious and blood-soaked—spewed out for her to pick apart. Somehow, I know I won't be able to scare her. Instead, she'll pick through them with surgical precision, separating the truth from the detritus.

Halfway through, she pulls up a chair beside the bed, her legs elegantly crossed. She doesn't interrupt me, not even once, just nods and takes notes on her pad until I slow down.

"I've heard about a situation where carbon monoxide was causing hallucinations," she says, frowning. "Do you have a detector in your house? That's one possibility." She makes another note and flips through the paperwork in her lap. "We should check for that on your next blood test."

"But what about last night? I was outside. Surely that wasn't carbon monoxide."

She tips her head to the side, considering. "True. You've heard the old adage 'The simplest explanation is probably true'? In this case, that would be the assumption that this is all related to the altitude," she finally says. "Though I would also add that trauma of any kind throws things off-kilter. As I'm sure you're aware. And your body has been through a lot these past few days. These past few years," she corrects, then references the chart. "I mean, even your birth could be classified as a form of trauma."

I can feel time slow, her words long and drawn out, my heartbeat loud, before it catches back up with me. "My birth?"

"Nearly a month premature."

I blink. "Yes. Because of my mom's—"

"Your mother's car accident." She shakes her head. "Frankly, I'm impressed she survived that. Speaking of trauma . . ."

I don't hear the rest, her words turning distorted, foreign. *Your mother's car accident.*

My mother wasn't in a car accident. My father was—

A series of seemingly unrelated memories crash into each other, vying for attention.

Kurt, insisting that we push on in the dark; Mom, resisting. Mom, pale and shaking, handing me the car keys. Kurt's outburst when I tried to talk to them about what happened. The fear on her face when I tried to tell her the truth. Her evasiveness when I asked if she had been here before.

Jesus, Teddy. We need to get off the road. It's not safe here.

There was another person in the car with him when he crashed.

And because she was eight months pregnant, that means I was there, too.

CHAPTER 23

I can't make my mouth form words. I gape at Dr. Archuleta like some kind of beached fish, but she's back to scribbling in my chart.

"That's . . . there?" I finally manage, gesturing to my chart in her hands. "About the . . . accident?"

"Whatever other faults your previous GP may have had, he kept meticulous records." She frowns as she takes in my heated face and tense jaw and slips her stethoscope back over her ears. "Let's take a listen to your heart one more time."

It's pounding so furiously she doesn't need the stethoscope. I can't even form a solid thought—they all wriggle past, red hot and slippery with anger. Mom was in the car. *In the car.* Eight months pregnant. Thrown free? Pulled from the wreckage?

Nearly a month premature.

So many times, I'd asked about my father. About his accident—what had happened, who was there. It bothered her to talk about it, I knew, but sometimes I just couldn't help myself.

And never, ever has she told me she was there.

"Lola." The doctor's voice pulls me back. "I'll have one of the nurses get your mom started on discharge paperwork so we can get you out of here. What do you say?"

"I . . . Yeah. That sounds . . ." I trail off, unable to finish. "Out of here" means home with Mom—who must know what's in my chart. After all, there has to be a reason Dr. K never discussed this with me. She must have asked him not to. I can't imagine why, much less why he agreed to it.

Is that why she was so anxious to leave?

Dr. Archuleta pats my arm.

"Excellent." She makes another note and goes to open the door. Mom must've been standing right outside, because she barrels in immediately. Hatred flares in me, white and stabbing. I bite my lip hard enough to make it bleed.

"We're going to send her home," she says.

I can feel Mom's gaze boring into me, but I refuse to meet it.

"I'd like to see her back in a couple of days. Let's say Tuesday?"

"Yes. Of course." Mom's voice is shaky.

"Grand. Lola, in the meantime, get some rest."

After the doctor breezes out, Mom perches on the end of my bed. "She seems—"

"Don't." I hate how tentative it sounds, how broken.

Mom inhales sharply. "What did she—"

"She told me. About the accident."

She stands to face me, her face tight but composed. She was expecting this. "I can expl—"

The nurse comes in, whistling Bobby McFerrin, oblivious to our tension. She wiggles a bag of IV fluid before tapping a code into the laptop on the IV stand. "Doctor says a couple more pints and we can spring you."

Mom clears her throat, but before she can speak, I ask, "Can I nap while we do that?"

"Absolutely." She swaps out the bag with quick, practiced hands, then pats my arm when she's done. "Rest a bit. Mama, how about you and I get started on her paperwork?"

Mom hesitates, but I turn over on my side, shutting her out.

It takes nearly an hour for the IV bag to empty. I don't sleep; instead, I spend most of that time staring at the wall and trying to make sense of the bomb my new doctor has detonated. I've heard that when someone close to you dies, your life becomes divided between "before" and "after." I'm sure that was true for Mom, but since I never even met my dad, my whole life has been lived in his after. Or, more accurately, hers. Because everything I know about him, every detail she's ever given me, has been deliberately chosen. This "after" has been her design. Facts were held back; secrets were kept. What purpose could she possibly have to keep this from me?

The amount of energy it must take overwhelms me.

I suddenly remember the box I'd found when I was maybe ten. Spying that old shoebox, lined with flattened tissue paper and tucked into the farthest corner of the highest shelf of Mom's closet, felt a little like discovering treasure. Inside, there'd been a book from my dad's funeral, full of messy signatures and tear-stained condolences. A copy of his obituary, clipped from the newspaper. A tribute written by a friend and published in their college newsletter.

None of it had mentioned her. Not an inkling of a suggestion that she'd been in the accident, or even anywhere nearby when he'd died. He'd been in Colorado; she'd been residing in their home in Michigan.

Was that deliberate, too? Had she scrubbed even those mementos of any evidence, on the off chance I might see them someday?

Or had she just gotten lucky?

Maybe I do sleep—briefly, fitfully—because I don't hear her come back into the room. I don't know she's there until she touches my shoulder and I wrench myself away from her.

"Lola. We're ready to head home."

The nurse removes my IV and helps me get dressed while Mom signs the necessary paperwork for my discharge.

"I thought about telling you," Mom finally says, pulling into the corner of the Target parking lot a few blocks from our house. She shifts into park but leaves the car running. "I was trying to find the right time. The right words."

"And when was that going to be?"

She clasps and unclasps her hands. "I hadn't decided."

"I don't know how you managed to convince Dr. K. to keep your secret, but you had to know there was at least a possibility this new doctor would say something. It was right there in my chart." So close. All this time. Dr. K's nurse must have known, too. Everyone, it seems, but me.

"I know. I was trying to find a way—"

"Stop. Lying." I grit my teeth. "I deserve the truth!"

She closes her eyes briefly, takes a slow breath. "I understand that you're feeling frustrated."

I scoff. "You have no *idea* how I feel."

She turns to me, finally, her mouth trembling. "You lost your father, and I'm not trying to excuse my behavior or minimize what you've been through. But"—she inhales sharply through her nose—"I lost my husband. My partner. The father of my child—" Her voice breaks, and it takes her another few moments to pull it together.

"I was scared and alone and I thought I was going to die. I thought *we* were going to die. I was grieving him and trying to hold on to you. It was the worst time in my whole life and I couldn't—I can't—relive it."

She leans her head against her window and cries, as quietly as a soft rain.

I roll mine down, the sorrow and the pain so stifling I can barely breathe.

"I know you want answers. Maybe you even think you're entitled to them," she finally says as she shifts into drive. "But I just want peace."

Neither of us speaks again for the rest of the drive.

But after she parks the car in front of the house, instead of opening her door, Mom folds her hands and says, "You believe my telling you the whole story will make you feel better, will heal some emptiness inside, but it won't. Knowing the gruesome details won't bring you any closer to him. It will only give you nightmares. I was trying—am trying—to protect you. And I don't owe anyone my pain. Not even you."

She still makes no move to get out, but I throw open my door. I can't be with her now, can't listen to her excuses, which somehow fill me with both rage and shame. When I glance back from the porch, she is sobbing into her hands, crying for the husband she lost, or maybe the baby she didn't.

I ache for her pain, sharp and sour in my throat. I want to comfort her, but I can't. She chose this—to keep this pain all to herself. To hoard it and box it up and shut me out.

And who am I to deny her that?

CHAPTER 24

We are all part of a lineage, stretching back and back and back through time. Linked by our blood and by our stories, passed down through generations. A collective memory, stitched together from snippets shared throughout our lives.

But what if the story is just that: A story? A fairy tale, invented out of whole cloth, fabricated by someone with their own agenda?

It's like what Mr. Zeller said. *History is written by the victors.*

Or maybe just the survivors.

If you hear something repeated enough times, you start to believe it.

My mother has been repeating the same story my whole life, and it appears all of my truths are actually lies. And if she isn't who I thought she was, what does that make me?

Tears blur my vision as I run toward the house. I need to be alone, away from her and everyone else. Instead, I barrel right into Sage.

"What are you doing here?" I snap, as he stumbles and steadies himself against the porch, his muscles no match for my anger.

"Yard work." He holds up a rake and gestures at the pile of leaves and debris at his feet. "I told Kurt—"

"You talked to Kurt? About last night?" Great. The last thing I need is Kurt on my ass about me messing around with "woo-woo shit."

He senses something in my tone and casts a worried glance toward the house. "I felt bad, so—"

"Why? What did you do?"

He blinks nervously. "I mean, you seemed really . . . sick. We were all worried. And Clare and I talked about it, and we thought maybe the best thing we could do is, you know, make things easier for you. So I came over to help clean up."

"Clean up? Like, get rid of evidence?"

He frowns. "Do you mean the wine?" he asks, lowering his voice. "Emory grabbed that last night. So you don't have to worry."

The wine is the least of my worries. "Are they here? Clare and Emory?" Did she use my incapacitation to try and get back into my house?

"I haven't seen Emory, but Clare's at home. I did talk to Kurt," he repeats. "But not about last night. Just about the yard work. I didn't want to, like, just show up on your property."

"Okay." He waits and I don't know what else he wants from me. "Thanks?" I finally offer, because it was a nice gesture and I'm not being fair. It's my mom I'm mad at, not him. And unlike Emory's visit, this doesn't seem to have any strings attached.

He nods vigorously. "You're welcome. You look better. But you're still really pale. Altitude's a bitch, especially if you're already . . . if you're not used to it."

Am I wearing some kind of neon sign? "How did you—"

"Clare told me." Of course she did.

"I should go in," I say, glancing back at the car. Mom is still bent over the steering wheel.

"Lola, wait." He kicks gently at the tines of the rake, not meeting my gaze. "Did you . . ." He takes a deep breath. "Did you really see her?"

The hair on the back of my neck goes up. "See who?"

He glances around nervously, as if someone might be listening. "You know. The witch." He whispers the last word in a way that makes me shudder.

Is that why he's here? For more stories he can take back to the group? "There is no witch," I mutter, pushing past him and up the stairs.

Kurt leaps off the couch as soon as I walk through the front door like he's spring-loaded. "Where's your mom?" He stops in the middle of the hall, blocking my way.

"In the car."

We both step to the same side, then the other.

I don't have time for this. I roll my eyes, try to push past him, but he grips my elbow.

"What's your little friend doing out there?"

I yank free. "You know what he's doing."

He jerks his head toward the door, and I use this distraction to try and make my escape, but I'm not fast enough. "Hold on. There are some things we need to talk about." He folds his arms across his chest. "What exactly were you up to last night?"

I swear softly under my breath, mentally kicking him and myself. I knew sooner or later someone was going to ask; I should've guessed it would be him. I straighten my shoulders and paste on a blank expression before turning back to him. "Just hanging out," I say. "Having a bonfire."

"Did you ask if you could have all those people over?"

It's my house. I almost say it, but bite my tongue. It's a childish impulse, and only technically true, but he brings out some kind of perverse animosity in me. "Mom wants me to make friends," I say, skirting the question.

"Yeah? Well, you and those friends trashed the house last night."

"We weren't even—"

"And nearly burned it down in the process. Lit candles? In the dining room?"

I flinch, and his nostrils flare with triumph.

Damn Sage and Emory and her candles. Damn that whole stupid séance.

You're possessed.

"And you're full of shit," I mutter under my breath.

"What did you say to me?" Kurt's jaw tightens, and his face goes purple.

"I was taken away in an ambulance!" I so want to be the rational one in this argument. And I almost manage it, right up until I scream the last word in his face. "So I am sorry if I didn't stop the paramedics to run back inside and tidy up!"

"I'm on to your little illness con. The nosebleeds and the dizzy spells that only seem to come on when your mom's attention is focused elsewhere. Very convenient." His sarcasm is so thick, I can feel it oozing over my skin.

"What's going on in here?" Mom stands in the doorway, backlit by the sun like some kind of guardian angel. But as she steps forward, her expression is less beatific and more dazed.

"Your husband was just accusing me of faking my illness to get out of having to clean up after myself." I'm getting short of breath again, but this time I'm sure it's from anger. "But he's wrong. I had—have," I correct, remembering Dr. Archuleta's words, "altitude sickness." I enunciate slowly and clearly, so even Kurt can follow. "Which, it turns out, isn't cured by *sucking it up*."

Mom makes a sound in the back of her throat that's either a gasp or a cough, then goes silent.

"I'm going to be okay, by the way. Not that you've asked." I tilt my head. "Do you know, you're the only person all day who *hasn't*?"

He looks from me to Mom, his face going from plum to a sickly lavender. "Tress. Please. I was . . ." His pleading whine fades as I head upstairs, and I almost feel sorry for him.

Almost.

I've got a half dozen messages from Bryn, so instead of crawling into bed, I keep going up the stairs to the attic. They want to know how the séance went. The last one—**WHY AREN'T YOU ANSWERING YOUR PHONE ARE YOU POSSESSED???**—sounds a bit more frantic than usual. Why does everyone go straight to possession? It's like I'm living my very own Satanic Panic.

Is this what everyone thinks? Sage seemed truly nervous when he asked me about the witch. And Clare didn't say much at the hospital. She looked uncomfortable, which at the time I chalked up to her thinking Emory crossed a line. But maybe they're all on board with the demon theory.

Fletcher, too? He's the one person I haven't heard from. I check once more, but no snaps or texts have appeared in the last thirty seconds.

I flop down onto the big red couch and call Bryn. Since I don't know how to even begin telling my best friend about all that's happened in the last twenty-four hours, I'm almost relieved when I get the familiar voicemail message: "I never listen to these, so feel free to try again, unless you're a motherfucking spammer, in which case I've already blocked your number."

I'm tempted to spill the whole story. They won't hear it, so it might be a good warm up. "Hey, Bryn. It's me. Not possessed. Yesterday—"

But that's as far as I get before I choke and hang up.

Yesterday was a lifetime ago. Since then, I've passed out in my own blood, been accused of demonic possession, and learned my mother has been lying to me my whole life. I need to process all of it before I can say it out loud. Or maybe not process. Maybe it's best not to think at all. Which won't be hard, given the screaming from the floor below me.

Apparently, Mom and Kurt are full-on fighting, and they've moved to their bedroom to do it.

". . . do not *ever* talk to my daughter—"

"All I said was—"

"Suck it up?"

So *now* she's jumping to my defense? This feels a little too convenient, like misplaced guilt is fueling her anger. But damn, does she sound pissed. I feel a twinge of something for Kurt I'd almost call empathy, except I'm not sure he deserves it. His attack crossed a line. Sure, he can be a self-centered dick. But accusing me point-blank of faking my illness? That's low, even for him.

My phone rings before I can decide where my sympathies lie. One more thing to avoid thinking about. I'll just file it with the others.

"Damn, Lola, I have been *freaking out*. What the hell happened?" Bryn's face is close to the screen, the camera jiggling as they walk down the hallway in their house, presumably from the bathroom to their bedroom, since their hair is soaking wet and they aren't wearing their glasses. "Why didn't you answer my texts?"

"I was in the hospital. But I'm home and I'm fine." The words are hard to say. I know how they're going to react, and I dread it. As long as I've been sick, there's always been someone quick to accuse me of doing it for the attention. But the truth is, I hate this kind of attention. I honestly can't imagine anyone who would enjoy it. It makes me sick to my stomach to even say the words, to watch Bryn's face fall as they try to backtrack and apologize.

They don't have to. But I know Bryn, and I know they feel like they've been insensitive, that they've offended me. And I hate every second of it.

"Oh my god."

I lean onto a throw pillow and prop my chin in my hand. "Apparently, I haven't been adjusting well to the altitude. That's why all the nosebleeds and headaches and shit. The good news is, I actually feel better today. Tired still. But my headache is gone."

Bryn props their phone, then steps out of view to throw on some clothes. "So no séance, I'm assuming?"

"No, we had the séance."

They sense something in my tone, rushing back to the phone and grabbing it up as they finish pulling a purple fleece over their head. "And?"

"And I had an episode."

Bryn pops on purple frames that match their sweatshirt and grabs a red Twizzlers off their vanity. "Tell me everything," they say, tearing off a chunk with their teeth.

I launch into a detailed account of the night before, and when I finish, Bryn's eyes are saucers. "You're killing us? That's what you said? As in murder?"

"Honestly, the details are a little fuzzy. Most of that came from Emory."

"And do we trust her?"

Leave it to Bryn to zero in on the question that's been rolling around in the back of my head. "I don't know. She and Clare came to see me in the hospital this morning. Supposedly, they were worried about me. But Emory seemed to have an agenda. She said . . . she said she 'knows what's happening.'" I make finger quotes. "That I'm possessed and she can help me."

Bryn snorts. "Un-fucking-likely."

"I mean, yes. But honestly, she's the only one who's picked up on the fact that something unusual is going on. I keep gushing blood and blurting out these exceedingly creepy things, and everyone else is treating it as situation normal. When clearly it isn't."

"Clearly. But they've got an explanation, don't they? The altitude. So even if they were suspicious, now they've got a plausible explanation."

"Right. But what about Emory?"

"That girl's not right in the head. She clearly rigged that séance for her own purpose, whatever that may be. She's fixated on the idea of a witch." Bryn shrugs. "Maybe you need to be straight with her."

"No!" My reaction is instant and possibly irrational. "I don't want to do that. Besides, what if she's right? What if this is all happening because Rebecca *was* a witch?"

They pause. "I mean, I feel like you'd have better powers than squirting blood from your nostrils. It's not exactly a classic sign of possession, is it? Channeling spirits through your nasal cavity?"

"I told you, I'm not possessed. I'm still me." I struggle to find the right words for whatever the hell happened. "It felt like a memory. But of something that never happened to me."

"You're literally describing déjà vu."

"No! It's the opposite of déjà vu." I pluck at the sofa cushion. "Déjà vu always feels like mine, you know? Like 'Hey, this thing has happened before. To *me*.' Whatever this is, it's different." I struggle to find the words to articulate what I've been feeling. "Last night . . . every time . . . it's like I'm inhabiting someone *else's* memories. And then I went to the park the other day, and I saw his statue. Dr. Clarett's. And I know how ridiculous this is going to sound, but I've seen him before. *He's the guy from my visions.*"

Bryn opens their mouth, but I don't let them speak. I need to get this all out before I lose my nerve. "And the dunking? Like I hallucinated at the reservoir? That happened. To real people. There are photos and newspaper stories and everything. I'm having memories of things that *actually* happened." I slap my chest for emphasis. "Just, not to me." I take a deep breath and lean back, bracing myself for Bryn's rebuttal.

It doesn't come. Instead, they say, "Actually, you're right. That doesn't sound like possession at all. It sounds like an epigenetic memory."

I squint at the screen. "Epi-what?"

"I heard about it on some genealogy podcast. Hold on." The connection gets muffled for a second, and then Bryn is back. "I'm looking at this guy's website. He's a doctor, and he was talking about the kinds of traits that get passed on. Like, we know that eye color and hair and shit are genetic. And talents, too, right? Say, if my mom had been a musician, I might've inherited perfect pitch or something."

I'd been expecting some kind of argument. Or at least a Bryn look, the one that says "You need to pull yourself together." This matter-of-fact agreement is throwing me off.

I can't sit still; I need to move. As they click away on their laptop, I move to the window. Sage's rake is lying in a loose pile of lawn debris, but he's nowhere to be seen. So much for his help.

"Here it is," Bryn says. "Epigenetic memory. The theory that a traumatic event can cause a change to a person's genetic code, which is then passed down through subsequent generations."

My shoulders sag. I should have known it was too good to be true. "That sounds like a bunch of pseudoscience bullshit."

"There's research to back this up."

"And how do you know that? Because some rando on a podcast said so?"

"He's not a rando. He's a doctor! And besides, it's fucking interesting!"

"We have very different definitions of that word," I say.

"Shut up. I haven't told you the interesting part yet." Bryn sighs. "After the Vietnam War, a lot of veterans came back really messed up. At the time, they didn't know about PTSD. Then they realized—duh!—even people who survived the war, who came home uninjured, they'd still suffered some kind of trauma. So scientists did all these studies. And one of the things they found was that a lot of them had anxiety triggered by loud noises. Which makes sense. But—and here's the interesting part—"

"Finally."

"Their kids had anxiety about loud noises, too!" Bryn pauses, and when I don't respond, continues, "Even though they had no reason whatsoever to fear loud noises."

"You're literally describing learned behavior."

"Wrong!" Bryn crows, as if they've been waiting for this. "How do you explain the fact their *grandchildren* were also affected? And those grandchildren's children?"

"I'm sorry, but it's a huge leap to go from 'anxiety is biologically inherited' to 'being scared can fundamentally change your DNA so much that your children will someday retain your memories.'"

"Not scared. We're talking big, life-changing trauma. And what about if the parent who experienced the trauma died? Before the child was born, even? That's not learned behavior."

My stomach drops. "Are you talking about my dad?"

"Maybe. I mean, you literally remembered something traumatic that happened to him. Before you were even born," Bryn says. "That's the textbook definition of an epigenetic memory."

"But what about these other memories? They don't have anything to do with my dad, or his accident."

"You're missing the point. It's not just your dad's accident. *Any* trauma can alter your DNA. And that shit gets passed down, generation after generation. You retain it, like, on a cellular level. You said it yourself—it felt like a memory of something that happened to *someone else*. You're killing us? Sounds pretty fucking traumatic."

Something that happened to someone else.

Someone like Rebecca.

Marguerite's hand, cold and lifeless. Mine, slick with blood.

You're killing us.

"Marguerite," I say, gripping the windowsill with a shaky hand. My heart is pounding and my head is swimming. "She was sick, Bryn. Like me." I sink to the floor, pulling my knees up close to my chest. "In her obituary, it said she was staying with the doctor *during treatment*. I don't know what the hell he was treating her with, but it didn't heal her. It killed her."

CHAPTER 25

"Oh my god. Do you think he was injecting her with creek water?" The idea makes me woozy and I drop the phone to put my head between my knees.

"Lola. Lola! Stay with me." Bryn pushes their face close to the screen. "I know this is some freaky shit, but we have to remember, it happened a long time ago. It doesn't have anything to do with you—"

I snatch up the phone. "But it does, don't you see? What if her illness is somehow connected to mine? What if *that's* why I'm seeing all her memories?"

"That conclusion you're jumping to is so big, it has its own zip code," Bryn says. "You've got to slow down."

I pull myself to my feet, using the windowsill for support.

Fletcher's Jeep is parked in front of the house.

"Did you hear me? I said—"

"Slow down. Yes, point taken. I have to call you back."

I shove my phone in my pocket and hurry down the steps, past Mom's room. She and Kurt are still arguing, the yelling punctuated only by the occasional sound of tears. I can't tell if they're Mom's or Kurt's.

I throw open the door before Fletcher has a chance to ring the doorbell.

"Hey!" he says, taking a step back. "Hi. I wasn't sure you'd be up and around."

My heart does a little stutter in my chest at his smile. I've been waiting to hear from him, secretly hoping he'd show up at my door.

That should probably worry me.

But I have so many other things to stress about right now, a crush on a boy who might already have a girlfriend feels downright normal. And somehow, his smile makes me feel safe.

"Hi," I say, smiling back. My mind goes blank.

Above me, a door slams in the front of the house. Shit.

"How are you feeling?" Fletcher asks, backpedaling as I step out onto the porch and pull the door shut behind me.

"I'm fine," I say. "What are you doing right now?"

He glances back at the Jeep and shoves his hands in his pockets. "Nothing. I mean, just visiting you—"

"Take me to see your bears?"

Mom won't even notice if I leave. I'm certainly not going to interrupt her to ask permission. Being with Fletcher after last night might be super awkward, but it's still better than being here, with their fighting and my churning thoughts.

Luckily, Fletcher's natural enthusiasm is strong enough to counteract my weirdness. He doesn't even ask why I need to get out of the house; he just takes it on faith that I've been stricken by a sudden need to meet the bears.

Either that, or he's so anxious to spend time with me he doesn't question my motives.

He drives to the sanctuary with Janis Joplin playing softly in the background, occasionally glancing over at me, then away.

"I'm not going to break," I finally say. "You can relax."

"Sorry. It's just . . ." He tightens his grip on the steering wheel. "Last night was so—"

"Don't," I say, shaking my head.

"—scary," he continues, ignoring me. "You might be fine, but I'm still on edge." He holds out a hand and wiggles it back and forth. "And I'll shut up, I promise, but first I owe you an apology."

"For what? Emory said you were the one who called the ambulance. If anything, I owe you a thank-you. I was in rough shape."

He shakes his head, sending a lock of hair tumbling into his eye. "And I should have warned you. You'd already had, like, what? Two nosebleeds around me? You told me about being sick, and how your symptoms were different here, and I still didn't think to warn you about the altitude." He pounds his forehead with his fist. "Dumb, dumb, dumb. I know better."

I reach up to swat his hand away, and he somehow flips it around so that we're holding hands.

"It's not your fault," I say, trying to keep my voice light despite the fact that my heart is beating like hummingbird wings. I pull my hand free and massage it with my other one. "I should've been taking better care of myself. It's just been a lot, you know? With the move and the house and starting school again. Anyway, it's all water under the bridge. Or should I say, blood under the bridge?"

He winces.

"Too soon?"

The sanctuary is only a few miles outside of town, in a round white building that looks like a circus tent. A sloping ramp winds up and around the building, extending out to an elevated walkway that stretches in both directions.

He parks in front and leans toward the dashboard. "This is the visitor center, as you've probably guessed. And on the other side of that"—he gestures at the walkway—"are the bears! In their natural habitat. Or as close as we can get."

He hops out and runs around to open my door.

"And we're going out there? With them?" It occurs to me that I didn't give this enough thought. Or any thought, really.

Fletcher lays a hand over his heart. "I will not put you in any danger. Pinky promise." He holds up his pinky, and I hesitate a second before linking mine through it. He tugs me gently from my seat.

The warmth of his touch sends a little thrill up my arm, and I drop his hand and wipe mine on my jeans, annoyed with myself.

"Are you nervous?" he asks.

His brown eyes are wide and warm, inviting me to share all my secrets. Just in time, I remember I might be mad at him.

I tear my gaze from his. "Nothing fazes me. Remember? Low-key." I make the same hand gesture he did the other day, complete with whistle.

"Right. Low-key. How could I forget?" He doesn't sound like he believes that anymore, and who can blame him?

"Why a circus tent?" I ask, making a twirling motion with my finger, hoping to get the conversation back on neutral ground.

He leads me toward the building. "I wish I had some cool, deep answer about how we're subverting expectations and metaphorically putting ourselves on display. But I think it was actually about the views."

At the top of the elevated walkway, I peer over the railing. It's at least thirty feet from the ground below, but the platform is tall and so solidly built that I don't feel worried about falling off. Unless—

"What if a bear rams the post and knocks it over?" I ask.

"They won't. The bridge beneath us is steel. A thousand elephants could walk on this and it wouldn't collapse."

"A thousand?" I raise an eyebrow.

"Honest. One tiny bear isn't going to be able to budge it."

"I'm more concerned about large bears."

"You don't have to be concerned about any of them," Fletcher says, so earnestly I believe him. He's never come across as artificial, but suddenly I know—this is the real Fletcher. This is his element. As much as he's been himself each time we've been together, here he owns it.

"Most people have only two associations with bears," he says. "Teddy bears and bear attacks. Everyone had at least one teddy, right?"

"Or still do."

He grins. "See? I knew there was a reason I liked you."

Is he flirting with me?

I shouldn't bring it up, but I'm too tired to keep playing these games. Instead, I blurt, "What about Clare?"

He blinks back. "What about her?"

"Won't she be . . . ?" But his expression of utter confusion is making me question the validity of Emory's words. "Emory told me you guys were a couple. *Flare*," I say with jazz hands.

Fletcher works his jaw. "When did she tell you that?"

I reach back, trying to remember. So much has happened. Was it after we talked about the séance? No, before. In class. "Wednesday?"

He frowns. "I don't know why she would say that, but we're not . . . We hooked up for a while, I mean . . ." His face is bright red. "What I'm trying to say is, we're much better off as friends."

That doesn't actually prove his point. "Does Clare feel the same way?"

"Of course. What, you think she has some secret crush on me?"

"That might explain why Emory talked to me. Maybe she's looking out for her friend."

He shoves his hands in his pockets and kicks gently at one of the posts. "First of all, Clare's honest. Like, completely. If she liked me, she'd tell me. In fact, that's why we broke up. She just walked up to me one morning and said she didn't like being my girlfriend anymore."

I have so many questions. How long ago was that? What did he do? Was he heartbroken?

"I swear, Lola. I'm telling you the truth. I wouldn't do that to you. Or Clare. I'm not that guy."

He's so sincere—and so worried—that I relent. After all, I've only got Emory's word to the contrary. And Bryn summed it up nicely less than an hour ago: *Do we trust her?*

Not enough to give this up.

I smile and hold out my hand. "I believe you," I say.

As he leads me farther along the path, the tree cover becomes thicker. Scattered over the ground beneath us are shelters that look like lean-tos, some boulders, and a tunnel made out of old tires. Another tire hangs from the tree like a swing.

"We get animals here who were injured or endangered, for whatever reasons, and they can't go back into the wild. They wouldn't survive. So we've created this sanctuary for them, and in return, we can study each of them and learn what makes them tick," Fletcher says.

"They can't go back because they've lost some of their . . . bearness?"

Fletcher's grin widens. "Yes! Exactly! You get it." His tone softens at my blank expression. "Even the behaviors they've lost, or better still, the human behaviors they've gained, those can all tell us something. Every bear has something of value to teach us. In return, we keep them safe."

"Are they in danger?"

"These bears would be, definitely." He jumps forward, alert, and crosses to the far side of the bridge. "See that dark shape, moving in the trees?" He pulls me close and positions me, our cheeks touching, as he points over my shoulder. "That's Kota, scratching himself on the tree bark. We got him as a cub. He was born in captivity; his mother was a circus bear performing with elephants and had picked up some of their behaviors."

"She thought she was an elephant?"

"She, at least, knew how to interact with elephants. Which was interesting to study. Most bears don't have the opportunity to socialize with animals larger than themselves."

"I mean, this is a nature versus nurture thing, right?"

"Yeah, but the cool thing is the more time you spend with the animals, the more you realize it's not an either/or question. It's both."

It's the same thing Perez had said, back on the first day of school.

"It's fascinating, right?" His face is animated as he talks. But now he slows and jams his hands in his pockets as he dips his head, his hair flopping over his face. "At least, I find it fascinating. Am I boring you?"

"Not at all," I say, somewhat surprised to find it's true. Did I ever expect to spend the afternoon talking about bears? No. But his enthusiasm is contagious, and it reminds me of what it used to feel like to get excited about something.

I have never been what one might call a nature girl, by any definition, and yet I'm enjoying Fletcher's tour immensely. And not just because the sun is warm and the air is sweet and I'm hanging out with a boy who geeks out over bears as much as I geek out over genealogy. In the bright light of day, with Fletcher beside me, it feels like last night happened years ago, to some other girl. Which, in a way, it did.

"So tell me what I should do if a bear attacks me," I say, trying to shake the thought from my mind.

"Bear attacks are much less common than you think," Fletcher says, turning so he's walking backward in front of me.

"How *much* less?"

He smiles. "I'm so glad you asked. You are *sixty-seven times* more likely to get killed by a dog. For every human killed by a bear, two hundred forty-seven others die from lightning strikes. In general, bears don't care much about us at all. We're the ones who keep encroaching on their territory."

"Those are some impressive facts."

He lifts a shoulder. "I may have done the tour a time or twenty."

"Okay, Ranger Hart. But what if the unimaginable does happen? Do I run?"

"Never run!" He sounds alarmed. "First of all, you want to stay calm. If the bear sees you, talk in a low, calm voice. Then, you're going to want to back up. Never turn your back on a bear, but you don't want to make eye contact, either. You want to give her as much space as possible, but slowly. No running."

"I'm sensing a theme here."

"If the bear does engage, you'll want to either play dead or fight back. If it's brown, lie down. If it's black, fight back."

"It's comforting to know that my survival depends on my ability to distinguish between two very similar colors," I say.

"Species, not color, but I get it. When in doubt, always use your bear spray."

"Bear spray." I remember that first night at my house; Sage said he never went anywhere without it. He was scared to be outside that night because he thought he'd seen a bear.

And yet, he didn't seem worried at the bonfire.

"In rare cases, mothers will attack to defend their cubs," Fletcher says. "It depends on the bear. Black bears are more likely to climb trees to escape humans than to attack them. Brown bears and grizzlies, there's more likelihood of a protective attack.

He continues, "Grizzly bears rely more on displays of aggression to keep people away than other species. They'd still rather posture than attack, though. The posturing is genetically coded into their DNA."

"Hold on." I stop walking. "Genetically coded? Are you talking about epigenetic memory?"

He raises his arms. "Yes! You know about epigenetic memory?"

"I just heard about it, actually." I can't wrap my head around this. "So it's real. I mean, it sounds like some kind of psychobabble nonsense."

Fletcher shakes his head firmly. "It's not psychobabble. It's necessary. For survival. Think about it. What if you're a baby bear whose mother has been killed before she has a chance to warn you about predators, or teach you what you can and can't eat?"

"Survival of the fittest?"

"In some cases, sure. But there are some dangers so important, they get encoded in the animal's memory. Predators, for one. Hibernation is another great example."

"That's different, though. That's just their body knowing what to do."

"But that's exactly what epigenetic memory is. Your body holding on to information it needs."

"I guess I never thought about it like that." The way he says it, it makes sense. At least for bears. But why would I need to remember whatever it is my weird déjà vu episodes are trying to tell me?

You're killing us. What is that even supposed to mean? Some kind of warning?

Or maybe it's more of a literal message: *So too will these waters heal you.*

Fletcher points to the next clearing. "This guy is a special case. Sherlock had a rare brain disease, a sort of encephalitis. It altered his behavior so much that he almost acted like a dog. He'd lost his fear of humans; in fact, the hikers who found him said he walked right up to them and wanted to play."

Beneath us, Sherlock stands and stretches, his nose pointing in the air. After a moment, he slowly turns to look in our direction, and I have the crazy thought that he knows Fletcher's talking about him. In fact, for a moment I'm convinced he understands everything we're saying. Then he drops down to all fours, turns, and lumbers into the woods.

"Most bears who are that sick end up being put down," Fletcher says as we watch him go. "But we had the space and his condition wasn't that advanced, so he was sent here. Now he's recovering, but he'll never be able to go back into the wild. It isn't safe for him anymore. We can try and teach him bear behavior, but we can't be certain he would retain it. And his condition makes him vulnerable."

I feel an affinity for Sherlock. I understand vulnerability all too well. "Why Sherlock?" I ask. "I mean, who names the bears?"

"The staff take turns. I'm not sure who picked Sherlock, but I'm sure it's because of the collective. Because a group of bears is called a sleuth. Get it?"

"That's clever," I say, although truthfully, I just have more questions. Why a sleuth? What are they looking for? And are they any good at finding it?

It seems like everyone is better than me at finding what they need. Everyone I've met recently, at least. Fletcher, Clare, Sage, Emory. They're all so self-assured, so confident. So . . . themselves. Is it the mountain air? Something in their magic water? How is it that everyone else has already figured out who they are, while I stumble around in the dark trying to figure it out?

Once, I thought I was strong. A runner. But that didn't last. Now, I'm someone completely different. My quickness, my lightness, my surety of foot have been replaced by slowness and unsteadiness. I've forgotten who I am; my entire identity shrunk down to my illness and my symptoms. But worse than that, I've stopped thinking about who I want to become. The longer this goes on, the less likely it feels that I'll ever get any answers. And how can I plan for a future without knowing whether I'll be sick or healthy? That kind of thought takes courage, and honestly, I haven't felt that brave in a long time. But watching Fletcher's excitement as he talks about his bears, something stirs in me.

Like an animal coming out of hibernation, I feel warm and alive and almost giddy with the thought that finally, this—this boy, this doctor, these new friends—might be worth the effort, and the risk. Since Michigan, I've been putting a lot of emphasis on what I've left behind.

It might be time to start thinking about what's ahead.

We wander on the rest of the elevated platform trail slowly, Fletcher pointing out the different bears and occasionally grabbing my hand to squeeze or hold. By the time we make our way around the whole loop, it's after three. My energy is waning fast, but I want to hold on to this day as long as possible.

On the way out, Fletcher stops at the gift shop to buy me a teddy bear wearing a purple T-shirt with the sanctuary logo.

"You don't have to do that," I protest.

"I want to. So you remember today," he says.

"I'm not likely to forget my first day with the bears."

"Now it's doubly memorable." He presses the fluffy toy into my arms. "I just have to check on something. Give me two minutes and I'll meet you in the parking lot."

As I wait for him by the car, I pull out my phone and turn it back on. Four missed calls and seven texts, all from Mom.

The last one is in all caps. **GET HOME. NOW.**

As if sensing my sudden shift in mood, a bank of clouds rolls in, eclipsing the sunny day.

CHAPTER 26

I don't call her. Her anger at not knowing where I've been is going to be tough enough to stomach in person, so why listen to the same lecture on the phone first? The most I can hope for at this point is to condense the argument into a single confrontation. She and Kurt have had plenty of time to reconcile, so this is probably going to be a them-against-me scenario.

Those never end well.

Mom is alone on the porch when we pull up, pacing, her phone pressed to her ear. When she catches sight of me in Fletcher's vehicle, she freezes for a second, then hangs up. I know her so well—she's the one constant in my life. Mom and I against the world. At least until Kurt came into the picture.

I'm expecting to see the two of them standing shoulder to shoulder. Anger coloring her cheeks, or worry lines furrowing her brow. Instead, she looks . . . eerily calm.

This is worse than I imagined.

"Thanks again," I say, waving Fletcher off before squaring my shoulders and turning to face her.

"I was worried about you," she says, her voice flat.

I walk slowly up the porch steps, rehearsing my arguments in my head. "Fletcher took me to the bear sanctuary," I say. I show her the stuffed animal.

When she doesn't respond, all of my righteous bravado leaks out of me like a deflating balloon, and I wait in silence for her opening blow. Where have I been? What was I doing?

But she says none of these. Just works her jaw in a move I know well—she's trying to hold it together. "When you weren't here, I thought maybe . . ." she trails off.

"Mom? What's—"

The front door bangs open as Kurt steps onto the porch, carrying two suitcases, his laptop bag strung across his body. When he sees me, his eyes narrow. "Lola. Thank goodness you're all right."

It's an empty sentiment, with no emotion behind it at all, simply stated to appease Mom.

Except this time, it doesn't.

She tilts her head to the ceiling and barks a sarcastic laugh. "You're not even *trying*. Just. Stop." She presses her hands to her cheeks and looks at me. "Has it always been this obvious? Am I really this . . . stupid?" She whispers the last word in horror.

This is maybe the most uncomfortable I've ever been. Clearly, they're still fighting. And I have no intention of getting caught in the crossfire. It'll be worse than when your friend dumps their partner, and you badmouth the loser, and then they get back together. Even if Mom is grateful I took her side, Kurt won't ever forget it.

"I'm just gonna . . . go . . ." I point at the door, waiting for Kurt to move aside.

"I'm going to drop Kurt off at the airport, and then I'll be right back. No more than half an hour," she says, forcing some energy into her voice.

"Tress, please—"

"Maybe less," she says through gritted teeth.

"I understand you want some time alone with Lola. I respect that. Just give me the keys. I'll go to a hotel for the night and come back in the morning so we can talk."

"I have to work in the morning," Mom says, in a way that makes me think they've already had this argument.

"Kurt's leaving?" I try not to sound too hopeful, but I'm not sure I pull it off.

"Just for the night," Kurt says, at the same time Mom says, "Yes."

"I'll drop you at the airport," she repeats. "If you don't want to fly, they have a rental car available. I checked."

"All my stuff is here."

"We'll send it."

This is both horrifying and fascinating, in a train wreck kind of way.

"I'm not walking out on you. We're *married*."

"I don't know what that means anymore. And you sure as hell don't."

I stare, open-mouthed, aware I'm mimicking Kurt's expression, but I can't help it. This is pre-lovesick Mom, the woman who doesn't put up with jerks and doesn't have time for bullshit. I haven't seen her in a long time.

"Let's go," she says, jingling the keys as she heads for the car.

Kurt watches her for a moment, then hefts his suitcase. "This is a temporary situation," he says, and I'm not sure if he's trying to convince me or himself. "I'll be back soon. In the meantime . . ."

I brace myself for whatever shitty advice is about to come out of his mouth. Suck it up? Grow up?

". . . take care of her." His voice is plaintive, and it hits me like a gut punch.

What does he think I've been doing all these years?

I watch from the porch until the car is out of sight. I have no idea how long she'll be gone and I don't trust her "half an hour" estimate. Their reunion could come at any time. Hell, she might have pulled over and they could be making up in the car right now, or at a hotel down the block.

The house looks the same as always; it's hard to believe that a major fight has taken place here. Their wedding photo still stands on the mantel, although his lucky baseball is gone. In the kitchen, there's more evidence. Someone—I'm guessing Mom—has pulled all of Kurt's good cookware out of the cupboards and piled it on the kitchen table. I go around the room, closing the cupboards and the basement door, which is also ajar.

I'm both tired and wired; I need a nap, but I also need to eat. But before I do any of that, I need to figure out if there is anything to this epigenetic theory.

I take Fletcher's teddy to my room and bring my laptop back downstairs so I can do research while I start dinner. After I put a pot on to boil, I sit at the kitchen table and type "epigenetic memory" into the search bar. The first link offers a definition in bold letters across the top of the page: **A heritable change in gene expression or behavior that doesn't involve changes in the DNA sequence. See also *cellular memory*.** I scan the rest of the page, slowing when I get to certain portion: *A growing body of evidence suggests that environmental stressors can cause changes in gene expression that are passed from parent to child.*

"A growing body of evidence" sounds more promising than Bryn's one dude on a podcast, so I keep reading: *Cells contain DNA inherited from parents, grandparents, and so on. What we normally think of as DNA-based inheritable traits, like eye color, hair color, nose shape, only make up a small percentage of your total DNA. The rest are things like personality and emotions.*

This gives me an unexpected pang. So much of who I am might have come from my dad, but those are traits I'll never recognize. On the other hand, I'm a part of my mom for sure. I see it in the shape of our chins, and in the slope of our noses. In our ability to ignore things we don't like. Our mutual love of folk music, and our weird fear of butterflies.

But what about all the ways we're different? Her inability to tell a joke, my recall when it comes to quotes. Her absolute need for order, my inability to organize anything. Her health, my illness. Are any of those from my father?

I swallow around the lump in my throat and click another link, a *National Geographic* article that describes a study where scientists shocked mice whenever they encountered the smell of orange blossoms. Very quickly, the mice learned to startle at the smell. Learned avoidant behavior. Exactly what I said to Bryn. But the pups of the mice, though never shocked, displayed the same behavior. As did the pups of the third generation. In essence, the pups *remembered* the scent and the danger it posed.

I click on another link, an article describing epigenetics as a kind of on/off system for genes. I can't help picturing a light switch as I read about chemical tags attaching to DNA and ultimately changing behavior based on whether they are turned on or off. Not just for an individual, but for the next several generations.

My gaze falls on a quote near the bottom of the page. *The work could provide information on how to erase aberrant epigenetic marks that may underlie some diseases in adults.*

I sit back, my heart pounding like I've run a sprint.

I was half hoping this would all be fake news—a bunch of links to some holistic faith healers and spirit guides. Not *National Geographic* and the University of Cambridge. Bryn was right. This is real.

The memories, when they come, are as sudden and brutal as an electric shock. I feel like one of those mice, bewildered and afraid.

I'm as helpless as they were to figure out why this is happening to me.

Even if there is a genetic component to all of it, I still have more questions than answers. Why me? Why now? And why these particular memories?

Are they connected to my illness in some way?

The pot on the stove is boiling rapidly, roiling and hissing. I grab a box of pasta from the pantry and dump half of it into the water, burning my hand in the steam.

"Shit! Shit, shit, shit!" I twist the faucet to cold and shove my hand under the water as I stare out the window over the sink. I know it's only my imagination, but it feels like the mountain is even closer than it was before. Like it's creeping slowly toward me, pressing in, pushing pushing pushing—

"Knock it off!" I say, my voice too loud in the empty house.

Above me, the floor creaks.

My heart stutters to a halt for a full second before thudding back to life with a roar that builds in my ears.

Someone's in the house.

The room seems to tilt as the footsteps above me move toward the stairs, slow and steady.

I'm going to pass out but I can't; it isn't safe.

I'm not alone.

Breathe, Lola. Breathe.

The box falls from my hand, scattering pasta across the floor, and I follow, crawling around the side of the counter, hard bowties cutting into my knees and palms.

My vision narrows to a pinprick, a dark tunnel that stretches out before me.

The tunnel seems to go on forever but I can't stop and back isn't an option, no matter how dark and scary it is here. I need to save her.

It feels like I've been walking for hours, but that can't be right. I've lost all track of time. The ground is so cold, my feet have gone numb. My arm aches where the needle has penetrated over and over. I'm so exhausted, I'm nearly dead on my feet.

But it doesn't matter. I'm almost there. "I'm coming," I whisper.

I hear a noise and whirl. James is standing in the tunnel behind me.

"What are you doing here? Did you follow me?"

"I've missed you," he says, the shadows contorting his features into a gruesome shape.

I take an involuntary step back. "I won't . . . I can't endure anymore. I'm only here for my sister."

He reaches for my hand. "I want to help you. I know about the baby."

I come to on the kitchen floor with a gasp, as if surfacing from underwater. I use a chair leg to pull myself to sitting, dizzy and disoriented. The broken pasta lies scattered around my feet into loose letters.

They spell out WITCH.

CHAPTER 27

The pot on the stove hisses as boiling water spills out in a river across the stovetop. I stagger to my feet to turn off the burner.

"Lola?"

I lurch away from the stove as Mom comes into the kitchen. She drops a bag onto the table and hurries over to me, kicking away the noodles. "Are you okay? The front door was wide open."

She takes my arm and guides me to a chair at the table. "Here. Sit. You shouldn't be on your feet. Why aren't you resting?"

I'm only half listening.

WITCH.

They were right *here*. While I was unconscious.

I shudder convulsively and lay my head on the table. Who would do something like that?

"The door was open?" I ask, turning my head to look up at Mom. "Did you close it? Lock it?"

"Of course." She smooths my hair and frowns. "Are you all right?"

I point toward the pasta with a shaky hand. "I was going to cook dinner," I say. "And I spilled the noodles." But the letters are gone, scattered by Mom's footsteps.

She makes a dismissive gesture. "I'll clean it up later. I got takeout from the Thai place downtown."

She bustles around the kitchen as I sit in a fog, trying to grab on to the disjointed thoughts that swirl in my head.

Someone was in the house. *Next* to me.

Are they still here? Hiding? Waiting?

I've heard about people who hide in the unused spaces of homes and live there undetected. Lord knows we have plenty of unused space.

Mom sets a plate down in front of me and I jump.

"They had the peanut butter curry you love. I also got some pad thai. And spring rolls."

I put a spoonful of each on my plate and swirl my fork through the noodles.

I closed the door when I came in. Which means whoever *was* here opened it to leave.

Unless that's what I'm supposed to believe.

My head is pounding. I press my palms against my eyebrows. "Someone was in the house," I say. I didn't plan on telling her, but it slips out. She needs to know. So we can do something.

"Kurt told me, at dinner—" she breaks off. "My god. Was that just last night?" Her eyes well up with tears and she clears her throat. "I'm sorry that happened. I'm sure it was really scary. But it was most likely someone who thought the house was empty and wanted to sneak a peek inside. Now that they know we're here, I'm sure they won't come back."

She's just parroting Kurt's words. Every single person I've met so far has known who I am and where I live. "That's not—" I stop.

She's crying silently, big tears slipping down her face and into her plate of food. She's a broken woman, and I can't break her anymore. "Can we do a sleepover tonight?" I ask instead.

I've never had a problem with insomnia. Usually, fatigue is my foe. I spend most of my time fighting to stay awake, grateful when I can finally give in and let sleep claim me. But tonight, I lie awake long after Mom has fallen asleep, listening to her soft snore in the bed beside me and the noises of the house behind her bedroom door.

Should I have told her about the intruder tonight? Clarified that this has happened more than once? This is more than some nosy neighbor or kids looking for an empty house to party in—I'm being targeted.

But I couldn't bring myself to hurt her more. Plus, I'm not sure she would have believed me.

What I need is proof.

What do I know so far?

They don't seem to want to hurt me, whoever they are; I was completely vulnerable tonight and all they did was try to scare me before running away.

That thought calms me. I don't know what they want—yet—but I've still got the upper hand. Because they don't know how strong I can be. They don't know that I'm a fighter.

Whoever this mysterious stalker is, I can't blame them for thinking I'm weak. Every time they see me, I pass out. The other night I ended up in the hospital. Tonight, I was out cold on the kitchen floor. That's maybe the worst thing about being sick—the loss of control. It's also the thing no one talks about. I can't control what makes me tired, or how bad my headaches get, or how long I need to sleep in order to recover some semblance of normal.

But finding out who's doing this?

That I can control.

I slip out of bed and crack the door, holding my breath as Mom snorts in her sleep and rolls over. The hallway is inky black and I almost lose my nerve.

But if I'm not going to sleep tonight, I might as well get some answers. As my eyes adjust, I make my way to my bedroom and shut the door before flipping on the light. Then I check under the bed and in the closet before settling at my desk with my laptop.

Bryn's not online, which doesn't surprise me. It is Friday night and unlike me, they have a social life.

WYA?

I send Bryn a snap, hoping they'll answer.

In a few seconds, they send back a blurry photo of a familiar neon sign.

Hanging at Erma's hbu?

Someone was in my house again. Left me a message—WITCH—spelled out on the floor

WTF

Bryn types.

Then,

Who was it?

Emory?

I respond: Maybe. But why?

I know what's happening to you. Who did you see?

Who? That very specific question knocked me off guard in the hospital, and there's no better explanation now. Either Emory does know what's going on, or she's a really good guesser.

She also didn't deny breaking in.

Then again, Clare also looked shifty when I mentioned the break in. And she hadn't been at school the day someone trashed my library.

And then there's Sage. He was here earlier, doing yard work that no one asked him to do. And he asked me about the witch mere hours before someone spelled out that very word on the floor beside my head.

But why? If it is any of them, why mess with me like this? Why pretend to be my friend and then try to scare the shit out of me? Because I'm the new girl? Because they've all lived here forever and I'm the outsider and they're bored?

Or is it something else?

Bryn is clearly thinking along the same lines.

What does she want?

Then:

It all comes down to motive

I roll my eyes and type,

This isn't CSI

Nah more like Paranormal Investigators.
Those guys stage shit all the time

This wasn't stag—

I delete my text. They're right. If I look past the absolute creepiness of it, there was definitely a theatrical tone to the noodle message. I could have opened my eyes at any moment and seen whoever it was. Why risk it? Just to scare me?

Or maybe someone is scared of *me*. From the beginning, everyone I've met has been strangely focused on who I am and who I'm related to. And more specifically, where I live.

What if this is about the house?

One need not be a house to be haunted.

Emily Dickinson, I shoot back. But point deduction for misquoting.

It's actually "One need not be a chamber to be haunted," and I shiver at the reference.

I'm not haunted, at least not in the literal sense. But I am becoming like everyone in this godforsaken town—obsessed with my house and the witch who lived here. This is where it all started, after all. The healing and the stories.

The dying.

When the intruder broke into the library that first time, they were looking for something. Something important enough they didn't care if they trashed the place to find it. My grandmother's scrapbooks are missing. But what if that isn't all they wanted? What if they didn't find whatever it was, so they had to come back?

Maybe some clue to what they were looking for is still here.

I eye my bedroom door, considering the darkness beyond. It's a false security, the idea that I'm safer in the daylight. Real monsters walk around us every day, and sunshine isn't going to keep anyone from hurting you if they really want to.

It hasn't yet.

Still, do I want to go wandering around this big old house in the dark by myself?

Then again, will I be able to sleep if I don't?

Gtg look for clues in the haunted house alone in the dark, I text, half hoping they'll try to talk me out of it.

Their response is swift.

GREAT IDEA TEXT ME AS SOON AS YOU FIND SOME!!!
Also isn't your mom home?

And finally,

If you turn on the lights it'll be easier to see the clues

Bryn is right. Again.

Plus, whoever was here earlier is gone. I hope.

I look around for a weapon, but don't see anything inherently dangerous in the immediate vicinity. For now, I give my new teddy a quick squeeze for courage, grab my phone, take a deep breath, and pull open the door, stepping quickly into the hall to throw on the lights. The warm glow of electricity floods the empty hallway and I breathe a sigh of relief.

Nobody's here. Just me and my shadow.

I listen at the top of the stairs, but the house is quiet, so I creep slowly down, one step at a time. I flip on the lights in the living room, the dining room, and the kitchen for good measure. If anyone is here, they aren't going to take me by surprise. And if anyone is considering breaking in, maybe they'll see the lights and think twice. After all, they don't know it's me. It could be my mom, suffering from insomnia. Or Kurt. Nobody knows he moved out yet.

This rational thinking makes me feel almost normal.

Time to search the library.

I love this room—in the daylight. At night it's gloomy, the lamplight throwing up odd shadows against the wood-paneled walls and turning the many windows into useless mirrors reflecting back my own distorted image. I grab a fireplace poker and set my shoulders, turning my back to the darkness beyond.

I straightened up in here the other day at Kurt's request, but not as well as I could have. The bookcase against the far wall is still a haphazard jumble where I'd attempted to reshelve the books. Now that I'm really looking, it's obvious that all the tossed books were from one section.

I pace slowly, studying the titles. What's so special about these books? Almost all are cheap mass market paperbacks. If I were looking for something important, this is probably the last shelf I'd go to. Nearer the fireplace, those shelves are filled with expensive-looking picture frames and other memorabilia—vases, a small clock, a gold-dipped rosebud. And the bookcase to my left is stacked with old leather-bound hardbacks, the gold-embossed spines faded from years of use. All of it looks much more promising than the entire bibliography of Stephen King.

Does that mean they *didn't* find what they were looking for? It's always in the last place you look, which means this chaos could be evidence of a last-ditch effort to find . . . what?

I grab a handful of the paperback novels and shove them from one side of the shelf to the other, my frustration mirroring what I imagine my intruder must have felt.

But as I reach for the next batch, something shifts.

I use the poker to brace myself as I lose my balance and catch the edge of the bookcase with my shoulder. I push away from the wall as the shelf gives way, spilling the books onto the floor.

I grab my throbbing shoulder and stumble backward, confusion clearing to understanding and then plummeting straight to horror as I stare past the tilted shelf and into the inky blackness of the opening beyond.

It's a secret passage.

CHAPTER 28

Is this how someone's been getting into my house?

The bookcase has only tilted about forty-five degrees, but it's big enough for a person to slip through. I fumble with my phone, turning on the flashlight to illuminate the darkness. The opening beyond is framed in stone, and stone steps twist down around a corner. The cold air wafting out smells dank, sour. Like wet earth and rotting fruit.

Where does it lead? To the basement? Or outside?

Is someone in there now?

My hand wobbles and the light jumps, knocking the opening back into shadow. I shove against the bookcase with all I have. Once the passage is closed, my gaze skitters around the room. The fear and the adrenaline have thrown everything into high relief. Is that the refrigerator, or someone kicking in the door? Is that fireplace real or another hidden passage? Nothing is what it seems, and everything is a threat.

My heart is a jackhammer and I press a hand to my chest, forcing the air out, then back in. *Breathe. Swallow back the bile. Think.*

The club chair. It's squat and solid. I shove at it, banging my hip against the arm, but it doesn't budge.

I work the chair legs onto a throw rug, one at a time, then slowly slide it across the floor. It takes all the strength I have, and I'm still not sure this is going to work. I don't know what kind of mechanism opens the shelf from the other side. Is it something with enough force to shove the chair out of the way? It toppled all the books, after all.

I don't have it in me to move any more furniture. Instead, I grab the bulbous hurricane lamp off the side table and balance it on the arm of the chair. It's not going to add any weight, but there's no way to move the chair without breaking the lamp. If I can't keep them out, at least I'll know they're here.

Whoever they are.

I need to know who's been using this opening, as well as where it leads, but even I'm not stupid enough to head down there in the dead of night by myself. Maybe in the morning. Maybe with—

But there isn't anyone I can trust.

If Bryn were here, they'd go with me in a heartbeat. But they're a thousand miles away.

I rub my eyes. I can't think about that right now.

I wander through the rest of the house, scanning the walls and scratching at my bare arms. I'm clammy and sweaty, my skin tight and hot. As the adrenaline wears off, I start to shake.

Who's to say that's the only secret door? An old house like this, it could be riddled with hidden tunnels. I don't know where to begin. In the kitchen, I eye the basement door, the one that doesn't latch properly.

I hesitate for only a second before shoving the kitchen table in front of it.

I'm not taking any more chances.

Moving the table saps my last bit of energy. I'm blurry eyed and buzzy, nearly dead on my feet. Too tired to search the rest of the house tonight. I leave the lights on and head to my bedroom, checking the walls and the closet before barricading myself in and collapsing on the bed, immediately falling into the deep pit of oblivion.

Bong, bong, bong, bong.

I wake to the sound of church bells, which is how I know it's Sunday.

Only as I crawl out of the depths of sleep and out from under my comforter, I realize it isn't bells. And I don't think it's Sunday.

It's that godawful doorbell.

I pull my dresser away from the door and stumble into the hallway as the bonging starts up again.

"Mom?" I call, my voice echoing down the stairs. "Someone's at the door."

I hurry down the stairs and peer out the window. Fletcher is standing on my front porch, flanked by Dominic and a pretty woman in yoga pants and a messy bun. He jumps when I throw open the door, and I'm not sure if he's startled by the movement or by my appearance. I touch my hair self-consciously, painfully aware of my thin tank top and pajama shorts.

"Hey, Lola," he says. He's wearing a Janis Joplin tee today—a nod to our date yesterday? His curls are wet, like he just got out of the shower. "Did we wake you?"

The sun is high in the sky behind him, so it's at least noon, if not later. Do I admit to still being in bed at this hour? Or is it better to let them think I just hang around the house like this all day?

"What time is it?" I ask instead.

Beside him, his mom glances at her smartwatch. She looks like the photos Fletcher showed me, and like the girl from the memory in the attic, a bit older but still recognizable.

"Two thirty. Totally understandable. You've been through a lot and you need your rest. I made you supper. Green chile enchiladas and my famous cornbread salad. Don't worry, there's no flour in it. Fletcher tells me you're gluten-free. Is your mom home?" She rattles off the information so rapidly, I'm almost out of breath by the time she's done.

"Thank—yes—I mean, no. I think she went to work." I stumble over the words as my brain plays catch-up.

"I'm Natalie. You can call me Nat." She shoves the casserole dish into Fletcher's hands and reaches for me, her smile large and her arms wide. "It's so nice to finally meet you!" She pulls me into a hug that goes on longer than I expect. "How are you feeling? We've all been so worried! Fletcher most of all."

"We just wanted to stop by and make sure everything was okay," Dominic says, rescuing Fletcher, whose face has gone beet red. "There are a couple things I wanted to check on, but we don't need to bother you if you're not up to it. We'll just leave the food and get out of your way."

He moves to take it from Fletcher, but he's too slow. Instead, Nat grabs it and moves toward me. "Absolutely. Right after I show you how to warm it up."

"Mom," Fletcher groans softly. "I'm sure she knows how to heat up food."

"It's fine," I say, stepping back to let them in, since it looks like Nat is coming in either way.

They file in, Fletcher lingering to whisper "I'm so sorry" as I close the door.

I smile at him, lips clamped shut since he's standing close enough to be knocked over by my morning breath. Or I guess afternoon breath at this point.

"Tress has done so much already," Nat marvels, looking around the living room. "It looks lived in again."

I can't tell if she means it as a compliment, or if "lived-in" is code for messy. "You can take that to the kitchen," I say, gesturing toward the hall, but she's already heading in that direction. It's clear she knows the house, but how well?

Does she know about the secret passage in the library?

I start to follow her, then detour up the stairs. "You can just . . . make yourselves at home," I call, hoping that's still something normal people say. "I'll be right back." I turn and sprint to my bedroom, groaning as I catch sight of myself in the mirror. My face is creased from sleep and my hair is flat on one side and sticking up on the other. I grab a bra and some sweatpants and then run into the bathroom to wet my hair and do a furious thirty-second toothbrushing.

Fletcher is waiting in the hallway when I open the door, but I catch myself before I scream. "What are you doing up here?" I glance toward my bedroom. The door is ajar, but I might have left it that way. Was he in there?

He scuffs his shoe against the floor and jams his hands in his pockets, then takes them out again. "I just wanted to apologize for my parents. I told them I wanted to talk to you and they insisted on coming along."

"Talk to me about what?" I ask, and he ducks his head.

He looks nervous.

Or guilty.

Does he know about the hidden passage? Has he been using it?

My heart plummets, *Titanic*-like. I really don't want it to be him.

"Fletcher!" Nat calls. "Come help your father!"

Fletcher grimaces. "Maybe we can talk later?"

"About what?" I ask, but when he doesn't answer I have no choice but to follow him back down to the kitchen.

Nat has brewed coffee. She definitely took "make yourself at home" to heart.

"There you are!" She clutches a mug to her chest when she sees us in the doorway. "I always knew our kids would be friends. I only wish Teddy were here to see it."

She has no idea how much I wish that, too.

"Fletcher, help me move this table while the ladies chat," Dominic says.

"How about you, Lola? You look pale." Nat peers at me closely, then sets down her coffee and fills a water glass. "Here. You need to stay hydrated."

I take the glass, struggling to speak over the surge of panic that tightens my throat as her husband shoves the table, exposing the basement door. "Why are you moving that?"

Dominic frowns. "It's dangerous to keep that door blocked. You've got your furnace and your water heater down there, not to mention all the electrical and pipes. If there's a problem, or a fire, you need to get at it quickly. You'd never be able to move it by yourself."

I don't tell him I did exactly that only twelve hours ago.

"Lola? Are you all right?" Nat asks.

"I'm better," I say, struggling to keep my voice even. "Altitude. Who knew?"

"We knew," she says fretfully. "And we should have warned you. Fletcher told us about the nosebleed the other day, and I am kicking myself that I didn't have Dom check in on you."

"Yeah," I say, only half listening. "It's just that . . . we like it there. The table." I slosh water onto the counter as I cross my arms over my chest.

Nat continues, "It's something we always tell the kids to watch out for." Her bun wobbles back and forth as she shakes her head.

"It's no one's fault," I say. "I'm not from the mountains. Sage says you call it a flatlander."

Dominic huffs out a breath that could be a curse or a laugh and Fletcher winces. "Mom, chill. She said she was fine. You're going to scare her off."

A weird choice of words, given that someone *is* trying to scare me off. Someone who knows the house. "That basement door keeps popping open. The table keeps it shut."

Dominic plays with the door for a second, trying to get the lock to catch. "We can install a hook and eye," he says. "That should solve the problem."

Will a hook and eye keep anyone out? Or is he suggesting it because it will be easy to bypass?

Nat, meanwhile, is still talking. "I'll just put everything in the fridge. The enchiladas can be heated at three twenty-five for about thirty minutes. The salad is ready to eat."

"Thank you. I wanted to—"

"Oh, it wasn't any bother. I was making dinner for Amber anyway. She's got so much on her plate, what with all those kids and being sick. I'm just glad she lets us. She used to be too proud—no charity, all that." She waves a hand. "But I told her, Amber, people want to help. Let them."

Let them help? Is this a subtle hint to me? Maybe they're here because they want to help. Or maybe they want me to make myself vulnerable.

"Speaking of helping, I told Tress I'd check the fireplace flues," Dominic says, heading toward the front of the house.

Is that a real thing? Or is he making an excuse to search the house? I set my cup down and go after him.

"Lola, wait." Fletcher follows me into the corridor, standing too close when I turn around. The warmth of the previous day comes flooding back. I like him; why does that feel so dangerous?

"Did you know about the secret passage?" I ask, the words coming out in a rush.

He pulls back, looking genuinely puzzled, but that could be an act. All of it could be an act. From the moment we met, he's seemed overly excited to meet me, to spend time with me. Why is that?

"What do you want from me?" It's a throwaway question born more out of exhaustion than any real expectation of an answer.

But his face goes beet red, and he runs both hands through his hair. "Look, I know this probably isn't a good time. I should have said something earlier. At the séance, or definitely yesterday. But I chickened out."

My stomach drops. "What are you talking about?"

But I already know. He's going to admit to everything—the break-in and the theft. And I am going to put on my big-girl panties and kick him out, and then put any ideas of romance away for good.

He reaches for my hand, tugging me gently to face him and I square my shoulders as I wait for the confession.

"There's a school dance. On Friday night. Will you go with me?"

I'm breathless and dizzy, in an emotional freefall, and I can almost hear the clunk as my brain switches gears. "Are you . . . asking me on a date right now?"

A crash resonates from somewhere deep in the house, the tinkling of shattered glass echoing in the silence.

Nat is beside us, wiping her hands on a towel. "What on earth . . . ?"

Fuck.

I run for the library, where Dominic is kneeling in front of my makeshift barricade, carefully picking up the larger pieces of the shattered hurricane lamp.

"What are you doing?" I ask.

"Why is this here?" he counters.

"You know, don't you?" I say, circling around the back of the chair, giving him a wide berth. Why was he trying to move it?

Fletcher stares at the ground and rubs the back of his neck, while Nat and Dominic exchange a look. Dominic hesitates before saying, "Teddy and I used to use it." He scratches his beard. "But that can't be . . ." he trails off.

"Where does it go?"

"Nowhere anymore. John Henry—your granddad—he blocked it off a long time ago."

"It was open last night," I say.

"You found it that way?" Dominic asks sharply.

"Well, no. I . . . fell against the shelf and it moved."

His shoulders sag in relief. "That's okay, then."

"What do you mean, it's okay?" I ask. "It's the opposite of okay. Someone's been using this to sneak into my house."

From over Dominic's shoulder, I see Fletcher checking his phone. His face is pinched as he slides it back into his pocket. Was he texting someone?

Dominic blinks. "That's not possible. The tunnel, technically, does still open on this end, but it's blocked off on the other end. Now it's basically just a hidey-hole."

The *tunnel*. Like in my memory.

He continues, "If someone was in the house, they didn't get in this way."

I think about the books scattered across the floor.

If someone was in the house.

Is he lying? Or just like every other adult in my life who thinks this is some pathetic bid for attention?

"Are there more tunnels?" I ask instead. "Other ways into the house I don't know about?"

"Not that I'm aware of."

I don't know why I bothered to ask. There's no way for me to know if he's telling the truth. I want to stomp my feet and scream in frustration. Instead, I take a breath and force myself to ask calmly, "Is there something about this house that I should know? A reason someone would want to break in? Something they'd be looking for?"

I stare at them all, wishing I could read their minds. Willing them to tell me the truth. When no one speaks, I continue, "I've heard the story about Rebecca. And the healing waters—"

"Fletcher, you didn't!" Nat cries.

"It was mostly Clare and Emory," he mumbles, shrinking under Nat's disappointed glare.

His phone chirps and he stares at the screen for a moment before slipping out of the room.

"Your dad *hated* that story," says Nat as the front door slams shut. "Said it made people crazy."

I look between them, my mind whirring. Does that mean this all happened to him, too? Is that why the tunnel got closed off? To keep weird witch-hunters off the property? "Did someone break in back then, too?"

"Break in? No." Nat shakes her head. "But there was always that stigma, you know? His house was haunted, he was the descendant of a witch. Even we got caught up in it. Like that time in the attic, with the Ouija board. The answer is in our blood—" Nat stops herself again. "But we don't talk about that. It's disrespectful to Teddy."

It takes a second, but then her words hit me like a dull hammer and I feel woozy.

I sink onto the window bench, my legs wobbly. "Where did you hear that?" I whisper, but Nat isn't listening.

"I actually think that stupid witch story is the reason Tress wouldn't consider moving back here until now."

Her previous words are still echoing in my head, so it takes me a second to latch on to the significance of these. "Wait. Did you say moving . . . back? Did my mom live here?"

"Nat! We talked about this—" Dominic lays a hand on her shoulder, but she pulls away.

"Well, I'm sorry. I know Tress didn't want her to know, but I really don't understand why it has to be this big secret." Nat is shorter than her husband, but as she pulls herself up and juts her chin at him, I wouldn't bet against her in a fight.

Dominic looks unmoved by his wife's determination. "I'm sure Tress has her reasons. And she asked me—us"—he gives Nat a hard look—"not to bring it up, and I respect that."

I don't think he's going to budge on this; his loyalty to my mom outweighs whatever pull I might have as Teddy's daughter.

Before I have time to test that theory, Mom clears her throat from the doorway. "Tell me again how much you respect me, Dom."

CHAPTER 29

For a moment, no one speaks. Mom's words hang in the air like heavy smog. Nat and Dominic's discomfort is so palpable it makes my skin itch. The grandfather clock in the hall ticks off eleven seconds that feel more like minutes before Mom speaks. "Lola, can you give us a moment?"

All I want is for somebody to tell me the truth. Whatever they're about to say to each other, I deserve to hear it. I set my jaw, ready to argue, but Mom knows me too well.

She folds her arms across her chest. "Lola Joy!" It's her "no arguing or else" voice. "Please go entertain your guest."

Fletcher. I've forgotten he's still here.

I turn away, my whole body vibrating with anger and humiliation. She knows she's been caught in a lie, and she doesn't even try and apologize. Instead, she sends me away like I'm some fragile child. I'm furious at Dominic, too, and at Nat. They're all lying. This whole fucking town is blanketed with lies. But Mom's lies are personal, so they hurt more.

Fletcher jumps off the edge of the porch wall when I come storming out.

"Hey!" His smile fades as he catches sight of my face. "What's wrong? What happened?"

"My mom happened," I say, clenching my fists.

"She didn't look all that happy to see me," Fletcher admits, "especially when I told her my parents were here, too."

"Damn it, Fletcher! What's going on? Why can't anyone just tell me the truth?" I'm so filled with anger-fueled adrenaline, I'm practically levitating. I pace back and forth, trying to burn off the energy. From the corner of my eye, I see him take a tentative step toward me, then retreat.

Finally, he clears his throat. "I know how this must look. Like some big conspiracy, right? Like we're hiding something from you. But I promise it's not what you think. The water story is just a story." He holds up his hands.

"What about the tunnel? And the break-in?"

He grabs for my hand. "I know it's a lot to take in. But I'm here. I want to help."

There's a weight to his voice that wasn't there before.

But before he can continue, I pull my hand back and ask, "Did you know? About the tunnel?"

He hesitates. "I . . . know. I mean, I know this town. And the people here. I can keep you safe."

He can't even give me a straight answer.

"Is that a yes or a no?"

"I would never break into your house. You have to believe that."

I want to believe it. And that's the problem. He denied breaking in, but he didn't deny knowing about the tunnel. What does that mean, other than that I can't trust my instincts, not with his stupid handsome face and goofy smile and all these feelings clouding my judgment? Maybe Fletcher's not the one who's been creeping around my house. But the odds are awfully good that he knows who it is. Because if it's not him, it's someone he knows.

"Who was that on your phone before?" I ask.

He frowns and lifts his hand to his pocket. "When? No one."

"You left the room to answer it."

An emotion ripples across his face, too fast for me to read it. Is it recognition? Fear? Pity?

"It was just a text. From Clare. I told her I was coming over and she asked me to grab their rake."

"Their rake." Right. Sage was doing yard work with it yesterday when we got back from the hospital. Was that just yesterday? "Why didn't Sage take it with him?"

Fletcher looks embarrassed. "I guess he left in a hurry. Something about your mom and Kurt arguing."

So much for keeping Mom's breakup quiet.

I've got more pressing problems, but Fletcher doesn't give me time to think about any of them. "So, what do you think? About the dance? Will you go with me?"

He stares at me with those big brown eyes, and a grave expression that is both serious and hopeful at once.

There are at least a dozen reasons I shouldn't trust him. I don't even really know him. Is he the shy, nerdy guy from the bear sanctuary? Or a calculating player? Does he really like me, or is this some kind of game?

Before I can decide, the front door opens.

"I'm sure it was just an act of charity," Nat is saying. She catches my eye as Fletcher and I spring apart. "People want to help—"

"By paying off those back taxes, you could make a claim on the house," Mom says.

A claim on the house? What the hell is she talking about? Why would they want our house? I look at Fletcher, who's watching his dad.

"It wasn't us, Tress," Dominic says, his voice tight.

"Who was it, then?" Mom asks. "And what reason would they possibly have to pay off my debt?"

Nat bites her lip. "I can't say. But it doesn't necessarily mean they're after your home."

Fletcher says, "Maybe it was Mr. Zeller. The tax thing, I mean."

Mr. Zeller? Why would Fletcher think that Emory's dad would anonymously pay off our taxes?

Nat fidgets with her bun again. "It's not a good idea to speculate—"

Fletcher says, "You're the one who said an act of charity. And Mr. Z loves this house. He knows how important it is to the community. Remember all that work on it he did, when he lived here?"

Random pieces of information click into place. Dominic and Mom talking on our first day about how the place had been rented out to pay for the upkeep. Emory's odd reaction when we first met, the way she wandered through the house. Like she'd been there before. *Where's your furniture?* she'd asked. Because she knew the things inside weren't ours.

My skin pimples with gooseflesh and I rub my arms. Emory used to live here.

Why didn't anyone tell me that?

After I say goodbye to Fletcher and his parents, I go back inside to find Mom in the kitchen.

"Have you eaten yet today? Nat made these lovely enchiladas. Would you mind grabbing the salad from the fridge?"

Someone who doesn't know her as well as I do might describe her tone as cool or breezy, but I can feel the bite of the finely sharpened edge. There's no Kurt here to soften either of our verbal blows, and while she's trying hard to keep her temper in check—as evidenced by the white-knuckle grip she has on Nat's casserole dish—I'm feeling reckless. Too much has gone unsaid for far too long, and I'm ready to rip all the wounds wide open and let them bleed.

"You're going to eat Nat's food? I assumed you'd dump it straight into the trash on principle."

She slams the dish to the counter and reaches to massage her temples. "Please, Lola. Can we not do this right now? It's been a long day. Let's just have a nice, quiet dinner."

"I know how much you love quiet." I fight to keep my voice steady. "It's that easy for you, isn't it? You just shut your mouth and leave me in the dark. How about you give me a list of all the things you'd rather not talk about? My dad's accident."

I start counting off on my fingers. "Emory. The fact that you lived *here* before dad died! There's a freaking tunnel into our home." I grab a fistful of my hair. "What am I missing? Do you actually know what's wrong with me?"

"That's not fair!"

"I know! I thought we were a team. That's what you always said, right? And now, it's like all of it was a lie! You've been here before. You know this house! Why would you lie about that?"

"All right." She pulls a bottle of wine out of the fridge and sets it on the counter, bracing herself before she speaks. "Yes, I lived here. Your father and I originally came out to spend some time with his friends and to clean out the house." She bites her lip. "But we fell in love with the possibilities here, and so we decided to extend our stay. We put the Michigan house on the market."

I stand frozen in place as she erases my whole life's history with one careless swipe.

She continues, "And then the accident happened and . . . it was something I never wanted to think about again. So I went back to Michigan. And for a long time, I didn't have to." She pauses, staring at the ceiling as she blinks and works her jaw. "I never made a conscious decision to lie to you about it. It was just . . . really hard to talk about. Nat had just found out she was pregnant with Fletcher when we were here. We joked about the two of you being friends. But then Teddy was gone and I was alone and it was all just too painful. They were this happy family, you know? I don't mean that we weren't happy. But I just . . ." She clears her throat. "I couldn't come back here. I couldn't face it. Everything Teddy and I talked about building, together—it's still here." She stares out the window, at another time and place, as she dashes a tear with the back of her wrist.

I brace myself, one hand on the refrigerator. Afraid to interrupt, afraid almost to breathe. This is the most she's ever told me, and I don't want to stop her.

"I was going to tell you, eventually. Then Kurt found out about the house, and he was so adamant about trying to sell it. But I knew that I owed it to Teddy to honor his wishes—to keep it for you, at least until you were old enough to make your own decision about it." She takes a ragged breath.

"Kurt was always so insecure when I would bring up your father. I mean, talk about a red flag!" She shakes her head once, hard. "The first time he mentioned the house, I told him I'd never been out here. It was a knee-jerk reaction, just to keep him from asking more questions. I said that I was holding on to it for you, which was true. And since I'd never told you differently, there was no reason for him not to believe it." Her lips quiver. "And then we all got caught up in the whole 'new family, new start' thing and it felt like it was too late to say anything." She chokes out a sob.

There are a dozen things I want to say, none of them good. Instead I ask, "Is it over? With Kurt, I mean?"

She balls her hands into fists and presses them to her eyes. "I made some rash decisions—and now I'm going to have to sort them out." She sighs, then continues, "A widow at twenty-three and a divorcée by forty. Great track record."

The end of her marriage is taking a lot of the wind out of my anger. It's hard to hold a grudge in the face of her obvious suffering. There were times I'd thought she was rushing into things with Kurt; Bryn and I had talked about that very subject exhaustively. But this is something altogether different. This split is lightning quick, a bolt of electricity that's cleaved her whole life in two, and I'm not sure what she needs me to say. What do I know about marriage? I don't have any role models in this particular area.

I put an awkward arm around her shoulders. "You can't help what happened to Dad. And you certainly shouldn't stay married just because you don't like the label." I pull her toward me, and she lays her head on my shoulder. "Honestly, we should probably be thanking Kurt. Like you said, if it weren't for him, we probably wouldn't have ended up here."

Her face is blank as she tilts her head to look at me. "And do you think that's a good thing?"

Our eyes lock and I know she's thinking about the trip to the hospital.

"I'm sorry," I say. "About the other night. If the . . . bonfire was too much. If that made things worse. I would have cleaned up . . ."

"None of that matters," she says, wiping her face with the back of her hand. "I'm just glad you're okay. When I got home and saw those lights . . ." Her voice catches on a sob and she reaches out to squeeze my arm, her fingers digging into my shoulder.

You're killing us.

I gasp and pull free, clutching at the counter for support. I spin around to cover my freak-out, wrenching open the fridge and grabbing the first item I see—a bottle of ketchup. I set it beside the enchilada pan. "What about Emory?" I change the subject. "Did you know she used to live here? When you invited her over that night?"

She takes her time pouring herself a glass of wine, filling it nearly to the top. "I didn't invite her. I invited Clare. When she introduced herself, I recognized her name. But that wasn't . . . I wasn't hiding anything. I just assumed she'd tell you. I don't know why she didn't."

"Because she's messing with me. She's the one who talked me into the séance the other night—"

"A séance? Is that what you were doing out there?" She looks at me, her eyes wide. "Were you trying to reach your dad?"

"I . . . No. Not like that." She's been honest with me, but it still feels like too little, too late. Like if she hadn't been pushed into a corner, she never would have shared any of this with me. I'm not ready to tell her about the memories. "There's a tunnel, in the library. I think Emory's the one who's been sneaking in; she probably found it when she lived here. Did Dom show you?"

She gulps her wine and fiddles with her wedding ring.

"You already knew." I slump into a chair, defeated. "Of course you did. Because you lived here." There's no end to the secrets. Just when I think we've uncovered them all, more surface. I feel like I'm falling down a deep, dark pit, and there's no bottom. Just darkness.

"I never used it, but Teddy mentioned it." She refills her glass. "Honestly, I'd forgotten all about it. Dom says it's been blocked off for years."

I sit up and bang my hands on the table, making her jump. "Someone is using it! They trashed the library. And stole Dad's albums. Kurt told you all this, right?"

She inclines her head, the slightest affirmation.

"So why are you so calm? They've gone through our things. Stole from us. All the pictures I had of him, they're all gone. Who knows what else they took!"

"Lola, honey. You need to calm down. The police seemed to think there was another explanation, other than an intruder."

What other explanation could there be? Does she mean she suspects me? Or Kurt?

I open my mouth and she holds up a hand. "As for the photos, they probably just got misplaced in the move. They'll turn up."

I gape at her, this woman on the edge of a nervous breakdown, so focused on her own pain she has no room for her own daughter. She's a stranger to me. A stranger who has been keeping her own secrets all along.

Maybe there's something in the albums she doesn't want me to see.

I tilt my head. "Did you take them?"

She trills a hollow-sounding laugh that is drowned out by the chiming of the oven as it finishes preheating. "Don't be silly. Why would I do that?"

It isn't actually a denial. And as she gets up to put the food into the oven and pull plates out of the cupboard, I can't help but think of her secret box, filled with clippings about my father's death.

What else is she hiding?

CHAPTER 30

Fletcher offers to pick me up for school, and given that the alternative is riding with Mom, I say yes and try not to overthink the implications. Does this mean he's going to ask me to the dance again? Does he think we're a couple? Is that just what other people will think when they see us together?

I need to get back to low-key Lola. I'm not sure she really exists, but Fletcher saw me that way, that first day. Low-key Lola goes with the flow. She's chill. No drama.

I wish I knew how I pulled that off, because I could use some low-key vibes today. I need answers, and no one is going to give them to me if I'm passing out and spewing blood all over the place.

I'm certainly not going to dwell on the fact that I woke up feeling crappy again, like my legs are filled with sludge. Whatever miracle drugs they'd given me at the hospital have worn off, and I'm back to struggling to stay upright. I guess it was too much to hope that the altitude sickness and my subsequent recovery might somehow wipe the slate clean.

When Fletcher's Jeep pulls up near the porch, something in me lightens, like an infusion of bubbles right into my bloodstream. Just seeing him makes me feel better.

And that scares the shit out of me.

"Just us?" I ask, peering into the empty back seat as I stow my backpack.

"That okay? Emory's riding with Clare."

"Fine. Great. Super!" I bite my tongue to hold back any further superlatives. I've bypassed chill Lola and somehow morphed into cheerleader Lola.

"Everything okay?" he asks, glancing over at me before he puts the car in gear.

Sweat beads on my forehead. I am literally the opposite of chill.

"No more . . . problems at your house?" he continues.

I fumble with the seat belt. "You mean the tunnel? Nope. It's closed off, right?"

"That's what my dad said." He flexes his hands on the steering wheel, and it occurs to me he might be as nervous as I am.

Because he likes me? Or because he's hiding something?

"How's your mom?" he asks.

"She's going through some stuff. Actually, she asked Kurt to move out."

He pulls a face. "That's gotta be tough. Have they been married long?"

"A few weeks?" I say.

Fletcher whistles. "That was quick."

"Yeah, well, it's possible she rushed into things. Because of the move."

And because of me. Kurt had better insurance, and although Mom denied it, red-faced and blustery when I'd asked, I can't believe it didn't factor into her decision at least a little bit. But I don't tell Fletcher this. It makes her sound cold and calculating, which she isn't.

"Has she been married before? Besides your dad, I mean."

"Nope. She rarely even dated before Kurt. She always told me she didn't have time for that. But Kurt was persistent. And, I mean, she probably doesn't want to be alone. When I go to college or whatever." I have to stop. I'm making her sound like some kind of lonesome, grasping widow. "I'm not being fair. It's just been a lot of changes, really quickly. For all of us. So I guess there's bound to be some . . . hiccups." As I say it, I realize that's all this is. She isn't going to get *divorced*. Not after a month.

The idea leaves me a bit deflated, as if I've been holding my breath, waiting for the inevitable disappointment. Which is a terrible thing to wish on my own mother. "I want her to be happy. She deserves the best," I say. Though I'm pretty sure "the best" isn't a petty and selfish daughter.

But I'm not sure it's Kurt, either.

I roll down my window and let the mountain breeze cool my face. "Honestly, it's probably not going to stick. The separation, I mean. Up until a few days ago, my mom seemed pretty smitten."

"Personally, I don't see the appeal." Fletcher gives me a lopsided grin. "He was kind of a dick the other night, after the ambulance had left. He was in a pretty big hurry to kick us off the property."

"Don't feel bad, he's a dick to everyone. Except my mom. Usually." I feel like I should say something about the fact that my mom is finally standing up for me, taking my side against Kurt, but I'm not sure I trust her rediscovered loyalty yet. "He certainly doesn't like me."

"Don't say that."

"No, it's true. He thinks I'm a hypochondriac. And that Mom enables me, or babies me. Or both."

"That explains why he was so weird that day, after I brought you home from the reservoir."

"He's an ass," I say. "But he has a point. I do rely on my mom a lot. Too much, maybe. She deserves to be happy, too."

I just don't know what makes her happy anymore. *I don't owe anyone my pain. Not even you.* Because she's already given me everything else?

"So you're saying you find it comforting to have your mom tell you everything's going to be all right? That doesn't make you weak. It just makes you human."

I have the sudden urge to kiss him. He barely knows me, yet he's being kinder to me than some of the people I've known all my life. For a second, I let myself forget that I don't trust him.

"Yes," I say.

"You agree?" He sounds surprised.

"Yes, I'll go to the dance with you."

"Really?!" He beams at me, his grin pure sunshine, and I bask in the glow of this pretend relationship.

It feels amazing.

Which is how I know it can't last.

The quad is quiet today. The energy of the first week has been replaced with weary acceptance as a smattering of classmates cluster together in groups, clutching coffee cups and talking softly. Clare and Isa are sitting under the big elm tree, Isa pulling Clare's hair into messy double buns.

Clare raises a hand. "Lola! Come sit with us!" She grabs my hand and pulls me gently to the ground beside her.

"Where's Em?" Fletcher asks.

Clare shrugs, and Isa adds, "She's in a mood this morning—took off as soon as we got here." She gives Clare's hair a final pat and turns to me, brandishing the brush. "Want me to do yours?"

I touch the ends of my shoulder-length hair. I normally don't "do" anything to it, just wash and brush. I lift one shoulder, about to decline her offer, when Clare bumps her arm against mine. "Let her. Isa's a genius with hair."

Isa crouches in front of me, her scrutiny intense, so close I can see the flecks of mascara on her lashes. Finally, she gives a quick nod and settles onto the ground behind me, pulling the brush through my hair.

"Can I ask you guys something?" I take my time choosing my words. "I just found out Emory used to live in my house. Isn't that weird? That I didn't know, I mean." I hold my breath as I try to gauge their reactions.

Isa pauses in her brushing, while Clare cranes her neck to look at me. "You didn't know?" I start to shake my head, but Isa holds it straight.

Fletcher is standing awkwardly over us, his face pink. "I guess we just assumed you knew."

"It wasn't a secret or anything," Clare adds.

How would I know?

"Did you guys know about the secret passage?" I try.

Isa leans over my shoulder, eyes wide. Her breath smells like peppermint. "What secret passage?"

Clare crosses her arms over her chest while Fletcher stares at a spot over my shoulder. They're united in their disbelief and their silence, which shouldn't surprise me. It's not like I expected anyone to raise their hand and volunteer information. But I thought I'd be able to gauge their reactions better. I was fooling myself. I don't know how to read people. Especially not these people, who were total strangers to me a week ago.

I give Isa the benefit of the doubt and answer, "There's a hidden passage. In my library. I guess it leads to the basement. Or maybe outside. I think someone used it to break in."

Isa yanks on my hair, hard enough to bring tears to my eyes. "Someone broke in? Did they take anything?"

"They stole my family photo albums."

Clare finally speaks, asking, "Is that all that was taken?"

It's a strange question to lead with. "I'm not sure. But the albums were my dad's. It's all I have of him and I want them back."

Clare frowns. "Did you call the police?" she asks.

I nod. "They didn't find anything. But they also didn't find the tunnel. It has to be someone who knew it was there."

"It could have been anyone," Fletcher says, furrowing his brow.

"So the tunnel is common knowledge?" The thought makes me sick to my stomach.

"That's not what I—That tunnel has been closed off. For years." He directs the last words to Clare for some reason.

She doesn't respond, just catches hold of an errant leaf and crumbles it in her fist, scattering it to the wind. The bits blow over the sidewalk and lodge against the front steps.

"I'm just freaked out," I say. "Between this and the séance the other night. All Emory's witch talk."

Isa shudders dramatically, her body rattling against mine. "I never want to talk about that stupid séance again." She rocks back on her knees.

I touch my head. She's twisted the top layer into a loose braid, the rest hanging loose.

"Gorgeous," Clare says. "Pic?" She leans her head against mine and holds up her phone. Isa pops her head up behind us, throwing up a peace sign with her fingers as Clare snaps the photo.

"What witch talk?" Fletcher asks.

Sage bounds up the walkway, trailed by Van, and shoulders his way between Fletcher and Clare. "Dude, it's *which witch*. Not what witch." He holds up his hands under the weight of our collective stare. "I don't even know what you're talking about. I just think which witch sounds better."

"Which witch. Which witch," Van chants, snaking an arm around Isa's waist. She wiggles out from under him and grabs her bag from the ground beside me. "Don't talk about her like that. It's disrespectful. I don't want to be cursed." She shivers dramatically as Van leans back his head and lets out a high-pitched cackle.

I duck my head. *What witch talk?* Is Fletcher kidding? It's all anyone can talk about, at least to me. Because my ancestor is the town joke—the story you pull out at parties to liven the mood.

Or when you want to scare someone.

That had to be the reason for the WITCH spelled out on my kitchen floor. Could Isa or Van be behind the prank?

I ask Isa, "Is that true? You think the witch curses people?"

Fletcher answers before she can. "No one says that. Right?"

Isa shakes her head. "I'm not taking any chances."

But Clare is done with the witch conversation. "What are you doing here?" she asks, poking a finger into her brother's chest.

"Um, getting an education?" Sage taps his temple and gestures toward the school.

She pulls out her phone and waves it at her brother. "You said you'd stay with Mom today. If I miss any more classes, I can't compete tomorrow."

Isa pauses with her backpack half off her shoulder. "Don't even joke about that."

"Relax. Clare's competing. And Mom's fine. I got the twins to school, and she was zonked. I left water and her pills next to the bed, but I'll bet she sleeps all day. We can check on her at lunch."

Clare is typing a furious text to someone. "You mean *I* can check on her."

He shrugs and waves at someone across the quad. "Thanks, Clare-Bear." He smacks her shoulder and takes off. Van follows without saying goodbye, and Isa gives us a finger wave before trailing after him.

Clare's face is red, and I can't tell if she's trying to hold back a scream or tears.

"I'm sure she'll be all right," Fletcher says. "I'll ask my mom to look in on her."

"Your mom's in Boulder for some court thing today," Clare mutters, and once again I'm reminded of how close they are, how intertwined their lives are.

"Right. I forgot." Fletcher thumps his forehead softly with his fist.

"Thanks anyway," Clare says, shoving her phone into her back pocket. "But I'll just do it." When she looks up, her face is resigned.

I watch her walk away with a mix of admiration and pity. Is this what it's like, taking care of someone who's always sick?

Is this how Mom feels? That she's traded off her dreams for mine?

I wonder how often she regrets that decision.

I find Emory huddled with Sage outside our AP History classroom just as the first bell dings. So much for talking to her about the tunnel. They're deep in conversation, or an argument, as she leans with her back against a locker and he boxes her in, one hand against the wall beside her. He smirks as she shakes her head and glares down at her phone. Then he whispers something in her ear and she goes stiff, shoving him into the sea of bodies in the hallway before slipping into class without ever glancing in my direction.

But Sage catches me staring. "Sorry about earlier. The witch stuff." He glances around furtively, then leans close. "Fletcher told me. About what you found. Are you completely freaked out?"

Of course I'm freaked out. What is he implying?

"It's gotta be like her secret lair, right? Where she conducted all her spells and shit?"

"Her—What are you talking about?"

"I mean, I just figured. A secret room in a witch's house? What else could it be? Did you go in? What'd you see?"

"No, I didn't—" The second bell interrupts us, giving me an excuse to back away from his macabre enthusiasm. "I have to get to class."

I enter the classroom and take my seat beside Emory. I still haven't figured her out. She seemed pissed off at me at the hospital, convinced I was lying. But I felt the same way about her. And she didn't look much happier just now in the hallway. Are she and Sage a couple? Were they fighting?

I'm not the best at social cues. Most of my conversations are with Bryn, who is brutally honest at all times. With Emory, I never know where I stand, or what she's thinking. I'm constantly misreading almost everything she says and does.

Except I'm more and more sure she's the one who's been sneaking into my house.

Hard to misread that as anything other than antagonistic.

She unpacks her bag, straightening her notebooks and pen on the desk. She's so deliberate, I'm sure it's some kind of snub. But when she turns her head and sees me, she does a double take, her eyes going wide. "I didn't think you'd be here today. How are you?"

How am I? It's a simple question—I feel like shit—but it's loaded. "I'm fine," I lie. "Why do you ask?" Because the last time she saw me, I was passed out on my kitchen floor?

She doesn't blink, just tilts her head slightly to the left and narrows her eyes in a way I find unnerving. "You were in the hospital," she says slowly, like maybe I've forgotten.

I'm not sure whether to laugh or slap her. "I'm not possessed," I say, lowering my voice as someone walks past my desk.

"Exactly what a possessed person would say." She tosses her hair and turns to face the front.

Is she for real? There's a hint of a smile at the corner of her mouth that makes me think she's just fucking with me. Keep me off kilter, so I won't accuse her of all the nasty things she's been up to.

If that's her plan, it's working. For now.

"Lola has been doing some research that I think some of you are going to find incredibly interesting. Lola, do you mind sharing with the class?"

What is Mr. Zeller doing? Sweat beads on my forehead as I sneak a glance at Emory. Her face is impassive, but I can guess what she's thinking. Basically the same thing she told me that day at the park.

You're going to piss people off. They're way too attached to the town mythology.

Then again, maybe she's got a point. Maybe it's time to shake things up. "I'm researching Claret Creek," I say. "The town's history regarding the healing water." Mr. Zeller nods encouragingly, so I continue, "I'm looking into where the story originated and if it has any basis in fact."

"It's all fact," someone calls from the back, but I can't tell who. The entire row of faces behind me all look personally offended.

"That's why they call it history," Emory adds. Her tone is mocking, though whether she's making fun of me or the others, I can't be sure.

"If that's the case, why isn't there more information about it? You've got miracle water, and yet no one's written any scientific papers on it. I don't think anyone even tested it." I'm talking to all of them, but I direct my words to Emory.

"We don't need science. Sometimes it's enough to just believe." This comes from a tall girl near the back with glossy black hair and an air of condescension that wafts toward me along with her Billie Eilish perfume.

"Dr. Clarett was a town hero." The freckle-faced girl in the seat behind me juts out her chin as she repeats the party line.

I can literally feel the amusement in Emory's smirk.

"If that's the case, then why all the secrecy?" I press. "Shouldn't he be famous outside this little town? Why aren't you bottling and selling this magic water?"

The first girl's jaw tightens. "No one cares what you think."

"Let's move on to today's lesson," Mr. Zeller says smoothly, oblivious to the tension in the air or else doing a great job ignoring it.

I can feel the glares of my classmates, hostile and silent, as I turn around.

If there's no big secret, then what are they all so afraid I'll uncover?

When the bell rings, I hang back to talk to Emory. "What happened to not buying into the town mythology? And the whole 'creek water is thicker than blood' thing? Are you one of them now?"

She takes her time packing her bag, finally looking at me as she zips it up. "Maybe some things should stay in the past."

"Says the girl who insisted on a séance. Talk to the people who were there, you said."

Her face turns red. "It was a bad idea. A joke that got out of hand."

We both know it wasn't. I'm not sure Emory is capable of joking.

"Whatever," I say. "You said you know something about my house. Is it about the tunnel?"

"Is this *you* asking?"

"Cut the crap, Emory! I know you used to live there."

"So? Everyone knows that." She tries for casual disdain but doesn't quite pull it off.

"So? That's how you've been getting into the house, isn't it? Does your dad know that you've been stalking me?"

She recoils like I've slapped her, but recovers quickly. "Stalking you? You know, I thought we could be friends. I thought you were different, but you're just like the rest. So caught up in your own drama, you can't be bothered to care about anyone else."

"My drama! You're the one trying to conjure spirits and accusing me of being possessed. I just want the truth."

But I'm talking to an empty room.

Emory is gone. And I'm late for bio.

"How are you all doing with the reading?" Ms. Perez is asking, giving me a raised eyebrow as I slide into my seat. "I know I've given you a lot, and it's a bit dry in these early days. But we're laying a foundation . . . Clare?"

Clare lowers her hand. "I've got a question about the supplemental reading, actually."

A smile plays around Ms. Perez's mouth. "Let's have it."

"It's about DNA collection."

Ms. Perez nods. "A sticky topic, ethically speaking. I presume you're talking about the use of private DNA tests to profile and identify criminals?"

"That's the article, yes, but I was actually wondering if those tests can be used to identify disease."

Ms. Perez pauses, clearly thrown by the question, and Clare adds, "I mean, say I do a DNA test through one of those genealogy sites. Can that be used to identify genetic abnormalities?"

"Technically, yes. And I believe there is a health risk assessment that comes with your report. At least, mine had one."

"You did a test?" Van asks. "Aren't you worried the cops can use that against you?"

"That's the dilemma, isn't it? Should the police have access? Or you can look at it another way—perhaps any potential criminals in my family will be deterred from committing crimes if they know our DNA is already on file."

"But what about crimes committed in the past? Before anyone knew anything about DNA," Van asks.

"Are you suggesting they had a right to be rapists and murderers because the *science* didn't exist yet to catch them?" Clare turns to glare at him. "Just because a crime was committed in the past, that doesn't make it less of a crime."

"It's an interesting discussion," Ms. Perez says, trying to defuse the tension. "Every society has ways of maintaining the status quo. Perhaps the surge of interest in DNA testing could be considered a tool for keeping order. Conversely, maybe it crosses a line. Using your unique genetic code for purposes you weren't intending."

"How far back does it work? I mean, isn't there a point where the DNA is so diluted you can't prove anything anyway?" Van asks. "Like, if my great-grandpa did some sh—stuff."

"You can think of DNA like a pie, if that helps." Ms. Perez moves to the board and sketches a circle. "This is you. Half is Mom, half is Dad." She divides the circle into halves, then into quarters. "Now we've got DNA from your grandparents"—she divides again—"and their parents, and so on. Regardless of how much or how little, it's all still a part of the pie."

"Mmmm. Inheritance pie," Van cracks, and the class giggles.

"Pie makes it sound like a good thing," Clare says. "But you inherit bad DNA, too. Which brings us back to *my question*," she says with great emphasis. "Can anyone *else* use that data? To identify abnormalities. The police can gain access. What about giving those results to scientists?"

"Yes, diseases and abnormalities can be inherited," Ms. Perez says. "So your question is an interesting one. Many of these companies are already doing research with the results. But the bigger issue here is privacy."

I tune her out, stuck on something she's just said: Diseases can be inherited.

This is it, the thing I've thought about pretty much nonstop ever since I first got sick. Is whatever I've got genetic? Is there someone in my father's family who suffered with the same disease? And if I found them, would it give me answers? Would it change anything?

Is this why I'm having these episodes?

"What about memory?" I interrupt without raising my hand.

In the back of the room, Van scoffs.

Ms. Perez frowns a warning at him as she perches on the edge of her desk. "What about memory?" she asks. "Can you elaborate?"

"Can you inherit memories?" Before anyone can laugh again, I push on. "I've been reading about epigenetic memory. Generated from trauma."

Ms. Perez rises to write "epigenetic memory" on the board and taps her chalk against the words. "Also sometimes referred to as intergenerational trauma. Trauma creates a change in your body—scientists call it a marker. And that marker changes how your body *reads* the DNA; it changes how your body responds. Think of it like a biological warning system." She sets down her chalk and dusts off her hands. "So the quick answer to Lola's question is yes. Memory can be inherited. Because trauma and memory are linked. Like cause and effect. Or action and reaction."

The fire alarm blares, jarring me so much I'm physically jolted from my seat, my fingertips tingling as I blink back dark stars.

A biological warning system.

Is that what these memories are all about?

"Line up! Straight out to the courtyard. Let's go!" Ms. Perez claps her hands, urging us along.

I shove my notebook into my backpack and follow the line of students out the door.

Trauma and memory are linked.

Bryn's podcast, Fletcher's bears, my internet research. It's all true. This is what's been happening to me. These episodes are real memories, and they're linked to the trauma Rebecca experienced.

But what if it's more than just these memories? My fatigue, my pain, my brain fuzziness—they all started long before Colorado.

What if they're all related?

Maybe the reason no one's been able to figure out what's causing my symptoms is because the change isn't recent. Maybe it was baked into my DNA a long time ago.

Figuring out where these memories are coming from could lead to an answer about my illness.

It sounds too good to be true, something impossible I have no reasonable right to wish for.

But that's the thing about wishes—they don't listen to reason.

CHAPTER 31

The class scatters as we hit the courtyard, and I nearly have to break into a run to catch Clare as she beelines for the parking lot. "Clare, wait up."

The familiar tightness in my chest yanks me to a stop, and I lean against the back bumper of a Ford F-150 as I try to catch my breath. It's too late—she's too fast and I'm too worthless. A year ago, I could have lapped the parking lot without breaking a sweat. Now I can't even follow Clare to her car.

As if sensing my distress, she turns, her pallid face a stark contrast to her dark hair. Her brown eyes are shiny, as if holding back tears. Perez's discussion has affected her as much as me.

It takes me a second, but then it clicks. She was talking about her mom.

"Are you all right?" she asks, jogging back toward me.

I nod, bracing myself on my knees. "Are *you*?"

"Yeah. No. I don't know." She spins around and starts walking away, then stops and comes back, shoving her hands through her hair. "It's just . . . so fucked up. Those idiots in there, talking about inheritance pie and using DNA for evidence, like it's some kind of scientific joke. But it's real. My mom's sick, really sick, and I love her, I do. But I'm so fucking tired of all this . . ." She waves her hands. "It's just too much, you know? Every day I wake up and my first thought is 'Will today be a good day?' "

She breathes in deep through her nose and tilts her face toward the sky. "And do you know what my second thought is? *What if it happens to me?*" A tear leaks down her cheek. "It's so selfish, but I'm terrified of getting sick like her. Or Rosie. What if it happens to Rosie?"

"Clare." I stand and put my hands on her shoulders, firm and steady. "It's okay. Look at me. I understand. I do," I say, and her brown eyes meet mine. "At least, the worry part. The sick part."

Other than Fletcher, I haven't told anyone about my illness. Part of me was hoping I'd never have to. Colorado was my chance to be someone other than sick Lola, and ironically, the altitude here bought me time. I don't have to share it with Clare, either; I want to. And there's a power in that choice.

"Because I've been sick," I continue. "Not just the altitude. Even before all that. And no one knows what's wrong." I shrug. "I know it's not the same. I don't have to take care of anyone like you do. That's gotta be hard. But I do know about the good days. And the bad days. The wanting answers and not getting them. It sucks."

She barks a laugh and nods. "It does."

"But you've got to remember, your mom is more than just her illness. And you're so much more than just her caregiver. Even though I know some days that's all you can think about."

"Shit. I'm sorry." She drags her hand across her face, smearing black eyeliner outward, giving her a lopsided cat-eye effect. "Listen to me. Feeling sorry for myself while you're . . ." She waves a hand at me but doesn't finish.

What was she going to say? While I'm what? For the first time in a long time, it doesn't matter what someone else thinks I am. "I'm fine," I say, and I mean it. "And I'm here, if you want to talk or scream or cry or whatever."

She juts out her chin. "Thanks. But I'm an ugly crier. Do you want to get out of here? The fire department has to come and clear the building before we can go back in. By that time, it'll be lunch anyway." She raises her voice as the sirens gain volume when the trucks pull around the corner. "Come on." Clare pulls me toward a compact yellow truck, the wheel wells lacy with rust.

I hop in, avoiding the tear in the fabric seat. "Where are we going?"

"I've got to check on Mom," she says. "It won't take long and we won't get in trouble. I promise." As she maneuvers her way out the back of the parking lot, I turn to watch the emergency vehicles stream in the front—two firetrucks followed by an ambulance and a sheriff's car.

"That's a lot of manpower," I say. "Are we sure there's not a fire?"

Clare shrugs. "Probably not. Some idiot pulled the alarm during the PSAT last year and this is what happened." She glances in the rearview mirror. As she speaks, more kids start peeling away from the front, heading toward various vehicles in the lot, apparently having made the same assumptions.

As we drive, Clare says casually, "I hear you're going to the dance with Fletcher."

"He told you?" I shift in my seat, my insecurities about the two of them flooding back. They used to date, he said, but she broke it off. Still, it seems weird that he'd talk to her about me.

"You're upset."

I forgot how perceptive Clare can be. "No. I just—"

"Look, I get it. Our relationship is weird. But we're just friends. Best friends, if I'm being honest. And yes, for a while, we thought that meant we should be more. But that was more other people's idea of us than our actual feelings. We were together all the time, you know? And our parents would joke about it. And our friends gave us shit about it. So it felt like a natural transition. But we tried it, and there was nothing there. It was like kissing my brother." She grimaces and rolls her eyes. "Okay, maybe marginally less gross than kissing my brother. But not by much."

"Wow. I did not need that mental image, but I guess thanks for telling me? Now I feel like an idiot. It's just . . . Emory sounded so certain that you and Fletcher were going to get back together. But maybe that was wishful thinking on her part."

Clare laughs. "Emory does *not* care if Fletcher and I are together. And even if she did, who cares what she thinks? What's important is whether you like him."

"I think I do . . ."

"But?"

"I haven't been to a dance—or on a date—for a long time." Or ever. "I don't have anything to wear."

"You're welcome to raid my closet." She smiles at me as she pulls over in front of a tall, spindly Victorian house with peeling baby-blue paint and dark gingerbread trim. A rickety front porch curves around the front like a gaping mouth with uneven teeth. The narrow windows, pitched roof, and gentle air of neglect give the whole thing the appearance of leaning.

"This is us. And that's Fletcher." She points across the street to a large house in the same style, but updated, with cedar siding and a bright white picket fence.

"You guys are neighbors." It doesn't surprise me, given how close they all are.

"Since birth," she says, leading me around the house to the side door, which opens into the kitchen.

Clare tosses her keys on the cluttered table and opens the refrigerator, which is covered with crayon drawings and photos. She grabs various containers of meat and cheese, a head of lettuce, one overripe tomato, a jar of mayo. "There's gluten-free bread on the counter," she says, gesturing toward the sink. "Help yourself. I'm going to make her some lu—"

"Sage? Is that you?"

Clare slams the fridge. "It's me, Mom," she calls back. "I'm just home for lunch."

"Who are you talking to?"

She drops the food onto the table, and I follow her toward a sunny room at the front of the house.

"Mom, this is my friend Lola. Lola, this is my mom."

Clare's mom is lying on a plaid sofa in the corner, propped up on a pile of pillows and facing a TV, which is tuned to some kind of daytime talk show. She has the puffy, waxy look of the chronically ill. I can make out Clare's features in the shape of her face and the arch of her brow, but they're distorted, like in a fun-house mirror.

"Hello, Mrs. Morales. It's nice to meet you."

"Lola." Her brown eyes widen, and she clutches a hand to her bathrobe. "Teddy's girl?"

With a jolt, I remember that this was my dad's high school sweetheart.

"Yes, that's right. You knew my dad." I sink in the chair next to her.

She struggles to sit up, taking her time straightening her blankets. "How are you settling in? The Creek can be hard for people . . ."

For what kind of people? People who weren't born here? People who don't belong?

"It's been all right," I say. "But it's hard. Being the new girl. There's so much history I don't know. Like, about my dad." I sit motionless, mentally willing her to open up.

"That was a long time ago," she says.

We sit in awkward silence, a commercial for erectile disfunction pills droning on in the background.

"I wasn't always like this," she finally says. "I've got a rare blood disorder. Genetic. And now they've diagnosed me with some kind of autoimmune thing, which apparently can lead to stroke or heart failure. Lucky me."

I'm all too familiar with that brand of luck.

The air in here is heavy and hot, thick with illness and despair. Is this my future? Too tired to hide my symptoms, instead spilling them to anyone with a sympathetic ear? The thought makes me break out in a cold sweat.

"So many tests, year after year. And then—bam!" Mrs. Morales claps her hands together and I jolt, my phone clattering to the floor.

She turns and stares, as if catching sight of me for the first time. I brace myself for some kind of comment about how much I look like my dad, but it doesn't come. "You've lost weight," she says instead. She's right, but how could she know that? "Itchy skin," she continues.

I self-consciously cover my arms and glance nervously toward the kitchen. Something's not right with this woman. Where is Clare?

"Dizziness? Headaches? Fatigue?" She recites my symptoms casually, each one hitting me like a bullet. "One invalid to another. I can tell."

I flinch. I'm not an invalid. Is that how she sees me? Whatever confidence I'd gained from telling Clare my secret is gone, and I feel exposed.

"Are you all right?" Amber Morales raises her voice. "Bring Lola some water!"

Clare is at my side, shoving a glass in my hands, and I clutch at it like a lifeline.

I haven't responded, but Amber goes on like we're having a conversation. "It was the genetic panel that finally gave us some answers. Before that, they said I was crazy. And they were sort of right. Being ill for so long, it messes with your head. The body is all one big, interconnected organism. When you're feeling shitty, you know in your gut that something's going on. And they run those tests and they come back negative, but you still know there's something wrong. But no one will listen. Especially if you're a woman." She smiles sadly.

I sneak a glance at Clare, who is studying her nails and scraping at her polish aggressively, her mouth set in a grim line. As if feeling my stare, she grabs the clicker to turn off the TV. "Where'd you get the flowers?" she asks, changing the subject as she straightens the bouquet on the table.

"From an admirer." Her mom runs a hand over her hair. "Amber Mistique gladiolus. Aren't they gorgeous?"

"You need to take your pills. And you should eat something."

Amber wrinkles her nose. "I'm not hungry."

Clare's composure slips, and for a moment I think she might cry. Then she straightens and goes back into the kitchen.

"Clare's a worrier. Just like me." Amber manages a twisted smile. "It doesn't do us any good, but here we are."

"Clare told me about the creek," I finally say. "She says it has healing powers. Or at least people believe it does." I want to ask her if she's tried it, which is a ridiculous question. Then again, if I were this ill, I might try anything.

"I'd be careful if I were you," Amber says, her face tightening. "It won't sit right with some people, you coming in and making fun of our past."

Her tone makes me shrink back in my seat. "I'm not making fun of anyone. If anything, it feels like the opposite. Like everyone knows something I don't. The water is magic, my house is haunted by a witch."

I've got her attention now. "Who told you about the witch?"

I wave a hand in the direction of the doorway. "They all told me the story, Clare and Emory and the boys. But even that was skimpy on details. It's all contradictory facts and hearsay. So it's not really a haunting; it's more like a memory of a haunting. Only it's not even a memory, is it? Because no one actually remembers what happened." I slump back, exhausted after my small outburst.

Amber says, "It's not that they don't remember. It's that they worked so hard to forget."

I sit up straight.

"You have to remember, it didn't start out as a story. They were real people, the ones he saved. Daughters, mothers, brothers. I think about them sometimes. Imagining what they went through. I mean, medical science is advanced now, but back then?" Amber's voice is soft, dreamy. "They thought they didn't have a chance. But then Dr. Clarett changed everything."

My pulse quickens. Is this finally where I'm going to learn the truth? "How many people did he save?"

"Oh, I don't really know."

I clamp my lips together to stop myself from screaming in frustration.

"But the doctor kept those journals," Amber adds. "It must all be in there."

I cock my head. How is this the first time I'm hearing about journals? Could they be in my house? "Do you know where they are?"

"We've got some of his personal papers." She lays her hands over her heart. "He writes so beautifully about his grief over losing his wife. And his daughter."

"Why do you— Wait," I interrupt myself. "What happened to his daughter? Was she one of hi—the victims?"

But Amber shakes her head. "She survived. We're her descendants."

Descendants of Clarett's daughter. Sage had told me that, in a roundabout way.

Clarett Creek royalty, he'd called himself. And at the reservoir, he'd said his great-great-grandad built the town. No wonder he wants to believe in the witch so badly. *Bewitched the doctor into giving her his house*, he'd said, that first night in the attic.

"The attic," Amber repeats, jolting me. I hadn't realized I'd spoken out loud. "That's where it all started, you know. The nosebleeds, the dizziness. Those hallucinations. *The answer is in my blood.*" Her lips twist into a sordid smile. "Turns out I was right. If only someone had listened to me way back then."

Her words crash into me like a wave, and I'm knocked sideways, the roar of my heart in my ears drowning out everything else.

Hallucinations? Nosebleeds?

I stare at her in horror, seeing a different time and place, another stifling room. Her voice, strange and yet familiar. The sound of my blood, rushing through my veins.

It wasn't my dad's memory I experienced in my attic, the first night I met them all.

It was Amber's.

CHAPTER 32

"Lola? Are you okay?" Clare's voice is coming from far off, somewhere beyond this room and the ringing in my ears.

"I don't . . . Can we go? Back to school?"

"You should eat something. And we were going to find you a dress."

I wave her off. They're both staring at me like I've grown another head. Oh god. Did I pass out? Say something? Am I bleeding? I touch my nose. Nothing.

"I'm fine," I say, plastering on a smile. "I'm just . . . warm. I need some air. And I remembered I have a paper I forgot to turn in." I push to my feet, holding myself steady by sheer force of will and it's only because I've been doing this for so long—pretending to be fine while inside I'm falling apart—that I'm able to pull it off.

"It was nice meeting you," I say to Amber, avoiding her probing gaze. "I hope you get well. I'll wait for you outside," I add to Clare as I hurry from the room.

I wait in the truck, mind racing, hands shaking. It was *Amber's* memory.

Amber, in my attic. Weak and bleeding.

But how can that be? If these are epigenetic memories from my ancestors, why would Amber share them?

We're her descendants.

Was she including me in that statement?

Clare wrenches open the door and I jolt, banging my head against the window.

"You all right? You're looking a little wobbly."

I sit up straight and crank down my window. "Yeah. Fine. Just tired. Sorry I ran out of there so fast."

Clare starts the engine and puts it in gear, leaning her arm across the seat as she backs out of the driveway. "I hope it wasn't anything my mom said. I know she can be . . . a lot."

"No. She was great."

Clare snorts. "We're friends. You don't have to bullshit me. No one wants to listen to her health complaints." She looks pissed.

"Clare, no! That's not it. If anyone is sympathetic to what she's been through, it's me." I take a deep breath. Can I trust Clare with this? *We're friends.* When's the last time anyone said that to me? "The thing she said about having hallucinations. That really hit home, I guess."

Clare glances in my direction, her face a mixture of sympathy and horror. "Oh shit. I didn't even think . . . I'm sorry."

"Don't apologize." I shake my head and turn halfway in my seat to face her. "Did it sound familiar to you? The thing she said? 'The answer is in my blood'?"

Surely she remembers that night in the attic. When I started spewing blood and other bullshit?

But Clare waves me off. "I know it sounds creepy, but she's just talking about her diagnosis. It's a blood disorder."

A *genetic* blood disorder.

Clare's mom suffers from a rare, genetic blood disorder, with symptoms that mimic my own.

And she's experiencing my ancestor's memories.

I need to look at my family tree.

Fletcher's already in his seat when I get to Spanish class, typing on his phone. He slips it in his pocket as I slide into the desk beside him.

Who is he messaging with? Clare? Did she tell him how weird I was acting?

"Hey. I was worried you'd gone home."

His phone buzzes but he ignores it.

Shit. What had Clare said to him? "Why would I go home?"

He waits a bit too long before answering, then shakes his head. "No reason. I just looked for you after the fire alarm. And couldn't find you."

"I was with Clare," I say, watching him from the corner of my eye as I unzip my backpack and pull out my notebook.

He nods, but I can't tell if this is new information to him. "Listen, about this morning . . ." he says.

I blink at him. What happened this morning? It feels like a hundred years have passed since I last saw him, and I have no idea what he's referring to. I have other things to worry about.

Like figuring out if I'm related to a murderer.

A drop of sweat slides down my nose and splashes my notebook. "Gross."

Fletcher's startled gaze meets mine as I blot at my face.

"Is it another nosebleed?" he asks, sounding worried.

I start to shake my head, then clamp my hands over my nose like a tent and nod. "Yep." I hurry to Profesora's desk. "I've got a nosebleed," I say, and she nods and hands me a piece of wood with the words HALL PASS burned into it.

I tuck it under my arm and half walk, half run out the door. The hallway is quiet between classes, but I pass two girls who do a double take before openly staring as I walk past. My cheeks burn as I break into a trot, hand clamped firmly over my face. I'm not actually bleeding. What the hell is their problem?

I back my way into the bathroom, which is mercifully empty, and drop the hall pass into the sink with a clatter before pulling out my phone.

I log into my genealogy page with shaking fingers, but instead of pulling up my own tree, I search for Dr. Clarett. He married late in life, after his so-called miracles, and gave birth to one daughter, Claret.

Jesus. The ego with this guy.

Claret was Amber Morales's grandmother—Clare and Sage's great-grandmother.

There's no connection that I can see between their family and mine. So how are Amber and I having the same epigenetic memories?

Unless.

I catch sight of my face in the mirror, my eyes wide as a theory takes root. The episode from the other night, when I'd passed out on the kitchen floor. What had James said to me—to Rebecca?

I know about the baby.

Rebecca only had one child. I'd assumed Daisy was James' daughter, born a few short months after the wedding.

But what if Clarett was the father?

There are a few more kids in the hall this time, each giving me covert glances and whispers as I retrace my steps, but I ignore them, my mind racing.

The idea that I was descended from Satan was disturbing but easy enough to dismiss as pure fiction.

Being related to a monster is harder.

Especially when I've seen his malevolence with my own eyes.

I step back to let a gym class go by on their way to the outdoor track; Emory is in the group. Her face goes pale when she sees me, and she jerks away, spinning and walking down the hall with a quick, stiff-legged gait.

"You're killing us!" a guy yells from the back of the group, shoving his friend as they pass by me. They burst out laughing.

The hair goes up on the back of my neck as his words register, and I turn slowly toward the sea of faces all staring back at me. Smiling. Leering.

Now that he has an audience, the guy goes full ham, falling to his knees and raising his arms. "You're . . . killing . . . us!" He mimes a spray of fluid, splaying his fingers and gesturing to the crowd, who cheer and shriek. Not in a confused way, but in the delighted understanding of a shared joke.

Somehow, they know.

They all know.

What happened on Friday night. Not just about the séance and the hospital, but the things I said. Emory must have told, well, everyone. Because how else could they . . . ?

"You're killing us!" This time, my own voice echoes back at me, tinny and echoey, from someone's phone.

She recorded it.

And I've gone viral.

CHAPTER 33

It doesn't take me long to find the clip.

I manage to stumble into an empty bathroom stall, where I sit and wait for the bell. Shaking. Sweating.

I don't know what I expected, but it's worse. Dark and grainy, the clip starts abruptly with me on the ground. Panting. Clawing at my own arm. The flames behind me distort the image, and whoever is holding the camera—Emory?—is moving. Blood pours from my nose as both Fletcher and Clare try to pull me safely away from the fire, even as I thrash and kick. "You'll . . . kill us both. You're killing us!"

The video zooms in on my face as I collapse. In the background, I can hear a scream and a slap and Fletcher's voice. "Someone call an ambulance."

Clare pulls my head into her lap. She looks up, her face going slack as her mouth falls open.

The screen goes blank.

I minimize the video with a shaky finger, then clamp my hand over my mouth.

It was posted at 1:17 p.m. on Instagram and TikTok, and has already garnered close to a thousand views. A thousand people, witnessing my pain and leaving comments like "Crazy bitch!" and "scary as shit" and "BitchBePossessed" and "#DemonGirl."

But the worst are the comments from the people I know, people I used to call friends. "All about the drama." And "Lola's a faker." And "Lol. In MI she was just a hypochondriac. Guess we lucked out."

I can't read any more. I barely manage to spin around before I vomit.

My throat burns and my chest is tight, so tight. I can't stay here. I can't face these people. I thought Emory was my friend. Or at least that we were friendly. Why is she doing this to me?

Because I wouldn't tell her what happened? Because I won't say I'm possessed?

I need to leave.

I wash up at the sink, dipping my face to the faucet to rinse my mouth and wiping it with a paper towel. I need to get to the office. Then I can call my mom. I don't know what I'll tell her—maybe that this was too much, too soon. I don't feel well. I've thrown up. Those are all true.

I can't tell her about the video.

I pull open the bathroom door and run straight into Emory.

She gasps and recoils. As if I'm the one who's toxic.

"You!" I hiss in a strangled whisper. It's all I can get out. My anger chokes back what I really want to say.

Emory straightens and pulls up her shoulders, jutting her chin at me. "Me what?"

"You know what."

Her voice echoes in my head. *So caught up in your own drama, you can't be bothered to care about anyone else.*

Is this some kind of retribution? I wouldn't play along with her possession theory, so she posts the video to prove I'm the product of some deal between a witch and the devil?

I feel like I'm in the Upside Down, like nothing is real and everything is wrong and I don't know the rules anymore.

"You recorded me. Without my permission. While I was having a . . . a medical incident. That's illegal. This is pure bullshit, but maybe she doesn't know it. "Why?"

She presses her lips together and ducks her head, texting something quickly into her phone. Checking out my lie? But when she looks up, her face is blank. "Why didn't you tell me you were sick?"

"Would that have made a difference?" My voice breaks.

Emory's chin trembles. "I didn't do th—"

"Bullshit!" I shriek, the sound echoing in the empty hallway. "I know it was you. This is what you meant, when you said you could help me?" I hold my phone out as the video plays, my hand shaking so violently, I drop it.

Emory is even paler than usual, her skin almost gray. "I didn't post that." Her voice gets louder. "Only a coward would do something like that anonymously. And I'm no coward."

I drop to my knees to retrieve the phone, and she takes advantage of the moment to pull away from me. "I never got the impression you saw yourself as a victim," she says. "It's one of the things I liked about you. So don't start now. Stand up for yourself." And then, over her shoulder, "She's fine. She just needs some air," as she vanishes into the restroom.

"Lola! I've been looking for you all over." Fletcher kneels beside me and wraps an arm around my shoulders. "What can I do?"

I force a shaky laugh. "Can you rewind time? Make this all . . . not have happened?"

"I can get them to take it down. My mom's an attorney. I'm sure she can threaten them with something. This . . . ConcernedCreekster."

I bark a laugh. "You mean Emory."

His brow furrows. "You don't think Emory did this . . ."

"Who else could it be?"

He works his jaw. "She wouldn't. She might be aloof sometimes, but she isn't mean. She's the one who texted me. She knew I was worried."

I appreciate his loyalty. I'd appreciate it even more if it were directed toward me.

"Someone did it. Someone who was there that night," I say, struggling to my feet. "I'm not crazy," I add, which might not be fair. After all, he hasn't suggested it.

I close my eyes, my stomach somersaulting into my throat. When I open them, he's watching the clip.

I can't listen to it again, and I can't be here. I duck away and Fletcher doesn't even notice; his eyes are still glued to the screen.

Mom doesn't question why I'm home early. Part of me is grateful, and part of me wants to tell her everything, curl up in her arms, and have her hold me and tell me everything is going to be all right. But we're miles away from that right now, and even if we weren't, there's no way I'd believe her.

I'm stunned and numb, but the numbness is fading and I don't want to feel the hot shame and embarrassment that are already creeping in. This is why people turn to alcohol and drugs—anything to escape this feeling of raw humiliation. I want to be anywhere but here—anyone but me. If I could peel off my skin and step out of this body, I would.

All I wanted, all I've ever wanted, was for people to accept me for who I am. When I was healthy, it didn't seem to be a problem. Running track, earning wins for the team—everyone loved me then. It's sick Lola they all can't stand. But we're one and the same. I'm still the same person inside; why can't they see that? Why does this illness have to define me?

So I pass out and channel dead people. Like they're so perfect?

My skin itches and I can't stand still. I'm shaking and aching and dizzy and nauseated and I'm not sure what's due to the altitude, or my illness, or just plain disgust.

I know Bryn is at school, but I call anyway, and to my surprise, they pick up.

"I'm trying to get a flight out," they say, their face pressed close to the phone. Their glasses today are black and square. "If I land in Denver, can you pick me up? How far away is Denver?"

"What are you talking about?"

"I saw it."

My stomach drops. Part of me expected this; after all, a former teammate had commented on the video. But I'd been secretly hoping it might somehow not find its way to everyone I know.

"What the fuck, Lola? Who did it? You know what, doesn't matter. I will kick all their chaps-wearing, Coors-guzzling asses!"

"No one is kicking anyone's ass."

"Who was it? Emory, right?"

I lift a shoulder.

"What the fuck is her problem?"

"I don't know. I think she broke into my house, too."

Bryn's eyes widen as I share the news about the tunnel.

The camera gets shaky as Bryn breaks into a jog. "Where are you?" I ask.

"Outside. I got a pass so I could try and book a flight. But the school has this stupid block on their internet, so I had to leave."

"You don't have to come here. I mean, I'd love to see you, but—"

"Fuck. Is your nose bleeding?"

I press two fingers to my nostrils and they come away wet. "Shit. I don't know. Hold on." I sit up fast, throwing open the door so I can grab some tissue.

Mom stands outside, her hand poised to knock. "Everything okay? I heard you talking . . . Oh no!" She gasps as she catches sight of the blood.

I press my hand over my face and shove the phone at her. "It's not a big deal. I just need a tissue. Talk to Bryn."

"Hi, Bryn." She waves at the screen half-heartedly, her eyes following me down the hall.

"Hey, Mrs. G. I was just telling Lola I'm coming to visit."

"That's nice," Mom says distractedly. "Over Thanksgiving?"

"I was thinking sooner."

I wash my hands and grab a wad of toilet paper to press to my nose. I can almost see Mom's thoughts. Kurt just moved out. I'm more of a mess than usual. She's got her new job to worry about.

"Don't worry," I say, taking the phone back. "I told Bryn it's not a great time."

"It's not that we wouldn't love to have you," Mom begins.

"Could you make me a grilled cheese?" I interrupt. "I need something in my stomach."

"Of course, honey. Bye, Bryn. We'll work out a visit soon."

Her voice is falsely cheerful, and I wait until I hear her steps on the stairs before closing my door and whispering, "She kicked Kurt out."

"What?!" Bryn stops abruptly. "I just talked to you on Saturday night," they remind me. "But clearly a shit-ton has happened since then."

I perch on the edge of my bed, my nose close to the phone. "Clare took me to meet her mom today. And Amber—her mom—she's had the same memories. And she's sick, with the same symptoms. I think we're related."

"How?"

"I think Rebecca had Clarett's baby. I was looking at the family tree, trying to piece it together. But then I saw the video, and I just . . . I freaked out and I came home."

"Look, I get it. The video is not great. It makes you look a little bit . . ."

"Deranged?"

"Off," Bryn corrects. "But so what? It was a fucking séance. And you were obviously in need of medical attention. So fuck everyone who commented. They're the ones who need to explain themselves. I mean, come on. You need to get angry. And then you need to get even."

"Revenge? That's the last thing I need. No, I have to let this die down. In a few days, someone else will be the internet sensation."

"They're calling you Demon Girl."

I flinch and peek at the paper. The bleeding has stopped. I toss it on my dresser. "Emory practically told my history class that I'm possessed. Which I'm not. I'm clearly just experiencing some epigenetic memories."

"Finally! Took you long enough."

"You have your way, I have mine. As for the right way, the correct way, the only way, it does not exist."

Bryn purses their lips. "Marx?" they finally guess.

"Nietzsche."

"Of course it's fucking Nietzsche. Still, I was right about the epigenetic stuff."

"You were," I admit. "I did a bunch of online research. And then my bio teacher laid out the link between trauma and memory. She called it a biological warning system."

"Hot damn." Bryn's face is practically glowing. "This is real. Forget Demon Girl. You're a scientific wonder."

"The thing *I* wonder is why. If epigenetic memory exists to make us stronger, or to gird ourselves for some kind of danger, then what's the danger here? All I've learned from these stupid memories is that the doctor this whole town worships was probably a huckster and the magic water story is bunk. Plus, thanks to these episodes and that stupid video, now everyone thinks I'm possessed. Or at the very least, some biological by-product of a tryst between a witch and the devil. How is any of this helpful?"

"That's what you have to figure out. Research!" Bryn's excitement is tangible and I wish it were contagious, because I feel nothing but exhaustion and despair.

Even if Perez is right and this is some kind of warning system, I'm too broken to care.

If the motive in releasing the video was to get me to back off, kudos to whoever's done it.

They've won.

CHAPTER 34

The library is full of people, strangers, huddled together near the fireplace, their backs to me so that all I see are dark suitcoats and black dresses. Beyond them stand three girls, like stair steps, their faces all covered by dark cloth. I'm afraid to move, afraid to breathe. I don't belong here, and if they see me, I don't know what will happen. The air is thick with the murmur of voices—words I can't make out—and the cloying scent of rotting flowers.

I press my fingers to my throat, as if to hold back a scream, or maybe coax it free. One of the girls watches me over the heads of the strangers, and I stare back, mesmerized, as she slowly raises her gloved hands to pull aside her veil.

The face looking back at me is my own.

I gasp and sit upright.

I'm in my bedroom, alone, bright sunlight streaming through the windows.

I grab for my phone, still shaken by the remnants of that awful dream. What time is it? What *day* is it?

It's turned off. Right. I'd done that some time . . . yesterday? After I'd begged off school and barricaded myself in my bedroom to wallow in private. I'd told myself that none of it mattered, but eventually the constant barrage of hateful comments became too much, and I shut off the phone and finally gave in to the dark pull of oblivion. I'd longed for a deep, dreamless sleep, but clearly that didn't happen.

I weigh the impulse to turn it on, but the thought fills me with even more dread than the idea of not knowing what time it is.

Mom mostly left me alone, popping in only to bring me tea and toast and to tell me she had to work early today. Clearly, she thinks I'm ill, which means

I haven't had to explain anything to her, but the guilt doesn't sit quite right. I've never been one to use my symptoms for sympathy or personal gain, despite what other people think. If anything, it's the opposite. I push myself too hard to prove that I'm normal, just like them.

But knowing that everyone has seen the video—Demon Girl, stumbling around and gushing blood and shouting proclamations—strips all of that strength away, reducing me to a quivering mess of shame and insecurity. How do I explain any of it without sounding like a lunatic? Sure, I could come clean, tell everyone that I've been sick. But the irony is, I doubt they'd even believe me now. Somehow my biggest secret has been reduced to a weak, unbelievable excuse. The thought makes me want to burrow under the covers and never come out.

It's official—I'm a coward.

I also feel like shit. The familiar heaviness is back in my chest, and my head feels stuffed with cotton, which ironically does nothing to muffle the buzzing.

It wasn't the altitude, then. Or it was, but not *just* the altitude.

Maybe this is all part of a blood disorder. Same as Amber.

Is that possible?

I only have her word about it, after all. But it can't hurt to ask Dr. Archuleta. Amber said she'd had a genetic panel done. I'd been asking—no, begging—Dr. K to do one for the longest time. His response was always the same: a patient, slightly condescending smile as he explained that those tests were expensive and unlikely to give us any results.

I switch on the phone, holding my breath as it begins to vibrate, the text messages and missed calls loading, one after another. Three from Bryn, seven from Fletcher. A handful from Clare.

I wipe the notifications aside and open the hospital's app. Dr. Archuleta had asked me to monitor my symptoms, and I've been doing a not-great job, forgetting to log anything most days. But there's also a contact button, and I use this to shoot off a quick question about scheduling a genetic panel.

Then I look at the string of text messages.

Both Fletcher and Clare reached out yesterday afternoon and again this morning, their texts an equal mixture of anger and concern. Fletcher vows to help me find "whoever was recording in the bushes" while Clare is less concerned with the who and more with damage control—**Fletcher's mom is getting the video taken down.** And **Don't read the comments. These people are assholes.**

I've even got one from Sage:

That was some party! Jk don't let the trolls get you down

The one person who hasn't reached out is Emory.

Because she feels guilty? Or because she said all she needed to outside the bathroom?

I kick off the covers as I stare at the ceiling, trying to remember her exact words.

I never got the impression you saw yourself as a victim. So don't start now.

Am I acting like a victim?

Hard not to be when someone is clearly targeting me.

She also accused me of being a drama queen. *So caught up in your own drama, you can't be bothered to care about anyone else.*

So what does she think I'm missing? Who do I not care about? Clare? Her mom is really sick. And it definitely took me too long to clue in on how hard things are for her and Sage.

I groan and hold a pillow over my face. Emory is right. I've been a shitty friend. But is that a reason to post the video?

Unless it wasn't her.

But who else would do it? It has to be someone who was at the séance. Someone who knows about my connection to the witch.

Van? Or Isa?

According to Clare and Emory, she was hysterical after I passed out. And she's terrified of the witch's curse. I don't think she'd risk it for a few hundred likes on a post.

No, this is personal. Meant to hurt me, or scare me away. It could be the same person who's been sneaking into my house, which means it has to be someone who knows about the tunnel.

Fletcher?

He's been here since day one, oddly attentive and strangely invested in my family history.

He's also the first person I told about my episodes.

And since he knew about the episodes, he had to have known that's what was happening to me at the séance.

I toss the pillow aside and sit up, too fast. Black spots swim into view. My head is hammering and my chest is tight, but they're both minor compared to the righteous anger coursing through me.

I'm going to figure this out, once and for all. Who's been breaking in, and why.

And to start, I'm going to follow the tunnel.

I dress, shower, and make myself a large cup of coffee as quickly as I can, given I feel like roadkill.

Dominic says the tunnel has been blocked off. But I need to stop taking everyone at their word. They're all keeping secrets.

Dust motes swirl as I shove aside the chair in the library. The bookshelf creaks and groans, taking much more effort this time. Once I've opened the tunnel, cool air, dank and damp, wafts through the crack.

I take a big gulp of coffee, take out my phone, and switch on the flashlight.

I'm going in.

It's less a tunnel and more a cramped stairwell that twists down, down, down into the bowels of the earth. I shudder and clamp my teeth together as something skitters across my cheek, keeping the light trained on my feet so I don't lose my nerve.

This might be the most terrifying thing I've ever done.

"You can do this."

Nope. Do not talk out loud. Somehow, that makes it worse.

I stumble down the next few steps and then mercifully I'm on solid ground.

The next section is longer, darker, and more claustrophobic. I walk for what feels like hours, though according to my phone it takes me less than ten minutes. I have no sense of direction—time and space seem suspended as I move through the belly of the earth, my hands close to my sides lest I touch something living and terrifying and grosser than the moss that fuzzes the old stone walls—yet I'm both exhausted and unsurprised when the tunnel stops abruptly.

I spin in a slow circle, phone out, finally capturing the trapdoor above me in the glow. By bracing my foot against the wall and shoving several times, I'm finally able to jimmy it loose.

Contrary to Dom's insistence, it's not bricked up.

I pause for a long time, dread filling up all the empty space around me.

A part of me hadn't believed him, but I'm still strangely bereft, as if I've lost something precious. A connection to my father, maybe. That his best friend would lie to me—worse, that he'd willingly put me in danger.

Still, I find it hard to picture Dom sneaking in this way. He has a key to our front door, first of all.

And trashing the library? Leaving behind a warning? That smacks of someone inexperienced. Younger.

Is Dom covering for *Fletcher*?

I shake the thought away like a cobweb and focus on the task at hand. Using the crude footholds chiseled into the wall, I climb up and through the opening, emerging into the middle of the old foundation.

Adrenaline courses through me like a drug. Somehow, I knew this is where I'd end up.

I let the door fall shut and it all but disappears, hidden as it is near the crumbling back wall behind a pile of rock and debris.

This is why Dominic told me not to come here, on our very first day. Not because he was protecting me from danger. But because he was protecting this secret.

For the first time since we moved here, I have the upper hand. I've found the tunnel, despite best efforts to thwart me. And I'm going to block it off. The door opens outward, so any barrier on the tunnel side would be useless. Something heavy on top, maybe? Though anything I can lift, Emory or Dom or Fletcher can surely take off.

His betrayal is fresh, tender to the touch, but it's a flesh wound and it will heal.

I gather as much debris as I can—crumbling bricks, tree branches, loose dirt—and pile it on top of the door. It's not a perfect solution—anyone can move it. But hopefully it will scare them. They'll know that I know. And after all, if I've gone to all this trouble here, surely they'll realize I have blocked off the other end. And who in their right mind would head into this creepy, claustrophobic passage without the firm promise of an exit?

I climb over the wall and toward the bank of the creek. The call of a northern flicker is answered in kind, and below me, the creek burbles softly, like a melody. It's so peaceful, no one would ever know that some kind of horror took place here. No one *will* ever know. Even I, privy to Rebecca's memories, still don't really know what happened to her.

I lean against the trunk of the tall aspen, tilting my head back to watch the tree branches overhead, the way the sunlight dapples and shimmers through the leaves, until my eyes burn and drift shut.

I'm in front of the fireplace, my skirts spread out around me. The iron poker is heavy in my sweaty palm, the smell of it like the tang of blood. I raise my arm to wipe my brow on the sleeve of my dress, the fire in the hearth blazing too high for the heat of the day.

Dr. Clarett stands in the doorway, watching me. "I don't know why you're so angry. I've kept my end of the bargain—"

"Bargain? Hardly. I may as well have sold my soul. And for something that should be rightfully hers." I add my signature to the line below his and tuck the signed deed into my bodice before he can renege on our agreement.

His eyes are dark, evil pools, the firelight dancing in them. "I don't know why I've bothered," he says. A lie.

"We both know why. The town may believe our playacting, but I know what you really are," I say, the words bitter in my mouth.

"It's not like anyone would take your word over mine. A woman? With a child born far too early in her marriage for propriety's sake. Plus, you've been ill. Everyone knows you are weak."

He's only trying to convince himself, but I tremble with rage as I readjust my grip on the poker, letting my fingers trace the loop of the handle and settle into the grooves of the twisted metal. "I am not weak. Your water has healed me, remember? And I can still ruin you."

"Seems an empty threat, since you're burning all of your so-called proof." He gestures toward the flames.

"Oh, I haven't burned everything. Don't look so surprised, Doctor. I kept records, too." His mouth twists as he leans toward the flames, as if to snatch something back. I jam the poker into the fire, narrowly missing his hand. Beneath it, my wedding photo turns brown and curls in on itself.

A spark leaps from the burning wreckage of his legacy, smoldering on the carpet. He leaps forward to stomp on it, as another ignites the curtains nearby.

"Be reasonable, Rebecca. Help me put it out."

He moves as if to grab my arm, but I duck under him to throw open the door, letting the wind rush in to feed the fire. "Don't you dare tell me to be reasonable! And don't touch me." I brandish the poker. "Ever again."

It takes all I have in me to stand before this monster, but I do it. For my family. For Marguerite, and for Daisy. He has already taken so much from me. He will not take this.

I press the tip of the poker to his chest, gently at first, then harder. Forcing him backward. "This is my property now. Leave it. Before I change my mind and tell everyone what you've done."

He stumbles backward, grabbing the porch beam to steady himself, but I keep going. "We're bound together by this secret, and perhaps we'll both go to our graves with it. But I take comfort in knowing that we shall never meet in the afterlife. I've done many things I regret, Dr. Clarett," I call after him as he flees down the porch steps. "But you've done so much worse."

I open my eyes, blinking into the darkness, trying to orient myself. The sun has almost set, and the rising moon is covered by clouds. My legs have gone numb tucked beneath me, and as I unfold them, blood rushes back in, painful and cramping. I wipe my nose with the sleeve of my sweatshirt, and it comes away smeared red. Ignoring it, I glance at my phone, but the numbers make no sense.

6:27 p.m.

I've been out here for hours.

CHAPTER 35

The first thing I do when I get back to the house is send a snap to Bryn.

I followed the tunnel

I'm so wired, I can't sit still. I pace my room as I wait for their response.

Bryn sends back a shot of their face, one eyebrow raised dramatically.

why are you covered in blood

I look down. The front of my sweatshirt is splattered with blood droplets.

Nosebleed. Not important

I thought that stopped when you adjusted to the altitude

I ignore the question and switch over to chat, typing out everything, beginning with the tunnel and ending with the memory of the fire.

Bryn takes a long time to send a short message: Are you sure you didn't fall asleep?

I shove aside the niggle of doubt their words raise. I know the difference between a memory and a dream. I choke back my irritation and send another snap.

Don't you get it? Rebecca survived.

Finding out what happened to her is not going to cure you

You're wrong. I'm sick. And Marguerite died. Maybe from the same disease

This time, Bryn's answer is swift.

over a hundred years ago

You're not listening to me!

My frustration is so strong I can taste it, warm and coppery.

Rebecca survived. I just need to see the right memory.

I watch the dots jump as I wait, mimicking their movement as I bounce on the balls of my feet.

What if the memories aren't about your illness at all?

I halt abruptly, sinking onto the edge of the bed.

what else could they be about?

Altitude? a residual reaction to trauma? It isn't magic. It's biology.

Bryn is both right and wrong. It *is* biology. Because Rebecca and I are linked, genetically.

And if I want to survive like she did, I need to figure out what really happened to her.

I'm feeling more clear-headed after a hot shower and a change of clothes. Mom's car is in the driveway, but she's nowhere to be found. I send her a text:

Are you home?

Lying down. I've got a headache.

Want me to handle dinner?

That'd be great, thx

I take the car and head to Snarf's, ordering two Big Fat Snarfs with everything, one on gluten-free bread.

When I pull into the driveway with the food, there's a car I don't recognize parked in front of the house and a strange guy standing on the doorstep wearing a trucker cap and holding a clipboard.

"Can I help you?" I ask, getting out and holding the bag of sandwiches between us like it might provide me some sort of protection.

"Tress Gunderson?" he asks, reading from the clipboard.

I shake my head.

He glances at the house and then back at me. "But she lives here," he says. Not a question.

"Maybe. What's this—"

"Do you? Live here?"

Who is this guy? My gut instinct is to lie. "No."

He narrows his eyes at me and brandishes a large manila envelope. "I've got papers for her. Summons to appear—"

I snatch the envelope. Is Kurt filing for divorce? I did not see that coming. But the sticker on the front of the envelope says something about property ownership. Is that asshole trying to steal my house?

"Wait." He's already got his car door open, one leg in. "What does this mean?" I ask.

He lifts a shoulder and clicks his pen aggressively, scrawling something on his clipboard before tossing it into the passenger seat. "She needs to produce a deed of ownership. Someone's making a claim on your house."

CHAPTER 36

Mom is in the kitchen uncorking a bottle of wine when I drop the envelope and the keys on the counter with a clatter. "Someone just served you with papers," I say.

She jerks on the cork with more force than necessary, droplets of wine falling to the countertop like rain. "Kurt?" she asks, trying for cool but failing.

I fight to keep my voice steady. My chest is tight and the pressure headache is building in my head like a stormfront, and neither has anything to do with my illness. "Nope. Apparently someone is making a claim on the house."

She sets the corkscrew down and walks toward me, her movements deliberate. I watch her face as she picks up the envelope and opens it, but I can't read her expression.

"Who is it?" I finally ask when I can't stand the suspense any longer. "Is it Emory's dad? Or Dominic?"

"Let's eat in the living room tonight." Her voice is falsely bright as she pours herself a glass of wine before she tucks the packet under her arm and walks away without waiting for my agreement.

I follow her with the bag of sandwiches.

She gets comfortable on the living room floor and turns the TV to *The Great British Baking Show*, sipping her wine as she waits for me to unpack the food. "I love Prue, but I do miss Mary," she says, her eyes on the screen.

"Are we really not going to talk about this?"

"I saw the video." She reaches for my hand, but the table is in the way.

Tears spring to my eyes. "I don't want to talk about that."

"We're a team. I don't want you to feel like you have to keep things from me."

Damn it, how has she turned this around on me? "Mom, who's trying to take the house?"

She sighs, pushes the envelope toward me, and picks up her wine glass.

I pull out the papers, but they're all legal documents and might as well be in Latin. Parts of them probably are. The top one reads *Petition to Claim Ownership*. I scan quickly to the bottom of the page. It's signed by Amber Morales.

My heart drops into my stomach, landing with a thud. This shouldn't shock me as much as it does. Mom had questioned Dom about this possibility. But he and Nat had dismissed the idea. And yet, Nat's signature is here, too, as Amber's legal counsel.

I swallow down a hot throatful of bile. "How could the house not be ours? This is a joke, right? Dad lived here, and Grandpa. They can't just take it."

"It says there is an anomaly in the transfer history. The house was built by her great-great grandfather and Mrs. Morales thinks it should have remained in the family."

"I just saw her. I can't believe she sat next to me and didn't say a word."

Although that's not entirely true. She told me she was related to Clarett, didn't she? Very deliberately. And she'd mentioned the house. Or at least the attic.

"She may have a rightful claim," Mom says. "Maybe this is for the best."

"The best? No!" I shove the papers off the coffee table. "It's our house! We're descendants, too."

"It's in the judge's hands now." She takes another gulp of wine before dropping her head into her hands. "I handled all of this wrong, from the beginning. Kurt wanted to sell, and I should have let him. But I wanted you to have the chance to see where you came from. I think now that was a mistake. After all that's happened—" Her voice breaks. "Maybe this is a sign."

"How can you say that? You want to just walk away? Without even trying to fight it?"

"This house is expensive, Lo." She sighs heavily. "I've been looking at the numbers, and I can't think of a way to keep it up. Not without Kurt's income."

"But we own it. I own it. We don't have a mortgage, right?"

"There are still expenses. Utilities, upkeep, taxes, insurance. It's a lot. More than we have. And with the added expense of a lawyer . . . ?" She leans over and fishes a paper out of her purse. It's a spreadsheet, house expenses in one column and her income on the right. The expense column is more—by a lot.

Fear thrums a steady beat in my throat. "There must be something we can do."

"Look, I know I screwed this all up. Big time." She reaches for my hand. "And it would be so easy to hate me right now, and I wouldn't blame you—"

"Is that what you want?" I snatch it away. I don't want her self-pity. I want this situation to be different; I want her to fix it. Maybe that isn't fair, but she's the adult here. "Will it be easier to give my house away if I hate you?"

She leans back and swirls her glass of wine, letting the red liquid coat the glass. "We don't have any ties here. A clean break might be for the best."

I shake my head, fast. "I do have ties to this place. It's in my blood."

She flinches. "Don't say that. This town. It's so small, you know, and . . . it just shouldn't be this hard. We're butting up against a lifetime of history that we weren't a part of."

"But we were," I argue. "At least our family was. Dad was born here. He left me this house for a reason. He wanted me to have it. I think he knew we were related to Clarett. This *is* our history."

"You want to talk about history?" Her laugh is dry and mirthless.

Why does she have to say it like that? Like I'm the one who's crossed a line?

"Do you want to know the real reason I hate it here so much? The real reason I never told you about your father's accident?"

I nod and bite back the urge to scream out no. Because of course I do. Except she looks like telling me is going to break something inside her, something I won't be able to put back together.

"When the car crashed, I was thrown clear. I woke up on the side of the road, disoriented. Confused. My head was bleeding and it was raining . . ." She touches her forehead, then her belly. "All I could think about was the baby. He was trapped in the car, tangled in the seat belt, and I didn't even try to save him. I was too worried about you. I saw the car, teetering there. And I just . . . crawled away." She sobs softly into her hands as the world shatters around me.

Finally, she lifts her head. "And I never told you. I never told anyone, because as long as no one else knew, as long as I kept that secret, deep, deep inside, it didn't have to be true. I didn't have to be a coward." She gets unsteadily to her feet. "But I am one. I didn't want to come back here, and I don't want to stay, because every day, I'm confronted by that simple fact. By the memory of him. I let him die."

She brushes her fingers against my head. "I'm sorry I waited so long. You deserve the truth."

I recoil from her touch, stumbling into the hallway and around the corner, sliding down the wall until I'm on the floor, where I sit alone with the awful finality of those words, as the grandfather clock in the hallway ticks quietly on, counting off the seconds of what to me will always be the "after."

I'm the reason my father is dead.

That's what she's really saying. They say it's a mother's instinct to save her child. It's biological. But all I have is her word on that, and after all this time, those words ring hollow. Maybe it wasn't even about me. Maybe that's just the story she's been telling herself all these years. Maybe the real choice was, simply, live or die. Human beings are wired for self-preservation. Is that why we're driven to keep these kinds of secrets? To protect ourselves, at any cost?

You deserve the truth.

Fuck yeah I do. I deserved it a lot earlier.

Because there's a power in knowing your history. Good or bad, it's what made us who we are. So I guess that includes this awful truth about my father's death. And my illness. And it also includes my family's trauma, and the secret that lives in this house and this soil.

And in me.

CHAPTER 37

I finally answer one of Fletcher's dozens of texts, agreeing to let him pick me up for school. Part of me thinks it's a terrible idea, but I rationalize it in a number of ways: There's no way in hell I'm riding with Mom. Besides, I need to confront him with what I know.

"How are you doing?" he asks as he reverses out of my driveway. "The other day was rough. When you didn't come to school, and then you didn't answer my texts—"

"Sorry about that." I fold my hands in my lap. "I just needed some time to . . . process."

"Don't worry," Fletcher says. "Soon some idiot will pour hot sauce down his pants and everyone will move on."

"I mean, I could probably pay Sage twenty bucks to do it if I get desperate." I'm going for breezy, but it falls flat. "Hey, while I was at home, I did some exploring," I add, partly to change the subject, but mostly because I need to say it before I chicken out. My emotions have run the gamut the past few days, from hurt to anger to resignation. Now that I'm sitting next to him, his eager cheerfulness engulfing me like a fragrant cologne, my resolve is slipping.

"I followed the tunnel."

His smile freezes on his face and my mouth goes dry, all the liquid in my body evaporating along with my last bit of hope.

I tense, breathing in hard through my nose. "You knew, didn't you? Where it led? That it was still open." He doesn't answer, and I choke out a groan that's half sob. "That's what I thought."

He pulls over and shifts the Jeep into park. "Let me explain."

I glance out the window at the deserted, unfamiliar street. "If you're trying to prove you're not a creep who's been sneaking into my house, this isn't helping."

His eyes go wide. "You can't think— It wasn't me. I would never break into your house. I mean, not while you're living there."

I bark a laugh. "Oh, I get it. If you can scare me off, then it's fair game."

"Look, Dad used to tell me how he and Teddy would sneak out and meet their friends at the creek. But as far as he knew, it had been blocked off for years. Then a couple years ago, Emory and her dad moved in. She's the one who opened it up. Since then, we've used it maybe a handful of times." He hastens to add, "Only before you moved in."

"Is that supposed to make this all right?" I cross my arms over my chest and stare at him. "Someone's been breaking into my house! And you didn't say anything. I showed it to you, and you let your dad act like I was crazy. Like there was no possible way anyone could be getting in. You knew, and you didn't say anything."

"I know I should have said something. I just . . . I thought I could figure out who it was. Make them stop. You have to understand, these are my friends."

"I thought *I* was your friend."

"You are! That's why I wanted to protect you. I asked everyone. Emory, Clare, Sage. They all swore it wasn't them."

"What if it was some psycho killer? You were going to let them just keep coming into my house?"

"There's a way we close the tunnel. A special log we lay on top. It hasn't been disturbed. I've been checking."

I throw up my hands. "Do you realize how this sounds? You admit you've been sneaking around my property, only you claim it's to try and figure out who's sneaking in! When clearly, it's one of your friends."

He shakes his head vehemently, but it's an empty gesture.

The log means nothing, other than it has to be someone who knows how to put it back. The fact that Fletcher doesn't realize it makes him ridiculously naive.

Or a liar.

We drive the rest of the way to school in silence. In the parking lot, he jogs to keep up with me until Sage joins us, stepping into the wide gap I've left between us.

"How're things in Romancelandia?" he asks, throwing an arm around each of us.

Neither of us answers.

I get about four "Demon Girl"s on our trip from the parking lot to my locker, which Sage deflects with his middle finger and wagging devil tongue, and Fletcher gets one attempted high five that comes with some ridiculous question about whether I'm a hellion in bed. Sage finds this hilarious, while Fletcher turns beet red.

Before he can choke out an apology, I duck away from both of them and head for my locker, spinning the dial three times before I can draw to mind the actual combination.

Dr. Archuleta asked me to keep a journal of the things that fatigue me. How will I even explain this? *Direct correlation between being trolled by my peers and onset of fatigue.* Or maybe just *School sucks. I need a nap.*

I'm not sure why either of them is still hovering nearby, but before I can ask them to leave, Clare joins us. They all chatter hellos while I ignore them, and just when things can't get any more awkward, Van walks up, the "What's new in hel—" dying on his lips as Clare bodychecks him, forcing him back against the locker.

"Relax. It was a joke." Van holds up his hands in supplication.

"A joke, huh? And I'm supposed to know that by the way we're all laughing?"

"Jesus, Clare. You're too fucking intense for this early in the morning." Sage punches her lightly in the shoulder and she shoves him back.

"Is everyone in this town an immature prick?" she asks.

"I'm not—"

"It was rhetorical, Fletcher." She turns to me, hands on hips, scrutinizing me in such a way that even Mom would be impressed. "This sucks. I'm sorry."

I lift my head from the locker. Everything is shit, and thanks to her and her brother, I'm about to lose my house, and she's *sorry*?

Sage's eyebrows go up and he and Van exchange a look, but Clare just nods. "The best way out is always through."

Is she really trying to play the game right now? After we just got served with papers? Then again, maybe she doesn't know that I know. I want to ask her, but not with this big of an audience. "Robert Frost," I say, pulling out a textbook.

She shoves her hands in her jean jacket and nods approval.

"I thought it was Nine Inch Nails," Fletcher says, his lopsided smile a desperate plea for approval.

Clare shakes her head sadly. "He's not illiterate, despite his best efforts to prove the opposite."

"Hey! I read. I just happen to like music, too."

She pats his head like a puppy. "Of course you do."

I chew on my lip, trying to calm my frenzied heart and my shaking hands. This all feels so impossibly normal, so *real*, and yet I know it isn't. These aren't my friends. It's all fake, like some TV drama. Van is playing the villainous dude-bro, while Clare is clearly setting herself up as the cool bestie. I'm the outcast, the new girl who definitely doesn't own enough flannel to completely fit in here.

I don't know if it's my illness, or the betrayal, or the fact that I'm this close to losing all of it anyway. Or maybe I'm just tired of trying.

I slam the locker door and clutch my books to my chest like a shield. "Any idea who posted the video?"

"It wasn't any of us." Fletcher looks flustered. "Back me up here, Clare."

But Clare stares pointedly at her cuticles.

"Sage?"

Sage lifts a shoulder. "Look, dude. I hate to say this, but Emory was recording that night. Still, we should hear her side of the story. Before we convict her. Otherwise, we're no better than the rest."

His solidarity softens me, but I'm not letting Emory completely off the hook. "No better than the rest? Meaning, the people asking me how empty my soul has to be to become a vessel for Satan?"

He leans his head back and hoots. "Who said that? Van?" He makes a finger gun at Van, whose shit-eating grin slides off his face when he sees my expression.

"Doesn't sound like me." He points toward the ceiling as the first series of bells chime. "Later."

Clare watches him go, her lip curled in disgust. "I asked Emory for her side of the story," she says as she turns back. "She admitted to recording it, but said she wasn't ever planning on posting it."

Not planning on it is not the same as not posting it.

Fletcher says, "Hold on. We've known Em for a long time. Doesn't that deserve some kind of benefit of the doubt?"

Clare squints at him like she's trying to figure out what language he's speaking. "It was a shitty thing to do," she says finally. "Knowing the person who did it isn't going to change my opinion on that."

Her words embolden me, and I take the leap. "Speaking of shitty things to do, I know about the lawsuit," I say, my heart in my throat. "Your mom served us with papers yesterday."

"What lawsuit?" Fletcher's gaze darts between us like a Ping-Pong ball.

"Your mom is representing her."

"Representing who?" he asks, at the same time Clare says, "I have no idea what you're talking about."

Is she lying? Her voice is flat, emotionless. But her fingers drum nervously against her books as she cuts her eyes to her brother, who smirks but keeps his mouth shut.

"Your mom is suing us," I say to both of them. "She paid off our back taxes, and now she's trying to take my house."

Clare starts shaking her head before I even finish talking. "No. We don't have that kind of money."

I shrug. "I don't know how she did it. But it's true."

Clare bites her lip and looks at Sage. "What did you do?"

"Moi?" He clutches his chest.

He's being dramatic, but he isn't denying it. Was the video just another way to get me to leave so they could have my house?

Fletcher is resolute in his loyalty. "Clare and Sage wouldn't take your home." He nudges Sage. "Tell her."

Sage lets out a frustrated sigh. "Dude, it was my family's house first. There were never even any papers signed. What if the house *was* stolen from us, all those years ago?"

I stagger back like he's slapped me. "Dr. Clarett gave it to Rebecca. He signed the deed. I saw—" I break off as I realize they're all staring at me with looks of concerned disbelief. "You know what? Forget it." I jerk my arm away when Fletcher tries to grab my hand. "I understand. I'm the new girl. The stranger. Who cares if I get hurt?"

"No one's trying to hurt you," Fletcher says, his brows drawing together.

"Chill," Sage adds. "It can't be good for you to get so worked up after the altitude thing. I think it's messing with your head."

They're not listening to me. Or rather, they have no intention of hearing me. Still, I give it one last try. "One of you has been in my house," I say quietly. "One of you posted that video."

"Okay, but—" Fletcher says, and I know I've lost.

"But . . ." I echo, letting it hang. How was he going to finish that? Maybe someone harassing me and stealing from me and *scaring the shit out of me* isn't that big a deal? Maybe the fact that someone wants to humiliate and violate my privacy isn't enough of a reason to shift loyalties? Especially not to a girl he just met.

"You called me your friend. I trusted you. *But*"—I lean hard on the word—"a friend would at least have given me a heads-up before trying to throw me out of my home." Clare flinches.

I turn to Fletcher. "A friend would believe me when I tell them someone is trying to hurt me. Or they'd at least believe *in* me, enough to hear what I'm saying before dismissing it out of hand."

This is the opposite of what they thought they were signing up for. No low-key Lola here. I'm putting it all out there, and maybe it's too much and I don't even blame them. I'm hurt and disappointed at their betrayal, but I can't fault their reasoning. This is their clan, their ride-or-die. I'm just the new girl. A nobody.

Mom was right.

This life was never meant to be mine.

CHAPTER 38

The bus drops me off at the foot of the driveway, and as I duck between the trees, the long afternoon shadow of the house covers me so completely, it's like walking into nightfall. I fish my keys out of my bag, but the front door is unlocked.

Goosebumps pucker my skin as I push it open.

Did Mom forget to lock it when she left this morning?

I stand just inside the foyer, leaving the door ajar.

I blocked off the tunnel completely last night, stacking everything that wasn't nailed down in front of the door in the library. If our not-so-mysterious stalker is feeling thwarted, maybe this is what they've resorted to.

I can't tell if this is a voice of reason, or one of paranoia. After a moment, I shake my head and push the door shut.

Listen.

The only sound is the incessant ticking of the grandfather clock.

Nothing looks out of place.

"Hello?" I call out, feeling foolish.

There's no reply.

I creep quietly toward the library. It's undisturbed, which is to say mostly bare except for the corner, where all of the furniture is shoved up against the bookshelf.

I can somehow feel the emptiness of the tunnel just behind the books. Dark and echoey and pulsing, an apt metaphor for my fear and my anger.

Whoever was using this to get in, they can't anymore.

As I turn toward the hall, a thud from above my head freezes me in place.

There *is* someone in the house. Upstairs.

The floor creaks, then the stairs.

I break from my temporary stupor.

I picture myself sprinting from the room, down the hall and toward the front door, calculating whether I can get out before the intruder makes it downstairs.

But I'm done cowering.

I'm ready to fight.

I grab a fireplace poker, a flash of déjà vu buckling my knees as I remember Rebecca brandishing it at Dr. Clarett. I fight against the woozy feeling washing over me.

Instead, I take it into the living room, catching the intruder as he tries to make his escape.

"Freeze, asshole."

Kurt stands between me and the front door, and I can't tell if this is deliberate or if he was trying to get out before I caught him.

The poker goes slack in my hands. "What are you doing here?"

"Hey, Lola." He shifts the box he's carrying to one hand and waves half-heartedly as he looks over my shoulder. "Is your mom here?"

I have the wild urge to lie. *Yes. She's in the kitchen. With a big knife.*

But this is Kurt. He's a dick, sure. But he's not here to hurt me. Right?

"What are you doing here?" I ask again, and then, "How did you get here? I didn't see a car."

He lifts a shoulder. "I took an Uber."

"And had them drop you off with no one home?" It's ballsy, even for him.

"Yeah, well, I had to pack up a few of my things. And I really wanted to talk to your mom. I figured, you know, she could always give me a lift back."

My mind is going a million miles a minute, each thought too fast for me to grab hold of. "I'm pretty sure she told you to get on a plane." I blurt out the first thing that comes to mind—maybe not the best choice.

An expression flits across his face—disgust, maybe. Or rage. "She did. I chose not to."

I don't know how to respond to that, so I say, "Well, she's at work. And I doubt she's going to be happy to hear you broke in while we were gone."

"I didn't . . ." He pulls back from the growl, straightening his shoulders. "I have a key," he says slowly. "We're still married."

I doubt Mom sees it that way, but this isn't my argument to have.

"Shouldn't you be at school?" he asks. "I thought you were healed now."

Something about the glint in his eye makes me think he might've seen the video. Or maybe I'm completely paranoid. "It's an early-release day."

He nods. "Right." He stares at me, a ghost of a smile on his upper lip. "Let me give you a little advice." He leans forward and lowers his voice. "The con only works if someone believes it."

"What is that supposed to mean?"

He shrugs. "I'm just saying, maybe it's time to pack it in. No one will blame you if you start to get better. Healthy mountain air and all that."

He still thinks I'm faking. For a second, I almost feel sorry for him. Maybe this is what a lifetime of being alone does. He's aware of human emotions, like empathy and trust, but he can't quite pull them off. Self-involved is his default, and maybe that's not all bad. Maybe I can learn something from him. For sure, I need to look out for myself more.

Starting right now.

"You need to go," I say. "You don't live here anymore, and Mom wouldn't want you here."

His face spasms as if I've slapped him. "I just need to talk to—"

"No," I say louder. "Get. Out." I point at the door, and my hand doesn't even shake.

He rolls his eyes, just a fraction, but I see it, and he knows I see it. He takes one small step forward as my face hardens.

I pull my phone out of my pocket, and he retreats.

"Fine. Calm down already. I see you haven't learned to dial back the drama."

My temper flares, but I don't lower myself to his level. "Nope. But you'll recall I do know how to dial 911. How do you think Mom will like it if you get arrested for breaking into her house? Can you say 'restraining order'?"

We watch each other warily for another long moment.

I don't know what he reads in my face, but he breaks first, turning away. At the door, he tries to say something. "Fine. I'm going. Tell Tress—"

But I don't let him finish; I just slam the door as soon as he's through, throwing the dead bolt and then backing away so I can't hear him. My whole body is shaking now, but it's okay. He can't see me, and anyway, this movement isn't out of fear or shame. It's pure adrenaline.

What was he really doing here? Picking things up, like he said? Or going through our stuff? I run upstairs to my room and throw open the door. It looks untouched, so I cross the hall to Mom's. Her closet door is open, as well as his, and there are clothes strewn across the bed.

Maybe he was telling the truth.

But damn, he made a mess.

A glint of metal in the driveway catches my eye, and I push the curtain aside to watch as his Uber pulls up. They must have been waiting around the corner after all.

I give the car the finger, and I'm oddly energized when he glances up toward the window.

"Adios, dickhead."

My vision wobbles and the room tilts. I lean against the window for balance, the glass so hot from the scorching sun that it burns my palms.

I shake my stinging hand and back away from the window. I know he's in there. The sun beats down on my head as I bang on the front door again.

Finally, he throws open the door, his eyes widening in surprise when he sees us standing on his porch. God, how I loathe his self-righteous, hypocritical face. It's killing me to ask him for help. But what choice do I have?

"What were you thinking, coming here?" he asks.

I hold the bundle up so he can see her, but he jerks away, cranes his neck toward the house. "You need to leave. My wife—"

"Please." I hold my voice steady. "I have nowhere else to go. If you won't do it for me, then do it for Daisy." His daughter wiggles at the sound of her name and begins to cry.

I blink as the memory recedes, replaced by the empty driveway, the ever-present ticking of the grandfather clock.

Daisy. His daughter.

I hurry down the stairs and wrench open the front door, stumbling out onto the porch. They were here, right here. With their baby. I squeeze my eyes shut, swaying in the cool shade. I press my hands against the stone, trying to will it back.

I need more time. I need to know what happened.

Daisy. Daisy. Daisy.

Somehow, my lips form the words. "She's as much your family as she is mine."

But he is unmoved by her cries, or my pleas. Why on earth did I think empathy would work on this man? This monster? I turn to go, but the hand on my wrist stops me.

It's Clarett's assistant.

I shrink back, but his steady hand holds me in place.

"Rebecca, wait." He steps out onto the porch with us and quietly pulls the door shut behind him.

"Go back inside, James. This doesn't concern you."

"But it could." He nods encouragingly at me. "You and the baby need a place to live. A respectable story to offset these . . . rumors."

He means the hideous things they've been saying about Daisy and me. "Rumors" is a bland word for the hateful talk of evil and dark magic. Talk they've done nothing to dispel.

"And you need to salvage your reputation, to move past all the whispers of malpractice,

the petty talk of sordid relationships," he says to Clarett. "What if there was a way for us all to get what we want?"

The doctor folds his arms over his chest. "I'm listening."

I turn too fast, and the dizziness takes over. As I crumple to my knees, I catch a reflection of myself in the glass in the wide front doors, holding my arms in front of me like I'm cradling a baby.

I'm bleeding again.

CHAPTER 39

I wake to the beeping of my phone, my room in dark shadow. I blink into the gloom, disoriented and afraid. Why am I here? What day is it?

I fumble for my phone on the nightstand. The screen says *Claret Creek General Hospital*.

"Hello?"

"Lola, it's Dr. Archuleta. I got your message."

"My . . . message." My head is throbbing, and my mouth is so dry I feel like I swallowed a mouthful of sand.

"Yes. About"—I can hear paper rustling—"scheduling a genetic panel?"

I sit up. "Yes, that's right." I'd used the health app to send the message, but that feels like a lifetime ago.

"I need a little more information," she says, "before we start ordering tests. I'm just not sure that type of screening is warranted."

Exactly what Dr. K had told me. Many times.

"My friend's mom has this rare blood disorder. She said it took years for her to get diagnosed, and they only finally figured it out through a genetic panel. Her symptoms are similar to mine, so I thought . . ."

"It can be tempting to hear about someone else's diagnosis and think it might apply," she begins.

"We're related," I blurt out.

"Okay." Her voice is neutral. "I'll make a note of that."

"And she said her condition is genetic. So that's why I thought . . . maybe. I don't know. Maybe it's a dumb idea."

"Nothing's a dumb idea when you're searching for answers," she says. "What's the name of her condition?"

"I don't know," I confess.

"Can you ask your friend?"

"We're . . . kind of in a fight right now." I cringe, hunched over the phone. *Plus, they hate me and are trying to have me thrown out of my house.* Could I sound any more ridiculous?

"Surely she'd understand."

I picture myself typing out the text to Clare, and imagine her immediately deleting it. "I don't think she'd answer me. But I can try."

"Let me know what she says. In the meantime, I think you're right. Some more blood tests seem to be warranted. Can you come down to the lab in the morning? Let's say ten thirty?"

"Okay. Thank you."

I hang up the phone and swing my legs around. I'm shaky and disoriented. When did I fall asleep? And how did I get up to my room?

Oh god. Did I pass out again? And Mom put me to bed?

That doesn't feel right, but I can't think past the pounding in my head. I need water and Excedrin.

I get up slowly, unsteady on my feet.

"Mom?" I call for her from the top of the stairs, and again at the bottom after carefully making my way down, clutching the railing.

She doesn't answer and the house is still.

I probably didn't pass out, then. Or at least, she's not the one who found me if I did. I doubt she'd have left me alone.

In the kitchen, I find a note.

Hope you got some rest. Betty called in sick so I'm heading back to the library for the evening shift.

Rotisserie chicken in the fridge, just needs to be microwaved. Also, Fletcher left you a letter.

She signs it with a tiny smiley face and a heart, but her handwriting is shaky and tentative. She has no idea where our relationship stands any more than I do.

There's a long envelope on the table with my name written across it in Fletcher's neat, tiny handwriting. I pick it up and set it back down. I'm going to need some painkillers and some food before I can face whatever he has to say.

After I swallow a couple Excedrin migraine pills and gulp a full glass of water, I turn to the fridge. My hand is on the door when I see it.

A magnet with a big red bird. Gayle Romero, Cardinal Realty.

Shit. Has this always been here? Mom just showed me those papers last night. She can't be moving forward with a sale already.

I grab the magnet to toss it in the garbage, but pause when I read the line on the bottom. *Serving Gunnison County and surrounding areas, including Claret Creek, Lansing, and Blue Mesa.*

There's a Lansing in Colorado? Did I know that?

I don't bother to heat the chicken, but just stand at the counter pulling bits of the cold meat off the bones. The meat is tender and well seasoned, but it does little to ease the ache in my stomach. I'm hungry, yes, but I'm also scared.

How did I get to my room?

This last memory had started upstairs, in Mom's room. It had been about Rebecca, visiting Dr. Clarett. With her baby. It had started to fade, and I'd done all I could to hold on to it, even running out to the porch and willing it back.

And it had worked! I'd seen Clarett and the baby—Daisy. I'd felt her in my arms. *His daughter.*

So it's true. I *am* related to Clarett.

After the memory had faded, I'd stared at my own reflection in the wavy glass of the front door, barely recognizing the woman looking back—eyes wide and worried, face gaunt, blood streaking her upper lip.

After that, nothing.

What had I done then? Gone to the bathroom to clean up?

That would have been logical, but I have no recollection of it.

I shove aside the chicken.

I've never been able to control a memory like this, to stay in it longer in order to gain more information. This is important—momentous.

But it's clearly taken a toll on my body. I'm shaking, buzzy. My head is throbbing. And maybe worse than the physical symptoms, I've lost time. Paid for Rebecca's memory with the loss of my own.

I put the chicken away and wash my hands before sitting down at the kitchen table with Fletcher's letter.

Inside, the letter is folded around several photographs. I let these fall to the table as I start to read.

Dear Lola,

My mom says I don't spend enough time around people. She's partly right—I prefer bears. They're easier to read. But what she doesn't understand is that bears can be social. They aren't pack animals, they're more discerning than that. But they do form attachments. They're just more selective about it. I guess I'm the same way when it comes to my friends. We chose each other, and I don't take that loyalty lightly. But you're my friend, too. I chose you, and you are important to me, and I'm sorry if I made you feel like you're not. I'm going to make it right. Prove that I'm worthy of being part of your sleuth.

I know this is probably too little, too late, but I hope you'll accept my apology. I'd still love to take you to the dance.

Sincerely,
Fletcher

I read it again, but it doesn't make any more sense the second time around. He's going to make it right? Does that mean he's going to confront Emory? Or convince his mom and Amber to drop the claim?

And what about "I chose you"? What does *that* mean? He could have just said "I like you." "I *chose* you" is so . . . formal. And a little bit weird.

I put the letter aside and pick up the photos. The first is of my dad and teenage Dominic, who looks just like Fletcher. They're mugging for the camera, one on either side of an aspen tree, leaning sideways into the frame until their heads are almost touching. My dad is laughing, an open grin that holds pure joy, while Dom is baring his teeth is an exaggerated bite.

The next photo is just my dad, his face in profile. He's holding a fishing pole and looking out at the creek as the sun sets. The last one is a group shot, a bunch of kids sitting on a wall of the old foundation, arms thrown around each other, Dad and Dom in the middle, along with another kid I don't recognize, and two girls on his right. I'm pretty sure the second from the end is Natalie.

I love this glimpse into his past, and I'm ridiculously grateful that Fletcher has shared it with me.

The gratitude is followed by an immediate pang of longing so sharp it brings tears to my eyes.

This is it. This is all I've have, once the house is gone. No more floors he walked on, no shared history. Just a few found photos that will never tell the complete story.

It won't be any better than what I had in Michigan.

I swipe my face with my hand.

No. I refuse to settle for that. I've come so far. I'm so close to him here. These photos were taken here.

In fact, I think I've seen this one before.

I squint at the last shot again, at the five teens with their arms around each other. It looks so familiar. These must be Dom's. I flip it over, and though the back is gummy with old adhesive, the printing beneath is still legible.

Teddy and his friends down at the creek, 2001.

Teddy and his friends. Not "Dom and his friends," like you might expect from Dom's photos.

This is one of my grandma's photographs.

CHAPTER 40

I'm on your porch.

I squint at my phone, trying to make sense of Clare's text. It's just after 7:00, so she should be on her way to school.

I think we should talk.

Between Fletcher's apology/confession letter and him sending me the photos he might have stolen from my house, I'm wary about whatever Clare has to say. Does she just need an excuse to come inside?

Pass, I text.

I'm not leaving.

I throw off the covers and make my way down the stairs. I can see Clare's shadow through the tall side window.

"Lola?" she says, rapping softly at the door. "Are you there? This is important."

I don't answer, torn between curiosity and dread. I want to hear what she has to say, but that other voice is my head is still whispering, *You can't trust her.* And I know the voice is right—I can't risk being hurt again. But there's another part of me that's tired of being alone and afraid all the time.

My hand hovers over the doorknob.

Just say what you have to say, I finally text, sliding down and leaning against the door.

"Really?" she says under her breath, then raises her voice. "Okay, then. Here goes. I really didn't know about my mom filing a claim to the house. If I had, I would have warned you. Probably. Ugh. Fuck, I don't know. But the taxes, that wasn't us. You have to believe me. We're broke. I mean, you've seen my truck. Any money we have goes to my mom's medical treatments. So I don't know where you got that information, but there's no way she'd pay off your debt when she can't even afford to send me to college."

A pause. "But you were right about the house. My mom did ask a judge to look at the deed history. Apparently, there's some question about title ownership or some fucking nonsense. I don't understand it, and anyway, it's out of our hands. But I'm sorry for the way you found out, and I'm sorry if you think it's personal. It's not. I really thought we could be friends."

I thought that, too, once upon a time.

"And I know you have no reason to believe me, or trust me, or any of us, for that matter. But I . . ." She inhales sharply. "I think you should give Fletcher a chance. He really likes you. The other day, when he told me he'd asked you to the dance, he was over-the-moon excited. And look, I know he sometimes comes off like an overactive Labrador. But he's had this idea in his head of you and him—Dom and Teddy's kids—ever since we heard you guys were moving here. I get that it's a little much. I told him to ease up. But that's Fletcher. He always goes all in and assumes things will work out."

All in. Is that what we're calling the breaking and entering?

But the picture she's painting sounds like the Fletcher I've spent time with. And I can't quite reconcile *that* Fletcher with whoever's been messing with me. The two images won't converge, no matter how hard I try.

But why did he have my grandmother's photographs?

For some reason, Natalie Hart's words float into my head. *People want to help. Let them.*

But that idea is terrifying—like letting go of the life preserver and trusting that someone is going to help me keep my head above water. Like I've been struggling against the strong current alone all this time, and now this stranger will somehow keep me afloat.

I want to trust her.

What about the tunnel? And the video? I text her, not trusting my voice.

She's quiet for so long I think maybe she's decided not to answer.

Finally, she texts back.

That wasn't Fletcher

Was it you?

The dots bounce at the bottom of my screen for three long minutes before disappearing.

When I open the door, Clare is gone.

But there's a dress bag draped over the railing of the porch. I bring it inside and unzip it, pulling out a black dress with sheer sleeves and a square neck. The skirt is short but full, with an empire waistline delineated by a ribbon that ties in the back.

"It's lovely," Mom says from behind me.

I hadn't heard her come down, and I wonder how long she's been standing in the shadows. Did she hear Clare?

She's right about the dress. It is lovely, and perfect for tonight. Fancy, but not gaudy, and not so tight or revealing that I would be uncomfortable.

"I've got some black heels that will work," she says, coming over to rub the silky fabric of the sleeve.

She's trying her darndest to make a peace offering, but I'm just as determined to avoid it. Her bombshell from the other night is still a fresh wound between us, and it's going to take more than strappy shoes to heal it.

I turn away. "Thanks. But I don't think I'm going to the dance."

In addition to the genetic panel, Dr. Archuleta has ordered a number of other tests, along with a lengthy questionnaire about my symptoms, so by the time I finish at the lab, it's after lunchtime and I'm starving and exhausted.

Do I go to school? Face the snickers and the whispers? The outright taunts?

Track down Clare? Make her tell me why she's so certain Fletcher had nothing to do with the tunnel or the video?

Sit next to Fletcher in Spanish class? Ask him about the photos? Try to gauge once again if he's lying to me?

Tell him I can't go to the dance with him?

It's the smart thing to do, the brave thing.

And still I turn the car toward home.

Maybe I *am* the coward.

Mom is standing on the front porch with a petite woman in a red suit. When she sees me pull into the driveway, she quickly tries to usher the woman inside, but Red Jacket takes little notice, pointing first at the stonework around the porch and then the French doors before flipping open a folder.

I drop my keys in the loose gravel on the side of the driveway in my haste to get out of the car, my movements uncoordinated and clumsy, as if my brain has stopped giving directions to my body.

"Lola." Mom is anything but happy to see me; "stricken" would better describe her expression. "You're home early," she says as I stumble up the porch stairs. "Why aren't you at school?"

"I had those lab tests." I glance past Mom at the woman, trying to figure out how I recognize her and why her presence fills me with such an overwhelming feeling of dread.

"This is my daughter, Lola. She's the inheritor of the trust. Lola, this is Gayle Romero."

The penny drops, as does my jaw, as I remember the magnet I threw in the garbage.

She reaches out a hand, and I barely withhold the urge to slap it. "Why would you call a realtor? We're not even going to try and fight this?"

Mom smiles nervously. "Can you excuse us a moment, Gayle?"

"Of course. Do you mind if I head back inside to take some notes?"

"No problem." Mom keeps her smile in place until Gayle closes the front door behind her. "Before you say anything, she's just here to give some options. We need to know what it's worth in case of a settlement—"

"A settlement? Do you mean, before you rip my inheritance out from under me and hand off Dad's history—my history—to the first person who asks for it?"

My heart is beating wildly, and my whole body is shaking. I'm in fight-or-flight mode, but my body hasn't decided which way it's leaning.

"Calm down, honey. It can't be good for you to get so worked up."

"Then don't get me worked up!" I sag against the wall, then leap back up to pace. "Something's going on here, Mom. There's a reason Amber wants the house. It's tied to me and my illness and to my family. If you just give it away, we'll never have any answers. Don't you see? That's why Dad left this all to me. In trust. Because he *trusted* me. To find the truth." I clench my fists and hold them to my chest. "It's in the name."

Mom looks perplexed. "Are you okay, Lo? You aren't making a lot of sense." She reaches over to press a hand against my forehead.

"I'm making total sense. You're the one who isn't making sense. Moving us halfway across the country to a house that belongs to me, left *to me*"—I pound my chest—"and then you turn around and tell me, 'Oh, sorry, that was a lie.' Like none of it matters. Well, maybe it doesn't matter to you. But it matters to me. And it mattered to Dad."

She flinches. "I'm well aware of your father's wishes. But he isn't here. And whatever he wanted seventeen years ago, we can't give that more weight than the things happening in our lives right now. It certainly can't come before your well-being. If he were here . . ." She takes a breath. "I'm sure he'd agree with me. This is just a building. Nothing's more important than your health."

"What does this have to do with my health?" I scream and she takes a step back. "I'm tired of you blaming me for everything! I'm getting better. Dr. Archuleta said so." I brandish the bandaged crook of my elbow. "She's running a genetic panel. She's helping me." I yell again as she steps closer. "This is *your* mess. Your web of lies that got us here. Why can't you just be honest? You can't stand this house because it reminds you of what you did. And you can't stand to look at *me*, because you blame me. I'm the reason he's dead, because you chose me over him. And all of this"—I wave my hand—"just serves as a reminder."

She shrinks back, her face drained of color. "Lola, no. I never . . ." Her voice breaks.

I shake my head. "You never do *anything*. That's the whole problem. Tell your realtor the deal is off. Whatever papers you need, I won't sign them. And you can't make me."

I run into the house choking back tears, past Gayle in her gaudy jacket and up the stairs to my room, slamming the door with a finality that should brook no argument.

Maybe I shouldn't have said any of it. I hurt her, and maybe it wasn't fair.

But she's hurt me.

Keeps hurting me, with her insistence on giving away my home, my history. My memories.

She says she doesn't owe me her pain.

What about my birthright?

What about the truth?

CHAPTER 41

I need to eat something. My vision has gone blurry, and the headache that's taken root at the base of my skull throbs like someone is trying to sever my head from my body. But I can't face my mother. And I certainly can't watch her sign away our home with a polite smile.

There must be something I can do.

I know Rebecca signed that deed. I *saw* it happen.

How could it have disappeared?

She wouldn't have burned it—not in a million years.

I know from my memory that she wore it tucked against her breast because she was afraid Clarett might renege on whatever deal they'd made that day on the porch with James. The deal that had ended up with her in this house and Clarett being hailed as a town hero.

But what about after he was gone? She'd outlived the doctor, so surely there was a time when he was no longer a threat. What had she done with it then?

I crack the bedroom door and tiptoe to the top of the stairwell. I can faintly make out the voices of Mom and the realtor, then the sound of the front door opening and closing. I retreat backward, out of sight, as Mom walks toward the stairs.

Her phone rings, and she pauses halfway up to answer it.

I duck back into my room, listening at the door.

"Dr. Archuleta. How are you? Yes, she told me . . . I see. Did you want to speak with her?"

There's a long pause and the stair creaks. "I don't . . . That sounds serious. You're sure?" and then, "Tonight? There's a dance at school. Surely tomorrow is . . . The hospital?" Her voice is shaky now, like my body, which has started to tremble.

It sounds like Dr. Archuleta wants to hospitalize me. It must mean she's closer to some answers. Hope flutters in my chest, warring with my rising anxiety. I can't leave the house now.

I need time. Time to find where Rebecca hid the deed. Time to figure out how she survived.

Clare's family has a legitimate claim, unless I can prove otherwise. Who knows what Mom will do if I'm out of commission and she's faced with another hospital bill? She hates this house as it is. And that realtor is breathing down her neck.

If I go into the hospital tonight, there's a good chance that I won't be coming home to this place.

I look wildly around the room, my gaze falling on the dress bag hanging on the back of the door.

Mom thinks I'm going to the dance, despite what I told her. Maybe I can convince her I've already left.

I snatch the dress off the hanger.

"I'll get Lola," Mom is saying, "and we'll meet you at the hospital."

I flip off the lights, grab my phone, and dive under the bed, holding my breath as she calls up the stairs. "Lola? Lola, honey." She nudges open the door. "That was the doctor. We need to—" She flips on the light and sees the empty room. "Lola?" She's back in the hallway, calling down the hall to the bathroom. I take a slow, quiet breath, praying this works.

"Shit." She's back, and by the creak of my door, she's found the empty dress bag.

Shit is right. What if she tries to call me? I fumble with my phone, my hands slick, managing to silence it just as her call comes through.

We both wait for it to go to voicemail, my heart thumping so loudly I'm afraid she'll hear it beneath the bed, a real-life Edgar Allan Poe scenario.

She sends a text.

Where are you?

I text back with shaky fingers.

At the dance

"Shit, shit, shit." She stomps out of the room and down the stairs, and I flip onto my back so I can take a deep breath without the pressure of the floor against my chest.

I need to talk to you. Call me.

She's not going to stop texting.

But I can stop reading. I switch off the phone.

I make myself count to sixty after the front door slams shut before climbing out from under the bed. I don't have much time before she gets to the dance and realizes I'm not there.

I head to the library. For whatever reason, I'm drawn here. I suspect Rebecca was, too, for no other reason than I feel like I know her now. If she was going to hide something important, I think it would be here.

And I'm not the only one who thinks so.

This has all been about the house—the tricks, the scares, the video. Someone is looking for the deed.

Trying to rewrite history.

Searching the whole place will take hours, and I don't have that kind of time.

Instead, I head outside, straight for the old foundation. From this angle at the top of the hill, with the sun staring to set, it's just a dusty pile of rocks, crumbling and broken.

This is all that's left.

This is my inheritance—my father's legacy. And I can't hold on to it, any more than I can hold on to a memory.

I read somewhere that a memory is really only a memory the first time you remember. Every time after that, what you're replaying in your mind is just a version of that memory. You add details, or subtract them. And with each recall, it gets weaker, corrupted and faded. In the end, maybe none of our memories are accurate. They could all just be figments of our imaginations.

Can I ever know the truth, if all I have to go on are someone else's memories?

When this house and this land are gone, what will I have left to tie me to my father? To my roots?

If Amber is going to take the house, at least I need to know that I tried to honor this blood commitment to my family. That I listened to Rebecca and her memories. That I did everything in my power to make it right.

I lay my phone on the wall of the foundation and slip off my shoes before I wade into the creek. I've thought about doing this a dozen times since we got here, but in the end I was afraid. Afraid to get this close, scared of how strong and visceral the memories will be in the water.

This magic, healing water.

I don't believe in the fairy tale, not for a second. How ironic that it's become my last hope.

I wade out into the middle of the creek, the icy water licking at my thighs.

The time for fear is long past. I need to know now—tonight—what exactly the doctor did to Rebecca and her sister, all those years ago. No matter how awful it was.

I need her to show me.

CHAPTER 42

It doesn't work.

I make my way to the deepest part of the creek, where the current is surprisingly strong. It pulls at me and I sink and float back up, gasping for air. I crawl closer to shore where I can anchor myself.

The water has always been a strong connection between the memories. It may not be magic, but it meant something to Rebecca. I'm sure of it, as sure as I am about anything else that happened here.

If only she could speak to me.

"Come on, Rebecca. Show me what you've got," I whisper.

But maybe I'm wrong. I've bet it all on this belief that my connection to Rebecca means that I can control the memories.

But this isn't how it works. I'm not channeling Rebecca; she isn't communicating with me.

Maybe the memories are just a biological anomaly, like Bryn said. Residual trauma, with no meaning and no resolution.

No.

I cling to the rocky bottom, shivering violently. I refuse to believe that. We're connected, her and me. By our pain, by our loss.

By our blood.

I take a deep breath and lie back in the shallow water, closing my eyes.

At first, all I hear is the rushing of the creek water, unceasing. A murmur that builds into a whisper. Then into voices.

"She's not breathing. What have you done?"

"Pull yourself together," the doctor snaps. "This is no time for hysterics."

I crawl toward Marguerite, cold and lifeless on the bed. The tube in her arm is still attached, the blood running in a river onto the floor beside her. I snatch it away, my own hands slick and wet, and press against the wound. "Mags! Mags, wake up." I moan and shake her, but it's no use. "You've killed her," I cry. I press my cheek against hers. "It's too much. I told you it was too much."

"We've got to get her to the creek," Clarett says. "The water will revive her. Help me move her." He pulls her to a sitting position, placing his arm around her waist. I stand, side by side with my sister. She's lifeless and heavy and I stagger, weak from my own blood loss. We walk like that together, half carrying and half dragging her down the bank of the creek and into the water.

He lets go, so suddenly that the momentum carries us both forward. I fall to my knees, but Marguerite goes under.

"No!" I scream, struggling against the current. I swallow a mouthful of water and choke it back.

From somewhere beyond my grief, the thin wail of an infant. "Is that . . ." I lift my head. Clarett stands on the bank, holding Marguerite's baby. "She's alive?"

"She's weak," Clarett snaps. "Sick. She doesn't have much time."

I scramble up the bank toward him, but something in his voice gives me pause. I study his cold, calculating stare. The one I once mistook for compassion and knowledge.

I snatch the baby from his hands, cradling her against my chest.

"Give me the baby, Rebecca," he says, but I slip away, into the water, humming softly in her ear to keep her quiet. It's a moonless night, and the burbling of the creek covers the sound as I work my way steadily against the current, ducking until we're both nearly submerged.

His eyesight is not the best, especially in the dark. From our hiding spot in the shadows, I watch him scan the creek. He's looking farther downstream, aiming his words at a tree stump. "You're grieving. Not thinking clearly. She's sickly and not likely to survive the night, especially in that cold water. Let me take care of her."

Take care of her. I know what he means by that. His face is pale in the moonlight, frozen in a sneer as he switches tactics. "You're unmarried, Rebecca. How will you explain her?"

The baby lets out a cry and his gaze snaps toward us. I stand straighter, my thighs straining against the constant push of the water. "You can't claim her," I say, shifting the squirming bundle into a firmer hold as I steady myself against the current. "Not without admitting what you've done. Marguerite was sixteen when she came here—a child herself."

"So what is your plan? To raise her yourself? They'll assume the worst. About both of us."

"I'm not worried about my reputation. And I certainly don't care about yours."

"I care," he says, taking a step toward the water. "I can drown her in the creek right now and no one will be the wiser."

"You're too late." My feet find purchase and I drag myself up the shallow embankment on the far side. I look at him, helpless and alone, the creek a dark slash between us—the before and after of both our lives.

"You think you're so powerful, but you're wrong. About this, at least. You can't wipe us out of existence. We will prevail."

I take my sister's baby and run, away from the creek, toward the trees and the darkness.

And that's when I see him, watching from the shadows.

CHAPTER 43

I sit up, choking and gasping, my lungs bursting.

I'm cold. So cold. And wet.

I'm in the shallow water along the bank of the creek and I need to get to dry land, but my legs are sluggish and heavy, as if filled with wet cement.

I turn onto my side and retch into the water, a thin stream of bile tinged red with blood. My head swims, and I clutch at the sandy bottom and hold on for dear life as the earth tilts beneath me.

Where am I?

When am I?

The air is cold, the water frigid, and the stars in the dark sky above blink out some kind of faint code I can't decipher. Somewhere in the distance, a coyote howls, and the splash of fear down my back, colder than the creek water, brings me unsteadily to my knees.

I need to get to the house. My house. Away from here.

Away from Rebecca's memories.

I stagger up the bank, swaying and clutching at the trees for support. My legs are like rubber as I move unsteadily toward the old foundation.

Dr. Clarett killed Marguerite, and probably would have killed her baby, too, if Rebecca hadn't taken her.

She'd saved her niece at the cost of everything else.

It was James who saw her that night on the riverbank. James who had claimed Clarett's baby as his own, but only when it had served him. Only after Rebecca had exhausted every other avenue, and gone to Clarett's house to beg for mercy. That was when James had said, *Maybe there's a way we all get what we want.*

Rebecca had wanted the house—not for herself, but for Daisy. *It's rightfully hers*, she'd said. In exchange, she'd helped concoct the story about Clarett and his miracle cure. She'd been his first success. Playacting for the crowds, but never letting him forget for one moment what a fraud he really was.

Maybe that was why he'd destroyed her reputation anyway, with the stories about her sister's death and the baby's birth. And she'd let him. As he'd pointed out, her word as a woman was no match against his.

I understand it all, as if I were Rebecca. In a sense, I *am* her.

Forced to give up my family, my home, my only connection to my father.

It may be too late to heal her pain, but knowing the truth is important. Unresolved trauma will keep repeating, generation after generation.

Only the truth can save us.

And maybe it can save my home.

Up on the hill, tiny lights wink at me from the library window. Like fireflies.

Or flashlights.

Why would mom be using a flashlight?

Then I remember: She's not home. She went to look for me.

I grab my phone and power it up, my fingers numb from the cold. Water drips from my hair onto the screen as I watch the notifications pile up.

Mom. Fletcher. Clare. Emory.

They can't find me, and they're worried.

They care.

Was I wrong not to trust them?

I lean back on my heels and scroll through the texts.

I skip the ones from Mom; I know what they're going to say.

Clare:

I'm worried about you. Can I help?

Emory:

Have you figured it out yet?

So cocky and smart, so typically Emory, I have to laugh.

Fletcher, concerned at first.

Do I have the time wrong?
Where are you?

Then pissed.

You could have at least had the decency to tell me to my face that you didn't want to go.

Then resigned.

Have a nice life. Wherever you end up.

Is it Fletcher, in my house? Pissed that I stood him up? Trashing things?

But try as I might to picture Fletcher as the intruder, the image won't come.

Clare was right. He's not that kind of guy. He's sweet and nerdy. Sincere.

So why did I push him away with demands and accusations? Why couldn't I just trust him when he said he'd help me?

Because I needed answers he wasn't able to give me.

And because the truth is always better, even if it's painful.

I cough up another mouthful of bloody phlegm.

I need to get home. Cleaned up. Maybe call my doctor.

Lights flash in the house again, this time in the upstairs windows. Mom's room first, then a moment later, mine.

Who the hell— But I don't need to ask anymore.

I know who it is.

CHAPTER 44

I try the back door first, but it's locked. So is the front, but one of the dining room windows is open, wide enough to squeeze through. A glint of metal in the corner of the front porch catches my eye and I lean over to pick it up, turning the can in my hands.

Bear spray.

Clare's words this morning broke something open inside me, a yearning to belong so strong it's threatening to wash away all of the boundaries I've so carefully constructed.

The walls around my heart can be rebuilt—I've done it before.

But maybe trust is easier.

I pull out my phone, hesitating a moment before sending the text.

I'm sorry. For everything. There's someone in my house. Will you help?

Then I take a deep breath, like I'm fucking scuba diving, and lift a leg over the sill.

The dining room is empty, the air hushed, like the house is holding its breath.

I fiddle with my phone. Do I turn on the light? Or will that give me away?

Something heavy falls, the crash reverberating through the house.

The library.

I feel my way down the hallway, fingers trailing the wood paneling.

I'm so far from frightened, I find it hard to believe I ever thought myself a coward. Instead, I am pissed. At the intrusion, at the absolute audacity.

I pause in the doorway and watch as he fumbles through a pile of books. He's the coward, sneaking around in the dark, posting the video and hiding behind his anonymous screen name.

I flip on the light switch.

"Hey, Sage."

He jerks and loses his balance, and I take a tiny bit of pleasure in his fear.

Behind him, I can see the destruction he's wrought. Most of the shelves are cleared, books piled on the floor in heaps, spines cracked. He holds one in his hand, a torn page in the other. His tie hangs askew and his hair is standing almost on end, as if he's run his hands through it a couple dozen times. He's disheveled, his eyes wide and wild like a cornered animal.

"You're supposed to be at the dance with Fletcher. What are you doing home? And why are you wet?"

The venom in his voice steals some of my resolve. "What are *you* doing here? It's my house."

"Not for long," he says, standing and wiping a hand across his brow.

Now that I'm here, I'm not sure what to say or how to reason with him. Somehow, I thought confronting him would make him flee. But he's acting as if he's in the right. Like I'm the one who should go.

He takes a menacing step forward.

I've forgotten how big he is, how solid and strong. I don't know if he's violent, but he's definitely angry. He makes a noise low in his throat, almost like a growl, and Fletcher's bear facts pop into my head.

Stay calm. If he sees you, talk in a low, calm voice.

"I think you should go," I say, keeping my voice steady.

"I'm not leaving without the deed. Where is it?"

The deed. I almost laugh. For some little piece of paper, he's been willing to do all this damage. Not just physically, but emotionally. He doesn't care who or what he hurts, as long as he gets what he wants.

And that makes him dangerous.

Back up slowly. Never turn your back.

He takes another step forward and I back up as well, trying to get between him and the French doors.

He says, "I heard you yesterday. By your locker. You said you saw it, so hand it over."

That's not what I said, actually. I almost said, *I saw Rebecca sign it*, but I caught myself. Or so I thought.

Give him space.

"Why would I give it to you?" I move slowly, giving him a wide berth while keeping him in my line of sight.

"Because it's my house!"

I know I shouldn't antagonize him, but I'm tired of cowering in fear. "Actually, the existence of the deed proves the opposite. That's why you want it, right? Why you've been sneaking in here? Trying to scare me? And when that didn't work, you thought, why not drive her out?"

It's the same thing Clarett did to Rebecca. First, he weakened her. Then, he took everything that mattered. And when she didn't bend, when he couldn't break her, he repeated the rumors, over and over. Until they became town lore. If he couldn't erase her, at least he could discredit her.

"So you posted the video. You thought you could drive me away. Or at least turn the rest of the town against me." The anger that washes over me is calm and cold, pure and untapped. Like I've slipped into it. Or rather, shed something. I've taken off my inhibitions, and this is all that's left.

Unadulterated rage.

But with that comes clarity.

I don't need Rebecca to show me where the deed is. I've walked in her skin; I've lived her pain. And I know exactly where she would hide something that important.

"You're right," I say. "I've seen it. And I can take you to it. There's just one thing I need you to tell me. How did you know about it? If you're so sure Rebecca seduced Clarett and stole the house, how would you know there was a deed to look for?"

He shrugs. "Some real estate agent contacted my mom. Said he'd been looking into the transfer deeds, and something was fishy about the way it was recorded. Rebecca took the house over during the influenza pandemic, and record keeping was lax back then. He said it could potentially have been an illegal sale, unless your family could prove otherwise. He wanted to know if my mom had the deed."

Do not stare.

I back slowly toward the mechanical bookcase, careful to keep my eyes averted from Rebecca's hiding spot.

"The deed is in the tunnel," I say. "I found it the other day. I left it because I figured if it's lasted there this long, it must be a good hiding spot."

He runs both hands through his hair before turning toward the furniture, shoving the big chair to the side. The end table beside it tilts, the knickknacks on top crashing to the floor. I flinch but make no move to stop him.

"What the fuck is wrong with you?" he asks.

Play dead or fight back.

This one's a no-brainer. I've had enough of playing dead.

"What the fuck is wrong with *you*? You broke into my house. Multiple times!"

"This house is rightfully ours! It was built by the town founder. And we're his descendants, not you. You wouldn't know that, of course, but my name means something here."

"Please. The town wasn't even named after him. It was named for the rhodochrosite they mined in the creek bed."

We both turn at the sound of Emory's voice, toward where she stands in the doorway, hand on hip.

Trust her to know this random fact that means nothing, yet everything.

Clarett was never the hero he wanted people to believe he was. And Emory is a goddamn legend.

She surveys the damage, her pert nose wrinkled in disgust. "You'd think the rightful heir would have more respect."

Sage whirls on her, fire in his eyes. "You want to talk about respect? My family deserves respect! And this town knows that. They remember. They know the good Clarett did for this town. The people he saved. And I'm not going to let some nobody waltz in and steal that."

"I'm not a nobody," I say, tension and rage tightening around my chest like a vise. "You may have roots here, but mine go just as deep. And your ancestor wasn't a hero. He was a monster. He murdered Rebecca's sister, after he knocked her up. That's how we got the house in the first place. It was a payoff—to keep quiet about all his crimes. Rebecca didn't steal the house. She earned it."

Sage rolls his eyes. "Spare me the drama. It doesn't matter what you think. No one's going to believe you, anyway. You're sick. A freak. And we all know what she did to 'earn' the house." He sneers at me as he finally succeeds in clearing a path to the tunnel.

And in his words, I hear the echo of our great-great-grandfather: *It's not like anyone will take your word over mine.*

This is what Rebecca had to fight against. It's what we both have had to fight against—the idea that the truth isn't enough. That one person's word, one person's opinion, carries more weight than our own. That some man, some boy, can decide who we are or how we're seen. That they can take whatever they want from us—our reputations, our stories. Our blood. All we've earned, all we've accomplished. Just because they want to. Because they think they matter more than we do.

And it has never occurred to them, for even one second, that they are wrong.

"You have no idea how hard I've fought," I say, my voice gaining strength. I'm not just yelling at him. I'm yelling at Dr. Clarett, and Kurt, and every other man who has ever tried to fuck with the women in my family. "For my health, for my family, for the truth about my past. For the chance to be accepted, to be a part of this stupid little town and your stupid little friend group."

"We're not the stupid ones," he says, pushing the shelf open and stepping into the tunnel.

"You think you're entitled to this house because your misogynistic ancestor built it? Well, mine bled for it! You're not the only one who has roots here, asshole. I belong here, just as much as you do."

I slam the tunnel door and slide the chair in front of it, trapping him inside.

CHAPTER 45

I sink to the floor in front of the chair, weak and breathless.

"Wow. That was . . . impressive."

I look up at Emory. "When did you know it was him?"

"After you accused me of breaking in," she says. "I used to do it all the time when it was empty. I'd sit in the middle of the library, waiting for my mom to talk to me, or give me a sign. But I've only come once since you moved in. There weren't any cars in the driveway and I didn't realize anyone was here. I just came to say goodbye. I didn't mean to freak you out."

That would've been the first morning I was here alone, when Kurt had gone to return the U-Haul.

She continues, "When you told me whoever it was had stolen from you, I knew something else was going on." She adds pointedly, "Something *other* than whatever supernatural stuff you were hiding from me."

Point—Emory. She came through for me; she deserves the truth. "I've been having epigenetic memories. Of Rebecca Payne."

"I knew it was something like that."

I cock an eyebrow and she relents. "Okay, so I didn't know *exactly* what was happening. But I knew you had tapped into something otherworldly. All I wanted was for you to acknowledge that. Do you know how hard I've tried to connect with the other side? To get just one more glimpse of my mother? To hear her voice one last time?"

"I get that," I say. "Trust me. But you don't need séances or witchcraft to connect with her. She's already in you. It's not just trauma we inherit. We get good things, too. Your mom's laugh. My dad's eyes. They're here with us. Always."

She puffs out her cheeks and exhales slowly. "Thank you for saying that."

I hold out a hand and she helps me to my feet. "Thanks for coming when I called."

"You didn't need me. This was all you." She fiddles with her phone. "I did try to talk sense into him. He denied it, of course. Said there was 'proof' in my video that it wasn't him. And because I was stupid enough to fall for that, I gave him a copy. I almost told you, that day in history class. But you were kind of a bitch and I was pissed at you." She quirks her mouth into a half smile.

"Ouch. But fair. I was kind of a bitch to a lot of people."

"You're the biggest fucking bitch I've ever met!" Sage hollers.

Emory eyes the shelves as if she'd forgotten he was back there already. "You didn't really lock him in there with the deed, did you?"

"Give me a little more credit than that." I walk over to the shelves beside the fireplace, to the books called *Recipes*. The deed is tucked inside the pages of the second book I pull off the shelf.

"Rebecca would never have left it in the tunnel. She hid it in a place she figured no man would ever look for it. They're always discounting women's work."

"Lola! Lola, are you in here? Dear Lord." Mom stops short when she sees the damage to the room.

"I'm okay," I say, grabbing on to the mantel for support. Now that the adrenaline rush is waning, I'm unsteady on my feet. I look over and do a double take. What's Kurt doing here?

Mom holds onto his arm with an expression so familiar, I nearly groan. Whatever has transpired between them in these last few hours, she's gotten sucked right back into his bullshit.

I gesture at the bouquet she's holding. "You brought flowers?"

Kurt lifts his shoulder and chuckles good-naturedly. "She mentioned a dance when she called, and I may have misinterpreted. I'm real proud of you, Lola," he adds. "Your mom is, too. But we need to get you to the doctor. And that deed somewhere safe."

I clutch the paper to my chest. What does he know about the deed?

"He's right, honey. Dr. Archuleta called me. The genetic panel flagged an anomaly. You're very sick. We need to get you to the hospital." Mom gently takes the paper from my hand and wraps her arm around me, but I duck away.

No. I shake my head. This is wrong. Somehow . . .

There's a connection here, but my brain won't make it. I close my eyes, trying to clear the fog.

"You bitch! Let me out! I am going to sue your fucking ass—"

"What the hell?" Kurt moves to the bookshelf, shoving aside the chair and pushing open the door.

Sage tumbles out, swearing and sweating. As he falls to his knees, trying to catch his breath, Kurt and Mom both turn toward me.

"Did you lock him in there?" Mom asks, sounding horrified.

"He broke into our house!" I say, the words coming slowly around the pressure in my chest.

"He's just a kid," Kurt says.

I look from Kurt to the tunnel and back again. "How did you know? That the tunnel was there?"

"I knew how worried you were," Kurt says, smoothing his shirt, "about someone getting in. I decided to check it out."

Something about his words rings false. "But you didn't believe me when I told you someone broke in."

"This again? I'm not the bad guy you want me to be, Lola. Of course I believed you! I just wanted you and your mom to be safe."

"When did you find it?" I ask, rubbing my temples and blinking away the dark spots. When he hesitates, I press on. "When did you have a chance to look for it? The other day, when no one was home? Is that what you were doing here? Or have you known about it all along?"

"Tress, she's in a bad way. We need to get her to the hospital."

I shake my head and press my back against the fireplace for balance. No. No. I've almost connected the dots.

"Give me the deed, Tress. I'll put it somewhere for safekeeping."

"Mom, don't. He's in on it somehow." I press my hand to my chest and concentrate on my breath, though my chest is so, so tight.

"Lola—"

And then I see it. Mom's bouquet. Gladiolus. The same flowers Clare's mom had on her table. From an admirer, she'd said. What were the odds?

It must have been her car the other day, not an Uber. I nearly slap my forehead at the revelation. No wonder it got here so quickly.

"*You're* the real estate guy," I say, watching Kurt's face. His eye twitches, but that's his only tell.

Sage is less savvy, his gaze shifting guiltily from me to Kurt and then to the pile of books on the floor.

"You're from Lansing, right? But not Lansing, Michigan. That cop said so. He recognized you. You're local. This has all been one big, long con." I'm amazed and disgusted in almost equal parts.

"Lola, do you hear yourself? Kurt is my husband! This isn't some vast conspiracy to get our house. And frankly, I don't care about some stupid piece of paper." Mom waves it at me. "You're very ill. All I care about is keeping you safe."

I waver. Is she right? Am I jumping to conclusions? But Emory shakes her head and gives me a thumbs-up of solidarity, so I keep going.

"It's not just a stupid piece of paper, Mom. Don't you get it? It's evidence! Of all the ways men use to discredit women. To take what belongs to them—their credibility, their families, their houses." I swipe at the trickle of blood I can feel on my lip and raise my fingers, shaking them at Kurt. "Their blood. You're no better than the doctor; you're a fraud. Not happy until you've bled us dry."

Mom's eyes widen. "Lola Joy. We are done messing around. We are going to the hospital. Now."

"She's delusional, Tress," Kurt agrees. "You need to get her to a doctor. I'll get these kids home and explain to Sage's mom that tonight was just a big misunderstanding. Hopefully she won't press charges."

I shake Mom's hand from my arm. "You're going to let him do that? Go over and compare notes with his new girlfriend?"

Kurt scoffs. "Amber is not my girlfriend."

"How'd you know her name was Amber?"

He hesitates, a fraction of a second. "You said it. Don't you remember? You're in a bad way." He shakes his head. "I don't even know the people she's talking about."

"That's not true," says Emory without looking up from her phone. "I saw you and Sage, the day after the séance. The two of you were talking on the porch."

"He came over here to do yard work," Kurt says.

"And that's when Sage recognized you as his mom's new boyfriend," I say, picking up the thread.

"This is ridiculous." Kurt throws up his hands. "The truth is, I caught him snooping around the house. But since I knew he was Lola's friend, I decided to cut him some slack. They were all shaken up from the night before, you know that." He directs this at Mom. "I told him he could do some yard work as punishment."

But Sage has had enough. "He told me you were sick. That he wanted to be with Mom, but he couldn't leave his wife while you were so fragile. He said it would be better for everyone if you just . . . went away." For the first time, he looks remorseful. "I knew it must be true. We all saw how you were at the bonfire. I thought if I posted the video, you'd give up and go back home."

For the first time, Mom wavers and looks at Kurt. "Is that true?"

"Of course not! The move hasn't been good for any of us," he says, taking one of Mom's hands. "I thought if I could convince someone to take it off your hands, we'd all be better off. I reached out to Amber after doing a quick reverse property search. We met one time. I don't know where she got the idea we were dating. I told her I was married."

"Did you tell her you'd paid off the back taxes?" I ask, taking a shot in the dark.

He pauses, and I can literally see him turning the words over in his head, trying to find his way out. Then he says, "I did that for you, Lola."

I snort, gagging and coughing at the coppery taste of the blood, before I manage to choke out, "The con only works if someone believes it."

His mask has slipped. I can see him, *really* see him.

And maybe for the first time, Mom can, too. She's looking at him like he's a stranger as she asks, "Why did you let me think Dom did that?" She jerks her hand away.

"Tress, don't listen to this. She's got a wild imagination, and somehow, she's pulled them all into this. Just give me the deed. Then we'll get her the help she needs."

"Hold on," Emory says, "let me get a better angle." She leans forward across the edge of the club chair, phone in hand. "I've been livestreaming this. Mrs. Morales, are you watching? Is this con artist your new secret admirer?"

"Hey! Don't drag my mom into this!" Sage tries to smack the phone out of Emory's hands.

At the same time, Kurt jumps forward and snatches the deed. He holds it above his head, soaking in his victory as he smirks down at me.

So egotistical. So convinced he's won.

So much like Dr. Clarett, like every man who has ever taken anything from a woman, just because he wants it. Because he thinks he's entitled to it, by virtue of his gender.

Because he can.

No wonder Rebecca wanted to burn everything to the ground.

"I was wrong," I tell him. "You're not a fraud." I take a step forward, swaying on my feet. "You're a predator."

And as his wolfish grin widens, I nail him in the face with the bear spray.

CHAPTER 46

I come to on a stretcher in the back of an ambulance, an oxygen mask strapped to my face. An EMT hovers nearby, attaching an IV bag.

"What happened?" I croak.

She pats my arm. "You passed out. We're administering oxygen and fluids, and we'll meet your doctor at the hospital."

"Where's my mom?" I try to move, but I'm strapped to the cart.

Clare sticks her head around the door. She's wearing a Gothic-looking dress with a high collar and poet sleeves in a wine color that matches her chunky highlights. "She's talking to the cops." She gives a little wave. "I'm probably the last person you want to see, but I told her I'd stay with you."

"When did you . . . ?" It's difficult to talk around the mask, but luckily Clare understands.

"Can I come up?"

The nurse gives her a hand up and offers her seat on the bench. "I'm going to finish this paperwork. Keep an eye on her."

Clare slides down beside me. "Your mom showed up at the dance in a real state. At first she was convinced you were there and we were hiding you. Fletcher wasn't much help. He got drunk after you stood him up—"

I wince.

"Sorry. Not your fault. He's an idiot. Anyway, he was babbling on to your mom about the tunnel and the photos and generally just freaking her out. Then Kurt showed up and they left and not long after that, Emory's livestream started. After that"—Clare snaps her fingers—"Fletcher was all business. I had to drive him, of course. We were almost here when we saw you shoot Kurt with the bear spray. I always knew you were a badass." She shakes her head admiringly. "Fletcher called 911 right then. He said bear spray is nothing to mess around with."

"I guess I have to thank your brother. He dropped it . . . on the porch."

"You don't have to thank him for anything." She bends forward and through the open door I can see Sage sitting in the back of the cop car.

"What's going to happen to him?"

"Depends on if you guys are going to press charges. On the breaking and entering. Harassment. Vandalism." She counts off on her fingers. "He'll get community service for sure."

Maybe it's the oxygen, but I'm feeling a lot more clearheaded. Charging him feels vindictive. He was preyed upon, just like us. "Where's Kurt?"

She jerks a thumb. "In the other ambulance. He was in bad shape." She grimaces, then laughs. "I can't believe your stepdad is my mom's internet boyfriend."

"What are the odds?"

"I mean, pretty good, actually. Since he targeted them." She smooths her skirt, one of her rings catching on the lace. "Once he saw the opportunity to get his hands on the house, he was playing both sides. Your mom for the quick sale, and mine when she proved harder to budge." She works the metal free, snagging a bit of the delicate fabric in the process.

I pull off my mask, which makes it harder to breathe but easier to talk. "I never liked Kurt," I admit. "But I didn't think he was an actual criminal."

Clare plays with the pill in the fabric. "It probably wouldn't have amounted to much if my brother hadn't convinced Mom we had a shot at the property. I'm sorry he was such a dick. I knew how much he loved this house, and the thought of our great-whatever being a town hero. But I never thought he'd resort to harassing you."

"I get it. The idea of losing the house made me a little crazy, too." The flashing lights outside are making me dizzy, so I stare up at the ceiling. "I accused you all of some terrible things."

She shrugs. "We're pretty shitty friends if we write you off entirely based on one fight."

I try to raise myself up, but have to settle for turning my head. "Are we? Friends, I mean?"

"Would I be here if we weren't? You could have called me, you know. I would've come."

"I knew it was Sage by then, and I didn't want you to have to make that choice."

The nurse pops back in. "Nope. Oxygen mask needs to stay put." She straps it back on my face and pushes a few buttons on the rolling cart beside me.

Fletcher sticks his head in the doorway. "Lola! You're awake!"

"It's getting crowded in here," the nurse says pointedly.

Clare rolls her eyes and climbs down to stand beside Fletcher.

"I've been watching them treat Kurt," Fletcher says. "I've heard what bear spray can do to a person, but I've never witnessed it firsthand. He's pretty messed up. So much leakage."

"Nothing he didn't deserve," Clare says.

"Is my mom with him?" I ask, afraid to hear the answer.

"Yeah," he says, and Clare elbows him. "Not *with* him, with him," he hastens to add. "She's being treated for some residual effects. She didn't get out of the room quickly enough."

"Oh my god."

I struggle to sit up, and the nurse presses me gently down. "She'll be fine."

"I'm going to check on Sage," Clare says, before turning away.

"Sorry about the dance," I say, fiddling with the mask, which earns me a glare from the nurse.

Fletcher shoves his hands in his pockets. "I'm the one who should apologize. I should have listened when you said one of my friends was messing with you."

Can't argue there. So I just stay quiet and listen.

He ducks his head. "To err is human; to forgive, divine."

I tilt my head. "Nicely played. But you have to know who said it."

A look of panic crosses his face, but he recovers quickly. "It's your turn. I gave the quote—you have to name the source."

"How will you know if I'm right?"

"I trust you," he says, giving me that smile that I can feel in my toes. "Plus, I'm grounded. So I'm going to have lots of time to look it up."

I raise my eyebrows, waiting for him to explain.

He scuffs his toe on the ground. "I got an underage drinking ticket."

"At the dance?"

"No, here. I was pretty wound up when the cops showed up, and one of them gave me a breathalyzer."

"But Clare said you were the one who called them."

"No good deed goes unpunished," offers the EMT.

"Oscar Wilde?" I say, at the same time Fletcher crows, "Idina Menzel!"

A cop steps up beside Fletcher and waits for our giggling to subside. "Ms. Boyd? I need to get a statement from you."

"Back off, Frank," says the nurse, jerking her head. "Her mom's being treated in the other truck."

"I've spoken to her already. She said it was fine to ask a few questions." He levels his gaze on me. "Are you aware that it's illegal to use bear spray on a person?"

I shake my head. I'm not. But it doesn't surprise me.

"Mr. Gunderson is filing assault charges."

Fletcher makes a choking sound as I struggle against the restraints. "Assault? He . . . conned . . ."

"That's not a defense," the cop says. "Were you in physical danger?"

I shake my head again, but this time Mom comes to my rescue. "That's enough. When you said ask her questions, I thought it would be related to the crimes committed by my . . . by Kurt. Not this"—she waves her hand—"ridiculous claim."

"As I explained earlier, this was an assault. Filmed by her friend."

"And she's not answering any more questions without a lawyer. Fletcher, can you be a lamb and have your mother meet us at the hospital? We're done here." Mom climbs into the back of the ambulance.

"You heard the woman," the EMT says. "Everybody out."

Fletcher backs up and gives me a little wave as the EMT slams the door in the cop's face.

Mom's face is red and her eyes are glassy.

"I'm sorry about the spray," I say, waving a hand toward her face. "I didn't mean for you to get hurt."

"No, I'm sorry, baby," Mom whispers, scooting forward to take my hand. "I'm sorry I didn't listen to you about Kurt."

"Kurt." I shake my head and slip the mask off, after checking the EMT isn't looking. "I just didn't like him. But I never thought . . . Did you know Bryn and I used to call him Inert Kurt? God, we were wrong."

She chokes out a laugh that ends on a sob. "We're going to get this taken care of. I promise he is not going to get away with any of this. We'll get you patched up, and we'll get these ridiculous charges dropped."

She's starting to sound more like the mom I know. A fighter.

"And then we're going to get the hell out of this godforsaken town."

"What?" I raise my voice in alarm, and the EMT whips her head around.

I shake my head even as she's reattaching my oxygen mask. "We're not leaving. The house is ours. I proved it."

"You did, honey. But that doesn't change much. We're still financially strapped. And now we'll have legal fees. I was going to wait to talk to you about this, but I think we should reach out to Amber and see if she'll agree to a settlement."

I've seen that look before. It means she's already made up her mind. She's the adult and I'm the child and she makes the decisions.

Not this time.

"We don't need to settle. It's my house. Dad's house." I cross my arms over my chest. I should be embarrassed that the EMT is witnessing this, but I'm not. Let her watch. I'm done apologizing for who I am and letting myself feel weak. It's time to be strong.

"I wish it were that easy. But it did belong to her family. Can you blame her for wanting it back?" She tries to smile, but her face crumples. "The thing is, I don't know if I'm brave enough to stay here. I didn't anticipate how hard this would all be—how the memories would affect me. How much I would miss your dad." Her eyes fill with tears. "I've made so many mistakes. Mistakes that have hurt you. And I'm just so tired." Her voice cracks. "And now there's Kurt."

He's broken something in her, and for that, I'll never forgive him. He played Mom and Amber against each other like they were pawns, all for his own gain. Like so many men before him, he thinks he has the absolute right to say who matters and who doesn't.

I've been fighting for so long, pushing against this idea that I'm less than, that I don't belong. Fighting to prove to the wrong people that I deserve their acceptance. But I don't have anything to prove.

I'm enough as I am.

And what I should have been doing was looking for the right people—the ones who were already in my corner, willing to take me at my word. Willing to stand with me. People like Emory, who came when I texted, no questions asked. And Fletcher, who called for help when I needed it, even though it got him in trouble.

Like Clare, who sees me as a badass and tells me so, even when I can't see it myself.

Maybe that's what Mom needs, too.

I take her hand. "We both made mistakes. But you're not a coward. You're one of the bravest people I know. You saved me, and you raised me on your own, and you've always done what's best for me. Taking a chance on love, even if it didn't work out. Moving across the country for a new start." I take a deep breath. "Staying in a place that has some bad memories, because you know we have a chance to make new ones? We don't have to wait for some kind of formal invitation to stay, Mom. We belong because we say we belong."

She grips my hand tight. "You remind me so much of your father. Did I ever tell you about our first date?"

I smile and close my eyes, letting the words of her story—my history—wrap around me like a warm embrace.

EPILOGUE

Spring

The doorbell bongs, and I throw the door open before the clamorous song finishes.

Clare and Emory stand on the threshold, each holding big boxes. "We've got to get that fixed," Clare says, wincing as the tones grind to a halt.

"Agreed."

"I kind of like it," Emory says. "It's got a murdery, don't-go-in-the-basement vibe."

Clare meets my horrified gaze. "We'll move it to the top of the to-do list."

I nod, relieved. "Do you guys need help?"

"Fletcher's got the rest. We're going to take this up to my room." I move aside to let them pass, then wait for Fletcher to bound up the stairs with a pile of boxes. He stops long enough to lean in for a kiss, but Orson jumps between us.

"Blocked by my own dog," he says, giving me that smile that still makes me melt.

I let Orson in ahead of us, then pull Fletcher close for a kiss I can feel in my knees.

"That's better." His dimple pops, and I brush the curls out of his eyes before I grab the top box. "Is this everything?" I ask.

"For now. Dad and Mr. Z are on the way with the rest of the furniture."

"Where do these go?"

I check the box labels. "Amber's room."

She and my mom come through the kitchen door just then. "Fletcher, you're a saint! I'm right down this hallway." Amber waves him over with her cane. She's looking better these days, slim and healthy, with color in her cheeks. "I don't want to have to do all the stairs." She squeezes his cheeks and turns his face to me. "He's a keeper, Lola. Don't let this one go."

"I don't plan on it."

He winks at me and grabs my box before following Amber down the hall.

The idea of sharing the house was weird, at first. But Mom had a point when she said it belonged to Amber's family as much as it did mine. And it was way too big for the two of us, anyway.

Nat's the one who deserves the credit, though. She knew Mom and Amber were both suffering, beating themselves up over a past they couldn't change. After spending months trying to tend to both their emotional traumas, she finally got them to sit down together and compare notes.

They've been inseparable ever since.

"Amber and I made cookies," Mom says, holding out the tray. "White chocolate macadamia."

"Yum. Where's Sage?" I ask, around a mouthful of cookie.

Her forehead wrinkles slightly. "Down by the creek," she finally says. "Don't—"

I hold out my hands in an "I'm innocent" gesture. "I didn't say a word."

It was harder to convince Sage and me of the benefits of cohabiting. At first, we couldn't stand to be in the same town together, let alone the same house. Mom never pressed charges, and I was in agreement; I'm not vindictive. But he did set out to hurt me. Manipulate me and scare me and prey on my weakness. 'Forgive and forget' wasn't going to come easy.

On the other hand, I locked him in a creepy-ass tunnel. He says he still has nightmares. Also, Amber made him sign up for community service, which of course he blamed me for. But his work with Habitat for Humanity must not have been all bad, because he's gotten this idea in his head of rebuilding the doctor's old quarters.

I'm not thrilled with his project, but it seems to bring him some kind of comfort. And it's like I told Emory—we're made up of both the successes and the mistakes of our ancestors. You can't claim the good genes and forget the rest. Ignoring the past doesn't change it, anyway. It still happened.

Our only path to growth is to acknowledge our wrongs, and try and do better. I can accept Sage's involvement in Kurt's scheme while also understanding that he was just another pawn. I can even recognize Dr. Clarett's accomplishments without sugarcoating his crimes. Though I will never see him as a hero, it turns out he was utilizing some advanced techniques in his treatment of Rebecca's blood disease.

Rebecca's journals were all hidden in the cookbooks in the library, and her meticulous notes have been lifesavers, literally, for Amber and me. Our shared disorder, like Rebecca's, is a myeloproliferative neoplasm, which means that our bodies produce too many red blood cells. While there is no cure, phlebotomy is a common treatment. Dr. Clarett went too far when he experimented with bloodletting on Marguerite, but he was actually on the right track. He was just too egotistical to investigate his failures. It was Rebecca who thought to document how she felt *after* the treatments, which the good doctor never bothered with. Why ask the patient when the doctor clearly knows best?

Clare and Emory hurry down the steps, the twins' little feet pounding behind them. "It's time!" Emory waves her phone. "Bryn's podcast is live!"

Bryn has visited twice this year, once over Thanksgiving and again last month for spring break. They were an instant hit with everyone. Fletcher sends them bear cam videos on a daily basis, and in return, Bryn shares shots of their new kitten, Pickles, in ridiculous outfits, which Clare sews for them. Meanwhile, Bryn and Emory are working on some top-secret project that involves busting fraudulent ghost hunters.

But today is the launch of Bryn's new podcast, one based on Kurt and his crimes. They dug deep, and found out that Mom and Amber weren't the first women he's tried to con. There were warrants out for him in three other states for a slew of fraud charges. In a weird way, knowing she wasn't the first of his victims made it easier for Mom to let go. Both she and Amber agreed to do interviews for the show. And in light of Kurt's other crimes, the district attorney quietly dropped the assault charge against me.

Clare plops down on the sofa and pulls me down beside her while Emory sets her phone on the coffee table. Fletcher helps Amber into a chair before squeezing in next to me.

Mom eyes the phone warily. "Why can't we watch it on YouTube?"

"It's a podcast, not a show," Clare explains patiently.

As I've explained to her at least a dozen times. She doesn't miss my eye roll. "I know that! But those nice young boys with the Ear Biscuits have a show. Why doesn't Bryn?"

"Ready?" Emory asks, giving us all a look before she hits play.

I take a deep breath as Fletcher squeezes my hand and Bryn's voice fills the room. "Welcome to *The Dirt on Kurt: The Down and Dirty on a Real Estate Con Artist*. I'm your host, Bryn Foster. The story you're about to hear is true; no names have been changed to protect the innocent because that's not how I roll. And Kurt Gunderson was anything but innocent. A narcissist and a petty criminal, for sure. He'd played the real estate con many times, and he usually came out on top. But this time, he let it get personal. And that was his ultimate mistake."

I still can't wrap my head around the fact that he was after the house all along. It turned out he'd grown up near here, just two towns over. Lansing, like he'd told Mom. He just hadn't bothered to mention it was Lansing, Colorado.

The house still belongs to me, at least on paper, though Nat has been urging us to decide what we want in the long term, and to make it legally binding. I owe that to Amber and Clare and Sage and the twins, whose family belongs here as much as mine. I thought that letting go would hurt more, but the longer I spend here, getting to know Dad's friends and hearing stories about his life, the less I feel the need to hold on so tightly to this one big piece of stone.

His memory lives on in so much more than this house.

As for memories, the epigenetic ones have subsided. I think it's because I'm feeling better these days, learning to live in this body and to take care of myself. I'm healing, both physically and emotionally, which is more than Rebecca ever got to say.

I may not feel her anymore, but I think about her every day. Thanks to her, I've got my health back. Mom and I are closer than ever, even though it's no longer just the two of us against the world. We've got a group of supportive friends and a big, new extended family.

Best of all, we have a home we get to share with people we love. Where we get to make memories of our very own.

ACKNOWLEDGMENTS

This is my third book, and I am still amazed and grateful every day for the opportunity to share my stories. I couldn't do this without some really special people on my side who keep me grounded and help make this dream a reality.

First up, the biggest thanks to Linda Davis, who in addition to always being my first reader is the best writing partner and friend a girl can have. Your many phone calls, pep talks, honest critiques, navigation of plot holes, and reminders to stay on track are the only reasons I have a writing career at all. You're always right—about all of it, including the blood! Sorry I didn't listen earlier.

I am eternally grateful to my amazing agent, Barbara Poelle, whose wisdom, tenacity, and talent for handling the difficult bits leaves me time to focus on the writing, which is all I've ever wanted to do. I couldn't do this without your hand on my back, guiding me gently and ever Onward! Thank you.

It takes a village to raise a child, and that is true for the editorial process as well, at least when it comes to my books. Liza Kaplan, you were the first editor to see something of value in those early pages. That encouragement means more than you will ever know. I miss you! Want Chyi, thank you for your kind words and your patience in guiding me through some of the changes behind the scenes. We never did get to reminisce about the Dells. Please let me know the next time you're in Wisconsin! Dana Leydig, thank you so much for taking on this project and helping me to shape it into something better and stronger than I could imagine on my own.

A huge thanks to the entire team at Viking, including managing editors Gaby Corzo and Ginny Dominguez, production editors Abigail Powers, Marinda Valenti, and Sola Akinlana, interior designer Anabeth Bostrup, proofreader Jessica Lack, and Kristin Boyle, Lori Thorn, and Maria Fazio for that stunning cover!

In 2021, the Council of Wisconsin Writers awarded me a weeklong residency at Ernest Hüpeden's Painted Forest in Valton, Wisconsin. It was in this beautiful, serene environment that I finished the first draft of this story. An enormous thank-you to the CWW for this incredible gift of time and space, and for making residencies like this available to writers like me.

Thanks to my family for putting up with me through yet another unpredictable cycle of drafting, revision, marketing, and publication. I probably owe you all at least one drink!

Emma, Ari, and Cameron, you are still the best things I've ever created. I love this book, but I love you more.

Josh, you asked for bullet points, but I've just got one:

You are my everything.